PRAISE F
THE SHELL HOUSE

'A cleverly plotted and thoroughly enjoyable book about deeds in beautiful places.'

—Elly Griffiths, author of the Ruth Galloway series

'A total delight.'

—Sarah Winman, author of *Still Life*

'Exquisitely written, set in Cornwall, great characters, and a gripping plot. Who could ask for more?'

—Jill Mansell, author of *Promise Me*

'This beautifully written cosy coastal mystery packs a real punch! With wonderfully atmospheric prose and twists and turns aplenty, the plot will have you riding a wave of suspense long after you've turned the final page. If you love Cornwall, you will adore this book.'

—Sarah Pearse, author of *The Sanatorium*

'Suspenseful, twisty and unputdownable . . . Loved it!'

—Claire Douglas, author of *The Couple at No. 9*

'Emylia was born to write detective fiction.'

—Veronica Henry, author of *The Impulse Purchase*

'An expertly plotted and hugely compelling murder mystery . . . Crime fans are in for a treat.'

—Lucy Clarke, author of *One of the Girls*

THE
HARBOUR LIGHTS
MYSTERY

THE
HARBOUR LIGHTS
MYSTERY

A SHELL HOUSE DETECTIVES MYSTERY

Emylia Hall

THOMAS & MERCER

Text copyright © 2023 by Emylia Hall
All rights reserved.

Published by Thomas & Mercer, Seattle

www.apub.com

Amazon, the Amazon logo, and Thomas & Mercer are trademarks of Amazon.com, Inc., or its affiliates.

ISBN-13: 9781662505157
eISBN: 9781662505140

Cover design by The Brewster Project
Cover illustration by Handsome Frank Limited – Marianna Tomaselli

Printed in the United States of America

For Bobby and Calvin

Prologue

JP can hear the sea hurling itself furiously at the harbour wall and he pulls his coat closer around him in response; it's too big for him really but it's warm, and that's what he needs on a night like this. The falling rain is as sharp as needles and he dips his head as he walks. At this hour the harbour lights are long gone, and the tourist crowds along with them. A feeble street light shows a patch of glistening black water, but the noise of the sea is everywhere. There's menace in the air tonight.

There were bad tempers at the Mermaid this evening too. Behind the scenes, anyway. Orders bellowed and knives hacked and oil hitting the pan with an extra hiss. That kind of energy always gets JP's blood up just the way he likes it: if you can't handle the heat and all that.

He bounces on his heels as he makes his way home.

JP's wired, like he's always wired after service. But in a place as dead as this he'll have to make do with a drink and a smoke back at his rental, on the sorry excuse that passes for a balcony, the view just silhouetted wedges of rooftop, the claustrophobic cluster of this village all around him. If he was still in London the party would have been just getting started, but not round here: the flat-footed waitresses plod home and fall straight into their beds; that dullard Butt trails upstairs to his disinterested wife; and Dominic was never much of a fire-starter, even in the old days.

Nah, I won't be here long. Just enough time for JP to make his mark, get people talking, then move on to better things in better places.

Mousehole village car park is full of boats pulled up out of the water and he weaves between their dark hulls as beyond the harbour wall the sea rages. He stops to get out his cigarettes, fumbling in the dark, as the icy wind licks at his middle. He can't remember the pocket he stuck them in at first, then he finds them; tugs the box free.

The blow comes out of nowhere. And it lands right in the middle of the back of his head.

JP staggers forward, his palms skidding on the asphalt. When he hits the ground, everything seems to stop. Only his lip twitches, and he thinks, in that moment, how even the concrete tastes salty here. Then white-hot pain consumes him.

And his lights go out.

1

THE NEXT NIGHT

Ally closes her hands around her cup of mulled wine, feeling its warmth through her knitted gloves. She takes a sip; it tastes like Christmas.

When Gus suggested going to Mousehole to see the lights she couldn't think of a good excuse not to. Ally's never been one for crowds, but Gus's face was shining like a little boy's as he said *I've heard it's about as festive as it gets*, and before she knew it, a plan was made. So here she is. Leaning against the harbour railing. The sweet voices of carol singers swirling through the cold night air, while wind rips at the strings of lanterns that swing high above their heads.

'It's a bit parky, isn't it?' says Gus, and whether it's intentional, or simply the jostle of other people around them, he moves a little closer to her. Then he raises his paper cup and bumps her own. 'Cheers, Ally. This is magic.'

His eyes twinkle, and she finds herself smiling. Then she looks quickly away.

Gus often ambles over the dunes from his place, All Swell, to hers at The Shell House, sometimes bringing a bottle, sometimes just a slice of conversation. Gus: the holidaymaker who never went home. And it always feels easy. Just two neighbours sharing an appreciation for their corner of paradise, their conversation running as surely as the tide. But they don't do outings – the odd fish and chips at The Wreckers Arms hardly counts – and they don't present as any sort of pair to the outside world. Because they aren't a pair. Not at all.

And now it's Christmas.

Christmas is a time for family. But Bill is gone – although that hardly seems true, when his absence is as tangible as any presence. And Evie and the children are on the other side of the world; they won't be in Porthpella until the early days of the new year – cheaper flights from Sydney, her son-in-law said. Maybe Ally's overthinking it but organising to do something with someone at Christmas just feels different. Maybe it's because of all the stage sets of decorations and twinkling lights: hope and expectation are everywhere. And is there anything worse than false hope? Or misjudged expectations.

'Is that an enormous fish pie I can see down there?' Gus's voice is easy with laughter. 'Not a classic Christmas prop, but okay.'

The pie is mounted against the harbour wall, perhaps six feet high. Three fish heads peep from the top. It crackles with blue and yellow lights, their reflections streaming like ribbons in the water below.

Gus's jollity is, as always, infectious. Although Porthpella has changed him in that way, she's sure. When he first arrived, back in the spring, Gus was a hesitant sort of man. Amiable, but you'd likely miss him in a crowd.

But then again, Ally's never cared for crowds.

'Surely you've heard of Tom Bawcock?' she says.

'Local lad?'

'Local legend.'

And so she tells him the story of the Mousehole fisherman who, hundreds of years ago, braved winter storms to make an epic

4

catch that saved the village from famine. How he's celebrated to this day by the making of Stargazy Pie – so-named for the fish heads peeping from the crust – and a lantern procession through the village.

'The twenty-third of December is Tom Bawcock's Eve, Gus.'

'Now why didn't that spread to Oxfordshire? I'd have got behind a festive fish pie.' He nods towards the lights. 'Especially one that size.' He counts on his fingers. 'Where are we? Today's Monday, so the twenty-third is Saturday. Shall we come here again?' As Ally hesitates, he takes a draught of his drink; flicks a glance at her over the rim. 'I mean, I might come here again. You don't want to spend all your time squiring about this old emmet.'

It's been some months since Gus last referred to himself as that. *You get to be an incomer now, mate,* Jayden told him back in the summer, *but the jury's out on whether that's actually an upgrade.*

'Though, of course, if you did want to come,' he says, 'it'd make it all the better.'

Before Ally can reply, the choir strikes up a new carol, 'I Saw Three Ships', and a section of the crowd joins in with gusto. Gus lends his voice too. It's as deep as a well – and surprisingly in tune. Ally smiles appreciatively, and the words dance a little in her mind, even if she doesn't sing them out loud.

> *I saw three ships come sailing in*
> *On Christmas Day, on Christmas Day*
> *I saw three ships come sailing in*
> *On Christmas Day in the morning*
> *And what was in those ships all three . . .*

As the carol ends, Gus turns to her.

'I mean it, Ally,' he says. And his expression suddenly becomes so serious that she wants to look away – at the carollers, the lights,

5

into the bottom of her cup of mulled wine. Anywhere but back at him. The choir starts up another number, 'O Little Town of Bethlehem', and Gus lays his hand gently on her arm. 'These last few months you've—'

But then his words are lost in a scream that cuts through the smooth notes of the carollers. It cuts, too, through the more distant song of the sea. It is, Ally thinks, a scream of pitch-perfect horror, and she instinctively grabs Gus's arm as the piercing note is held. His mulled wine tips in his cup and splatters his jacket.

As a wave of panic washes over the crowd the singing scatters to a stop, only a lone voice continuing unknowingly: *the hopes and fears of all the years are met in thee tonight.*

'What on earth . . .' begins Gus.

Ally realises she's still holding on to his arm and she drops it quickly. There's only one thing, surely, that would provoke a scream like that.

2

Jayden is lying in the dark. Well, kind of lying. His upper body is twisted, his hand slipped through the bars of the cot; his left foot thrums with pins and needles. He thinks of the yoga that Cat does out in the barn, and whether the downward dog – or any other kind of dog – would help him now, because this is one hell of a contortion. He shifts himself, by the smallest increment, then holds his breath as his daughter moves in response.

Please. Don't. Wake. Up.

I love you I love you I love you. But please don't wake up.

The truth is, Jasmine has the pair of them wrapped around her little finger; Jayden, in this moment, literally. The thought of walking away and leaving their daughter to cry herself to sleep has been beyond them both since day one. *They have to learn*, his mum-in-law, Sue, once said, with a practicality verging on coldness that surprised Jayden. *Catherine was in her own room from six weeks old. We couldn't be up all night with a farm to run.* Whereas Jayden's own mum simply says, *Do what feels right. She's yours. Only you know.* But do they? Really? Sometimes it feels like Jasmine, for all the nine months that they've known and loved her, is a visitor from outer space. And one they live in fear of displeasing.

Right now, Jazzy's big thing is not sleeping. Which means every night is not just broken but shattered, Jayden and Cat crawling out of the wreckage into the next endless day. Like everything else, people tell them it's a phase, *this too shall pass* and all that. Meanwhile, Jayden's quickly learnt the rules of relativity. Back in the day he used to think the beeping of his alarm for work was brutal; well, it's got nothing on a baby's full-decibel scream. And five hours' sleep? These days that's a gift from the gods, that is.

He can feel his phone buzz in his pocket, but he can't reach it. It could be Ally. And he never wants to miss a message from Ally.

Carefully he begins to extract his fingers from his daughter's grip. Slowly, very slowly, then he stops, feeling her tiny fingers tightening. She makes the snuffling noise he knows only too well: it initially suggests contentment, but it could turn into a furious cry at any given moment.

'Shh, baby,' he murmurs, 'it's all good. Sleepy babe, you sleep.'

He restarts the gradual movement, millimetre by millimetre.

His phone buzzes again.

Jayden goes for it. In a single fluid movement, he wins his hand back and performs a kind of half-roll away from the bars of the cot. He sits up, pressing his back against the wall. *Victory.* Now he just needs to get to his feet without the boards creaking. Then push open the door – the hinge of which he lashes with WD-40 on a regular basis – and make his escape down the corridor. There are at least seven things that could go wrong in this sequence. So, first, he pulls out the phone.

It's Ally. And a message at this time of night might be something important.

This time of night. It's only 20.08. But he's tired. So tired. They both are, he and Cat.

He cups his hand to shield the glow of the screen and reads.

There's been a murder in Mousehole. The body of a man found on a boat in the harbour. Hit over the head,

Jayden, multiple times. The police are on their way, so we're going to wait too.

He draws a quick breath.

The second message: *'We' being Gus and I. He wanted to see the lights.*

Jayden feels a jag of adrenalin. They were in Mousehole just a couple of days ago, seeing Old Fran, Cat's cousin once removed. And now Ally – and Gus, let's not forget Gus – happens to be in the seaside village at the exact same time that a murder took place?

Interesting.

Since Jayden and Ally officially started up the Shell House Detectives, their cases have been pretty lo-fi. In early summer they traced a missing man out towards Truro, only to discover that the whole thing was an attempted insurance scam. And then, in the autumn, there was the online gallery selling rip-offs of some of Cornwall's best-known artists' work – including Fiona Penrose. Fiona hired them to prove the faint line in the sand between inspiration and imitation, and they managed it too. These cases were involving, and satisfying, but a long way from the crazy days of their first job back in the spring, the one that set them on this path; the body at the foot of the cliffs, a missing woman, and a killer who'd never been brought to justice. It wasn't that Jayden wanted murder and mayhem to come again to this corner of Cornwall, far from it. But something to get their teeth into? To make his old mates from the force up in Leeds quit their smiles? Smiles that were well-intentioned, maybe even lit by a little bit of envy for what they saw as the good life, but smiles, nevertheless. Well, he wouldn't mind that.

Do you want me there? he messages back. And he's willing the answer to be *Jayden, yes, report for duty instantly!*

But murder is police territory, pure and simple. So, it's no surprise when Ally messages to say they'll be at the scene shortly: PC Mullins and Detective Sergeant Skinner. They'll be setting up boundaries and talking to witnesses. Forensics doing their meticulous business. The Major Crimes team jetting in from Newquay. What did he expect?

'Jay!' Cat's voice is a whisper on the stairs. 'Is she down yet?'

Jayden climbs to his feet and eases through the doorway; treads stealthily along the landing. When he emerges into the light, he sees his wife's pale, enquiring face.

'She's down,' he says. 'What shall we do? Put the telly on so we can fall asleep in front of it?'

'I don't even think I've got the energy for that.' She looks at him questioningly, then checks her watch. 'You've got a spark about you though. I suppose, yeah, quarter past eight is basically a win. Though we'll pay for it later. In an hour, probably. And the hour after that.'

'Cat, there's been a murder in Mousehole.'

Her mouth drops open.

'Ally's there.'

'What, called to the scene?'

'No. *No*, she was there for the light display. With Gus.'

Cat grins. 'Ally's there with Gus?'

'Erm, that's not the news here.'

'Jay, who is it?'

'I don't know.' His phone's in his hand and he turns it, willing another message to come in.

'God, that's sad,' says Cat. 'I better check in with Old Fran.'

She was Cat's dad's cousin, Frances Thomas, who'd apparently earned the nickname 'Old' when they were just kids, because she was the oldest of all the cousins by about fifteen years. Now it finally suits her – a tiny woman in her early eighties with a loose

10

grey bun and eyes as pale and blue as sea glass. She lives just one street back from the harbour, in a miniature cottage that Jazzy loves to visit, because Old Fran usually gives her a saffron bun to chew on, and she can sit in the window-seat and watch people walk past, just steps away from her nose.

Jayden likes Old Fran too. Sometimes he thinks she's the only rebel in Cat's family. She married twice, lived in New Zealand and Spain, and finally settled down back in Mousehole with a lofty Frenchman called Bernard.

And now there's a murder on her doorstep.

Jayden moves into the galley kitchen. It's nothing like the vast flagstoned farmhouse kitchen in the main house – the house he can see the lights of from the window – but it's theirs, and he's grateful for the breathing space. He loves Cat's parents – well, maybe *love* isn't quite the word, but he definitely appreciates them – although the months when he and Cat lived with them made Jayden's life in Cornwall feel only temporary. And like it wasn't his choice to be here. But it was his choice. Well, it was *their* choice. Cat is Cornwall through and through. Jayden should have known that about her when he first met her in Leeds, but Cat is one of those people who fits in wherever she goes. He took her for a city girl; albeit a city girl with marine-blue eyes, and sea-salt waves in her hair.

As for Jayden, he had needed to change something. After Kieran, his friend and partner, was killed on duty, there was no way he could carry on with his old life in Leeds. Nothing about it felt right. So, with a heavy heart Jayden quit the West Yorkshire Police, and he and Cat moved down to this westerly spot together. To start their family and find a new path. Hard to believe that was over a year ago now.

Jayden takes a beer from the fridge and stares at it. Does he even want it? It's Monday night and he's on autopilot; it's a small reward to mark the end of the day.

He's got the opener in his hand when he hears a noise from above. He freezes.

'Was that Jazz?'

'Can't hear a thing,' says Cat, sending him a look of appeal. She's stretched out on the sofa, a blanket pulled up around her shoulders.

'I've got it,' he says, putting the beer back.

But halfway up the stairs he pauses, hand on the banister. All is quiet. He tiptoes on. He might as well look, now that he's here.

He treads carefully to her cot and peers down at his sleeping daughter. In the dim light he can make out the fullness of her cheeks, her forest-dark lashes, the whorl of her hair. She's heart-stoppingly beautiful, this baby of theirs. And there's nowhere else in the world he wants to be right now.

Except, perhaps, in Mousehole.

3

Monday night in The Wreckers Arms and Mullins is halfway down a pint. He's perched at the bar, beside the sparkling lights of the Christmas tree. Not that he'd tell anyone, but he chose this seat because you get the best smell of the tree. For years, Mullins didn't even realise Christmas trees had a smell – unless you counted the slightly musty pong that their plastic tree sends out when it's first brought down from the attic. *Who wants to spend their life hoovering up needles?* his mum always says, her voice prickly. *Anyway, nature doesn't do them in silver and I like silver.*

The Wreckers is the most festive place Mullins knows. There's always a fire, no matter what time of day or night you walk in. They're big on tinsel, and it's strung along every beam: red and gold and silver. The tree itself is massive and loaded with decorations; stuff you wouldn't think of, like birds with gold beaks and bright tail-feathers, little blokes with drumsticks, love hearts.

Did he, Mullins, just say *love hearts*?

And people – there are always people at The Wreckers. Even if they aren't talking to him directly, he likes their presence. In another life, Mullins might have liked to belong to one of those big families you see on telly; the kind where they all sit round the table together and argue and banter and snatch, but the love is real, and anyone can see that. At the house he shares with his mum on Ocean Drive it feels like the wind whistles clean through it sometimes: just two flimsy figures – okay, you'd never describe Mullins as flimsy, but that's how he feels at times – and all that space between them.

He's just thinking on whether to order a bowl of chips when his phone goes.

'Sir?'

Mullins's eyes widen as Detective Sergeant Skinner speaks. He instinctively reaches for his pint – then draws his hand back again when he hears that one word: *murder*. He wasn't on duty, but now he is. It's going to be all hands on deck, isn't it? He feels a thud of reluctance. Right before Christmas too.

'You want me there now?'

'I want you there yesterday. Bobbies on the beat might have stopped this.'

'There hasn't been a bobby on the beat since Bill Bright back in the day, and—'

'Metaphorically speaking, Mullins. Now stop dithering and get yourself to Mousehole.'

Mousehole! He straight away thinks of the lights. The last time he saw them he was a kid, and he remembers it like it was yesterday. He had a pocket full of treacle toffees and a scarf wrapped tight around his neck; an itchy tartan one that he didn't much like, but he wore anyway because his dad had one just like it. *Chequered mates!* his dad used to say, something Mullins didn't get at the time because he was no kind of a chess player, not then and not now, but the mate bit was good. They were in Mousehole together that night, the three of them, looking like a family out of a Christmas card. It was one of the last times.

And they were great, the lights.

With that thought he's up and at 'em, scattering his coins on the counter, pulling his coat over his shoulders, saying, 'Gotta go, police business!'

14

Mullins parks at the edge of the village. He half expected the place to have emptied – the discovery of a dead body not exactly fitting the festive mood – but the narrow streets are full of bustling people togged up in hats and scarves and coats. He breaks into a trot, and his breath comes in white puffs like a carthorse in a winter field. When he hits the harbour, he slows down and takes in the full spectacle of the light display; he feels his cheeks ache as he sees the three ships, their electric reds and yellows and blues making the water glitter with a rainbow.

The boats. They were the ones he liked the best back then.

One for each of us, he remembers saying. His mouth so sweetly clogged with toffee, looking at his mum and dad and not seeing anything in their faces to worry him at all. Well, people are liars as it turns out, and there is a murderer here in Mousehole tonight. Merry Christmas, eh?

Mullins follows his nose to the end of the harbour where blue tape flickers and bright lights turn, as if the cops are trying to outdo the village display. That's when Mullins sees that he's been beaten to it. Not just by Skinner – there he is in his black coat, tall as a crow, barking orders – but by the Major Crimes lot, down from Newquay. What are they doing – crouching on their starting blocks just waiting for someone to fire a gun?

A blunt object, actually. Multiple blows. A clear head wound. That's what Skinner said on the phone.

'Better late than never. Get yourself over here. There's witness statements to take; they've been lining up freezing their behinds off this last half hour.'

Mullins blinks at his senior officer. Skinner's moustache looks frosty, like the cold night air has settled on it, or he's just taken the top off a pint. Mullins sees him wipe it with the back of his hand, then lick his finger.

'Hot chocolate,' he says. 'But don't you get any ideas. Witness statements. Go.'

'Do we know who it is?' asks Mullins, craning past Skinner towards the boat. Like most of the harbour's craft, it's been hauled up in the car park for the winter; there's a bright blue tarpaulin pulled all the way back. He sees a crouching figure and the flash of a camera. The name *Sea Pup* on the stern.

'John Paul Sharpe. Goes by the name JP. A chef up at Mermaid's Rest. Not one of your watering holes I should imagine, Mullins.'

Mullins rubs his nose with the back of his hand. Well, Skinner's right there. All he knows about Mermaid's Rest is that it's a place that fancies itself. Back in the day it was a decent old pub with a community attached, but now it's for people with more money than sense. And depending on the time of year, there's plenty of that lot about down here.

'What about the boat?' he asks.

'Word is it belongs to Trip Stephens, local fisherman.'

'You'd have to be a special kind of idiot to hide a body on your own bloody boat,' says Mullins.

'Stranger things have happened at sea,' says Skinner, and then he's already turning away, his eyes on the Newquay lot.

Mullins spots the neat bob of DS Chang. Their paths crossed back in the spring with the Lewis Pascoe and Helena Hunter case, and Mullins remembers wishing she could have done a swap with Skinner. He's pretty sure DS Chang would never attend a crime scene with a hot-chocolate moustache.

He tweaks his collar and walks towards *Sea Pup* and the cluster of people gathered round her. He feels a shifting in his stomach as he gets closer, and his mind goes to the chips he never got to order at The Wreckers. Hunger? No. The thought of chips – oily, salty chips, dolloped all over with blood-red ketchup – makes his insides churn. He presses his hand to his mouth, as if he might actually puke.

Then it hits him.

There's a body on that boat. And this is Mullins's first proper murder.

4

'Tim, good evening.'

Ally sees Mullins jump as she says his name. When he turns to face her his cheeks are sallow and there's a sheen to his forehead, detectable even in this half-dark.

'Are you feeling alright?' she asks.

'Mrs Bright. Ally. Um, yeah.' He glances back towards the boat. 'Did they call you too?'

Ally shakes her head. While her work with Jayden back in the spring earned them some respect from the Devon and Cornwall Police – grudging respect, in the case of certain officers – they're hardly going to be on anyone's first-responder list. She explains that she was here to see the light display, just part of the crowd, when they heard the scream.

'What, you and Jayden?'

'Me and Gus.'

'Oh, he's here, is he?' says Mullins, appearing to brighten.

Ally finds it touching, how much Mullins likes Gus. Back in the summer they talked rural police procedure over a pint or two at The Wreckers, research for the detective novel that Gus came to Cornwall to write. Maybe it's because the young officer likes feeling like an authority on something. Or maybe it's more than that. Gus has a solidity to him; a reassuring presence that perhaps Mullins doesn't find elsewhere.

Ally finds herself capable of thinking this about Gus, while simultaneously feeling a swell of panic at whatever he was about to say before the scream. *These last few months you've . . .*

'Kids found the body,' says Mullins. 'Couple of teenagers, wanting a cheeky can and a place to neck. Pulled back the tarp and whammy, there it was.'

Ally sees his eyes flick back towards the boat. He scratches the side of his head.

'Not a nice sight really,' he says.

'Do you know who it is yet?'

Mullins opens his mouth then closes it again. 'Bloke. Forties? I shouldn't be telling you much more than that.' He starts to turn away.

'There's already talk,' says Ally. 'Talk of who it is.'

She nods back towards the crowd. A sizeable group of villagers and curious tourists remains, huddled on the other side of the tape. Since the scream, fragments of information have swirled through the crowd, like flotsam and jetsam caught in fast currents. And Ally's found herself reaching out to catch every single one of them.

That bloke from Mermaid's Rest.

Nasty piece of work. God rest him, obvs.

'And we'll get it all down in our notebooks, Mrs Bright. Don't you worry. Wait, what, how do you know anyway? Are you interviewing people?'

'Of course not.'

How strange it is, that he sees her this way. Ally has been invisible for so long she's still getting used to the idea of being seen – and as some kind of a detective too. Ally thinks of herself as strictly amateur and Jayden would probably say the same thing about himself – but no, Jayden's professional through and through. Ally can't help feeling that whatever they're doing here together, there will come a day when it won't be enough for Jayden anymore. But until that time comes, she's going to enjoy every moment of both his company and his experience.

They don't advertise. There's no website or social media or anything like that. But people round here call them the Shell House Detectives.

'I just overheard a few things,' she says, casually.

She turns, sensing Gus approaching.

'Evening, Tim,' he says. 'Terrible business.'

Mullins gives a stoical bob of his head. 'All in a day's work.'

Just then there's a shout from the boat.

'Found something on him!'

Mullins shoulders off towards the huddle of police, and Ally watches him go.

'So . . .' hedges Gus, 'what did you want to do?'

I want to stay, thinks Ally. *I want to know what's happened here.*

'If I was any kind of bona fide crime writer I expect I'd be taking notes,' he says with a shiver. 'Making the most of being at a real live crime scene. But I haven't got the stomach for it. All I can think is how nice it'd be to be at home with the fire going. Couple of crumpets. I know it's late, but did you fancy . . .'

Two young women jostle past, arm in arm, and Ally steps aside to let them go.

'Bev will be dancing on his grave, mind,' one says, followed by a cackle.

'Don't,' cries the other, 'that's awful!'

Ally watches them go, resisting every urge to follow them. Instead she pockets the name, like a shell from the strandline. She'll take it out later, look closer at it. Share it with Jayden too.

'Ally?'

And there's the slightest tinge of impatience in his voice. She knows Gus deserves her full attention.

'Sorry! Yes?'

But as she says it, she's glancing towards the boat, wondering whether she should pass on this name she's heard to Mullins and Skinner. There's a cluster of officials at the railing, their heads bent over something. As she watches, she sees Mullins step backwards – his eyes are wide and round as saucers, and he mouths an unmistakable swear word.

Through the space he's created, Ally can see the flash of a piece of white paper. Then the circle closes again; Mullins's professionalism resumed.

'I think they've found something,' she says, turning at last to Gus.

5

Trip Stephens chucks another log on the fire and watches the flames take a hold of it, licking all the way up to the top of the burner. He settles back on the sofa, and the busted springs creak beneath him. All the lights are off and the uneven walls of the old cottage dance with shadow. Trip picks up his mug of tea and takes a slug. This room of his feels very small on evenings like this. Life feels very small.

When he's cutting through the waves on *Night Dancer*, that's when Trip feels like all is right in the world. Fishing isn't just about the catch, or the cash – though it is a bit, because it's his livelihood – it's about being out in it. Being part of it. Keeping his feet, keeping his head, through all the pitch and toss. Steaming out just before dusk – now that's his kind of all-nighter – leaving the lights of land behind him. Shooting out the nets under the stars, silver haul upon silver haul of finest Cornish sardines. Then back to Newlyn in the pink dawn, Trip all lit up inside and out.

When he stays too long on land, a strange sadness settles in his bones and the only way to shake it out is to pull on his boots, up anchor and get back out. He knows he isn't the only fisherman to feel like this. Years back, Wilson said that's how it was for him. That was when Trip was a boy, and school was just another thing getting in the way of fishing. Wilson seemed to be the only one who understood it, then. When it came to Wilson hanging up his skipper's hat, Trip knew how lucky he was to get it – he's only twenty-four himself – however temporary an arrangement it might turn out to be.

Trip picks up his phone and weighs up whether to message Wilson and ask him if he's alright; see how his dinner with the missus went last night. But he decides to leave it. It might sound like he's on the make.

When it's too rough to fish, there's no pay. Trip knows that, it comes with the life. You can't help the weather, just as you can't help how the fish come and go. No point losing your head over things you can't control. Maybe that's why fishermen are a superstitious lot. Or maybe that's just Wilson. Yeah, that's mostly Wilson, with his little black pottery cat tucked up high in the wheelhouse, blessing every voyage. No whistling onboard. Don't even think about wearing green. Old sailors' stories, but why not?

It hasn't helped lately though. These last months, they've had a slew of bad luck: a run of lousy catches, chasing shoals that turned out to be nothing but piss-poor scad; the engine packing up out of nowhere, thousands it cost to replace it; Wilson's fall, catching his foot in a stray rope and going over and staying down – still, even now, not quite back up. And this weather – you'd have to be desperate to go out in it.

On top of it all, there's Mermaid's Rest, and the kick in the teeth that was. Trip shakes his head, and it feels like something's loose in there, banging at his temples. He knows that when they lost the contract, it was because of what happened at the end of the summer, when he took JP and that loser Leo on the boat. Their feet hardly touched the deck, but still, it was long enough for Trip to realise that it had been a very stupid idea. Long enough for the damage to be done.

Does Trip really believe that? He's getting as superstitious as Wilson. But the fact remains. It used to be good business having a fancy place like Mermaid's Rest on the books.

He puts the phone down. He doesn't want his boss thinking he's looking for a handout. Though with Christmas around the corner, it would be useful.

Trip settles back on the sofa, stares into the flames. Fire and water. That's where it's at. Maybe it's the things that can hurt you that he admires the most. He's just rolling that troubling thought around his brain when there's a smart knock at the door. Followed by a ringing of the bell.

Trip gets to his feet. He doesn't really think about who it might be or what they might want, he just pulls open the door.

And it's the police. Standing on the doorstep, side by side, like salt and pepper pots. But their hats are on. When his brother died, their hats were off; they held them in their hands, as if that changed anything about what they were about to say.

Hats on. Okay.

'How can I help?' he says.

And Trip's calm as you like.

6

Bev Potter sees off the last fish finger in two bites. Cold peas are no one's idea of fun though, and she tips them into the bin. The chips, obviously, are long gone. She drops the ketchup-smeared plates into the washing-up bowl and reaches for the tap, then stops. It'll keep.

She can hear the television on in the other room; some loud-mouthed cartoon that has her boys hooked. She flicks on the radio and it's the news, so she turns it off again just as fast.

It doesn't take much to knock her down these days.

The worst of it is that the boys' letters to Santa – the ones they think she's posted off to the North Pole – are burning a hole in her knicker drawer. She daren't show them to Neil because she knows he'll say it like it is: *We just can't do it this year, Bev.* Then she fills in the next bit herself: *If you hadn't gone and lost it . . .* Though she knows he'd never do that to her. Neil is always on her side, and he'd go toe to toe with anyone in her name. This time, though, she did it for herself – she fought her own battle and lost that too. And she still can't bring herself to tell Neil what really happened. No, that ship has sailed, and all that's left in its wake are massive great waves of guilt.

This is what Bev keeps coming back to: it was her tips from the moneyed lot up at the Mermaid that would have made the Lego possible. Every time she plastered on a smile or held her tongue was worth a handful of bricks, until it added up to the kind of sets the boys had written off to Santa about. How many fully magical Christmases do they have left in them? Because it isn't that their mum will be letting them down on Christmas morning – it'll be Father Christmas. The man who, against all odds – against playground gossip and someone's older brother and just the biting bloody reality of the world – they still believe in. It's a miracle that they do. And now she's about to tear it all down, all because she let the job get to her.

Bev moves to the window, presses her face up against the glass. Her breath mists the pane and she wipes it with her sleeve. From here she can see the lights of Newlyn stretching below her; the sparkling outline of a reindeer on a rooftop, a string of flashing blue lights wound around the fuzzy-headed palms; the dark glimmer of the water beyond. It isn't much, their house, but it has one hell of a view. If they put it on the market some out-of-towner looking for a fixer-upper would snap it up in seconds. But she can't do it. They can't do it. She was born in this house, upstairs in their avocado bathroom; that'd be the first thing to go, if anyone bought this place. No one else giving a fig that thirty-seven years ago in this very room she flew into her dad's waiting hands, like one of the rugby balls he caught every Sunday, and as he took the catch, all six foot four of him started to sob, or so the story went. Her mum comforting him: *Come on now, Davey, we're alright, you're a dad now, we're alright.* She who just gave birth. *There, there, Davey.* Her lovely mum, who was there for Cody and Jonathan's births too, not on the bathroom floor but in a birthing pool, in that same room where the boys are now stretched out on the sofa with their gazelle-legs, their shoulder-length surfer hair, just babies who believe in Santa and want him to bring them a little bit of Lego for Christmas.

Bev can't sell the house. But maybe they can't afford to live in it either.

She hears Neil's key in the lock and instinctively she moves to the sink. She needs to look busy; the least she can do is keep things in order. There's the rustle of his coat as he shrugs it off, the clunk of his boots landing in the heap beneath the stairs.

She sets the hot tap running.

'Daddy!'

Two voices in unison.

Bev takes a step back, so she has a clear view: the boys hurling themselves at him like he's a returning hero. Neil dropping kisses on their heads. She feels her face aching with a smile.

What about one more kiddie? she said to him the other night, in a moment of madness. *I can just see you with a little daughter.*

But the expression on Neil's face said it all. The baby phase: they've been there done that – and of course they can't cope with another mouth to feed. Bev quickly reassured him that she was joking. But, just occasionally, she does find herself wondering what it'd be like to have a girl – and who could blame her, what with the fart jokes and the wrestling and the little puddles of urine left on the rim of the toilet. She's outnumbered around here.

'Bev!'

He's looking past the boys and straight at her. It's been a while since he's looked at her like this: a good-news look.

'You won't believe what's happened, love.'

Neil extracts himself from his sons and comes down the hallway. The bruise on his cheek gives him a roguish look; dangerous job, decorating. He folds her into his arms, and she lets herself exhale; leans into it with everything she's got. She can smell the paint and dust on him. He lifts a lock of her hair and whispers, his voice hot in her ear.

'JP Sharpe's dead.'

7

It's late when Ally opens the door to The Shell House. Fox gives her an ecstatic welcome, planting his paws on her legs and pushing his nose into her hand. She bends to fuss him, her back gently protesting the move; she turns sixty-five next year, but forty years of beach walks have kept her in good working order. Tonight though, she's carrying extra tension; she creaks with it.

As they said goodbye in the dunes, she turned down Gus's offer of a nightcap. There was something half-hearted in his suggestion and who could blame him, really? He never picked up from where the scream made him leave off – perhaps he thought better of it, or simply read her signals: that she was more interested in what was going on at the crime scene than an intimate conversation with him. It wasn't that simple, of course it wasn't. But Ally suspects Gus was about to say something fond, maybe even tender.

She walks to the kitchen and pours herself a small glass of red wine. Here she's strung tiny white lights along the cupboards and a silver star hangs in the dark square of the window above the sink. Her fruit bowl, piled high with oranges, has a sprig of holly, planted like a flag on a mountain's summit. *Nice, Al*, Jayden said last week, and even though decorations don't have to be for anyone but yourself, somehow that made it worth it.

Ally looks through to the sitting room where Fox has returned to his basket and is settled for the night now. She joins him and soon gets the wood burner going. The kindling catches and blazes, the whoosh of air from the vents nothing to the roar of wind outside. Ally already knows that when she steps outside tomorrow there'll be sand in her flowerpots, and pale drifts of it along the veranda and against the door to her studio too. The dunes beyond her garden will be quite reshaped. She lives in a landscape where nothing stays the same, change the only constant. And, most of the time, that's what she loves about it.

But now, Ally suddenly feels very alone.

She straightens up and goes over to the bookcase where she draws out a record. It's an old album of Cornish Christmas carols that used to belong to Bill's mum, sung by the Mousehole Male Voice Choir. They played it every year. Every year except for last year, when she couldn't face it.

She sets the record on the player and lifts and drops the needle. There's a moment of silence, when all she can hear still is the thrum of the incoming tide through the wooden walls, the moan of the wind. Then comes the music. The first strains of 'Lo! He Comes, an Infant Stranger'. So mournful sounding, until the hallelujahs come in.

Ally's eyes fill with tears.

He was here, he was just here. Wasn't he? In his chequered winter shirt; his so-solid shoulders. *Think I've got the voice for it, Al?* as he joined in with the carol's chorus.

She closes her eyes and listens to the music.

Mousehole is a village that knows of loss. Tomorrow, the nineteenth, is the anniversary of the Penlee lifeboat disaster, when the entire crew of the *Solomon Browne* lifeboat was lost to the sea. Ally and Bill were still living in Falmouth when it happened, before Evie was born. Ally can remember the wild storm that lashed the coast that night, and the terrible news the next morning; how Bill stood in his uniform and wept. He talked of volunteering for the RNLI after that, but despite living so close to the water, he was never a man of the sea; Bill's beat was on the land. But they always gave money to the lifeboats. And since that day the famous harbour lights seemed to speak of something else too, perhaps: of hope in darkness. Every year they're dimmed on the nineteenth as people remember those who lost their lives; the courage and selflessness of the *Solomon Browne* crew.

Was it hope that Ally felt tonight with Gus – and is so afraid of? The truth is, if letting Gus in means letting go of her grief for Bill then she can't do it – because some days it feels like that grief is the only thing that still tethers her to her husband.

She FaceTimed with Evie this morning; her daughter sun-tanned in the Sydney summer, Ally's grandsons pushing their faces to the screen, then wandering away distracted mid-conversation.

'I know this time of year is hard, Mum,' Evie said. And Ally didn't want to tell her that it was all hard, so instead she said how lucky they were to have so many good memories – grand memories – of family Christmases.

'Do you remember when Dad laid all the reindeer prints on the beach? I got upset because reindeers were supposed to fly. I thought they were the wrong kind that'd come, not the magical ones at all.'

'Your dad was so pleased with himself too. He'd gone out with his torch, catching the tide just right.'

'But then you said, "Who doesn't see a beach and want to walk on it?" That did the trick.'

Ally can still remember the grateful wink Bill sent her. *Good save, Al.*

Ally sinks back in her chair. Anyone who thinks their life is mapped out – who's foolish or selfish enough to think it even for a moment – is surely in for a shock. Ally has been widowed for a year and a half now. Her only daughter lives on the other side of the world, happily – and quite right too. Sometimes Ally looks at

Fox, no young buck himself, ten years old and counting, and thinks *please don't leave me too*. But, of course, he will. One day.

Not today though, she thinks. And not right now. Ally does her best to sink into the moment. She reaches out her toes to touch his snoozing form and he offers a grunted murmur in response; a twitch of his tail. She takes a sip of her wine; savours its spiced red-berry taste. The male voices of Mousehole wrap around her.

Ally closes her eyes. Immediately, she sees the turning of blue lights and the unspooling ribbons of police tape; the shocked move-ment of the crowd. Mullins's face: his wide-eyed, open-mouthed response, when he took in whatever was found on the victim's body.

Discomforting, but also distracting.

Ally takes up her notebook, and in her meticulous handwriting she sets down all that she saw and heard – including the hearsay too. Then a list of questions to follow up in the morning.

> *Presumed victim: JP Sharpe. Chef at the Mermaid's Rest. Unpopular?*
>
> *Who is Bev and why would she be 'dancing on his grave'?*
>
> *What was found on the body that shocked PC Mullins?*

She glances at the clock. She can wait for the morning, or she can just make a start now. She goes over to get her laptop. Ally has spent more time on the internet in the last nine months than in her whole life before that. Not idly surfing, but sharply focused; as if Google is a giant magnifying glass and she a beady-eyed sleuth.

As she picks up the laptop, she catches sight of the small stack of Christmas cards on the shelf beside it. The image is a reproduction of one of her collages – frost-licked fields, a winter-blue sea – made from ocean plastics she's gathered over time. She started to write

31

the cards at the beginning of December, signing *With festive wishes, Ally*. But her name on its own just looked so incomplete, after Bill's beside hers for almost all her adult life. Now it's the eighteenth and she's probably missed the last posting date. Which, she tells herself, is why she's writing lists of questions connected to a murder case instead of a card to her cousin in Norfolk for instance, or Bill's sister in Yeovil.

Jayden would no doubt turn his kindly eyes on her and gently suggest that what she's doing now is a displacement activity – probably followed by a more forceful reminder that when it comes to murder, it's strictly police business. But Jayden is at least two miles away as the crow flies and almost certainly in bed, whereas Ally has the infinite acres of the internet in which to roam, and questions needing answers.

For all she knows, by morning it could be more or less an open-and-shut case. A guilt-ridden perpetrator turning themselves in, or that flash of white paper being a piece of evidence so damning that the police know exactly whose door to knock on first. The whispers in the crowd seemed to suggest that there would be no shortage of suspects – or people willing to talk. A tragic death, and a crime quickly solved, then on with Christmas – for all except the victim and the bereaved. Or . . . it might be more complicated than that.

Ally opens up the search engine. Her fingers hover over the keys as if on starting blocks, and she feels her heart quicken in anticipation. She begins to type.

8

Saffron wakes up on Tuesday morning and, at first, she doesn't know where she is. The room slowly comes into focus. Her room. Not the Ahangama beach house. No jungle palms outside her window or the croaking calls of pelicans. No warm body beside her.

'Happy birthday, Mum,' she says quietly.

It was a restless night – jet-lagged, uncertain – and she's glad to leave it behind. Saffron swings her legs out of bed and the coldness of the room hits her: yep, she's home alright. She pulls back her curtains and squints out at the day. As if in consolation, it's a near-perfect Porthpella winter morning. The sky is a piercing blue. Only there's a wild wind out there; she can see how it's tearing through the palm in her garden, shaking every frond. She thinks how skinny the palm looks compared to the ones she just spent three weeks beneath, but it marks the garden and she loves it.

Her mum loved it.

And her mum is why Saffron's here. Here and not in Sri Lanka. With Broady.

She was always due to fly home yesterday, but Broady had been working on her to stay. *You've got to be here for New Year, babe.* And it wasn't that she didn't see the appeal of it: paddling out before sunrise in beautifully consistent swell, retreating to the shade for the crushing heat of the day, then barrel rides at sunset; their skin turning golden brown; those lit-up nights and Broady's coconut kisses. The living was free and very easy. Until Saffron found out that Dee, who worked at the surf school, was an ex; and not just any old ex but *the* ex. The one you dread. With hair to her waist and a smile full of secrets, and so damn nice too.

Saffron has never thought of herself as insecure, but she feels like things aren't quite settled between her and Broady yet. He's slippery as a fish – that's his reputation, anyway, she knew that going in – and, so far, she's done a pretty good job of pretending it doesn't matter to her.

Saffron didn't love leaving Broady in Sri Lanka. But she can't miss today. She can't miss any of these days.

The nineteenth is the day her mum came into the world, and Saffron always takes a birthday poinsettia to her grave. She then sits there a while, with a flask of coffee laced with rum, and always tries to think about how lucky she is to have had her mum at all. After that it's the run-up to Christmas, and that's Mum-time too: Saffron has to be in Cornwall for it. She can't be stroking out in azure waters, riding that perfect right-hander; or dancing at sunset with a beer in her hand, the bass bringing the sky down, all those people – old friends, new friends, friends of friends – having the time of their lives. No, she has to be here.

Christmas was always magic with Mum; she made everything beautiful. They'd come back from walks in the woods with their arms full of holly and mistletoe. The kitchen would be full of the smell of gingerbread, the star-shaped cookie cutter in overdrive. And then, on the twenty-third, on Tom Bawcock's Eve, her mum always made a Stargazy Pie just for the two of them; a giant thing, with fish heads winking at the heavens. It was hot and creamy and tasted of the sea.

No, Saffron needs to be in Porthpella. Even if it feels like she's the only one who is. Jodie is still in Australia, backpacking with her sister, and Kelly has more or less moved in with her boyfriend in Newquay. The house on Sun Street is empty. And that's okay. Saffron can be as weird as she wants and not have to explain it to anyone.

After she's been to the churchyard, she'll get a tree and bring out the decorations. She'll play some Sister Nancy, because her mum was all about the Sister Nancy. Then she'll have herself a merry little Christmas. Or something. Maybe a surf, if there's one to be had; after the sweet, warm waters of the South it'll be an ice-blast, but that could be just the reset she needs. And it won't hurt to look in on Hang Ten and see how it's holding up without her. She knows storms have been battering the coast here for the last week. Broady laughed at her for caring what the weather was doing in Cornwall when they were so far away, but she'll be opening up the café again in a couple of months. And she can never tune out completely.

Saffron pads downstairs, pulling on a hoodie as she goes. In her exhaustion last night, she forgot to turn the heating on, and the house is an icebox. The clock on the wall says nine o'clock.

Nine o'clock in Ahangama and the sun would already be high in the sky. She'd be stepping into the shower, washing off the salt water, then having a second breakfast. They had smoothies pre-surf, then often grabbed egg hoppers for after, loaded with perfectly zingy coconut sambol. The two of them sunk side by side in hammocks. Some of the guys would be off exploring, trekking in the interior. Dee off doing whatever Dee did: being hot and nice, basically.

'I could live out here, y'know,' Broady said. 'Couldn't you?'

'And leave Porthpella? Never.'

'I'm serious.'

'What about the surf school you're setting up?'

Which was probably also code for *What about me?*

'The cash would go further here though, hey?'

She couldn't argue with that one.

Now Saffron gets the kettle boiling, opens a new bag of coffee.

It will be quiet, the churchyard. Her mum's grave is in the wilder stretch at the back and even though Saffron hates it, she kind of loves it too. It's always the first place to find snowdrops, and crocuses and daffodils soon follow. In summer it's all big-headed daisies and buttercups, and in the autumn bright red leaves the size of dinner plates scatter the ground. Now though, in midwinter, you have to work hard to see the beauty. But Saffron's always been pretty good at that.

The kettle's just reaching boiling point when she thinks she hears the door. She steps out into the hall and sure enough, through the dimpled pane there's the shape of someone.

She kind of wanted today to be a quiet day; no desire to babble about the trip or hear what she's missed since she's been away. There'll be time enough for all that. Saffron wants to haul up the drawbridge and be selfish for once.

She pulls open the door. And one of the last people she'd expect to see is standing there looking back at her.

'Mullins!'

In his uniform. Hat in his hands.

'Alright, Saff.'

And he says it so gravely, he doesn't sound much like Mullins at all.

'I didn't know if you'd be here. But then I remembered the date.'

She gives a quick nod then says, '*You* remembered the date?'

He shrugs. 'You always go to the churchyard, don't you? Anyway.' He glances back towards the road. There's a woman Saffron hasn't seen before, with a sleek, dark bob and a woollen coat. She walks smartly up the path, heels clicking.

'What is it?' asks Saffron. 'Is everything okay?'

Mullins looks uncertain. He rubs at the back of his head.

'Saffron Weeks? I'm DS Chang. Do you mind if we come in?'

Saffron leads them into the kitchen, clicking into autopilot. 'Coffee, or . . . ?'

Mullins is chewing his lip. And it's the other officer who speaks.

'I'm afraid we've some bad news. Do you want to sit down?'

Saffron leans against the counter, and her whole body is clenched from head to foot as mentally she runs through a quick roll call of everyone she knows and loves.

'No, tell me,' she says.

'It's John Paul Sharpe,' the officer says, then waits for a moment, as if expecting a reaction.

Saffron simply shakes her head again.

'I'm afraid he's been killed.'

Saffron looks to Mullins. He looks back, and the sight of his familiar face is grounding. She realises she's been holding her breath, and she finally lets it out.

'I'm sorry,' she says, 'but I don't know who that is.'

9

Jayden feels the knots of the night loosening just as soon as he gets out in the fresh air and starts walking. The lane down from the farm to the village winds like a helter-skelter and they're moving fast, Jasmine riding up top in a carrier. The wind is at their backs; all the better to head over the dunes with. He's got a coffee date at The Shell House. Not that Ally knows it yet. But murder on their patch? She'll be expecting him, surely.

'Hey Jazzy, you all good up there?'

Jayden presumes she'll tell him if she isn't. Not that she can speak yet. But she can definitely express herself – and she's particularly good at dissatisfaction. Delight too. The extremes, basically. In fact, when Jayden thinks about it, his daughter seems to pendulum from one end to the other, hardly ever occupying any kind of middle ground. Cat's pretty mellow. Jayden's pretty mellow. His whole side of the family is pretty mellow. Maybe she gets it from Jayden's father-in-law – Cliff is quite a force – though he'll be sure to keep that thought to himself around Cat. Jayden thinks of how the last few months have tested the two of them. How their baby is the sun, and Jayden and Cat are separate planets in her orbit; mostly spinning in time but, sometimes, on a definite crash course.

Like this morning.

'I don't think you should be taking Jasmine to Ally's if you're going to be talking about the murder.'

And they'd obviously be talking about the murder. Not that they'd be getting involved any time soon: it was police business, no doubt.

'Cat, she can't understand anything.'

'Don't count on it. She understands *everything*, Jay.'

'Not the M word.'

'Still. It's not a good vibe.'

'I'll give her a bottle and some carrot sticks, and as far as she's concerned, that's a great vibe. And Ally'll get her grandkids' toys out. All good.' Then Jayden said it – and as soon as it was out of his lips, he knew it was dumb. 'If I've got her today, it's up to me what I do with her.'

'What do you mean, *if* you've got her today. *If*. You were always having her today. It was planned ages ago. Don't make me feel guilty, Jay.'

'I'm not. Course I'm not. But when I'm on childcare duty, I make the—'

'Childcare? It's not childcare when she's your own daughter.'

He held up his hands. He didn't even mean it. Of course it wasn't childcare. He and Cat are, on balance, fifty/fifty (or sixty/forty, if you count all the times he does that little bit more). She knew that and he knew that, but couldn't you be forgiven a slip of the tongue when you'd had, like, three hours' sleep?

Cat left for her morning out with the girls with the sour vapour of the exchange still hanging over the pair of them.

Have fun, babe, he texted. *Don't rush home.* Then, *I love you.*

And a string of kisses came back his way, which, in their dating days, he might have tried to interpret the subtext of: effusive, or dismissive? Careless or heartfelt? But they're way past that.

And they're both so damn tired.

The hedgerow dips and Jayden's rewarded with his favourite view on this route. The deep blue of the water. The grey rooftops of

Porthpella. Bright red berries erupting from some tree – a tree that his wife would almost certainly know the name of – framing the view. He pauses for a second, taking it in. For all that Jayden misses the city – feeling, sometimes, like a fish out of water – Porthpella has proved a healer. He's found something here that he didn't expect to: purpose. And quite a bit of pleasure too.

'Check it out, Jazz,' he says. 'Pretty nice place we live, huh? Mummy grew up here and now you are too.'

His daughter gurgles and taps out a drumbeat on his head, which he takes as an invitation to talk on.

'Where did Daddy grow up, you say? Well, sure, if you're asking. Daddy grew up in a pretty cool place too, as it happens. Really cool. Leeds is a little bit busier than Porthpella. Streets and streets of houses. Lots of brum-brums. But parks too. We did have some green, right on our doorstep. And people, so many people: black people, brown people, white people. You'll be visiting in a couple of weeks, babe. And your cousins are going to be coming up too. We are going to have some fun fun fun.'

Jazzy makes an enthusiastic noise. And Jayden takes that word, *fun*, and spins a little song out of it, clumping them down the lane to its beat. There are definitely some freedoms to living in the country – though maybe he'd have been a singer of silly songs on ram-packed urban streets too. *Yeah probably.*

They carry on in that way – *fun fun fun da da dum dum* – the wind whistling along with them, until they're into the outskirts of the village. They go past short terraces of grey-stone cottages and low-slung bungalows with names like Landlubber and Kittiwake and Tidal Reach, as if everyone's vibing on being here. Though if Jayden had a choice he'd live down in the dunes where Ally does. The bright painted beach houses and sugar-white sand remind him of childhood trips to see his great-grandparents in Trinidad. And the view from every veranda there is killer. He nods and smiles to a passing dog walker. Jayden always feels stupidly proud, being out and about with his daughter like this. She's got a bright red knitted hat on; the cherry on the cake.

Just a couple of days ago in Mousehole, he was down at the harbour with Jazzy, just the two of them, while Cat and Old Fran were back at the house. Jayden was totally engrossed in pointing out the little island that lies just offshore, when a voice said, 'A hands-on dad, eh? You don't see many of your kind.' He turned to see a young woman, standing with a sad sort of smile on her face. 'Mine wasn't like that, that's for sure,' she said. Jayden told her that he wouldn't have it any other way.

He stops, now, as they peel out on to the square, spotting a familiar figure; a flash of pink hair, and the quick-turning wheels of a bike.

'Hey, Saffron!' he calls.

But Saffron doesn't hear him. She's cutting down the alleyway that leads to the church. He thinks he's missed her, that he'll have to hear her traveller's tales another day, which is a shame because it would have been cool, to be lifted up and taken somewhere different. Not that he doesn't love what he has here – after all, he's got the best person in the world up there on his shoulders, pulling at his ears. But being footloose like Saffron, surfing her way around Sri Lanka while her café is closed for winter, that's a story that he'll take a vicarious pleasure in.

Another day.

But then Saffron's riding back out into the square; skidding to a halt in front of him.

Jayden grins, expecting to see a grin back, because Saffron is always smiling. She's the perfect beach café owner: bright, buzzy, and makes flat whites that outdo Leeds's hipster-finest. But today Saffron's beanie is tugged down low, and when she looks up at Jayden her eyes are blurred with tears.

'Hey,' she says. She looks down again, spins her pedals back-wards. 'I didn't want to see anyone. But it's you. And maybe you can help. Maybe you'll know more than they're telling me. Mullins is useless. Obviously.' She rubs her hand across her nose. She looks, and sounds, suddenly a lot younger than twenty-four. 'Sorry. Jayden. Hey. How are you guys? Hey, Jasmine.'

Only Saffron, in a state like this, would still bother greeting a baby.

'Hey, what is it?' he says gently. 'What can I do? You want to go somewhere?'

'I was on my way to see Mum. It's quiet there.'

He hesitates for a second. Wasn't Saffron's mum . . . Then he puts it together with the church.

Ace detective, Weston.

'Sure,' says Jayden.

'You've got time?'

'Always.'

They dip into the alley, Saffron walking ahead with her bike. He wonders whether he should fill the space. Ask about the trip. Unless this is about the trip. Or about Broady. But why mention Mullins?

'Sorry,' she says, glancing back over her shoulder. 'This is all just really weird.'

'I'm good with weird. I promise.'

They push through the church gate, and Saffron leaves her bike leaning against the wall. She reaches into the basket and pulls out a small bottle of Captain Morgan rum.

'I forgot the coffee though,' she says, waggling it.

She tucks the bottle under her arm and then they're cutting round the side of the old church, heading down the slope. Jayden can feel a shift in Jasmine's weight, and reckons she's probably nod-ded off.

'Hey,' he begins, 'back there, Jazz, is she . . .'

'Asleep. She looks like an angel.' Saffron blows air from between her cheeks. Then stops, suddenly, by a newish-looking headstone.

Stephanie Weeks. Daughter and beloved mother. Gone too soon.

As they stand together, Jayden starts rocking gently side to side, foot to foot, in case stopping makes Jasmine wake up. That would be bad, when Saffron needs his full attention.

Saffron turns to him. She's unscrewing the lid on the bottle and takes a quick swig.

'So, I just found out two things,' she says.

And her eyes are so full of tears that he can't believe they're not running down her cheeks. He wants to offer her a tissue, but all he has are Jasmine's wet wipes. Saffron turns slightly, and it's as if she's talking half to Jayden, and half to her mother's headstone.

'The first thing . . .' she says. 'The first is that a man called John Paul Sharpe was murdered last night in Mousehole.'

Jayden stops his rocking. In the tree above them a wood pigeon takes off with a clapping of wings that sounds like gunfire.

'And the second thing,' she says, 'is that John Paul Sharpe was my dad.'

10

Ally looks up from her breakfast as Fox starts barking. It's his happy bark. In fact, she thinks, it's probably his Jayden bark. With Gus there's more of a questioning note: or is that her imagination?

She moves out to the veranda. Jayden's crunching down the path, Jasmine riding high in her carrier, bundled up in a snowsuit and knitted hat; she waves her arms and legs, excited by the sight of Fox.

Ally thinks how natural this feels, and how lovely, to have these two people drop by. Their easy presence in her life lessening – and, very occasionally, deepening – the absence of her own daughter and grandsons.

'Good morning!' calls Ally, and Jayden raises his hand in greeting.

But as he gets closer, she sees his face. And she realises it doesn't look like a good morning at all.

'What is it?' she says. 'Jayden, what's wrong?'

Inside, Jasmine is settled on the rattan mat surrounded by cushions. Entirely occupied, she's digging around in a wicker basket full of wooden blocks. Every so often she exclaims, but it seems to be more for her own gratification than to draw their attention. Meanwhile

Jayden sits on the sofa just by his daughter, his long legs stretched out. He cradles his cup of coffee in both hands.

Ally hasn't taken a single sip of hers.

She woke up earlier feeling heavy, as if the shock of being there at the moment of the body's discovery had finally settled in her, quietly calcifying. Last night she made all those notes with such purpose, but this morning she knew it wasn't their case, and that it never would be their case. For her and Jayden, there was no way in.

But now Saffron is involved. Poor, dear Saffron. And that changes everything.

'They're doing a DNA test,' says Jayden, 'so she won't know for sure until, I don't know, could be days.'

'And all these years she's never had any idea who her father might have been?'

'No. She said her mum never told her. And that she was always okay with that.'

Ally thinks of Stephanie Weeks. She never knew her well – Ally has come to realise that she's never known any of the villagers really well – but Saffron's mum was a familiar face in Porthpella; a tall woman, with hair in a thick plait and an explosive, joyous laugh. She died of cancer three years ago, and the church was overflowing.

'JP Sharpe though,' Jayden goes on. 'The victim.'

'Forty-six,' says Ally. 'A career chef. Trained in London and Paris, and moved down here at the end of the summer to take up the role of head chef at Mermaid's Rest. No other connections to Cornwall, as far as I can see.'

Jayden narrows his eyes. 'Al? Have you been . . .'

'Not a popular-sounding person, by all accounts,' she goes on. 'They were saying as much in the crowd last night.'

Jayden gives a low whistle. 'How the hell did word spread that fast?' He shakes his head. 'What am I saying. It's Porthpella.'

'Actually, it was Mousehole,' she says with a smile.

She knows that Jayden misses city life sometimes, and she's often wondered how Porthpella looks through his eyes. The fast currents of tourists in summer. The long and empty winters, locals rattling around like buttons in a box. How everyone here knows everyone – and most of their business too.

As if he's reading her thoughts, Jayden says, 'Did you know him then?'

'Not at all. What about you?'

As far as she can see, Jayden has slotted into Porthpella more or less effortlessly. He has an easy way about him that means he can make a friend out of anyone. And he knows more about people's lives round here than she does – and she has forty years in the village to his one.

He shakes his head. 'No. I remember Cliff saying Mermaid's Rest had gone downhill though, on one of his classic rants. Upmarket and downhill, that was what he said. Did you and Bill ever go?'

'Not together. But, years ago, when it was a different sort of place, I think he played darts there once or twice.'

It's tucked away on a country lane, a few miles outside of Mousehole. The kind of out-of-the-way spot that fills up with motoring tourists in the summer months but is far quieter the rest of the year; not a pub with a community attached, these days.

Ally thinks of the Facebook page she unearthed for Bev Potter and how her employment is listed as Mermaid's Rest. It has to be the same woman. But why would she want to dance on JP Sharpe's – Saffron's father's? – grave?

'Saffron said she was in shock,' Jayden says. 'So, she hardly asked the police any questions. They just told her about the letter and what it said. From what Sharpe wrote, it was clear he didn't know if Saffron knew who he was or not. It was the first time he'd tried to contact her, in all these years. But then he didn't even sign

46

his name at the end, so maybe he thought she did know who he was. Or maybe he planned to hand it over to her himself. The police even asked Saffron where she was last night, as if she was a suspect.'

The expression that Ally saw on Mullins's face last night makes sense now.

She tries to imagine how it might have gone, with the police turning up on Saffron's doorstep. The letter from the father she never knew, and the fact of his death – and which way round they would have presented these two pieces of information. Ally's heart tugs, thinking of the young woman. Bill would have been boundlessly kind, if he'd had to deliver that kind of news.

'I'm glad it was you she saw afterwards, Jayden,' she says.

'Yeah,' says Jayden, his brow wrinkled, 'though I don't know how helpful I was. We called her housemate, and I waited till she came. Broady's still travelling, apparently. Saffron was running away with the idea that JP Sharpe was definitely her dad, but I told her to wait and see what the DNA test brought back. Because if he isn't, well, it's a different stress, I guess. But if he is . . .'

Jasmine hurls a block towards Jayden and he bends to pick it up. She plants her hand on top of her dad's then topples over, laughing delightedly.

'She's going to need her friends,' Ally finishes.

Jayden gets down on the floor, scoops up his daughter and swings her upwards towards the ceiling. Her laughter bubbles and he does it again.

'So, where do we go from here?' she says.

'What, us? Well, nowhere, I guess. Be there for Saffron, that's all we can do. She knew I'd be telling you about it, but I doubt she's broadcasting it otherwise.'

'Last night in Mousehole I heard the name Bev come up.'

'Come up how?'

Now he holds Jasmine over his arm, her limbs draped as if she's a leopard in a tree. The little girl looks the picture of contentment. Ally's sure she can't remember playing with Evie quite so much. As Jayden rocks his daughter back and forth, Ally tells him about the talk in the crowd, and how she then looked the name up online and discovered that Bev Potter works at Mermaid's Rest.

'Al, if you've got anything you should give it to the police.'

'Of course. And I haven't really got anything, I just joined a few dots.'

'We can't get involved in a murder.'

'We did in the spring.'

'It was different in the spring.'

And Jayden is right; it was different. Lewis Pascoe came to Ally for help, and the police made their minds up about what happened to him all too quickly. She and Jayden were united in their shared belief that there was more to it all than met the eye. And they were right in the end.

'But it's Saffron,' she says.

'I get it,' he says. 'And I want to help her too, okay? But I figure the way we do that right now is, like you said, by being her friends.'

Ally wants to tell him that it's more than that – and doesn't he feel it too? The tingling anticipation of a new case. Perhaps he doesn't. Ally's often wondered if it's enough for Jayden, his life here. He and Cat are getting their campsite started, but she knows it isn't exactly his dream job – Jayden has said that what he loves is the detective work. But can he really mean the detective work with her? Over the summer they had a missing persons case that the police had stopped pursuing, and a plagiaristic artist and a swindling gallery. Both puzzling, and satisfying to solve, certainly; for Ally, that kind of thing is more than enough on both the excitement and occupation front, but it's different for Jayden, surely. He's only just thirty, and had a good career in Leeds before he decided to leave it behind. City policing must be so different – not that he talks about it all that much: losing his friend and partner while on duty coloured everything for Jayden, and was part of the move to Cornwall too. Ally is sure it's only a matter of time before a role opens up in the force down here, or even further afield; and if it does, surely he'll take it?

Jayden's professionalism means he plays by the rules, but for Ally, perhaps there's liberation in the fact that, a lot of the time, she doesn't know what the rules are. Now that they have a stake in the case, her determination is renewed. She'll tell the police about Bev Potter, for what it's worth. Then she'll carry on finding out everything she can. Just in case it proves useful. Just in case it helps Saffron.

She knows she's frowning, the lines on her face deeply etched. Jayden nudges her.

'Talking of friends,' he says, a mischievous look on his face, 'how was your night with Gus? Before, you know, everything.'

She realises – not a beat too soon – that Jasmine is grinning gummily up at her. She puts her hands out and Jayden passes the baby to Ally.

'You are the sweetest thing,' she says, cuddling her close, 'yes, you are. And please tell your daddy that he shouldn't poke his nose into things that don't concern him.'

'Yeah, okay,' he says. 'Bang to rights.'

And it's the first proper smile she's seen from him all morning.

'Jayden,' she says, a sudden idea landing. 'What are you doing this evening?'

'Same thing I do every evening,' he says, gesturing to Jasmine with a flourish.

'What about a drink up at Mermaid's Rest?'

He gives her a look. 'Just to see the lie of the land, that what you're thinking? Nothing more?'

'What possible more could there be? We're hardly going to start interviewing suspects.'

'Though if a certain Bev Potter happens to be your waitress then . . . a little friendly conversation, right?' Jayden shakes his head. 'I can't escape tonight. But don't let that stop you. You want to go, you go, Al.'

'Oh, I wouldn't go on my own.'

'So, ask Gus.' Then, 'What do you mean, you wouldn't go on your own? I don't want Jazzy hearing that chat.'

Jayden's smiling as he says it, but she knows he's dead serious too. Ally looks down at Jasmine. Already she seems like the kind of girl who won't have trouble doing anything.

'But I'd stick out like a sore thumb, an older woman in there by herself.'

'To be honest, I think it's the opposite, Al. No offence, but you'd be pretty invisible. And that's your secret weapon, right? Our secret weapon. Perfectly placed to observe.'

'Suddenly, you don't sound so much like someone who doesn't want to get involved.'

'So long as we know where the lines are,' he says after a pause. 'There's no harm in watching, listening, is there? Anything of note, we just pass it along.'

'Agreed.'

'But . . . it can't just be a drink. Not enough interaction with staff. You've got to go for dinner. The full three courses. And you'll want to compliment the replacement chef, afterwards. It's only polite, right?'

'Jayden . . .' begins Ally. And she wants to say that she's sixty-four years old and has never gone out for dinner on her own in her entire life. But then she looks down at Jasmine again, and thinks, *Well, why not?*

11

Saffron sits hunched over her laptop. She's wearing a hoodie, a parka and her woolliest beanie – basically everything she had on at the churchyard earlier. Even with the splash of rum inside of her, even with the mug of hot coffee she's now holding with both hands, Saffron is ice-cold.

When she got back home, the heating hadn't kicked in and the house was as she'd left it. She flicked every possible switch on the boiler, turned radiator dials clockwise and anti, but nothing made a difference. Saffron is a practical person; she grew up in a house where her mum did everything, and so she has become the kind of woman who does everything too. But busted boilers are different. On any other day she'd call Daz, the same guy who kitted out Hang Ten, but not today. The thought of having someone else in her space is worse than being alone in it.

Kelly has been and gone. She's on placement on a maternity ward for the final part of her midwife training and she couldn't say no when the hospital called saying they were short-staffed, and could she come in.

'They need you,' Saffron said.

'But you need me.'

'Not as much as those mamas.'

'What about getting Jayden back? He's so nice, Saff. Plus, he'll know what to do.'

'But there isn't anything *to* do.'

'I'll come straight back here after my shift, I promise.'

'What, to a sub-zero house, when you've got a super-warm place, with a super-hot boyfriend, in Newquay? I don't think so, babe.'

'Then you have to promise me you'll come and crash on Jonno's sofa. Because this is major, Saff. This is crazy stuff. You can't be alone with it.'

Saffron made all the right noises in reply.

'And listen, until you know who this guy really is, don't fill your head—'

'*This guy?*'

Kelly chewed her lip; her coat was half on and half off.

'I know it sounds like he's your dad,' she said. 'And he definitely could be, right? But he could also have no connection to you whatsoever, Saff. Remember that.'

Saffron didn't know what to say after that.

As soon as Kelly left, Saffron layered up, then positioned herself in a patch of feeble sunshine by the kitchen window. She booted up her laptop and sat back, eyes blurring.

Could she be further from Sri Lanka in this moment? The sky outside is trying its best but from this sad, cold house, even the blue looks, well, *blue*. She picks up her phone and sees the message from Broady.

Landed okay, babe? xx

She tries to imagine him taking a call from her, leaning against the banana tree in the beach house garden, sunshine all around him. Dee in the background in a tiny bikini. The others lounging about post-surf; yoga mats tossed down, mellow beats wafting from the veranda. Saffron can't bring all of this – murder, sudden fathers, total head-wrecking chaos – into all of that.

So, she puts the phone down again and turns her attention back to her laptop. Mermaid's Rest fills the screen. It's a rangy old white building with a slate roof and two tall chimneys. The window frames and sills are shiny black.

Celebrate good taste at Mermaid's Rest this Christmas.

Saffron likes keeping an eye on the scene – the good places gone bad and bad places gone bust – so Mermaid's Rest was already on her radar. In the past it was just another country pub, owned by an elderly couple who couldn't afford to keep it going and then ended up selling to a developer from upcountry. At the end of the summer it was given a serious makeover and relaunched as a kind of fine-dining gastropub. Word on the street is that it's way too expensive, and staff come and go as rapidly as tourists. Nice addition to the neighbourhood: not.

Saffron clicks through to the picture of head chef JP Sharpe. Her fingers are trembling, whether from cold or nerves or both. She peers at him, searching for any familial resemblance. And that's when she feels it: a bolt of recognition.

She's seen this man before.

It's a pose-y headshot, JP in his chef's whites with his arms folded across his chest and his chin tipped towards the camera. He's half smiling, but it gets nowhere near his eyes. His skin is pale, cheeks stubbled. His hair's dark brown and slick with some sort of gel. There is, she thinks, a kind of rodenty look to him – which isn't a criticism, she loved *The Wind in the Willows* as a kid. And Ratty was the charmer, wasn't he? Everybody's mate.

His face is definitely familiar. She just can't think where from.

Saffron has always considered herself a 'live and let live' kind of girl, but whenever someone comes in the café, she makes a quick judgement. Not in a harsh way, just . . . observational: she picks up on the vibe. And this man, this head chef, this JP Sharpe . . . she knows their paths have crossed somewhere – and that she had an opinion on him, even then. And she's also pretty sure that he didn't leave her with a matey kind of feeling. She just can't think when it was, or why, or where. He must have come to Hang Ten. Surely that's it.

Could you give me half a chance?

That was how the letter ended. Why not sign his name? It felt like an evasive move, even if he'd been planning on hand-delivering it.

JP Sharpe. Her dad. What if it's just nuts enough to be true?

Saffron peers closely. His eyes are small and set close together. *Beady* would be the word. He has a look of furtiveness. And tiredness, too, with a couple of panda rings around his eyes.

Then it comes to her. Not the backdrop, but his words to her.

That wasn't bad, actually. And then he handed his plate back to her. A scraped-clean plate, no less.

Thanks, dude, she said, all sweetness, then kicked herself afterwards, because it was such a half-hearted compliment that she should have served up a little spice in her reply.

And now Saffron knows exactly where it was and when it was. She ran a couple of cook-outs down on the beach back in the summer and they were a hit: Sri Lankan curry served on enamel plates just as the sun went down. Hunks of butter-smooth fish and sweet blasts of ginger and coconut. She had some coverage in the local paper and the second night drew quite a crowd. And this JP Sharpe was at one of them.

Saffron's hand goes to her mouth. Did he deliberately come along to scope her out? Watching her from across the sand, the daughter he never knew? She was buzzing on those nights – and busy too; she wouldn't have noticed. But if he was her father, why didn't he say anything then?

That wasn't bad, actually.

It doesn't sound so irritating, now she knows he was a chef. Quite annoying, sure, but . . . contextualised, maybe. And he wasn't a seasonal jobbing chef, but a fully trained-up, passionate, talented chef. Saffron scrolls through his list of accolades, the places he worked at in London and Paris. She looks at the dates, counts back on her fingers. She reckons he's in his late forties. Saffron's mum was twenty-five when she had her. According to his bio, JP Sharpe was just getting his start in a restaurant in Marylebone at the same time – *in fact, jeez, the very same time* – that she knows her mum was studying at nursing college in London. She presses a hand to her forehead, feeling herself burning up at the thought of it. It's another connection. Did her mum and JP get to know each other in London?

In that moment it strikes Saffron that, as far as she knows, there isn't anybody alive who can possibly answer this question for sure. And it feels like the saddest thing, that those London days – the two of them learning their trade, JP in kitchens and her mum on wards – could slip to nothingness, as though they hadn't existed at all.

Now someone has murdered this man who could be her dad. Who looks, from the facts – London, the cook-out – like he might be her dad. Is he, in fact, her dad until proven otherwise?

My dad.

Saffron says his name out loud. Then she takes a juddering breath, before exhaling in a white cloud. She takes another, and it's rapid, uneven. She shivers, cold to the bone, and it feels like it's more to do with the reality of the situation finally settling into her than the busted boiler. How can someone have no father at all one day, then a murdered one the next? What kind of move is that from the universe?

Saffron pulls her coat around her and her eyes go to the window, hunting out the steadying horizon. On a day like this, up close the cresting waves will look as if they're laced with snow; the foam crackling over the sand like frosting.

She's never looked at the sea on a blue-sky day and not felt better for it.

Instead she turns back to her laptop. She asks Google Maps how long it'll take to cycle out to Mermaid's Rest.

12

Mullins sits upright in his chair. His pen is pinched between his finger and thumb and his notebook rests on his thigh. The low winter sun is shafting right through the window and he's squinting to avoid it. It's not working though. Just like avoiding thinking about yesterday's conversation with Saffron isn't working either.

She was all tanned from her travels, and that pink hair of hers was a little bit sun-bleached. And even though Mullins knew it was her mum's birthday and that was a sad day for her, her smile was pretty close to bright. Until DS Chang started talking, that was.

Saffron seemed surprised he remembered the day, so she'd obviously forgotten about that time he found her at the churchyard two years ago. Someone had reported signs of a rough sleeper, but when Mullins had got there all he found was Saffron sitting on the grass by her mum's grave. It was like she was having a picnic, with a thermos and a biscuit tin and everything. No wonder he used to call her Hippy-Dippy back in school. She'd offered him a gingerbread star and he'd said no thanks, then regretted it afterwards. If it'd been anything like the brownies at Hang Ten it would have been A1 too.

'So, the victim has been identified as John Paul Sharpe, commonly known as JP. Head chef at Mermaid's Rest, about four miles from Mousehole, under new ownership since the end of the summer.' Skinner is doing that thing where his chest is puffed out like a turkey cock's. It's because the Newquay lot are here again. He struts back and forth in front of the whiteboard, waving his marker around. *Gobble, gobble.* 'He moved down here to take the job in September. Originally from London. Only surviving relative – *confirmed* relative, anyway, and we'll get to that in a minute – is Lisa Sharpe; cousin, based in Reading. She identified his body this morning and then was out of here as quickly as she came. Not a lot of love lost there. They had nothing to do with each other.'

'Is she a suspect, the cousin?' says Mullins.

'Cast-iron alibi. She's into her amateur dramatics, and she was on stage last night. Agatha Christie's *The Mousetrap*, funnily enough.'

Skinner goes on: 'Sharpe was hit over the head, several times, with a blunt object. Possibly a rock. We've got a diver in the harbour looking for it but . . . well, the whole bloody beach is full of rocks. Time of death estimated to be around midnight on Sunday the seventeenth. The body was discovered by a couple of teenagers, Hannah Bowland and Jesse Maddox, just after eight o'clock in the evening on Monday the eighteenth. They thought the boat would be a prime spot to watch the lights from – and have a little canoodle while they were at it.'

'Canoodle?' says DS Chang. 'Is that technical language?'

Skinner adjusts his tie. 'What passes for it round here. Now, the boat wasn't floating in the harbour but drawn up in the car park. Safest place from winter storms, apparently. And with a prime view of the festivities. The kids dragged back the tarp and hey presto. There was Sharpe.'

Mullins sees Chang shake her head. He wonders if it's 'hey presto' that she's not a fan of – or Skinner more generally.

'Theory at this point is that he was killed elsewhere, possibly nearby, and the body was hidden in the boat. Not the cleverest of hiding places, as it sees a fair amount of action, that harbour car park. Chances are it was spontaneous, and the attack itself took

57

place in the immediate vicinity. The boat, *Sea Pup*, is a dingy, owned by a Trip Stephens, local fisherman. He fishes out of Newlyn but lives in Mousehole.'

'Is Stephens a suspect?' asks Mullins.

'He is. Claims he was home alone on the seventeenth, nobody to prove it. Also claims he'd have to be stupid to kill someone and hide them on his own boat in plain sight. And he's got a point there.'

'Double bluff?' offers Chang.

'A risky one. But we'll be considering his motive, nevertheless. Stephens claims not to know Sharpe well, but what he does know, he doesn't like. Distinct animosity.'

'What about Saffron, Sarge?' Mullins can't help it. It blurts out of him like a whale shooting water.

Skinner narrows his eyes. 'Saffron Weeks. Twenty-four years of age, born and bred in Porthpella.' He tracks the briefing room. 'A letter was found in Sharpe's coat pocket, addressed to her. Had a stamp on the envelope, but no postmark. An important letter though – as, in it, he claims to be the father she never knew she had. She's been notified. Meanwhile she has an alibi. She was in Sri Lanka at the time of the murder, and on a coach from Heathrow when the body was found.'

He points to a photograph taped to the board.

'In it, the writer expresses regret for the years lost and suggests the possibility of a meeting. He doesn't sign it, instead he writes the words *could you give me half a chance?*'

'A weird sort of letter, isn't it?' says Mullins. 'To send it out of the blue, with this big announcement, and not actually say who you are. He sounds like a jerk to me, this JP Sharpe.'

'Ever considered a career in profiling, Mullins?' says Skinner, with a roll of his eyes.

Mullins knows he mustn't get emotional – only it's difficult; it's Saffron. He chews the inside of his mouth, collects himself.

'Maybe he didn't finish it,' he says. 'Maybe he meant to sign it but then didn't for some reason. There's that, isn't there?'

'And the fact that the envelope wasn't sealed does support that possibility,' says Skinner.

Mullins nods. Encouraged, he goes on. 'The DNA test is in progress, by the way. I pulled a couple of strings to fast-track it.'

'Good. Now let's get back to the letter,' says Skinner. 'There's more.'

A face appears at the door then.

'Sharpe's cousin was just on the line, Sarge. She's dredged up a few names for us. Blokes that Sharpe fell out with at catering college, apparently. She says she doesn't know anything about his life after that. But she remembers these tiffs.'

He holds up his notebook; the page is full to the brim.

'Might be going too far back, this lot. But speaking as someone who knows him – or knew him – she reckons our problem in this case is too many suspects. Not too few.'

13

Phil Butt needs to get started on this Tuesday morning, but the truth is he feels terrible. Yesterday's hangover is back for more, as though lethargy and faint nausea have settled deep in his bones and won't let him go; not to mention a full-body sense of unease, too. This is what happens when you're heading towards fifty. Hurtling towards fifty, actually, with no way of hitting the brakes. No sensible way, anyway. You pay the price for a single night's excess for days to come.

What he really needed yesterday was a sound night's sleep. But that was the last thing he got. It started with his wife bursting into the bathroom just as he was cleaning his teeth. Phil in his pants, swilling and spitting; Melissa wearing a pair of silk pyjamas he hadn't seen before.

'Read that!'

She pushed her phone right up to his face; her voice high as a bird's.

He squinted at the screen – he wasn't wearing his glasses – then spat into the sink again.

'Well, say something!' she said.

So this was what it took for them to have a conversation, was it?

'It's rubbish,' he said. 'What's she talking about?'

'Why would she make it up?'

His wife's face was sheet-white, her eyes rimmed red. Her mouth – the mouth she used to kiss him with – was slack with . . . what, exactly?

'Where's she getting this?' And there was a nip of venom in his voice. Which was understandable, because it was gone midnight, he'd worked a twelve-hour shift, the new waitress kept keying in the wrong orders, and JP hadn't even bothered to tell him why he wasn't showing up.

It was also understandable because JP was, yet again, invading their space.

Phil felt strangely vulnerable there in his pants, toothpaste-spittle dribbling down his wrist. But then he always felt vulnerable these days.

'Coleen's niece was in Mousehole for the lights.' Melissa's voice went up another notch, as if that were possible. 'You don't believe me, do you?'

'I don't believe Coleen's niece more like.' He set his toothbrush back in its pot with some force and regarded her steadily, his minty-fresh teeth gritted. *And it's not like you and honesty are known for being best mates, is it?* he wanted to add, but he didn't. There was never any point in speaking his mind.

'Melissa,' he said, and his fingers fluttered lightly on her shoulders, almost a touch, but not quite. 'Are you really telling me you think JP is dead?'

Her breath came in a gulp. 'Well, was he in today, Phil?'

'No show.'

Melissa chewed her lip. 'Did you call him?'

'Course I called him. I left three bloody messages.'

And the truth was, that wasn't like JP. He was a lot of things, JP Sharpe, but he wasn't uncommunicative. He was too communicative, as far as Phil was concerned, always whining or railing or ranting about something.

61

'You need to call the police,' she said with finality, then went back to her room.

But then the police called on Phil, early the next morning. Just as he was fixing himself a coffee in the bar downstairs.

And they confirmed his wife's suspicions that her friend Coleen's niece was, in fact, bang on the money. JP Sharpe was dead.

Now the police are gone, and Mermaid's Rest is quiet again. Phil has a full mug of cold coffee. He watches a spider – one of the pathetically skinny ones – do something elaborate in its web by the beam above the bar. He picks up yesterday's paper and rolls it up. Then he stands on his tiptoes and sweeps down the web, swatting the spider for good measure. He tosses the lot in the pedal bin.

Housekeeping need to pull their finger out.

Overhead, he can hear the boards creaking: Melissa. She'll have heard the tyres crunching on the gravel, and that sharp knock at the door.

They said they'd be back later and wanted to talk to everyone, the officers. To build a picture of who Sharpe was, they said. But the younger cop's nose was twitching like a rabbit's and Phil knew what this meant: they already had their suspicions.

Phil plonks down on a stool and runs his hands through his thinning hair. He tries to get to the bottom of this desolate feeling of resentment, as if JP is continuing to inconvenience him, even in death. It doesn't need a lot of figuring out, to be fair. And it isn't like the kitchen will fall apart without its head chef, either. Sharpe was a leader, sure, but he was also an antagonistic presence. Sharpe's second-in-command, Dominic, can do the job just as well – and with a whole lot less aggro too. Dominic's had a few days off for sickness, but he's due back in today and can take the reins then. The foul publicity will be a problem, though. The last thing they need in the run-up to Christmas is a cloud of police buzzing around the place; it hardly says 'merry and bright', does it? Bookings are down on what they should be, even without this.

Although . . . rubberneckers? Will the grotesquely curious flock to order guinea fowl and dauphinoise and chocolate orange mousse? Perhaps there'll be a silver lining, after all.

He hears the boards creak again, then footfall on the stairs. Melissa. And he honestly doesn't know how her features will be arranged when she walks in. She'll have been listening in on his chat with the police, he's sure of it.

Phil's heart tugs in his chest and he rubs his hand over the pocket of his shirt; it's as sore as a pulled muscle. What is it that people say about there being a thin line between love and hate? Phil's not sure that's true. But then he's not very sure about anything these days, is he?

14

Dominic is hurrying over the gravel forecourt, in a world all of his own, when he hears someone call out to him. He starts, then swivels to see a pink-haired girl standing with a bike. She doesn't look much like the usual clientele of Mermaid's Rest, in her swamping green parka and bright yellow beanie.

'Sorry,' he says, with a laugh of recovery, 'I was miles away.'

'I said, are you open yet?'

Dominic's late in on his first day back, but he messaged JP on the way over and explained he was running behind. He glances down at the phone in his hand: 11.04.

When Dominic called in sick three days ago, he told JP it was a sickness bug, and thanks to the head chef's self-absorption, he only had to put up with JP's blast of irritation that he wouldn't be in, rather than fielding any more questions. It was a response that suited Dominic hands down, because if he'd told JP the truth about why he needed the time off he'd have got out-and-out laughter – and a ribbing about Dominic being a hopeless romantic. No one needed that.

'Sorry, did you hear?' the girl says again. 'Are you open?'

For a moment, Dominic wonders how she knows he works here, then he realises the broadcast of his black and white check trousers. If she looks closer, she'll see the dead giveaway of his scarred-to-bits chef's hands too. He stuffs his phone back in his pocket.

'We open at twelve,' he says, offering her a grin.

Lena told Dominic that it was his smile that first drew her to him. Every one of her compliments felt like sunshine on his face, back then. So, yeah okay, maybe he is a hopeless romantic. He turns to go, but for all that Dominic's mind is elsewhere, there's something about this girl that holds his eye.

She stands there looking all forlorn, her arms wrapped tightly around herself, and she's staring up at the swinging pub sign with a weird kind of intensity. He follows her gaze to the mosaic of the mermaid's tail and the sweep of her long blond hair. To Dominic, she's always looked like Lena, this mermaid. A constant reminder of what he temporarily lost, but also what he now stands to regain.

My God, the last few days.

Lena walked through the door of his dreary rented cottage the other night, and immediately brightened the whole place up. She'd come all this way just to see him, and he knew what that meant: it was true love that made someone head west on a train in the dead of winter. Of course, it wasn't long before he found out there was more to it than that: love, yes, but also life. New life. He'd never have guessed it, looking at her slim form, but when Lena turned to the side, he could just see the slightest bump.

What did he feel initially? A whole cocktail of emotions swirling in his gut, to be honest. But then, resolution: he would be a good dad. *No, a great dad.*

In an instant, Dominic's comprehension of his responsibilities changed.

He knows it isn't that simple. He knows that technically they're broken up and maybe a baby isn't enough to bring some people back together, but he and Lena are different. He knows where it went wrong for them: all those late nights in the kitchen; never giving the best of themselves to each other. And then he went and moved to the other end of the country. Well, he can fix those things. He loves his job – he trained hard to get where he is – but the truth is Dominic loves Lena more, and these last few days he's come to realise that it's all about choice. And he chooses her. He chooses their family. *My God, a family.* He sure as hell doesn't choose Cornwall. So, hasn't it, after all, made everything simple?

Even though Lena has left now, back on her train to London, the love hasn't gone anywhere: Dominic still glows with it. Lena said she has a lot of thinking to do, but he knows he's stacked the odds in his favour with this stay: freshly made Thai curry the night she arrived; clean sheets on the bed as he took the sofa like a proper gent; passing her a massive bar of Dairy Milk as they cosied up and binge-watched *The Sopranos* together, while outside the wind rattled the windows of the rental. It's the small gestures, as well as the big ones, that matter. As he hugged her goodbye on the platform in Penzance, he let his hand pass just lightly over her middle, thinking about the life inside. He said, *I'll give you all the space you need.* And he's been as good as his word. He hasn't contacted her at all. Except for one emoji-filled text message.

Hopeless romantic.

No, Dominic has a good feeling about the future. And this time of the year is all about the good feelings, isn't it? Not that you'd know it from the look on this pink-haired girl's face.

'Is there anywhere I can wait?' she says. And despite her cool style, it's a small, hesitant voice.

'The garden? Though it's kind of chilly. Better to keep moving!' And he makes to carry on round the side of the building to the kitchen entrance.

'You've all heard the news, I guess.'

Dominic stops. He's late and getting later by the minute, but there's something about the way she says it.

'What news?'

'Oh!' She holds a hand to her mouth. 'You don't know?'

Then she tells him: *JP Sharpe is dead.*

Dominic freezes. He's misheard her; that's his first thought.

'He was found in a boat down in Mousehole. It was out the water for the winter. Some kids were messing about watching the harbour lights and they found him. He was hit on the head.'

Dominic blinks rapidly. How could this random girl walk up and say a thing like that?

'What are you talking about? JP's in the kitchen.' He jerks his thumb back as he says it. And for some reason he laughs.

But her face is all sorrow, and she gives a quick shake of her head. 'No, he's dead. Last night. The police are investigating. I'm . . . sorry.'

There's a moment where the only sound is the creak of the pub sign. Dominic feels dizzy. This, he thinks, is *reeling*. Whenever he's heard people say that word, he hasn't understood it – what was it, a camera film unspooling, a fishing line whipping in? Or this: standing in a pub car park, feeling like the ground has come out from under your feet.

Where has she got this from? And, more to the point, how come no one else told him first? Surely he's the obvious person to contact. Unless this girl isn't random. Unless she's someone important to JP. He looks at her again, then shakes himself. *Get real,* he thinks.

'Dominic, come inside now, mate.'

And it's Phil, clamping a hand on his shoulder. Phil stinking of that cheap aftershave he always wears, the one that goes so well with his polyester shirts. Dominic can hear the crunch of his soles on the gravel so he figures they must be moving. He leans into Phil, sourness rising in his throat. Together they duck through the door, then Dominic's dropping into a chair; a whisky glass is pushed into his hand.

'Drink it,' says Phil. 'I'll be right back.'

Dominic closes his eyes; beneath his lids they feel burning-hot. Outside, he can hear the two of them talking, but he can't catch what they're saying. He turns the glass in his hands. He doesn't want it, but he drinks it down anyway.

You've all heard the news. He never would have imagined the next words to leave that girl's mouth would be *JP Sharpe is dead.* Then all those theatricals, those big, swimming eyes: who was she to care, when it was him, Dominic, standing there, being told by a complete stranger that the guy who mentored him, who brought him along for this Cornish gig, was dead? No police knocking at his door; only this girl, dropping her bombshell in a pub car park. He hasn't listened to the radio or looked online recently. He's been too wrapped up in his own world. His new future.

'I wanted to tell you about it face-to-face,' says Phil, coming back in and sinking down in the chair opposite him. 'I didn't stop to think you'd hear about it some other way.'

Dominic pushes his fingers to his eyes; refocuses. *Spineless suit* is what JP calls Phil. *Cheapskate middleman.*

'It seemed like a good idea at the time, but I should have phoned you. I'm sorry, Dominic.'

Dominic chews at his thumbnail. In a lot of ways, he loves JP. Not in a romantic way, not even in a brotherly way, but he admires him; is grateful to him. He's happy to put him on a pedestal. And he likes the fact that other people don't get it, that they bitch and moan about how harsh JP is in the kitchen, but that's the genius's prerogative, isn't it? Licence to be an arsehole. Dominic has always known how to handle him. And he knows he's the closest person to a friend that JP has.

Had.

He can feel his eyes stinging with angry tears, then the feeble press of Phil's fingers on his shoulder. He stiffens at the touch.

'You feeling better, by the way?' says Phil. 'You don't look so great.'

'Yeah, I'm better,' says Dominic. 'Was better, anyway.' Sweat prickles at his brow, and he trips the lie out with ease. 'Sickness bug. Should have been twenty-four-hour, turned out to be . . . yeah, quite a bit more. I reckon I've lost a stone. Look, Phil, JP can't really be dead, can he?'

Dominic realises, then, that this tale that he's telling might come unstuck. The police will surely be asking for alibis. If everyone at work knew that Dominic's ex-girlfriend was coming to stay, then it'd be easy: alibi central. But, instead, his pride made him tell a lie and now he's stuck with it. Just because he didn't want JP needling him: *What, you really think she'll want to get back with you?* And then, afterwards, the assault of questions: *So then, go on, success or what?* And the truth is, with Lena it's all a little too close to the bone. Newsflash: love hurts.

But, of course, Dominic hadn't known about the baby when he made up his dumb lie. And now the sickness story means he has to say he was home alone, with nothing but a turbulent gut for company. And what if anyone unpicks that? He'll look stupid, that's what. Or worse.

Dominic wipes his forehead with the back of his hand, says, 'He didn't message me back.'

'What's that?'

'JP. This morning. I sent him a message saying I was coming in but that I'd be late. He didn't reply. I didn't think that was weird but course it was. He would have been down my neck, wouldn't he?'

When Phil doesn't say anything, Dominic shivers and looks over at the giant fireplace. There's a fire set in the grate but a match hasn't been put to it yet. The surrounding tables are laid with heavy cotton napkins and cutlery; sprigs of holly in skinny vases, the only obvious nod to the season. He stares at it all dumbly.

He wants, in this moment, to be held by Lena. Not fussed over by bloody Phil.

'We opening up today?' he says, trying to get himself together.

'Of course,' says Phil. 'The flag'll be at half-mast, but the show will go on.'

Dominic gnaws at his lip. 'There isn't a flag.'

'Figure of speech.'

'Phil, who the hell would kill him? She said he was hit over the head, that girl. Murdered. I mean, what the—'

He stops. Phil has one eyebrow raised.

'What?' says Dominic.

'What's the first question the police always ask? On telly anyway. Did the victim have any enemies? I think we both know that JP was pretty good at rubbing people up the wrong way.'

And doesn't Phil know that better than pretty much anyone?

'They've been here then? That's how you knew?'

'What, the police? First thing this morning.'

'And did they ask about enemies?'

'They did,' says Phil, straightening his tie.

Dominic heaves a breath. He has a sudden picture of the first day he met JP at The Peppercorn: the pure snow of his chef's whites; the way his knives gleamed like no one else's; the wolfish smile that said, *I'm better than you, and we both know it.* But none of it intimidated Dominic. He just admired JP's hard focus and obvious talent. But other people? To say that JP was pretty good at rubbing people up the wrong way would be a definite understatement.

'She was upset,' says Phil, cutting into Dominic's thoughts. 'That girl outside. She wanted to talk about him, with someone who knew him. I got the feeling . . .'

'Got the feeling what?'

'I don't know.' Phil's eyes drift to the window, and Dominic watches him carefully. He seems calm, considering. Or has he just given up? Dominic has only known Phil for a few months, but he's noticed that he's become a paler version of himself – and he was pretty limp to begin with. *Ghost Boy*, JP called him once, because anyone could walk right on over him and all the way through him.

'I said we all needed a bit of space. To process it. That's the word everyone uses these days, isn't it? Melissa's certainly a fan.'

Phil picks up Dominic's empty glass and stands up. He's almost smiling, in a way that makes Dominic feel like he can't quite catch his breath. Is this how Phil was with the police too? Because, if so, the guy will be going straight to the top of their list, surely.

'Where did she go?' asks Dominic. 'The girl.'

Because she looked like she cared; like she had something invested. Some people – people like Phil, for instance – inspire indifference, but not JP. If this girl wanted to hear good things about JP, then Dominic figures he's pretty much the only person round here who is capable of telling her them.

Phil shrugs. 'I offered to call her a cab, but she said she was on a bike.' He holds up the whisky glass to the light. 'Look, your fingerprints, clear as day. That's how we're all thinking now. It's like being in bloody Cluedo or something. The police will want to talk to you too. I gave them the names of everyone who works here. Said you two went way back.'

As Dominic nods, Phil skids the glass down the bar and it comes to a stop with a chink. A sudden thought strikes him.

'Whose boat was he found in?'

'Whose boat? They didn't say.' Phil drums his fingers on his chin; a strange gesture Dominic's never seen him do before. 'Though you're right. That's relevant, isn't it?'

In fact, Phil's whole manner is unfamiliar. The guy's got more life in him than Dominic's possibly ever seen. What would the police make of that? Then, as though Phil becomes aware of his vitality at the exact same moment that Dominic registers it, he suddenly changes, as easily as if a switch has been flicked.

'I know you two were friends, mate,' he says, dolefully. 'And this must be hard on you.'

Despite everything, Dominic shimmers a little with that 'friends' line. He's always been so proud of how he gets on with JP when other people can't.

Got on. Past tense.

'Now, though, it's got to be all hands on deck. In fact, whatever management say, I'd like you to take the reins in the kitchen. Until they send a replacement in, anyway. Can you do that?'

Dominic nods. Because what else is there to do? So much for telling Lena that he'd drop the job in an instant.

The door opens then, and the girl from before peers in. Her cheeks are flushed red. And in that moment, there's something about her that looks almost familiar.

'I know you're closed, but please . . . JP Sharpe. I'd really appreciate it if you'd tell me a bit more about him.'

Phil narrows his eyes. 'Are you a journalist or what?'

She shakes her head. 'He . . . he reckoned he was my dad.'

And for all that Dominic's mouth skids open, in that moment he thinks, *Well yeah actually, that could be true, couldn't it?*

15

Ally and Fox skirt the strandline, heads bent, making their usual patrol. The waves are as high as houses, each one breaking on the shore as if hit by a wrecking ball. Seafoam fills the air like a snowstorm. Everything feels shaken up.

Ally thinks of Saffron over in the village and wonders what she's doing right now. Ally wouldn't put it past her to take her board out in conditions like this, and she can understand the urge; let the elements and her body fight it out, leaving all the things that are swirling around her head back on land. Her eyes scan the churning water and she's relieved to see there's no one out there.

What a tangle of emotions Saffron must be feeling. She's a resilient young woman, shiningly so, but this is too much for anyone. Are condolences appropriate? Perhaps just a simple *I'm sorry*: two words that can hold so much. Ally resolves to write a card and drop it in to Saffron later. Or is that intrusive? She's sure that other people don't agonise over decisions like this. She should ask Jayden: he always knows what to do.

What Ally does know is that the thought of Saffron hurting makes her heart clench in sympathy. Saffron needs answers, and Ally hopes that the police will be able to give them to her soon. But she and Jayden can't just stand by and watch, can they? She understands his reservations, but to consider themselves detectives

– no matter how informally – and not do anything feels wrong. In fact, it feels like betrayal.

Ally glances down as a spot of pale pink catches her eye. It's a Smarties lid, one of the old ones from the seventies, with an alphabet letter. She stoops to pick it up, because she always picks up litter, plus this salt-bleached pink will be perfect for her collages; the orb of a setting sun or a child's ball lofted in the sky. But she already knows she won't stick it down. Not this one; not this B.

Is this superstition, or something else? She never knows what the sea will bring in, and that's the magic of it. Only last week Ally found a tiny buttermilk-coloured cat, the ceramic cracked like a spider's web but otherwise perfect. Three days ago, a trio of cowrie shells, implausibly clustered in the sand just a few steps apart. Had they travelled across the ocean like that? It seemed too strange. More likely they were shaken from another beachcomber's pocket, landing together in the sand.

And now this B; B for Bill.

What would Bill say about her plans for the evening ahead? He'd say, *Go for it, Al*, wouldn't he? She stops, trying to imagine the look on his face. But it won't come; not in fullness. Perhaps the reason that Ally can't picture his response is because, if he were still alive, she simply wouldn't be planning a solo dining excursion to Mermaid's Rest.

She walks on, drawn by the glint of light up ahead. It's the sun catching the face of Sea Dream, the vast glass-fronted property that, since the day it was built, has stood out in the dunes like a space-ship. It's still empty, as far as Ally knows, the new owners having not yet taken up residence. And less than a hundred yards away lies All Swell, a typical wooden beach house – dinky and cheerful, with blue-painted weatherboard and a bright red gable. Ally slowly breathes out.

Gus's place.

Or, his place for as long as he keeps on renting it, more accurately. He came to an arrangement with the owners for a longer-term let, extending it through the summer, the autumn, and now the winter. Ally has found herself, on and off, wondering why Gus doesn't just buy his own place if he likes it here so much. Or rent somewhere on a long-term basis. He could probably afford it, if he manages to keep living in a holiday cottage. Perhaps being temporary suits him though; no mollusc-like clamping to the Porthpella rocks for him. Of all the things she and Gus have talked about, this specific point has never quite come up in conversation.

As she walks on, Ally feels a pang of discomfort, thinking of Gus and last night's abruptly halted conversation. It's akin to embarrassment; but whether it's embarrassment for him, or exclusively limited to herself, she can't be sure. Just like she can't be sure if Gus's muted farewell was down to him picking up on her distance, or the shock of the murder. She shakes her head as she thinks it; how preposterous of her to blend the two.

'Now that's what I call perfect timing!'

Gus – appearing to have entirely recovered his spirits with the new day – calls out to her with zest; he's wearing a flour-dusted apron, his hand raised in a wave.

Ally realises she's been standing with her boots planted in the sand outside his house. Meanwhile Fox, thinking a visit is on the cards, has charged to the gate; paws up and barking.

'Mince pies are just out of the oven. Tell me you'll be my taste tester.'

She hesitates.

'You'll be doing me a favour,' he adds.

'I didn't know you were a baker,' says Ally, heading up the path.

'Well, you're probably about to discover I'm not.' He throws the door wide and steps aside for her to come in. Ally notices he has a puff of flour on his left cheek, but she doesn't say anything.

Would she have, before yesterday? 'If they're any good,' he says, 'I'll make another batch to bring on Christmas Day.'

It must have been mid-November when Jayden asked her what she was doing for Christmas. Ally's reply – that she was getting ready for Evie and her family's visit – didn't cut it.

'But they're not coming until into the new year,' he said. 'I mean Christmas Day. Have you got plans?'

Jayden was an easy person to say yes to usually. But this wasn't just him, and it wasn't just Cat and Jasmine either. It was Sue and Cliff Thomas, Cat's parents. Innumerable cousins. A whole farmhouse full of people, all of whom belonged there.

'Oh, Jayden, it's very good of you, but . . .' she began.

'Have a think, Al. We'd love to have you.' Then: 'Gus is coming.'

'Gus is coming?'

'Bit my hand off. Unlike you.' Jayden grinned. 'Though he did ask if you'd be there.'

Now Gus jiggles the coffee pot. 'Shall I? Or . . . is it too early for a nip of port instead? This time of year, I'm not sure it's ever too early.'

'I can't stop for long,' says Ally. 'Fox is restless.'

But the dog has slunk over to the fireplace and is settling himself on the mat.

'How are you doing?' Gus says, meaningfully. 'It was a shock and a half last night, wasn't it though? That body turning up. It's all over the news now. And the whispers in the crowd had it right: chap called JP Sharpe. A chef.'

'Gus, how portable are those mince pies? Perhaps we could walk?'

'About as portable as any.' Gus is already kicking off his slippers and reaching for his boots. 'Coffee-or-port conundrum still stands though.'

He takes down a thermos.

'Oh, go on, port,' says Ally. 'I think it's needed.'

Five minutes later they're down on the sand. She can feel him watching as she takes a bite of mince pie.

'Any good?'

'Very good. Delicious.'

'Too light on the filling,' he says, chomping. 'I was too stingy. Didn't know how much the pastry could take without it collapsing.'

'The pastry,' says Ally, 'is . . . extraordinarily strong.'

'*Tough*, I believe is the word you're looking for. I left them in too darn long, didn't I?'

'Lovely shine to them though,' she says, suppressing a smile.

'I brushed the best part of a box of eggs on that pastry.'

'Ah, so it's egg. I wondered what flavour I was getting.'

Gus groans. 'God, total fail. Ally, spit it out. Don't take another bite.'

'The port,' she says, taking a sip from her cup, 'really does help matters.'

'I'll drink to that,' he says, with a grin.

Ally can't go on any longer. 'Gus,' she says. 'It's Saffron.'

And she explains. The letter, the words, the fact it could just all be true. It's only after she's finished talking that Ally wonders if it's even her place to talk about Saffron's business with anyone other than Jayden. Doubt blasts in, like a sudden gust of wind.

It's because it's Gus, that's the trouble. She's forgotten the hesitations of last night and slipped back into their old ease. And it's dangerous, that ease. It makes her act unlike herself. She's never had a runaway tongue.

'I shouldn't have said anything,' she says abruptly.

But Gus doesn't seem to hear. Instead he stares out to sea, both hands wrapped around his cup as if the port is something warming instead.

'What an awful mess. I can't quite believe it.'

The creak in his voice catches Ally unawares. It moves her, his reaction, and she feels her own eyes prick in response.

This is the trouble.

'To never know your father,' he goes on. 'And then . . . never get the chance. It's . . .' He visibly shakes himself; rolls his shoulders and puts one foot in front of another.

'The letter wasn't signed, remember,' Ally says. 'It's not necessarily him.'

But she knows she sounds punctilious.

As they walk, Saffron's beach café, Hang Ten, is just visible in the distance. Even shuttered for the winter it's a dash of colour in the landscape; relentlessly cheerful. *Just like Saffron*, thinks Ally.

'Perhaps I'll go and see her,' Gus says. 'If that's not overstepping.'

'I'd wait, I think. Give her some space.' Then, more honestly, 'I'm not sure I should even have said anything to you about it, Gus. She told Jayden, not me. I'd hate for her to think—'

'Don't worry. I'll be discreet.'

She sees Gus take a breath, and Ally thinks how hard it's hit him. Though he has always had a soft spot for Saffron – and her flat whites.

'I'm sure she'd love to see you,' she says quietly.

'I won't take her a mince pie though.'

Ally's looking for the start of a smile, or at least a lip twitch, but nothing; his face is quite straight. 'Wenna sells some very nice ones made along the coast,' she offers.

'Along the coast, eh?' And it's as if he's about a hundred miles away. Then, 'But I really think Saffron should keep out of it all. Not get . . . entangled.'

'She can hardly help it. A letter like that can't just be ignored.'

'Can't it? What does Jayden make of the murder?' asks Gus.

'Jayden makes it to be police business.'

78

'Which of course it is.' He raises an eyebrow. 'You want to be involved though? I could feel it last night, even before.'

'Before what?'

'Before Saffron.'

Ally sips her port and shifts on her feet. 'I'm actually going up there this evening. To Mermaid's Rest. For a meal.'

'A meal, eh?'

'Undercover,' she says. 'To . . . observe. Not actually to . . .'

'What, you and Jayden?'

'I'm going on my own.'

There's a beat of quiet; Ally absorbs the surprised – then hopeful – look on his face.

'It's so that I can quietly observe,' she says quickly. 'You know, not stand out.'

'I'd have thought you'd stand out less if you were part of a couple.' He looks flustered. 'I don't mean a *couple* couple. I just mean two people dining together . . . that's ordinary, isn't it? Normal. Boring, actually. But if that's the idea, you know, to blend in and such, it might be a good idea to go with Jayden. That's what I meant.'

For some reason, Ally doesn't tell him that Jayden isn't free to come. Instead she offers him what she hopes is a reassuring, non-committal smile.

It would, in so many ways, be much nicer to go with Gus. Easier, too. So much easier. And he is very possibly right: the two of them together wouldn't turn a single head. But then Ally imagines candlelight and tall-stemmed wine glasses. Sitting face-to-face across a table, like actors taking their place on a stage set, where certain lines are expected to be delivered. What if Gus picked back up where he left off before the scream in Mousehole?

No. Going on her own is a much less intimidating prospect.

16

Jayden can see the police tape fluttering in the wind. The bottom section of the car park is cordoned-off and right now there are more boats than cars; mostly fibre-glass dinghies with bright painted hulls. Nothing like the ones down at the harbour in Newlyn, fishing boats as big as double-deckers and rigged with all kinds of elaborate and mystifying equipment.

Jazzy's pointing and giggling, her eye drawn by a slightly bigger boat up on wooden blocks. Clusters of neon buoys hang from the sides like baubles on a tree.

'*Summer Daze*, that one's called, Jazzy,' he says. 'You like it? We're looking for one called *Sea Pup*. See, there it is. The blue and black one.'

To a passer-by he'd look like a holidaymaker, enjoying the picturesque harbour. And it *is* pretty, no question; a picture-postcard view. There's a ring of grey stone cottages and a tempting-looking quayside pub. The Christmas lights aren't lit yet, but the bright lanterns strung along the harbourside are full of the last of the day's sunshine and have an almost neon glow. The slim strip of beach leads to clear water, the low tide revealing rusted chains and old ropes and a bank of tangled seaweed – just the kind of stuff that Ally would be poking about in, given half a chance. Jazzy too, to be fair, but she's still up there on his back; bobble hat firmly on her head, mittens on her hands. *Okay, Cat, I did take her to a crime scene, but at least she was warm.*

Forensics will have come and gone, taken everything they needed. Evidence – if there was any – bagged. Photographs taken. They could cut the tape down now, probably. Visitors here for the Christmas holidays won't want the reminder that this is a place like any other, after all. Where Old Fran lives – where Jayden's headed next – has holiday lets on either side. Cat said that once a tourist peered over the wall and complained at the sight of Fran's washing on the line. Apparently, her bedsheets were obscuring the last of the evening sun from the patio. If Jayden knows Old Fran, she'll have had a sassy response.

'Okay,' he says, 'we better go. Ready, Jazz?'

This trip isn't going to hold up in the court of Cat, but that's a risk he's willing to take.

Oh really, Jay, just three days after we pay her a visit you decide you just have to go back again? This relative of mine that you see, maybe, every couple of months at best? That you've never, not once, gone and just visited on your own?

Jasmine's idea – that's what he'll say. That'll fly.

He's pretty sure that if his daughter could speak, she'd ask to see Old Fran every day of the week. She has a parrot, an actual parrot, bright as a bag of Birds Eye peas, who says *pieces of eight* in a French accent, because it was Bernard who taught him. And Old Fran's chocolate-biscuit tin is always full to the top.

As they turn from the harbour, Jayden glances back but, really, there's nothing to see. Whatever happened here will be pieced together in a lab by people whose job it is to do just that. As much as Jayden wants to cut down the slope and lift that tape, he won't, he can't, and there's no point anyway.

But if Ally's representing out at Mermaid's Rest tonight, then the least he can do is connect with his own sources – and he knows Old Fran sure likes to talk.

His head's down, thoughts buzzing as he powers up the slope, and it's only when a shadow falls over him that he comes to.

'Sorry, mate,' Jayden says, stepping sideways.

The man walks on without replying. Did Jayden hear a muttered 'watch it'?

He turns, thinking, *Okay, I'll do that.* Jayden observes the man as he moves fast and with obvious purpose. He makes a mental note: Caucasian male, well built, average height; black fleece, brown boots, a knitted hat pulled low.

'Daddy, hurry up!'

A girl in a yellow raincoat appears from a side path, a crabbing bucket in her hand. The man's face changes as he catches up to his daughter, splits wide with a grin.

'Steady, petal, it's slippery.'

The girl laughs and charges on without him.

Jayden walks onward, one hand reaching up to cup Jazzy's swinging foot. He tries to imagine not getting to see his daughter grow up. And he can't. No way.

Since he saw Saffron this morning, all Jayden's thoughts have been with her and how she must be feeling. Now he finds himself thinking of the dead man and the letter in his pocket that he never got to send; how before this final tragedy, there was perhaps another. A story that would maybe never be told now – not with Saffron's mum dead too.

Could you give me half a chance?

Jayden squeezes Jazzy's foot all the tighter and heads up the hill to Old Fran's.

The cottage is in a grey stone terrace, with bright yellow windowsills and a stained-glass picture of a lighthouse set in the old wooden door. A beady-eyed seagull sits on the rooftop watching them approach. Jayden knocks and the door opens to reveal an already smiling Fran. She's wearing the same kind of thing as always: pale denim jeans, thick woolly socks, and an oversized chequered shirt. She looks cool – and it's totally where Cat gets it.

'My two favourite Js!' she trills, her face a mass of wrinkles as she smiles. 'Back again so soon? Come in, come in.'

Jayden ducks his head and carefully wrestles off the baby carrier. Jazzy immediately throws up her arms to Fran, and he watches as she scoops her up. His daughter looks huge in the tiny woman's arms.

'Is Bernard here?'

'I've sent him to Penzance to do a bit of shopping.'

As Fran makes tea, Jazzy sits on the floor staring up at the parrot's cage. Jayden settles into the sofa, and a heavily embroidered throw slips down over his shoulders; he lets it settle, as it's kind of cosy. Fran and Bernard's tiny place is cluttered to the max. Every inch of wall is covered with a picture or painting. A grandfather clock, made for a mansion not a doll's house, gongs out the hour. Old-style lamps with tassel fringes send a warm glow. It's not his style, but he kind of loves it.

'So, Jayden,' she says, her eyes glittering, 'I can guess why you're here.'

He rubs at his chin. Takes a sip of her sweet, strong tea.

'Well, you know Jazzy loves to come, and . . .'

'And there just happened to be a murder. Are you working on it?'

'No, we don't get hired for that stuff, Fran. But . . . I wanted to see if you're okay.'

'Of course I'm okay.'

'It's a shock though, right? Especially in a small place like this . . .'

'They'll catch him, I'm sure. Or her. There's been plenty of police swarming about.'

She's watching him closely. *Eighty-three and sharp as a tack –* that's how his mum-in-law describes Old Fran. Last year it was *eighty-two and sharp as a tack.* Once you get a label in Cat's family, it tends to stick. Jayden briefly wonders what his own is.

'It turns out that a friend of mine, Saffron, is the daughter – or possible daughter – of JP Sharpe, the man who was killed. I guess that's why I'm here.'

Fran's cup clatters in its saucer. 'Ah. Oh dear.' Then, 'So you are working on the case a little, then?'

Jayden gives a brief shake of his head. 'Did you know the victim? He was pretty new to Mousehole, right?'

Fran crosses her ankles. Nods slowly.

'Knew him by sight. But I don't think we ever swapped more than a passing "good morning", if that. He hadn't been here very long, as you say. And he worked away from the village.'

'Up at Mermaid's Rest.'

'Quite right. Late hours too, I expect. Bernard did a spell in the kitchen years back and it's a profession that does take its toll in the end. Though not as much as walking from the harbour car park apparently.' She holds up a hand. 'Sorry, poor taste.'

'I expect you know how the body was found?'

'Oh yes. Bernard went down to the harbour last night. We saw the blue lights, you see. And a neighbour knocked. Word travelled, as it does.'

Fran sets her cup on the coffee table.

'Mousehole isn't like other places,' she goes on. 'We pull together, those of us who properly live here. People talk about the streets full of holiday houses, nothing but dark windows for a lot of the winter, but let me tell you, at this time of year our lights shine brightly, and I don't just mean the Christmas decorations.

Community: that's what I'm talking about. Today, the nineteenth, we mark the loss of the *Solomon Browne* lifeboat. You know about that, don't you? We'll dim the harbour lights tonight, honouring the bravery and selflessness, reflecting on the lives lost. After, they burn bright again. Then on the twenty-third we celebrate the legend of old Tom Bawcock. You know, the fisherman? Everybody comes together for the party. Community matters here, my love, that's what I'm saying. That's what it means to live in Mousehole.'

Jayden nods, moved by the tears in Old Fran's eyes.

'Did JP Sharpe get that?'

'I can't speak for him. And I'm not sure there's anyone here who could. He kept himself to himself. Didn't drink in the pub. Didn't make an effort to get to know his neighbours, far as word went. He argued with one once though, Terry Harris, about access rights through a shared yard. But it blew over soon enough. Terry's not the type to hold a grudge.' Fran takes another sip of tea. 'No, it's Mermaid's Rest that's the sticking point, I'd say, Jayden.'

He reaches for his mental notebook. 'How do you mean?' he says, all cool.

'Well, back in the day, Mermaid's Rest was doing local before it became trendy. Everyone was, it just made sense. If you ordered chicken and chips, those spuds were growing in Cornish fields and the chickens were scratting in Cornish yards. Word got around that when the new lot took over up there a few months ago, they changed all the suppliers. And the worst of it was the fish. An ocean full of riches at their fingertips but they went and shipped it all in from elsewhere.' Fran shakes her head. 'So, when you ask if JP Sharpe "got it", I'd say all in all no, no he didn't. Not as far as most people round here were concerned.'

'It's not a motive for murder though, is it? Hospitality contracts?'

Fran narrows her eyes. She reaches down to gently stroke Jazzy's cheek. Jazzy, entranced by the parrot, hardly registers it.

'P'raps not. You know much more about that than me, motives and such. What I would say, is that a decision like that – to get your fish out of county when there's people on your doorstep trying to make a living, and a hard one at that – that's a slap in the face, that is. We live at the edge of things here, Jayden, and we should be pulling together, not pushing each other away.'

'Do you know who supplied fish to Mermaid's Rest before it was taken over?'

'It came from Newlyn, as I remember. So, your friend – Saffron, is it? – she never knew him then, this dad of hers?'

'She never knew him,' says Jayden. But he's still thinking on the fish thing, and how much a decision like that might upset certain people. Was it a coincidence that JP's body was found in a fisherman's boat? He'd be chewing that over with Ally soon enough.

'This friend of yours isn't a suspect, is she?' asks Fran.

Jayden lowers himself to the carpet and huddles his daughter into him. 'No way. Anyway, she was flying back from Sri Lanka. Come on, Fran, what's the word on the street? Because people must have been talking, right?'

Fran crumples a smile. 'The word on the street, eh?'

'Uh-huh. Lay it out for me.'

'You miss it, don't you, sweetheart? The police.'

Jayden shakes his head. 'I like what Ally and I are doing.'

'It has its limits though, doesn't it? I should think it does. And you strike me as a young man who should be going all the way. A case like this, for instance, you shouldn't be on the sidelines, Jayden.'

He holds her eye for a moment, then says, 'Fran, you're changing focus, dodging the question. Oldest trick in the book, that is.'

'Oh, I am, am I? Well, the word is . . . that someone, or something, must have caught up to him.'

'So not a case of wrong place, wrong time then.'

'I shouldn't have said so, no. But, of course, whoever you're looking for could be long gone by now. Disappeared upcountry.'

Or still right here. But he doesn't want to scare Old Fran.

'Or they could be sitting pretty right around the corner,' she says. 'There's always that. Now, more tea, my love?'

17

Trip takes the hill to Wilson's place on foot. There are gusts peeling in off the sea and the hedgerows are shaking with it. Maybe if this wind can get inside his brain too, then things might even up a bit: right now, it's a mess in there.

Is someone out to get him?

That's the thought that's holding him to ransom – and it's the police that put it there.

There are better places to hide a body, the officer said. *It feels . . . considered.*

It wasn't the first time Trip's given a statement to the police, but he isn't about to worry that he's under suspicion. Because for what exactly? Having the bad luck to own a boat that's out the water for the winter and some lunatic goes and dumps a body in it?

But why his boat? There are more than a few answers he could give to that one. Because it wasn't just any body. It was JP Sharpe.

Ever since Trip was a teen it's been Wilson he turns to when the going gets rough. He always has the answers, even if they aren't spoken out loud: just by standing shoulder to shoulder with the man you have the feeling that things will be okay, one way or another.

And that's what he needs now.

At the rock etched with the name Bay View, Trip steps off the road and heads down the driveway. The slope pitches like the face of a wave, then breaks evenly on a gravel pathway in front of the bungalow. A gnome with a fishing rod sends a wink in his direction. Dawn's work. Her idea of a joke – and not a bad one, because there is something of Wilson in the bearded bloke, the twinkling eyes. But there's no catch on the end of the gnome's line and that most definitely isn't Wilson Rowe. No one knows fishing like him.

Trip rings the bell and waits. Inside he hears yapping and, as he leans close, the scratching of claws on the lino floor. Clementine and Suma: the two terriers Dawn took on three Christmases ago, a rescue-centre brother and sister. *No manners, those two*, Wilson likes to drawl. *Best sent back where they came from*. But Trip's seen the way he bends down to stroke behind their ears, the way he gives them beef trimmings on a Sunday, even though he calls them *Dawn's mutts* and won't walk them for love nor money.

'It's only me,' Trip calls through the letterbox, thinking his voice might calm them down. He hits the bell again. The yapping goes stratospheric.

Trip sees then that Dawn's little blue Nova isn't in the driveway. So, it'll be Wilson making his way slowly from the conservatory. It's getting on for three months since he did his leg in and it seems to have aged him twenty years.

Trip tries the door and it's open. He pushes it and the dogs surge to his ankles. One – is it Clementine or Suma? – gets his laces between its teeth.

No manners.

'Alright, Wilson, it's me!' he calls.

'Come in, son.'

A low voice, and one with effort in it. Down the hallway Trip sees his friend and boss lowering himself back down into his armchair.

Trip peels off his boots, risks his feet with the terriers, and pads down to the conservatory. Mercifully the dogs don't follow. They can smell the fish on his boots and are licking them.

'How do?'

'Ideal,' says Wilson. It's what he always says, but these days it's not exactly true.

Trip drops into a chair across from him. 'Dawn's out?'

'At her sister's.'

Trip's eyes settle into the glittering view. This is why Wilson moved, so his story goes. For years he lived in a cottage just a street back from the harbour, an old granite terrace with ceilings that grazed your head and a sitting room you could stretch out your arms in and near enough touch the opposite walls. If Wilson wanted sunshine then he'd sit on a bench by the harbour, swarms of tourists admiring his quaintness, an actual fisherman in a knitted jumper and stinking boots, taking his ease by the waterside. Then they buggered off for half the year and this watery front garden was all his again. But then he met Dawn, and when her mum died this bungalow became available and well, you couldn't top the view, could you?

Since he's been off the boat Trip doesn't know if it makes it better or worse for Wilson, seeing the sea all laid out like this; like being an artist with a canvas you can't paint on.

'You've heard, then?' says Trip.

'I've heard.'

'My bloody boat.'

'Good as any for it, I suppose.'

Trip shakes his head. He expected more outrage. 'Police have had me answering their questions. Where was I the night before last. All that.'

'And could you tell them?'

'Course. Same place I've been since the weather turned. Shut up at home.'

'Not down the pub? That would've been better.'

'Better?'

90

'Alibi. That's what they're wanting is it?'

'Yep. But I was home alone. Just like the film.' He wrinkles his brow. 'Where were you?'

'Me?' Wilson is holding his binoculars in his lap. He lifts them again, trains them on the water. 'It's not me they're asking after,' he says.

'They might.'

'Hauling a body about, in my condition? Yeah, good luck.'

'You're strong as an ox,' says Trip, partly because he wants to believe it. He doesn't want this man to fade away – much as he's loving his time in the wheelhouse. 'You could have done it if you wanted to.'

'What, killed JP Sharpe?'

Trip chews his lip. The quietness of the house pulses. Even the dogs have piped down. If Dawn were here, she'd be bringing through tea, bustling and chattering, setting down a plate of fairings. Or maybe something Christmassy, because she's gone to town on the decorations alright. There are loops of gold and silver tinsel at the wide windows, and cards strung down the walls. A tree decked with baubles as red as cherries.

'Not worth the trouble,' says Wilson.

'Someone thought it was.' Trip's eyes follow the line of Wilson's binoculars. There's nothing much to see out there. No day-boats lifting up and down, streams of gulls in their wake. No supersonic trawlers muscling out either. 'He wasn't a friend of anyone down the harbour, was he?'

'Water under the bridge,' says Wilson, his eyes glued to the water still.

But that isn't true. The day JP Sharpe cancelled the Mermaid's Rest contract and started shipping fish in from out of county won't be forgotten by any of them. It wasn't just the income; it was two fingers held up to the men scratching a living right there in front of him. Risking their lives, day in, day out. Some people don't think there are consequences to their actions, but there are, aren't there? Like Tommy Roberts, over in Newlyn. He was a consequence, alright. Two months ago he lost his job on Spike's boat because they weren't getting enough catch in, and not enough cash for it when they did; Tommy disappeared into the Bermuda triangle of pubs, carrying his heart in his hands, then reappeared two days later only to fall into the harbour and drown. Tommy Roberts is blood on JP Sharpe's hands, as far as Trip is concerned – or the likes of Sharpe, anyway, and all those other suits who don't get it. And he knows Wilson thinks it too.

But a fisherman wouldn't stitch up Trip, and everyone knows that *Sea Pup* is his little daytime run-around. He isn't the kind of guy to carry grudges or go off like a firecracker; he's pretty steady, all in all. So that body was either in the boat by accident – and fishermen don't do anything by accident, not when it comes to boats – or it isn't one of theirs that killed him.

The more Trip thinks about it, the more that seems right.

He looks at Wilson again, blood pumping in his ears. The bad luck that keeps following them, that they can't shake, all started after JP Sharpe set foot on Wilson's boat, *Night Dancer*. Trip knows that, but what if Wilson does too, despite his best efforts to hide it from him? JP and that idiot Leo, being stupid on the boat. *Leo – could he know something?*

'You were taking Dawn out, weren't you?' Trip says. 'The other night?'

'What night?'

'The night Sharpe was killed.'

Wilson pulls at his beard. He's got the binoculars pushed tight to his eyes again, staring out at all that blue.

'Where did you go for food?'

Trip doesn't know why he's pushing it. He feels like a little boy stretching an elastic band, his mum cautioning, *It'll snap!*

'Nowhere we enjoyed,' says Wilson gruffly. He lowers the glasses. 'Dawn's sister called just as we got our mains. Thought she was having a heart attack.'

'What, seriously? Why didn't you say anything?'

'Saying it now. It wasn't, mind. Just her angina. But they'd been having some trouble and it'd got her riled up. Course we didn't find any of this out until we'd zoomed over there. That bloody son-in-law of hers playing games and causing stress again, working up her Jen. I'd only had one bite of steak too.'

The day Trip started working properly for Wilson, he laid it out: *I don't have many rules, but I do have one: no drama. Whatever's going on for you on land, don't go bringing it on the boat.*

'Steak, eh? Fancy. Where was that, The Manor?'

Wilson nods. 'I won't be going back, that's for sure. Nasty taste.'

Trip watches him. 'She's alright though, is she?' he says.

'Who?'

'Dawn's sister? And her niece?'

'Oh, they're always alright, that lot. Lot of fuss about nothing.' Wilson turns to face Trip properly for the first time. 'Family. You're best off out of it, mate.'

Trip kneads his hands together. Sometimes he pictures a chair at Wilson's table and Dawn fussing over him. It's not a bad image.

There's the faint sound of a car in the drive then, and the dogs are set off.

'Sun's up,' says Wilson. Which is his little way of saying *here's Dawn*. Trip's heard Wilson say it a hundred times, and he can never keep the tenderness out of his voice.

What's Trip thinking, asking questions of this good man? But maybe it's contagious, a visit from the police. Because if he, Trip, is under suspicion for murder, then that's just as stupid as it being Wilson. So why shouldn't Wilson be asked for an alibi too?

Especially because the place that Wilson said they went to has been closed for the last week. Trip's mate Dev works the bar there sometimes. Apparently, a guest upstairs left the bath running and the ceiling came down. There's no way Wilson and Dawn had their steak dinner – interrupted or not – down The Manor.

18

Out on the water the wind is a wall of sound and fury. Saffron wears a hooded wetsuit, and her gloved hands cut clean strokes. As she goes into the massive wave she's as slick as a seal, and when she gets to her feet it's with a lion's roar.

This is it. This is what she needs.

She's caught it, she's riding it in, but then out of nowhere she's flung face down into the water. She feels the salt burn in the back of her throat. Saffron thrashes back to the surface, a flash of unaccustomed panic hitting her, but then her feet skid on the sanded bottom and she stands in shoulder-deep water. She hauls on the leash, her board like an unruly dog, tugging to get away from her.

Today, not even her faithful friend, the surf, is working out.

She snatches at the board and rolls on to it. Strokes her way back to the beach with effort, a feeling of bone-deep failure following her in.

As Saffron trudges over the sand, she can feel the sky blazing, the tint of neon at her feet. She stops, slowly turns. The horizon behind is a riot of pink. The waves are lashing silver. It's a startling winter sunset, the kind you just can't ignore – no matter what else you've got going on.

'Yeah, okay,' she says. 'I see you.'

She's about to turn away when she stops and looks again. Hippy-Dippy, that was Mullins's name for her back in school, and maybe he had a point, because right now she's thinking this: is it a sign? Her mum trying to tell her something, filling the sky with such epic beauty.

But what?

Yes, he's your dad.

There was this moment, this one moment, when her mum knew she wouldn't make it, and she said to Saffron, *Did you want to know about him, sweetheart? Because if you do . . .* Saffron remembers feeling a spark of anger at the thought of it – to have someone else, a third, crowding them right at the very end of her mum's life. There was no way she was going to make her mum feel like she wasn't enough.

I don't, she said.

And she meant it. Then.

Now, she realises her teeth are chattering, and she stamps her feet in the sand. Then she abruptly turns and hurries on.

Inside Hang Ten, Saffron lights candles, mostly because she doesn't want to advertise that she's here. She keeps the curtains closed and peels off her wetsuit, stands shivering on the wooden boards. The little portable heater is noisily getting itself going and she feels the faint puffs of warm air on her bare calves. She dresses hurriedly: hoodie, leggings, beanie over her wet hair.

She knows this small space will heat up, and when it does, it'll be cosier than home.

Her mum never saw Hang Ten, and while that makes Saffron sad, it also means that it's a space that she doesn't connect with her. She built the business from her mum's money – a nurse's set-aside salary, a little every month for two decades, and also a small inheritance from her own father, Saffron's grandad – and Saffron knows the café probably wouldn't exist if she hadn't died. But it's always been a place of positivity. Of looking forward and smiling through it.

Today, it feels a simpler place to be.

The epic cheese plant is curling its way across the ceiling, and the rainbow-coloured skateboard decks on the walls flicker in the candlelight. She scoops up an armful of cushions – tie-dye and ikat, fabrics gleaned from her winter travels – and builds a den against the counter.

Saffron closes her eyes and thinks back to this morning at Mermaid's Rest.

Phil Butt and Dominic Brook. Two men who had spent every working hour with JP Sharpe. Did they act as though they'd lost someone close to them?

Dominic, maybe. But not Phil. He behaved as if JP's death were an inconvenience, not a tragedy. But maybe some people are better at hiding how they feel. They sent Saffron on her way just as the first of the lunch crowd began to roll in. But then Dominic caught the sleeve of her coat as she was heading out the door.

'They'll find who did this,' he said.

And he looked so deeply into her eyes that she wondered if he was sizing her up. Trying to see if there was any JP in her.

'What did you say your name was again?' he said.

She told him. And how stupid that she heard her own voice lift a little with hope. What was that about? As if JP might have mentioned her to this guy? Side by side in the kitchen one day, casually saying, *So, Dominic, apparently there's this daughter . . .* It wasn't like she wanted it.

Or did she?

Now, she shifts on the cushions, feeling the warmth from the heater slowly wrap itself around her like a sort of airborne hug. Should she sleep here? She hadn't planned to. But the cold and empty rooms on Sun Street just seem to hold too many shadows. Kelly would kill her if she knew, she's sure of it. And she's had three messages from Jodie, all the way out in Australia. *Saff, are you okay? Can we FaceTime?* And sweetly, ridiculously, *Do you want me to come home?*

Nothing more from Broady. But then beyond her brief reply – *landed! All good xx* – she hasn't messaged him either.

Saffron pulls off her beanie and tugs her fingers through her still-wet hair. The trouble is, she doesn't know how to tell him what's happened. Perhaps she should leave a voice note instead; find her way through it in a more natural way. Or wait until the DNA test is back.

There are so many ways to react to this, that's the problem.

'How am I supposed to feel?' she says out loud, her eyes filling. 'How am—'

Her words disappear in a yelp.

There's a face looking in on her, at the tiny window without a curtain. It crams the pane like a dark moon. Saffron drops low to the floor, her hand clapped to her mouth. Outside, she can hear feet creaking on the boardwalk. Then the door handle rattles. Her heart thunders in her chest as she wonders if she even locked it.

19

Bev lowers herself on to one of the pebble seats on the promenade. Her feet are sore from pounding Penzance's pavements; her ego's sore too, and it was pretty squashed to begin with.

Despite the wind shoving from every direction, the horizon line is all serenity. Out on the water the sun's going down in a fizz of liquid gold. On any other day Bev would be snapping it on her phone, but now she shuts her eyes. She wishes it'd all disappear. She wishes she'd disappear.

Is JP Sharpe really dead? And a murderer still on the loose?

It should put Bev's own problems in perspective, but somehow it doesn't.

Her bag is at her feet and there are still at least ten copies of her CV inside. The closest she came was at an Italian restaurant with plastic tablecloths and plastic menus and a plastic Christmas tree – and probably a plastic promise of *we'll let you know*. She can't bear it anymore; drawing out a copy, proffering it with a cheerful smile. *Just in case you get a chance to take a look!* While all the time trying not to let her hope – no, more than that, her need – get the better of her. Bev knows she isn't the only person who needs a job and doesn't have one; there are plenty of people around here who are a lot worse off than her family, God love them. No, what she hates is that it feels like her own fault.

Bev didn't always hate Mermaid's Rest. That first shift, when she turned up in a freshly ironed blouse, a dab of lipstick on, she was up for it all. They sat at one of the elegant wooden tables and the boss used words like *community* and *togetherness*. There were homemade biscuits and tea in china pots and a view across the fields to the sea. Bev knew waitressing was always waitressing once you got down to it. The backache and sore toes were the same everywhere. And you'd need a trip to the dentist for all the teeth gritting – *the customer is always right!* She also knew that most kitchens included at least one tricky bloke. But she thought Mermaid's Rest might be different. She hadn't reckoned on a relentlessly tricky bloke – an arsehole, actually – like JP Sharpe.

She got so fed up with his bad moods and endless arrogance, the way he talked to the waitresses. No one seemed to stand up to him. Certainly not Phil, the so-called manager. So, a little over a week ago, she finally snapped and told JP what she thought of him. She didn't mean for all the swear words to come into it. And she definitely didn't mean for the kitchen door to be wide open to the dining room, Phil standing there with his mouth wide open.

I can't believe they sacked you for that, Neil said afterwards, his face pale with anger, fists balled. But her husband did believe it. Or she let him, anyway. And maybe that added up to the same thing: that she, Bev Potter, was a liar.

Her phone trills in her bag and brings her back to the present. To her cold cheeks – face *and* bum, for that matter, whose idea was it to have stones for benches? – and the disappointment sitting heavy in her chest.

'Deb, hello love, you alright?' Trying for bright. But what she really means is *are the boys alright?*

'Oh, they're fine, good as gold. They're making comics.'

God, she adores them. With their folded A4 and erratic stapling and fingers smudged with felt-tips. *The Attack of the Flying*

Paint Can was last week's edition, because Jonathan loved his dad's story about how he got his cheek bashed.

'Just to say, Neil's home, so I'm heading off early. Unless you want me to stay anyway? Give them their tea?'

'Neil's home?'

'He said he finished up ahead of time.'

She checks her watch. It's been jinxed from the start, the Pollock job. The fixing up of a second home above Mousehole, with an owner who spits directions down the phone from upcountry. Problem after problem. It brings out the worst in Neil too; she's heard him at it, deliberately slowing himself up, drawling *dreckly, dreckly* in an exaggerated accent whenever the owner shifts the timings and makes even more impossible demands. She can't imagine Neil getting ahead on that job any time soon. She feels a sudden pang of unease; sharp as heartburn in her chest. In truth, she's had her suspicions about the paint can story. Did Mr Pollock from Epsom make a site visit? Did he and Neil come to blows? If he's gone and lost his job too, then they'll be in the worst possible mess. The renovation project Neil was working on up near Porthpella back in the autumn ended suddenly when the London owner ran out of funds: another greedy incomer taking out one too many loans for their second, third, fourth home. And they were the ones to suffer.

No, the Potters need every inch of the Pollock house.

A paint can? she said, when Neil came home with that bruise last week.

Ruddy great one. What, you think you could have dodged it?

And the boys laughed so hard – once they got over concern for their daddy and his bashed cheek – that Bev laughed too.

Why does her mind do this anyway? Take hold of a thing and then make a break for it, running away to all the worst places. Is it because she knows more about Neil than he thinks? And sometimes this knowledge – these words not spoken – presses at her chest. But his temper's been under control for years now. It's not even an issue. The boys have softened him in all the right places.

Get a grip, Bev.

She realises she's frowning; her forehead aches with it. 'I'm just about on my way back now, Deb. You go, if Neil's there. And thank you. Thank you so much.'

The wind rushes harder as she gets to her feet. She stoops to pick up her bag and for a moment her head spins with the effort. She missed lunch. She doesn't know what tea is.

'Any luck?' her friend asks.

'What's that?'

'With the job hunting?'

'Nothing solid. But something'll turn up. It always does.'

She rings off. Takes a breath; then another.

The dark is settling around her and it feels like a long walk home. As Bev trudges along the promenade the sea hisses at her shoulder, taking her worries and doubling them. She turns from its blackness; fixes her eyes on the garlands of twinkling lights as they lift and twist in the wind.

Comfort and joy, that's what Christmas is supposed to be.

Maybe they can get the snakes and ladders out. Or stick on a family movie. It should be a good thing that Neil's home early. So why does it feel like it isn't? Probably because wherever Bev goes, the lie – and the guilt – go with her.

20

Mullins leaps clean out of his skin. Saffron is lying face down on the floor, and for a moment he thinks she's dead. Around her, the whole room flickers with creepy shadows. And there's a tall, dark figure standing in the corner.

'Saff . . . ?' he edges, his voice disappearing in a gulp.

'Jeez, Mullins. What are you *playing* at?'

She's on her feet, hands planted on her hips. For a second she looks just like the usual Saffron – not the girl they gave the news to that morning. He quickly rights himself; though, in truth, his heart's still all rat-a-tat. He shoots a glance at the figure in the corner – okay, the *wetsuit* hanging up in the corner.

'I thought you'd be here,' he says.

'Ten out of ten for detection.'

'Well, I tried you at Sun Street. Then Wenna's. I even knocked at Broady's place . . .'

'He's still in Sri Lanka.'

Mullins raises an eyebrow. What kind of guy doesn't come home for this? 'And then I came here,' he finishes. 'So maybe it's a nine out of ten, Saff.'

'Have you got news?'

He hesitates; rocks on his heels. And then he decides to lie. Not because he wants to, but because he thinks he has to.

'No. No news.'

'So, why are you here?'

Good question.

'Checking in. The police do that, you know.'

She drops down on to a stack of cushions; pulls her knees up to her chin. 'Have you got suspects?'

'I can't talk about that.'

She shakes her head, and even in the half-light he can see her hair's wet.

'But yes, there are people helping us with our enquiries.'

'God, Mullins, drop the act. Now's not the time to suddenly pretend to be professional.'

He feels his cheeks burn.

'I'm sorry,' she says. 'I didn't mean that.'

The truth is, this time last year she'd have been right. But since the spring he's been trying – really trying. It isn't just about Ally and Jayden either. It was that whole thing with Lewis Pascoe.

'Thing is, Saff, they don't really tell me that much,' he says. 'I'm involved, but I'm not *involved* involved, if you know what I mean. I'm not a DC, am I?'

Not just anyone can be a detective, everyone knows that. Though the Shell House lot don't seem to play by those rules. Jayden was only a PC in Leeds, even though he had more years under his belt than Mullins. And Ally being married to the local sergeant all those years – well, that doesn't exactly qualify her for anything, does it? Even if Bill Bright was the best of coppers, or so everyone says. Alright to be able to hang that sign over your door – Shell House Detectives, *yeah yeah* – without taking a single exam.

The truth is, if they offered Mullins a job, he'd take it in a shot. Throw off the uniform and go and hang out on the veranda of that beach house and eat biscuits all day: that's how it looks to him. Nice work if you can get it.

'Here, Saff,' he says, 'what are you doing here anyway? You're not thinking of opening up?'

'No. And there's no brownies around, in case that's what you're thinking.'

'As it happens, I come bearing gifts.'

He ferrets in his pocket and draws out a crumpled box of Jaffa Cakes. He waggles it triumphantly.

'There's three left. Two for you, one for me.'

'Wow. Sure you can spare them?'

'Anything for you,' he says, grinning at her sarcasm. This is better. This is Hippy-Dippy. He thinks about sitting down beside her on the cushions but that seems a bit much. So, he shifts on his feet and takes out the cellophane-wrapped biscuits; tosses them in her direction. Saffron catches them deftly. Mullins has a sudden memory of her on the rounders pitch at school. Her hair wasn't pink then, but you couldn't help noticing her. Long tanned legs, and a very short sports skirt. She could whack that ball further than any of the boys.

He takes a chair from a stack by the door. Plonks himself on it.

'Phil Butt and Dominic Brook,' she says, through a mouthful of Jaffa Cake. 'Have they been helping you with your enquiries?'

'Restaurant manager and deputy chef from the Mermaid. Yep. They have. Least . . . we've spoken to Butt. He lives above the restaurant.' He takes a glance at his watch. 'They'll be talking to Brook now. Between lunch and dinner, it's quiet up there, they said. Hang on, how do you know all this?'

'I went up there.'

'Not a good idea. Leave it to the police.'

'It wasn't about him getting killed. It was just about him. I wanted to know about him.'

Mullins doesn't really know what to say to that.

'I don't think Phil Butt liked him,' she says. 'But Dominic and JP Sharpe were close. I felt awful, that I was the one breaking the news—'

'Not a popular bloke, is what we're hearing,' Mullins cuts in. Then he checks himself. 'Sorry, Saff, it's just, I mean . . .'

'I don't care.' And her voice is higher than usual, unsteady, 'He's a total stranger to me.'

He's not sure he believes her.

'So, the DNA test . . .' he begins.

'Nothing yet. But—'

Her voice breaks. Mullins looks down, uncomfortable suddenly. He studies a thumbnail; tears at a ragged edge. He knows he can't tell her what he learnt today – the thing that's got Skinner and co. all excited. The fact that they had the letter fingerprinted and while Sharpe's prints are on the envelope, they aren't on the paper inside. There are other prints though – prints they have no match for – on both the interior and the exterior.

'So, Sharpe didn't write the letter,' Chang said.

'Bingo. Sharpe didn't write the letter,' Skinner echoed. 'So, the question is begged . . . who did? And why didn't they sign it? And what's Sharpe doing with it? Is it, in fact, the letter that got him killed?'

And Mullins just sat there, dumbstruck; thinking through what it all meant.

'I should have brought more biscuits,' he says to Saffron in the end.

'Yeah, what were you thinking? Three. I mean, what's even the point?'

'There were more than three at the start of the journey,' he admits.

'Figured as much.'

They sit a little longer. Outside the waves crash and roll and the wind sends up a piercing whistle, but inside Hang Ten it feels like a small and cosy cave. He can see why Saffron came here looking for peace. He hates the thought of that peace now being smashed to bits.

'Where are all your mates anyway?'

'Away. Working. I've had a ton of messages.' She pulls a breath. 'I'm okay, you know. It's good to be on my own. I need to think.'

'Is that a hint?'

'What? No. Just . . . You must have places to be. Haven't you?'

'Not really. I'm not on shift till later.'

'Well, okay. I mean, I get it. I'm amazing company. Best I've ever been.'

The way she says it, it's like she feels bad for feeling bad. Maybe when you're nothing but sunshine, you think that's all people want from you; that you aren't allowed to be anything else. Well, stuff that.

Mullins picks up the empty biscuit box, flattens the cardboard with his hand. He doesn't know which is worse: that Saffron's dad has been murdered, or that Saffron's dad, whoever he is, might actually be the murderer.

'Saff, if you want to know what I think about all this . . .' he says.

'Not so much.'

'Okay.'

'Mullins, I was joking.'

He huffs a breath. 'Dads. Fathers. You know.'

'Yeah?' she says softly.

He turns the cardboard over; rips it in two. 'Well, they can turn out to be more trouble than they're worth, I reckon.'

21

'Al, you're not bailing on me, are you?'

'Of course not. Just . . . seeing if you've got any last-minute instructions.'

Ally sits behind the wheel of her car, peering through the windscreen at the rather haughty-looking exterior of Mermaid's Rest. She knows she's being a little needy phoning Jayden. In the background she can hear Jasmine snickering, then the ping of a kitchen timer. He doesn't need the interruption.

'Keep your eyes wide open,' he says. 'Your mind too. And if you want to be loyal, don't order the fish.'

Jayden messaged her earlier, telling her the one thing he found out from Cat's great-aunt over in Mousehole: Mermaid's Rest get their fish in from out of county. Now, who does that, with Cornwall's finest on their very shore? And the living hard enough to make as it is, too. It isn't just the contract for that one restaurant; it's the principle.

'Right, no fish.'

'Seriously, enjoy it, Al. No pressure. And fill me in later.'

'Tomorrow. I don't want to bother you again tonight.'

'Alright, tomorrow. Unless, you know, you nail the killer or something.'

She gives a low laugh and hangs up, wishing Jayden were with her. Not only for the company, but for the particular charge that she always feels in his presence: as if anything might happen.

Inside the restaurant Ally's greeted with a look that sweeps up and down and left to right, as though a dining companion might materialise out of thin air.

'Have you a booking?'

'Oh, I'm sorry, I didn't think to.'

Wrong-footed, already; so much for blending in.

It seems to Ally like the man is making a show of scrutinising his computer screen. He purses his lips, says, 'Ordinarily we don't take walk-ins, but maybe we can squeeze you in. Just yourself this time, is it?'

'Well, two of us actually. The website said you're okay with dogs?'

She expects a smile – scruffy little Fox always draws smiles – but instead she gets an officious 'If it's well behaved'.

He turns on his heel, whipping through the dining room at quite the pace. Ally follows him with some reluctance, reminding herself that there's no point reacting to his rudeness; she's here for business, not pleasure. He sets the menu down on a table at the very edge of the space, an undesirable spot for most, probably, with the kitchen doors just behind and the corridor to the toilets adjacent. The table is set for two, and as he gathers up the superfluous napkin and cutlery, the unrequired wine glass, Ally wonders if he'll take the candle too, and the twist of holly and ivy. She wouldn't put it past him.

'There,' he says, 'all yours.' As if he's done her a huge favour. Then he skates off.

Ally slides herself into the seat, feeling self-consciousness prickle in her chest. If there were a rock, she'd scuttle beneath it, or burrow into the sand like a shore crab. Fox, on the other hand, settles beneath the table as if he's done this a hundred times before. She puts her hand down to feel the comforting touch of his nose, while her other hand adjusts the napkin. But when she looks about the room, no one is taking the slightest bit of notice of her. Her shoulders, ever so slightly, relax. She feels Fox rest his head on her foot.

There's a sudden blast of noise behind Ally as the kitchen doors spring open. A waitress shimmies past, her arms loaded with plates; her skirt swishes the edge of the table.

No, not a prime spot. But for her purposes, it's perfect. If she were in a country house, she'd be perched between upstairs and downstairs.

'Have you decided?'

He's back, this man who she presumes is the manager. The shirt and tie suggest it – as does his air of affected superiority. But it's insubstantial. His face is pinched and drawn; his shoulders rounded. There's no charge to this man in charge. Perhaps it's the shock of JP Sharpe's murder.

His speed at asking for her order suggests a desire to rush her through rather than any particular attentiveness. But knowing why she's here gives her a quiet confidence; removing any expectation of pleasure makes everything easier.

'I'll just have a drink first, please,' says Ally. 'A small glass of the Sauvignon Blanc, I think.'

Then she settles back in her chair and takes in the room.

It is, she thinks, *almost* well done. Certain boxes have absolutely been ticked – seascapes on the walls, polished wooden floorboards, a vast fireplace with flames flickering in the grate – but there's also an absence of something. Maybe because it looks like it was designed in one fell swoop, rather than built up slowly with love and attention.

The diners seem content enough, though. What she guesses is some kind of a work Christmas do takes up a large table in the middle, a group of rather mismatched companions, paper crowns askew. A spindly-looking older couple – she with pearls, he with red trousers, both with an air of obvious prosperity – are seated nearby, and from the pointed looks they keep sending the big table they clearly consider it an unfortunate placement. Ally notices another woman eating by herself, then, and she's immediately intrigued. She's deeply glamorous, her leather jacket matching her razor-sharp bobbed hair for jet-black colour and shine. She's tapping into her phone, with what looks like an untouched meal in front of her. Ally watches as the woman reaches for her wine, takes a sip then sets it back down, all without her eyes leaving her screen. *She's used to eating out alone*, Ally thinks. *This is nothing to her.*

'Decided?'

'Gosh, do you know, I haven't looked yet. Sorry.'

'Do you need more time?'

Her eyes run over the menu; the prices are almost laughably expensive. The bill for this one meal will amount to more than her weekly shopping. But, she tells herself, it's her duty to be here. And the longer she stays – rather than eking out a single bowl of soup, which is her natural instinct – the more she might learn.

'Perhaps I could just order a starter then make my mind up later . . .'

He gives a quick shake of his head. 'We need to put them through together. Starters and mains.' Then, as an afterthought, he adds, 'I'm afraid.'

Ally looks up. But he's not even looking at her – his eyes are watching the room. She wonders, for a moment, if she's blundered, but her request doesn't seem unreasonable to her. Surely, when it comes to a menu, you can order what you want, when you want it? She and Bill didn't eat out often, it's true, and when they did, it was pub style; Bill was always the one who went up to the bar.

'Well, in that case, I will need a little more time. Perhaps some bread and olives, to be going on with.'

In for a penny, in for very many pounds.

'Still or sparkling?'

'Just tap water is fine. Thank you. Did you get the bread and olives?'

'I did.' And he pushes his hand to his forehead as if he's in sudden pain. 'Bread and olives. Tap water.'

Then he's off. She watches him go; notices the sweat patch blooming across his lower back. When he swaps words with a waitress, his arms are snapped across his chest defensively. As the same server barrels back towards the kitchen, Ally catches her.

'Excuse me, what's the manager's name?'

She looks defensive, as if she's a schoolgirl who's about to be reported to the headmaster.

'Phil. Why's that?'

'I thought I recognised him, that's all.' Ally's fingers pinch the stem of her wine glass. She's not nearly practised enough in this smooth talk – but, she has to remind herself, this woman doesn't know that about her. *Fake it till you make it, Al*, Jayden would say. So she offers a smile. 'Is Bev working this evening?'

There's a moment when Ally thinks this woman might say, *I'm Bev!* and where would she be then? But she's certain she's not. Ally saw her photograph on her Facebook profile, and Bev Potter looked broader and fair-haired.

The woman narrows her eyes. 'Bev doesn't work here anymore.' She glances back towards where the manager, Phil, was. Then says, 'Do you want to order?'

Ally knows she needs to keep her talking.

'I'm torn between the sea bass and the chicken. Is it local, the fish?'

112

'Um, yeah, I think so.'

Either the waitress just has no idea, or she's saying what she thinks customers want to hear.

It could be relevant, Al, Jayden said earlier. *The body in a boat as a kind of symbol.*

Ally says she'll have the chicken. Then, 'When did Bev leave? I felt sure she still worked here.'

'Two weeks ago. Something like that.' Then, sharply, 'Are you a journalist too?'

'Not at all.'

'That woman over there's a journalist.' And she nods to the other lone diner, the one with the phone. 'What about a starter?'

She chooses the soup. Not that Ally has much appetite – she's too distracted for that.

'Do you happen to know where Bev works now? I wanted to catch up with her.'

'No,' the waitress says. 'I'm new here. You should ask Phil. But he's . . .' She hesitates, searching for the word, eventually landing on one. '. . . busy.' Then she's pocketing her notebook and carrying on towards the kitchen.

Later, after Ally has chewed her last olive and picked her way through the chicken – not a patch on Bill's cooking, she has to admit – she's thinking about asking to see the dessert menu. Not through any desire for crème brûlée or Eton mess or whatnot, but because she wants the excuse to stay longer. Now that she's settled in, she feels enjoyably undercover; posing as a slightly nervous solo diner, her stealth intentions well hidden beneath her linen tunic, her string of sea-blue beads. So, Bev Potter, who used to work here but doesn't anymore, is rumoured to want to dance on JP Sharpe's grave. Why? Was it the reason Bev left? Already, the trip to Mermaid's Rest has proved worthwhile.

Ally sees the manager coming towards her, an unreadable expression on his face. He's reaching into his back pocket and Ally think he's going for his notebook, wanting to get her dessert order and hustle her out, but instead he draws out his mobile phone. He doesn't even glance in her direction as he turns down the corridor towards the toilets.

Ally sits for a moment; then, whispering an assurance to Fox that she'll be back, she follows.

The corridors in the old inn are labyrinthine, and away from the showy dining room, there's an unfinished feel, and a sharp tang of disinfectant. She can hear a voice – hushed but insistent. She sees the sign for the ladies and walks on by. In the low light it's perfectly plausible for her to have missed it, isn't it? She rounds the corner and sees a set of stairs. Phil is sitting on the bottom step, leaning against the wall – and everything about his posture suggests defeat.

Ally steps back, aware that she's intruded on a private moment.

'Just call me back, okay,' he says. 'I deserve that, don't I? At least tell me where the bloody hell you are.'

Ally feels a pang of sympathy, realising, at the same time, that this is a prime eavesdropping opportunity. Is this conversation connected to JP? She hesitates, her breath held. It would be good to have something solid to tell Jayden, for this solo mission to have yielded some fruit – other than a rather primped and preened chicken breast and a glass of overpriced Sauvignon.

But she can't do it. Whether it's through fear of being caught, or just discomfort about the act itself, she starts to hurry back the way she came. In no time at all she hears movement behind her and knows that she made the right choice.

The footsteps quicken, and so therefore do Ally's.

'The ladies is that way,' Phil calls out as he catches up to her. And she's surprised by the latent accusation in his voice, as if he's known her game all along. Over her shoulder, Ally offers what she hopes is a breezy *thanks!* – then plants her hand on the door to the toilets and pushes her way in, heart thumping.

As Phil goes past her, she hears him start whistling 'We Wish You a Merry Christmas', and it strikes her as either grimly determined or deliberately ironic. Or perhaps both.

22

After closing, Phil wipes down the bar with smooth strokes, back and forth and back and forth. It's already sparkling but he carries on anyway. *Wipe, wipe.* He has the feeling, suddenly, that if he stops this one small act of maintenance, everything else will fall apart.

Without the noise of conversation and the clattering of cutlery, the music that has been playing softly-softly in the background all night breaks through: Dean Martin crooning that it's cold outside. *Same here, Deano.* But luckily for Phil he doesn't have to venture out; there are definitely some advantages to living above the restaurant. Only Dean hasn't exactly got a weary commute ahead of him either, it's all nothing but an angle to get some woman – the one who's piping up now – to stay over. Phil turns and snaps off the music suddenly, a bitter taste rising in his throat.

'I'm off then.'

It's Dominic, pushing through the door from the kitchen like a baby bull. He's got his winter coat on and a hat pulled down low. Phil refocuses. Dominic's done well tonight: no dramas in the kitchen. They were down on numbers, a few of the bookings pulling out last-minute, citing illness and so on, but the real reason was obvious: Mermaid's Rest has an air of trouble about it just now, and that isn't exactly compatible with a festive dining experience.

Dominic stops by the bar, drums his fingers on the countertop. 'Was it just like this,' he says edgily, 'two nights ago? When JP left?'

'What do you mean, was it just like this?'

'A normal night. Did you see him as he left?'

'Yes, I saw him. He was belly-aching about the cold.'

'But nothing seemed off?'

'If you mean, did he look like a man who knew he was about to get himself killed, then no, I'd say on balance, he didn't.'

Phil regrets his tone as soon as the words are out of his mouth. He needs to keep him on side, this man; the kitchen really will be in trouble if he goes too.

'How was it earlier?' says Phil, making an effort. But his teeth are gritted; he can feel a muscle going at his jaw. 'With the police? I meant to ask, but then we got swept up in service. Not much to tell them, huh?'

Dominic sniffs noisily. 'As it happens, I did have a few things to tell them.'

'Well, you knew JP better than most.'

'I didn't hold back. I told the truth.'

'What are you saying?'

'You know exactly what I'm saying.'

And Dominic sounds to Phil like a peevish little boy now, lashing out in the playground. Maybe this is what grief does. Maybe what Phil's feeling himself is not so very different to grief.

Dominic goes on, puffing his chest out like one of the turkeys they've got heaped in the freezer. 'Quite a few people round here had grudges against him, didn't they? I just filled the police in on that. They said I was very helpful. Once they stopped getting excited about me not having an alibi, anyway. What else are you supposed to do if you've got a sickness bug? Not exactly people-friendly, is it? I said, "Check my bathroom pipes, they've seen some action. Do a swab of my toilet bowl if you want proof."'

Phil has stopped hearing him now though. He picks up the cloth again and wipes the bar, back and forth and back and forth. His hand trembles as he does it.

'What did you fill them in on?' he says, not looking up. 'I've a right to know. I'm the boss.'

Why does Phil sound so feeble when he assumes his rightful authority? That was always the trouble where JP was concerned too: round the head chef, Phil was always too easily thrown. Pathetic that it dogs Phil still. He knows he needs to shake JP off once and for all. He glances to the ceiling, even though he knows Melissa isn't up there – though that's about all he does know of her whereabouts. Phil can feel his jaw jutting; jutting so hard it might dislocate. Melissa hasn't answered any of his texts. And he's had no call back after his voicemail earlier; the voicemail that woman must have heard him leaving earlier, as pathetic-ness poured off him, swilling down the corridor like floodwater.

Dominic says nothing in response to his question, and a feeling suddenly overcomes Phil: it's all doom. He blinks at Dominic, wondering if he can feel it too – or if it's exclusively his own.

'Because,' Phil goes on, clutching at straws now, 'if you're stirring up anything around this place, it's only going to impact the business, isn't it? Which means your job, as well as mine. We can't afford to lose the bookings this time of year. You do get that, don't you? I mean, it's not rocket science, is it?'

Dominic gives a maddening smile in response – or is it a grimace? – and, in it, Phil sees something of JP.

'Calm down, Phil. I just gave them the names of people they should speak to. Nothing you don't know already.'

'You mean Bev Potter? Bev wouldn't hurt a fly. Who else? You didn't go gossiping to that journalist, did you? Damn cheek, showing up here.'

118

But Dominic is heading towards the door. He turns as he gets there, and whatever bravado he was attempting seems to slip. There's real anguish in his face.

'Someone killed him,' says Dominic. 'Okay? JP left like this, just like I'm doing now, two nights ago. Finished his night's work and went home – only he wound up dead. Excuse me for wanting whoever did that to him found.' He passes a hand across his eyes. 'Even if it's inconvenient to you. Even if it's inconvenient to this place.'

The door slams and Dominic's gone.

Phil groans, and there's real anguish in that too. But then a thought dawns and he brightens fractionally: if Dominic knew anything about Melissa, then he'd have come straight out with it there and then, wouldn't he? Maybe Phil can save face, after all.

On that thought, he locks up and turns out the lights. As he wearily makes his way upstairs, the old wooden steps creak with every step. Any angry energy he had through the exchange with Dominic has gone. He's ready to drop. At the top of the landing he hesitates outside the bedroom door: he can't hear anything in there. And when he nudges it ajar, he sees the bed is empty.

Of course it is.

Phil goes into the sitting room and stares dispassionately at their unlit tree. He bends and clicks on the lights, blinking as they flash manically, a hectic pattern that seems neither festive nor magical. He's about to chuck himself down on the sofa when he notices an envelope propped on the mantelpiece. It has his name on it. And there's a bubble as the 'i' dot.

She's the only person he knows who does that. He used to think it was cute.

Phil tears it open and sees the same Christmas card they've sent to all of their friends and contacts. Well, he says *they*; Melissa had no interest in doing cards this year, so Phil took up the mantle.

He even aped her signature pretty well too. The picture is a bland snowy landscape that isn't Cornwall but could be Cornwall. *Season's Greetings* embossed in gold. *All going well down here!* That's the kind of thing he scrawled inside, to the likes of Lynn and Jeff and Bri and Anya. *Watch out Rick Stein!* Etcetera, etcetera. Cheery as you like.

He flips it open and starts to read. His eyes widen like a cartoon character's.

Melissa actually wrote this one. And how he wishes that she hadn't.

~

Half an hour later, Phil's made a decent dent in a bottle of gin, despite never being a gin man. He feels like he's on board a ship in wild seas; everything around him appears to pitch and toss – his mind, his gut, the bloody three-piece suite and the lunatic, flashing tree. His wife's words blur in front of him, random sentences breaking and reforming before his eyes.

I need space.

I should have done this months ago.

We're finished, Phil. Don't try to get in touch.

It's not about him.

And that last is the kicker. The sheer lie of it. He dies, and then she takes off? Like hell it's not about JP Sharpe.

Phil reaches for the mantelpiece, knocking over a candlestick, sending a gilt frame crashing to the floor. His fingers fasten on a box of matches. As he strikes, the first match snaps in half. The second won't take. But the third blazes instantly and he stares at it; for a moment he forgets what he's doing. He feels the flame reach his fingers and lets out a squeak. In a panic he throws the match on the card, and sees the flames take hold, the paper curling at the edges. Just like that, Melissa's cruel words will be obliterated.

He watches the card twist as it burns, skittering its way across the glass-topped coffee table.

What did he hope to feel? Erasure? He takes another slug of gin. When he opens his eyes again, he realises he's looking straight into rising flames.

How the hell is the rug on fire?

He scrambles to his feet, staggers backwards. Agog.

Seriously, the rug? Phil watches the fire spread, as if he's risen outside of himself; some part of him is lost in marvel: *How quickly it moves! How bright it burns!* Then panic crashes in. And the devastating realisation – as up go the curtains, the cushions, Melissa's chenille throw – that he's really gone and done it now.

23

When Dominic's phone rings in the early hours of Wednesday morning, he thinks of only one person: Lena. It must be. He's scrabbling for it, and in his rush, it hits the floor. He hangs off the side of the bed to get it and sees the name all lit up.

Phil Butt.

The disappointment is a gut-punch. Quickly followed by confusion: why is Phil Butt phoning him at two o'clock in the morning?

Ever since the news of JP's death, Phil's been trying to butter him up – and Dominic isn't sure he likes it. He's never wanted the extra status in the kitchen; never wanted to be anyone's right-hand man except JP's.

The fact of his death hits Dominic again.

The phone rings on, and it feels like it's drilling right through his skull. He flicks it to silent. He could just not answer it. But somehow his fingers are hitting the button and he's saying, 'Phil?'

At first there's just a crackle, like a bad line. Has Phil bum-dialled him? But the crackle turns to more like a roar. Then, in the background, he hears what sounds like a shout. A loud hissing. Whatever it is, it's major interference.

'Phil?' he says again, hitching himself up on his elbow.

Dominic fumbles for the light and suddenly the room's flooded with it. Down the line, the background noise is chaos. He rubs his eyes; none of it makes sense.

'Is that Dominic?' says a voice.

It's authoritative, steady. And, most of all, it's not Phil. Dominic goes hot from top to toe.

'What's going on? Who's this?'

'Your friend's been involved in an incident. He's worse for wear, but he's not injured.'

Dominic breathes out.

'We're up at Mermaid's Rest, about ten to fifteen minutes from Mousehole,' the voice goes on. 'The boys are getting the blaze under control.'

'A fire at Mermaid's Rest?'

'He did well to get out, the state he's in.'

'State?'

'Inebriated.'

Dominic's on his feet, adrenalin surging through him.

'He could do with someone up here with him. He gave us your name to call.'

He agrees to come, then hangs up. Only then does Dominic wonder where Phil's wife is. But they'd have said, wouldn't they – that fireman or whoever he was – if Melissa was hurt? He steps out of his pyjama bottoms and looks around for wherever he threw his jeans. As he quickly dresses and makes for the door, Dominic's got a weird energy about him. Questions spin in his head, propelling him down the stairs and out into the cold night air towards his car. He turns the key and the engine protests, then coughs into action. Dominic blows on his hands, realising he's freezing; his teeth knock together.

Thoughts of JP blast in.

There was a kitchen fire at The Peppercorn a couple of years ago. It was on JP's watch. He, Dominic, was the hero of the hour then, grabbing the fire extinguisher and dousing the blaze within seconds of it starting. He can still remember the shock on Lena's face as she walked into the kitchen and saw the jump of the flames. JP's volley of swear words. The way the kitchen porter knocked over a stack of plates in panic, shattering every single one. A few seconds of chaos, then calm restored. A clap on the back from JP (the KP got both barrels though).

It didn't sound like there's any calm to be had at Mermaid's Rest tonight. And Dominic is too late to be any kind of a hero this time.

What the hell happened? And why does he have a horrible feeling – a toxic feeling, that's quickly spreading inside of him – that this is somehow to do with JP?

Ten minutes later and Dominic is pulling into the jam-packed car park. Two shiny fire engines loom out of the darkness, looking just like a couple of kids' giant toys. He clambers out of the car and stands with his hands held to his head, acrid smoke catching in the back of his throat.

The building looks, he thinks, like a slayed beast. It's already a bare-boned carcass in places, with its blackened walls and gaping holes. Flames lick from what's left of the roof. And suddenly it feels like there are people everywhere. That's when Dominic tunes in to the presence of the ambulance. The police car too. A regular circus. And Phil Butt somewhere in the middle of it.

An officer comes towards him, his arms spread wide, as if shepherding Dominic away from the scene. Dominic tries to say something, to explain he has business here, but the attempt erupts into a cough.

'Are you Dominic?'

He nods, coughing still. *What am I even doing here? Why does Phil want me?*

'I'm PC Mullins,' the officer says. And he looks like an overgrown schoolboy, with streaks of soot on his big round cheeks. 'I'll show you where Phil is. Tell you what, he's a lucky guy. This place went up like a box of fireworks.'

'Any idea what caused it?'

'Not yet, but we're working on it.'

At that moment Phil steps from the side of the ambulance. There's a blanket wrapped around his shoulders, and he stoops as he comes towards them. He stumbles into Dominic, a hand clawing at his shoulder. Dominic fights the urge to shrug him off.

'It's all my fault,' Phil says messily. 'All of it.'

Dominic glances uneasily towards PC Mullins. The officer offers a raised eyebrow in return – a comical sort of gesture, in the circumstances. Then he says, 'What do you mean, *all* of it, Mr Butt?'

24

In what has become a ritual, Ally turns on the radio as she walks into the kitchen. She's spent her whole life loving the quiet, but now that quiet is mostly all that she has, she's come to value the voices of these presenters; their reassuring chatter always there at the turn of a dial. Outside it's still dark. Sunrise won't come for at least another couple of hours at this time of year.

Ally opens the door so Fox can do his morning business, and a gust of cold wind pulls at her dressing gown. The tide's in and it's hurling itself at the beach, the sound filling the air. As she pokes her nose out of the door, she can practically feel sea spray on her cheeks. When the wind's blowing right, salt crystals form in crusts along the windowsills. She looks down at her sheepskin slippers and sees sand heaped at her doorstep like a snowdrift.

These winter storms are the best for wrecking – what they call beachcombing in Cornwall. Ordinarily Ally would be planning on heading out as soon as the tide drops, seeing what treasures have been deposited along the shore, but this morning her head is full of other thoughts. It's full of Mermaid's Rest.

Ally sets the coffee going and takes a ginger biscuit from the tin. She picks up her notebook and turns to the pages she wrote last night when she got home.

Just as she was settling up her bill, Ally mentioned JP to the waitress.

'I was so sorry to hear of the death of the chef here.'

The reply seemed mechanical: 'It's a shock.'

'Were you friends?'

'No. I didn't really know him. I'm new.'

The girl passed Ally the card machine, and Ally slowly, deliberately, entered a decent tip.

'What about Bev?' she said then, looking up with a smile. 'Was she close to JP Sharpe?'

But then the manager appeared from nowhere, passing Ally her coat which she couldn't actually remember handing over in the first place. Was he purposefully chivvying her?

A flash of boldness overtook her, as she said, 'Oh, I almost forgot, I wanted to compliment the chef on that wonderful pudding. Could I?'

She said it loudly enough that the adjacent table nodded in agreement, dessert spoons halfway to their mouths. 'Hear, hear!'

The manager hesitated. 'I'll pass that along. Good to hear.'

'I couldn't tell him myself?'

'Not in the middle of service. He's flat out.' Then, 'But we'll tell him.'

'He's actually just on a fag break,' the waitress said, oblivious to Phil's scowl.

And that was how Ally came to meet the faintly smoky-smelling Dominic, who took her praise for his chocolate tart in his stride.

'It must be difficult circumstances,' she said, as she shook Dominic's hand. But then Phil ushered the chef back to the kitchen before he could reply.

In one evening, Ally learnt that Bev Potter no longer works at Mermaid's Rest, and that the manager Phil was definitely upset with somebody – although she has no idea who. That's pretty good going. She got little sense of the other chef, Dominic, other than the fact that he's a dab hand at chocolate tarts and has a sturdy handshake. Oh, and the fact that Bev's replacement has a thing or two to learn about being customer-facing – but at least the woman was honest with it.

Do any of these people know what happened to JP Sharpe? And do any of them know about the existence of Saffron? Ally can't wait to fill Jayden in, to speculate and ruminate, and just see if they can't put something together.

Now Fox bursts back into the house, his little body whisking past her ankles.

'Good boy,' she murmurs. Then she stops, cocking her head to the radio as the local news comes on.

> '. . . *Mermaid's Rest. The blaze broke out at this upmarket eatery in the small hours of Wednesday morning. Phil Butt, general manager, who lives on the property, sustained minor injuries but did not require hospital treatment . . .*'

Ally hurries to turn up the volume.

> '. . . *flames engulfed the building, devastating its structure. Dozens of firefighters attended the scene from across West Cornwall, bringing the fire under control after more than two hours. The cause of the blaze is not yet confirmed . . .*'

She's glancing round, already looking for her phone.

> '. . . *Mermaid's Rest suffered tragedy just two days ago as head chef John Paul Sharpe was found dead in Mousehole. The murder investigation continues.*'

The report ends, but the insinuation continues to hang in the air. Is the fire connected to JP Sharpe's death?

Ally looks to the window. Her reflection stares back from the black rectangle and she feels a ripple of unease.

'There's more to this,' she says out loud. 'There has to be.'

She's just about to dial Jayden's number when she remembers it's six o'clock in the morning. Far too early to call anyone, even a man with a baby who's probably been up since 4 a.m. She's just putting her phone back down, thinking she'll wait at least until eight, when it pings with a message.

Jeez, have you turned on the news, Al? Mermaid's Rest.

She can't help a smile – which feels callous, given the circumstances.

I sort of feel like you've replaced me, Evie said the other day on FaceTime. *I need to meet this Jayden when I'm over.* Ally replied that unless she and Evie were ever partners in a private detective agency, then, dear daughter, she wouldn't call it 'replacing' at all.

I know, she messages Jayden now. *But they said it was started accidentally?*

Fishy though, he texts back. Then, *I don't like it. I'm going to check in on Saffron. How was it there last night?*

Ally starts to message, then changes her mind and presses the Call button instead.

'It was definitely worth me going,' she says as Jayden answers.

Behind her, Fox barks indignantly, demanding his breakfast. But for once her little dog can wait.

25

Gus asked Wenna to tie a ribbon round the mince pies but now he's wondering if that's too frivolous a touch. And pushy, actually, because the fancy dressing demands that the recipient coo over it, and that's not what he wants at all. They're just mince pies. Better than his, undoubtedly, but just mince pies, nevertheless. And, really, they're mostly to give Gus something to hold as he stands on her step; a sort of pass for entry – or at least permission to knock. He's never dropped by Saffron's house before.

Wenna. As soon as the bell clanged at his entrance she said, 'Have you heard what's happened to that fancy place down Mousehole way? Near enough burnt down.'

And Gus hadn't, so she filled him in on the details. Which was little more, in truth, than what Wenna said as he first walked in. But she pushed her glasses up and down her nose, blinked at Gus expectantly and said, 'And coming after that chef was killed as well. I wouldn't like the look of that if I was police, no, I wouldn't. What do they make of it down at The Shell House?'

Wenna didn't mention a word about Saffron, and Gus wondered if she even knew of the connection then. He kept his mouth tight shut and didn't say where the mince pies were bound. Saffron and Wenna were pretty close, and if Saffron hadn't said anything to her, he wasn't going to be the one to do it.

Gus rounds the corner on to Sun Street. It's right at the top of the village, a gently sloping road with most houses built into the hillside to take advantage of the view. Though it's not much of a view this morning: the sea is the colour of dull metal with the sky hanging heavy and portentous above it. Gus walks on, feeling slightly out of breath.

His thoughts turn to Ally, as they often seem to. It feels like something in the air has changed between them, only he doesn't quite know what or why. In Mousehole the other night he was building up to pay her a compliment – to tell her how much he values their friendship, and that it's more than that, if he's really honest with himself. But the discovery of the corpse put paid to that. A case of saved by the bell? Maybe. Because ever since, it hasn't quite felt right to say it.

Asking what Ally and Jayden make of the fire would be nice, sure ground though. Because they will undoubtedly be making something of it, those two. In Gus's work-in-progress novel – *don't ask, long story, literally* – he's just written the line 'you don't need imagination to be a good detective; in fact imagination gets in the way, you just need the facts'. He popped it in the mouth of his central character, but Gus isn't sure he believes it, let alone whether the guy who's doing the talking does. This is perhaps one of the reasons why Gus's novel is in go-slow mode: a lack of conviction.

He walks on. Feeling less certain with every step.

For the most part they're bungalows up here, mid-century builds, or tiered family houses with cars in the driveway; bird boxes, garages with bikes, BBQs under tarps. Where Gus is staying, at the edge of the water, in a house that's hardly more than a wooden hut, he feels perfectly at home. It's only when he's faced with what looks like normality – the bird boxes, the bikes, the garages – and he imagines people inside such houses, shaking cereal into bowls and pouring orange juice and sitting down together, that he feels rootless.

But then there's Saffron. At number 21. And there's nothing normal about what's going on with her.

Whenever Gus feels himself sliding towards peevishness, he forcibly puts the brakes on. He makes a mental list of all the good things – the very many good things – about his life. Lack of perspective has always got his goat: Mona, his ex-wife, was born with a silver spoon in her mouth but didn't she like to bemoan her lot, nevertheless. The opposite of someone like Ally, who, it seems, needs very little to be happy. *Gratitude journal*, Saffron said to him once, as she handed him his flat white on a blueish kind of day. *You should give it a whirl.* But Gus doesn't need one, not really. And he certainly doesn't need to bring more writing into his life when he's still scratching out his godforsaken novel.

And, to be honest, that's a state of affairs he's okay with. Because he's told himself that the book is his excuse to stay here in Porthpella – that's the story he tells, to anyone who asks – in the tiny little holiday house that he can't bring himself to leave.

And anyway, did you need an excuse when you were in your mid-sixties? Couldn't you do what the heck you wanted? Especially when you've been through an unpleasant divorce. And when you've found yourself, on occasion, looking back on your life and wondering if you were ever really *in* it – and what a terrible waste it would be if it turned out that you weren't.

Gus walks up the short driveway of number 21. It's a neat-looking square house, with a built-in garage. Not the kind of place he imagined for Saffron. Up here is as close as Porthpella comes to suburbia. The palm tree in the garden is the only Saffron-ish touch as far as he can see, but they're ten a penny in these parts and Gus is learning to take their easy glamour for granted, as any emmet-turned-incomer should. No, number 21 is the home she grew up in. Her mum's house: Stephanie Weeks. And when Stephanie died, Saffron stayed on, renting out the rooms to her friends. Girls who are probably with her now, and who'll raise an eyebrow to see an old man like Gus turning up at her door.

But he really does need to speak to her.

He rings the doorbell, feeling oddly nervous. Or, perhaps more accurately, appropriately nervous. He's about to tell Saffron something he's never told anyone face-to-face. Not even Ally. And he's wanted to. Mostly because he finds himself wanting to tell Ally more or less everything.

'Gus, hey. How are you doing?'

Saffron doesn't look surprised to see him. But she does look as if she's about to head out; she's in a big coat and a hat with an implausibly large pom-pom.

'Oh, morning,' he says. 'I hope I'm not intruding. Are you off out?'

She gives a small smile; a shake of her head. 'Not at all.'

'Oh. I mean, I know it's not Hang Ten. I know people can't just turn up.'

'Course they can,' she says. 'Coffee? Go on, I haven't had one yet either. I spent half the night at the café then was like, what am I even doing? This is mad.'

Saffron has, Gus thinks, a strange sort of energy about her. On the way here he pictured her diminished, and hated the thought of that, but maybe that's just how he reacts to intense experiences: curls up inside his shell like a whelk. He looks at his watch. It's past nine thirty. Which makes it more or less his coffee time (which is always).

'Mince pie to go with it?'

Saffron takes the box. 'Thank you. That's, erm, sweet.'

'Oh dear. You can't stand them, can you?'

She pulls a face, and she looks just like a little girl then. 'Is it that obvious? Sorry, the thought's super nice . . . but mincemeat is the worst.'

Gus grins. He can feel himself warming up. Maybe this will go okay after all.

'I've got some cookie dough in the freezer,' she says. 'We won't go hungry.'

He's following her in, nudging the door closed behind him, when Gus realises she hasn't asked him why he's here. And for a moment he wonders if, on some level, she already knows.

26

It's only when they're in the kitchen, and Gus hasn't taken off his jacket – in fact is zipping it all the way up to his chin – that Saffron remembers to say about the heating.

'But that's a nightmare!' he cries. 'You can't be without it.'

'Gus, it's cool. Someone's coming to fix it today.'

She spoons coffee into the stove pot, and sets it going.

'What about your housemates?' he says.

'What about them?'

Gus has an uncertain look on his face, but then that's often a default expression with him. Actually, less so these days, but when he first arrived in Porthpella he looked like he could be knocked down by a single onshore gust.

'Well, Jodie's in Australia. Having an amazing time. She won't be back until end of February. And Kelly, Kelly's at work.'

She doesn't add that Kelly is rarely at Sun Street these days. Gus's look of concern makes her feel like it won't go over that well if Saffron says she's here on her own right now. That said, Gus hasn't mentioned anything yet – not about the murder, the letter, her mum – but that must be why he's here.

'And the travels,' says Gus. 'You had a good time, did you?'

'The best. But . . . the homecoming was kind of mixed. I guess you heard?'

She watches as Gus slowly exhales. 'I'm so sorry. Really. Ally told me. Afterwards she was worried that it wasn't her place to.'

'She doesn't need to worry.'

'I couldn't believe it, Saffron.'

'Which part? It's all pretty crazy.'

'Well, quite.'

Gus sinks into a chair, rubs at his shaven head. He looks at her with such intensity that Saffron is suddenly glad of the coffee-making job at hand. She was feeling quite free before Gus came. Weirdly free, in fact.

'Did you hear the news this morning?' she says. 'There was a fire up at the place JP Sharpe worked at. Mermaid's Rest.'

'I heard about it. Terrible.'

'It was a beaut old building too. Who'd do that?'

Gus flicks another glance at her. *He's treading carefully around this too*, Saffron thinks, *because he presumes there's a connection.* Well, maybe there is. But right now, her head is filled with something else. And perhaps it's strange that Gus should be the second person to know, but hey, why not? It's probably even stranger that Mullins was the first. Anyway, if she doesn't say it out loud, she feels as if she might actually burst. It's like she's way underwater, and her air's running out, and the only thing to do is kick towards the surface. Breathe in all that light.

'Things have kind of changed, actually, Gus.'

'Changed?'

'The man who was killed in Mousehole. John Paul Sharpe. He wasn't my dad.'

Gus blinks. 'He's not?'

Her voice is jumping all over the place. 'I just got the DNA test back. It was sent through this morning. There's no match whatsoever. He wasn't my dad. He had a letter from my dad in his pocket which . . . yeah, is very weird . . . but he's not my dad.'

Saying it, Saffron can feel her eyes fill, and a push of emotion inside her chest. Is it only really sinking in now? She was quite calm when she called Mullins earlier – initially, anyway. Then he told her about the fingerprints; the fact that while JP Sharpe's prints were on the envelope, they weren't on the letter itself. *So, we're one step ahead, Saff,* Mullins said, and she wanted to punch him through the telephone then. Not so calm after all, it turned out.

Gus nods quietly. And the feeling that slammed her as she opened up that DNA email hits her again now – and it's a feeling so nuts that it forces the tears from her eyes; sends them running down her cheeks.

'Oh, Saffron,' he says, and half gets out of his chair, then stops. Instead he stretches over and pats her arm. 'It's okay.'

'The stupid thing is,' she says, sucking in a breath; steadying herself. 'I wanted him to be. I mean, not *him* exactly, not JP Sharpe. Not him at all. But . . . the knowing part. That someone out there was. And he was here, wanting to meet me. But dead. God, it's so messed up.'

Saffron looks to Gus. He seems pretty level, apart from a swimmy look in his own eyes, but then she, Saffron, does that all the time. A *sympathy well*, Jodie calls it.

'It's like when you toss a coin to make a decision. But, deep down, you already know what you want to do. So, the coin toss isn't really to leave it to fate at all. It's so that if it's, say, tails, and you're like "oh crap, not tails" then you should go with whatever heads was. It's like that. As soon as that email came through, and it said there was no match, I . . . I was gutted. Only, like, for a moment. A really, really brief moment. But . . . . Yeah. Does that even make sense?'

'I think it makes a lot of sense,' says Gus quietly.

'So, I've decided.'

'Decided?'

'I want to find him. Whoever really wrote that letter. Whoever my real dad is.'

'Saffron . . .'

'And I'm going to ask Ally and Jayden if they'll help. Do you think they will? Is it the kind of case they take? I just . . .' She stops. Gus is slowly shaking his head. 'What is it? What's wrong?'

Gus looks up at her. His eyes appear very big in his face suddenly.

'Oh, your coffee,' she says. 'Crap. I forgot your coffee.'

'I don't need the coffee. But I do need . . . I wanted to tell you something . . . It's not easy for me to . . .'

'Tell me what?' she says.

Gus's mouth opens but no sound comes out. All of a sudden, it's like he doesn't know where to look.

A thought starts to dawn on Saffron. It gathers pace, filling the room with a fierce bright light. Her head starts to ache with it.

'Gus . . .' she says very carefully, 'are you saying . . .'

'Don't. Don't go looking, Saffron.'

'Don't? Why? Why not?'

'I know it's not my place,' he says. 'It's absolutely not my place. But I went looking once. And I regretted it probably, oh, I don't know, probably every day of my life since. That's why I'm here. I wanted to tell you how it was for me.'

Saffron drops down into her chair. She almost wants to laugh. Is this how it's going to be now? Looking at every man of a certain age, as if they could be her dad?

But Gus's face. His purpose, then his hesitation. His emotion. *Could you give me half a chance?*

But no. It's just Gus. Gus with a story of his own to tell.

So, Saffron listens to him as he says to her how he grew up without a dad too. His mum never telling him much beyond the fact that he was Bad News. But then came a day when Gus needed more than that; when he wanted to make his own mind up, thank you very much. Because by then he'd started to think of his mother as unreliable. So, he went looking, and it wasn't too hard, in the end, in the small town that Gus grew up in. People remembered.

'He wasn't a good man, it turns out,' Gus says. 'He was violent. And I'm sure he had reasons for that because people usually do, don't they? But the fact remains. As a husband, as a dad . . . well, bad news. I met him for myself, and then I ran as fast as I could in the other direction.' Gus looks up at her. 'I haven't actually told anyone this in . . . over forty years. I'm ashamed of it, you see. Ashamed that I didn't trust my own mother's word. Something broke between us, after that. I don't think she ever really forgave me. Which isn't fair either, probably, but . . . that's how it was. And I'm ashamed that I didn't . . . well, that I perhaps didn't try and understand him a little better too.' He exhales. Shakes his head. 'I'm not really sure I ever came back from it. Not fully.'

Gus passes his hand across his mouth. For a moment he looks almost impossibly sad.

'That's what I wanted to say to you, Saffron. That afterwards, I very much wished I hadn't gone looking. That I wanted to keep my own story of who my dad might have been. When Ally told me what'd happened with you, I had this very strong . . . I don't know, protective instinct. I hope that's not overstepping.'

Saffron feels her eyes fill again. She shakes her head.

'I don't want you to feel like I did, Saffron,' he says. 'Not for a moment.'

Saffron stares out of the window at the run of grey rooftops; the sky looking ready to drop its load; the whiskery palm tree all torn up in the wind.

'Gus, the thing is though, my mum's dead. The only person I have to upset is myself.'

He drops his head at that. So, Saffron tells him that she appreciates it, that he bothered to come and offer this piece of himself. She thanks him, too, because, instead of putting her off, it's actually only strengthened her resolve. She really does want to know who her dad is. And she's going to go and see Ally and Jayden today.

'But Saffron,' says Gus, 'have you thought about the fact that—'

'I haven't really thought about very much, to be honest. It's all just happened. But I do know how I feel.'

'Just . . . the fact that the letter was in a dead man's pocket. What if—'

'What if what?'

'Well, isn't the author of the letter a suspect, as far as the police are concerned? If Ally and Jayden find who wrote it—'

'My dad, you mean.'

'Your dad . . . they might—'

'Also be finding the murderer?'

'Well, yes.'

Saffron looks again to the window. There's the smallest strip of blue above the horizon line; it looks painted on, just for her, in the middle of all those shades of grey.

'Yeah,' she says, 'I thought of that. But then I also thought, there's just no way, is there?' And she feels about eight years old, fiercely insistent, based on nothing but instinct. 'No dad of mine is a murderer, Gus.'

27

Jayden stares at his laptop in frustration. It's only been two days since he was last working on the website and he's already forgotten how to change the page layout. How is that even possible? He's always thought himself pretty decent with tech, but nothing about this Build Your Own Website package is intuitive.

He clicks on another incomprehensible icon and waits to see what happens. Not much, is what. Jayden groans and rocks back on his chair, the floorboards adding their own music. He stifles a yawn.

The murder in Mousehole, and Saffron's connection to it, kept him awake last night; he was almost grateful when Jazzy refused to settle, because he had a reason for being awake – it was something to actually *do*.

And then the news this morning: Mermaid's Rest up in flames.

Jayden's already read everything he can find online about the blaze. He's clicked through the photos of the destruction, inside and out. He's gone through the comments beneath the article on Cornwall Live, every man and his dog weighing in as they always do.

RIP Mermaid's Rest.

What a shame. Real piece of history. But then it was ruined well before the fire.

Had a lovely meal here in the summer. Pricey but worth it. Sad news.

Hmm, head chef murdered and then pub burnt down, what's that about?

After he and Ally spoke this morning, Jayden checked in with Saffron. She replied quickly – she knew about the fire too – but he's heard no more from her since.

In the latest piece that he saw, there was an update: the fire was thought to have started in the upstairs apartment. An accident. Which doesn't exactly fit with the theory that the two events – murder, and well, as it turns out, probably not arson – are connected. Jayden knows from experience that fire investigations can take days. Observations are made at the scene – burn patterns, smoke, heat – but then studies take place afterwards too. This, though, was fast. Phil Butt, the manager, must have confirmed the origins of the fire.

There was something going on with the manager, Ally said earlier. *That phone message I heard him leave, he was angry. Sad and angry.*

But sad and angry seem to Jayden to be a reasonable state of mind, given the fact that Phil Butt's colleague was murdered.

But what of this Bev Potter? Ally already had a bee in her bonnet about Bev after what she overheard in Mousehole. Now that they know Bev no longer works at Mermaid's Rest, well, there could be a story there. Ally intended to pass the information along to the police after she spoke to Jayden – but, on his advice, downplay her own trip to Mermaid's Rest. After all, they don't need accusations of interference coming their way again, do they? There was enough of that back in the spring with the Lewis Pascoe case – though Skinner had to eat his words in the end. Even after all this time, Jayden doesn't quite feel easy when he comes into Skinner's orbit. And he doubts Ally does either.

He sighs, refocuses on the screen in front of him. Cat overheard him on the phone to Ally earlier and reminded him that the police would be doing their job and that he should do his – which is, this morning, to push on with the website for the campsite. And so here he is. Isn't he? Pushing on. In body, if not in spirit.

No, his spirit is definitely elsewhere.

Jayden goes back to the main menu for his web build and studies the options. He hits Pages again, then Preview. But the display is all wrong, images cropped in weird ways, gaps in text.

'Maybe we don't need a website,' he says, through a groan.

His eyes travel to the window: nothing but a grid of fields from here to the sea, but it's grey and green out there today, the blue skies of yesterday all gone. He imagines the same view full of tents and caravans; kids streaming about on bikes and grown-ups in dressing gowns trudging to the toilet block. A toilet block with a turf roof and wooden beams ten times fancier than the cottage they're living in, but hey, speculate to accumulate. Isn't that what some people say? Not him, personally, but other people. It's amazing, really, that Cat's parents agreed to it all. But when they ran the sums, Cliff's eyes lit up. Jayden knows that he and Cat are travelling optimistically with their business plan, imagining themselves fully booked through a long summer season, but if they get it right, their campsite could be the kind of place that people return to again and again.

I want to share the love, Cat had said, back when she first pitched the idea to him, *I was so lucky to grow up here, Jay. It's the best place in the world.*

And while Jayden wouldn't go as far as all that – really? In the whole world? She was there too wasn't she, when they went to the Caribbean? – he has to admit they're super lucky to have this place and be able to take a shot at making it work. Hopefully earning enough through the summer to last the winter; with the detective work to fill in the gaps – and feed the soul.

Ally prefers the idea of their work coming to them organically, rather than them shouting about it, and Jayden's mostly good with that. No website for the Shell House Detectives! At least it saves him the hassle of trying to build the damn thing . . . Sometimes he thinks about raising it with her: *We have to get professional, Al!* But most of the time he likes it lo-fi, too. Heading to The Shell House in flip-flops, working out ideas in a Moleskine notebook. Ally getting the coffee going as soon as she hears his feet on the veranda. Jayden's uniform days feel like a different life altogether. Parts of it he's well glad to be out of: the hierarchies, force politics, squeezed resources, institutional racism. But there was more to it than that. Like that feeling of heading out with Kieran, radios buzzing their next move, the city at their feet. Jayden still misses his partner with an ache that he suspects will never go away. The job itself though? That's more complicated. When his old training mate Fatima said, *What you're doing down there, it's just you keeping your eye in, right, Jay?* he didn't correct her.

'Babe, how's it going?'

Cat's hand on his shoulder makes him jump. Jayden shifts in his chair, spins round to her.

'They're saying the cause was accidental now,' he says. 'That it started in the upstairs flat.' Her face is blank, so he adds, 'The *fire*.'

'I meant the website, Jay.'

'Oh yeah, right. Well, this thing's tricky. But I'm getting there.'

'Have you uploaded my copy yet?'

His daughter's balanced on Cat's hip and she grins at Jayden with a pirate's leer. She's teething and her top is wet through; the girl drools more than a bloodhound.

'Some of it. She needs a bib-thing on, Cat. A bandana. Neckerchief. Whatever it's called.'

'I think I want to change it a bit, put more about us in there. Living the dream, family affair, that kind of thing.'

He reaches out to tweak Jazz's top, feel her clammy little chest.

'You're soaked, honey. Ask Mummy to sort you out.'

'Jay.'

'What?'

'Er, passive-aggressive vibes, is what. Jazzy, can you tell Daddy to stop talking to me through you? And, also, while you're at it, tell him that I know how to dress my own daughter.'

Cat throws him a smile but it's a forced one. Jayden doesn't blame her; back-seat baby driving is never a good look. Though he's sure she's just as guilty of doing it when Jazz is on his watch too.

Does any couple survive this stage unscathed? Some days they walk about, the three of them, as if they're bathed in light: all love, pure love. Okay, never exactly whole days, but moments, definitely. And sometimes a whole bunch of moments close together, too. But other times a different sort of energy follows them around: low-level bickering, punctuated by transactional interactions, as they cycle through the never-ending tending and chores.

How can one tiny human generate such chaos?

How can one tiny human inspire such devotion?

Jayden isn't the only hands-on dad around, but he and Cat are the only couple he knows who split it all down the middle. Maybe that woman in Mousehole was right – there aren't too many of his kind about. He likes knowing that his daughter will grow up seeing literally no difference between her mum and dad. Gender roles, anyway. There are other differences. Like there's no way he'd leave her so long in that soggy top.

'When you're done here, fancy a walk with us?' says Cat, and her smile has a bit more in it this time.

'I'm nowhere near done here. But I am up for a walk.'

The perfect weather of yesterday blew out overnight and they woke up this morning to a sky so heavy it felt like it might actually be coming for them all. But there's one thing that Jayden has learnt about living by the sea: you never regret that walk, that swim, that surf – well, attempt at a surf, in his case.

He's out of his chair and just hitting Sleep on the laptop, thinking how the right moves on the website might come to him this afternoon, when his phone starts buzzing.

'It's Saffron,' he says to Cat.

'We'll get ourselves up together. Meet you out front.'

'Okay.'

'And Jay, take your time with Saffron, she's having a nightmare. But, also . . .'

'Also what?'

'Don't make more of it than it is. The fire, I mean. It was an accident, right?

'Yeah. So, they're saying, anyway.' He picks up the call. 'Saffron, hey. How's it going?'

As Saffron speaks, Jayden sits back down. It takes a moment for him to catch up to what she's saying.

She wants to trace her dad. Her dad who is not, after all, JP Sharpe. And she sounds completely determined.

'So, what do you think? Can you help?'

'Of course we'll help,' says Jayden. Then, with a breath, 'You can count on us.'

Which sounds dangerously close to a promise; one he's not sure he's able to make.

28

It's just gone noon when Trip gets to the empty skate park, which is about right for the guy he's meeting. And, sure enough, here Leo comes, punting himself along: hoodie to his knees, wide-leg trousers billowing in the wind. He enters the park with a flourish, spinning his board and then missing the landing. He swears as he hits the ground but tumbles over as easy as a puppy.

'Alright?'

Leo blinks, bleary-eyed, looking like he just rolled out of bed. Or rolled a very fat joint. Or both, probably.

'Mate,' he says, getting to his feet.

And this means *hello*. Or *I'm sorry*. Or *I agree*. Or pretty much anything, basically.

Mate.

'Long time.' Leo sniffs, dragging his sleeve across his face. 'What's up with you?'

Maybe Trip does look like something is up, because he doesn't normally go looking for a guy like Leo. And there isn't much point hanging about in a skate park without a board. Plus, his face, don't forget his face, which Trip is pretty sure is set in a default worried expression: his forehead feels like someone's lashed a rope around it and is hauling with all their strength. His eyes ache. Even his beard's itchy. He hardly slept at all last night, his mind buzzing with questions, like, when are they going to get back on the water and start earning again? Why was the body in his boat? Why did Wilson – a straight man through and through – lie to him about The Manor? And this morning, what the hell's all this about a fire now?

Trip drags in a breath. Says, 'You heard about JP Sharpe, right?'

Leo makes a sound of acknowledgement, at the same time as sticking a cigarette between his lips; Trip watches it bob up and down and fights an urge to snatch it from him and grind it beneath his shoe.

Trip realises then that he really kind of hates this guy. Well, maybe *hate* is too strong a word, but he despairs of him: that's closer. Leo is one of those kids who's been given everything – and then done nothing with it. His parents owned a holiday home along the coast and then moved here full-time. They gave it a couple of years then changed their minds, horrified to discover, no doubt, once the sheen of summer was over – all lobster lunches and sun bouncing off the 4x4 and posh accents swashing from beach to beach – that Cornwall is a real place with real people. *Newsflash!* Leo stayed though. Putting his expensive education to use with small-scale drug dealing, and even-smaller-scale DJing.

'He was found in my boat,' says Trip. And he watches Leo closely as he says it.

'No,' says Leo. 'Really, yeah?'

'Really, yeah.' Trip grits his teeth. 'You didn't hear that bit?'

Leo shakes his head. Snaps his lighter in his fingers.

'That's heavy,' he eventually says.

'You and JP. Were you still mates?'

'On and off.'

'More on than off?'

'He liked to party.'

'I keep thinking it over. Not just who'd kill him, but who'd stick him in my boat. What kind of a point they'd be making there.'

Leo tucks a strand of his lank hair behind his ear. 'Yeah, it's weird, man.' Then it's as if something dawns on him. 'You had the police coming around?'

'No,' says Trip. 'They decided no need.'

'Nice.'

Trip almost laughs. Rumour has it that Leo went to Eton; what an advert for private education. 'Course I had the police coming around. He was murdered, and then found on my boat. And now there's been a fire up at the Mermaid. Which feels like too much bad luck.'

'But you didn't tell them anything?'

'I didn't tell them that he liked his drugs, no. And I didn't tell them that he bought them from you. And I didn't tell them about that little chat the three of us had back in the summer either. And what happened after.'

'Cool.'

Cool?

How did it start? With Leo calling out Trip's name in the pub, he can't even remember which one now. *Hey, here's a fisherman. Trip, mate. This guy wants to make friends with a fisherman.* And, so, a night followed with JP Sharpe getting the drinks in, and talking of business opportunities, how those neat little fishing boats could putter out into the channel and get up to all kinds of things without anyone turning an eye. Catch more than a few fish in their nets.

'Just saying,' JP said.

'Yeah hashtag just saying,' Leo added. Then, 'I've been saying this forever, by the way. Blatant business opportunity.'

And Trip listened to their dumb chat because the beers were flowing, and why not, but there was no way – just no way – that he'd get involved in anything like that. Nor would anyone else down at the harbour either.

'There's a long and valiant history of smuggling in these parts,' JP said, as if he could be the one to tell them about Cornwall. 'That's what they tell me, anyway. That's what I'm hearing.' And he tapped his nose and winked.

Trip's memory is sketchy at this point. He's pretty sure some kind of toast was made, the knock of glass against glass, and Leo doing that sniggering laugh of his. They ended up on Wilson's boat. Which was stupid, so stupid. But JP wanted to see it, asked so many questions, and Trip dumbly felt like a big man, so took them down the harbour. Just as soon as they were aboard *Night Dancer*, Leo was sparking up in the wheelhouse, then Trip heard a smash and JP was standing there kicking at fragments. The little black porcelain cat, Wilson's lucky charm, lying in smithereens. Trip, even through the drink, had the most sinking feeling – right there and then. He got the pair of them off the boat as fast as he could. Then he stumbled home, not thinking of hauling cocaine, but just this: *Idiots, idiots, idiots.* And he was including himself in that.

And, above all: *Wilson can never know I did this.*

'You remember, right, Leo? How when I said no to JP's big idea, he really didn't like it. And when I explained why – and I guess I didn't mince my words – he really *really* didn't like it. And that's when he cut the contracts.'

What Trip realised then was that JP didn't like being made a fool of. It was really that simple. Laughing at him was a bad move. Afterwards, Trip thought it was forgotten. But apparently not. JP never broadcast his reason for cutting the contracts around town. And, as far as Trip knew, he didn't try to rope anyone else down at the harbour into his plans either. Because the fact is, there were no plans. Just idle, stupid pub talk. That's what Trip thought, anyway. But now JP was dead.

'Did you and JP keep those conversations going?' he says to Leo now. 'Or include anyone else in them?'

Leo throws his butt to the ground. 'No, mate.'

'What about whoever you work for?'

'Work for? Hah, no. I'm a freewheeler, business leader.'

Leo cups his hands as if thinking about beatboxing, then drops them. Sticks them in his pockets.

'If this is about drugs, I don't want it coming back to me,' says Trip. 'And I don't want it coming back to Wilson.'

'Why would it? You're Mother Teresa, aren't you, yeah?' Leo plants one foot on his board, pushes it back and forth. There's a very smackable sneer on his face. 'Why Wilson?'

Because of the little black cat, thinks Trip. And that's when he realises: this is what he's really afraid of. Because as stupid as it sounds, their luck was fine until that moment in the wheelhouse. Then came the series of poor catches. The engine packing up, costing thousands to fix. Wilson's accident onboard, the worst of all. And now this weather stopping them from even trying. What if Wilson found out that JP was to blame for the change in fortune? What then?

Leo, clearly bored of the conversation, pushes off on his board. He attempts another flip of some sort, the board clattering to the ground, and Trip feels a flash of short-lived satisfaction. Quickly followed by this thought: *If JP was killed by anyone, please let it be a drug dealer.* Which is basically the same as saying, *Please not Wilson.*

29

Ally, Jayden and Saffron are gathered around the big wooden table in The Shell House. Outside, the wind tears up and over the dunes, a gale made of sand and salt. There've been nights out here when Ally's felt as if the house might escape its concrete mooring and take off: timber splitting, roof tiles skidding. But it hasn't got to that yet. Right now, a thin stream of afternoon sun, the first and only brightness of the day, is filtering through. *It's trying its best*, thinks Ally.

Saffron is trying her best too. It's the first time that Ally's seen her since what happened in Mousehole, and she looks tired, but nevertheless lit with a kind of energy.

'So, will you do it? Will you – what do people say? – take the case? I've never done this before. Obviously.'

Ally can feel Jayden watching her, waiting for her response.

'I'll pay you,' Saffron says, her fingers smoothing the knotted surface of the table. 'Whatever the going rate is for tracing a missing person . . . if that's what he is? It's not though, is it? Because he's only missing to me. And if someone's never been found in the first place, they can't exactly go missing, can they?'

'You don't have to pay us,' says Jayden.

'Not a penny,' adds Ally gently.

'So, you'll really do it?' Saffron's eyes are full of emotion.

'Of course we'll do it,' says Jayden.

'My only nervousness,' says Ally, and here she looks to Jayden, '*our* only nervousness, is the murder investigation. The fact that there's a . . .' – she searches for the right word – 'a closeness to it.'

'I know. The police are going to be looking for my dad too. But for a different reason. I know that, guys. They'll be following every lead. And that's what they'll see the letter as – a lead.'

Ally and Jayden swap looks again.

Saffron gives a low laugh. 'Mullins probably shouldn't have told me about the fingerprints on the letter, should he? The fact that they weren't JP Sharpe's?'

'No, he shouldn't have,' says Jayden. 'But now we know, we know. That was all he said, right?'

Saffron nods.

'Okay,' says Jayden, 'So if they can't get a match through their database – they'll only have the fingerprints of anyone who's had a conviction – then they're back to square one. So, I guess they might want to talk to you again, to see if you've any idea who might have written it.'

'But how would I?'

'They don't know that, remember. For all they know, this person could have made contact with you already, and they'll want to check that out. Not signing the letter could suggest a kind of familiarity, right? Like, the author expects you to put two and two together, maybe. Connect it with some past meeting or something.'

Saffron told them earlier about the Hang Ten cook-out, with JP Sharpe and his scraped-clean plate. But she shakes her head. 'There's just no way.'

'Saffron, right now,' says Jayden, 'you might be the closest actual thing they have to a lead in this investigation.'

She tips her head back and laughs; sort of. 'But that's wild. I'm not a lead. I'm a nothing. A nothing who doesn't know anything.'

'I keep thinking about the fact that the letter wasn't sealed,' says Jayden. 'Maybe the reason it wasn't signed is that he hadn't finished writing it. Did JP interrupt whoever was writing it? Or even take the letter from him?'

Ally sits forward. 'That's an interesting thought. What if JP Sharpe didn't want the letter to be sent?'

'But why would he care?' says Saffron.

'It's a decent line of enquiry,' says Jayden. 'Whether there was a different kind of connection between JP Sharpe and your mum?'

'You said that you and your mother never talked about your father,' says Ally. 'And that you'd never really given any thought to it, that you were happy it being just the two of you.'

Saffron nods vigorously. 'I didn't need to know that bit of myself, to feel . . . like a whole person. Mum was more than enough. I wanted to be all of her, not half. I *was* all of her. Does that sound mad?'

'Not at all,' says Ally.

Ally thinks of Saffron's mother, Stephanie, dead for three years now. Can she see the remarkable woman that her daughter has become? Can she hear these words, the tenderness and pride with which Saffron speaks of her? All that love. Ally's no churchgoer, but the truth is, how can anyone really know where the dead go? She's always distrusted people who have too much certainty.

'So, Saffron, to help us,' says Jayden, 'maybe think about anything your mum might have said, or maybe even something among her possessions, that could give us a place to start. Can you do that?'

Because unless there are fingerprints on the letter and the police get there first, we don't have anything, Ally thinks. *And if the police do get there first . . .* She stops herself. But if they're doing this properly, it isn't about avoiding uncomfortable truths. And this is the burning question: was Saffron's father, the author of the letter, the last person to see JP Sharpe alive?

'We just want you to be sure that this is something you want to do,' says Ally.

'You guys are as bad as Gus,' says Saffron. And Ally does a double-take at that. 'But I know it's because you care and I'm so grateful that you do. But, look, I'm really sure. It's weird how sure I am.'

'You can change your mind at any time,' says Jayden. 'You know that, right?'

'I won't. But thanks.'

'Whatever we discover, if it has a bearing on the murder case . . .' Ally glances at Jayden. He takes it from her, as neatly as a passed baton.

'We'll have to tell the police,' he says. 'If it's relevant to their investigation.'

Saffron nods. 'Mullins has been sweet. I can't believe I'm actually saying those words. Though in the scheme of unbelievable things, his sweetness ranks pretty low, to be fair.'

'Perhaps it's better that you don't tell Mullins about this for now,' says Ally. 'The police might not take kindly to us being involved, even in the peripheries.'

If they are in the peripheries, that is. Ally has an uncomfortable feeling that they're right in the middle of this.

'Okay,' says Saffron. 'I already told Gus though. Is that alright?'

'Gus?' Ally smiles in what she hopes is an even sort of way. 'Of course that's okay.'

'You know what, Mullins might be useful to us,' says Jayden, 'even by accident. But Ally's right, let's keep this under the radar. Okay . . . Saffron, can you write a list of anything you think might help?'

'It's going to be really short. I'm sorry. I already got in touch with Mum's two oldest friends. I emailed them and they don't know anything, and never did. God, it felt weird asking. I hated it. Like

I was going behind Mum's back. Or like the two of us had never even had a proper conversation.'

Saffron's pen hovers over the blank sheet of paper. Ally watches her, feeling the return of her nervousness. It's so important that they do everything right by her. But what if they end up discovering the worst kind of truth? Ally looks to Jayden, and she knows he must be thinking the same thing. Outside, the wind howls, as if it already knows the answer.

30

The doorbell rings just as Bev is getting ready to go out. The boys have been desperate to get to the park all day, and despite Jonathan's insistence that he's old enough to go on his own – *yeah, yeah, alright, Mum, I'll keep an eye on Cody if I really have to* – Bev can't quite bring herself to agree to it. It isn't so much the roads, because they're pretty good at stopping, looking and listening, her boys. It's not even the people, the strangers that might be lurking in shadowy corners. It's just the fact of letting them go, right now, when her nerves are so jangled. She heard about the fire on the radio: Mermaid's Rest is all but gone. For all of her mixed feelings about the place, the news sucked the breath from her. They're saying it was accidental and straight away she thinks of her boys, the way they claimed the broken vase, the punch on the arm, was an *accident*. In their house, it's one of those convenient, not-quite-a-fib words. Though who is she to talk?

There is one thought that's sort of calming though: if she was still working at Mermaid's Rest, she'd have lost her job anyway, because of the fire. She'd be exactly where she is now. Just with a few more weeks' pay in her pocket.

'I'm coming,' she calls as the doorbell goes again. Her hip catches Cody's scooter in the hallway and sends it crashing, whacking her calf on its way down. She squeaks, rubs the spot, then yanks open the door in a half-temper, her hair falling into her eyes.

'Beverley Potter?'

A woman she's never seen before is standing on the step, flashing her white-teeth smile. Her hair is cut in a shiny black bob and she looks so put together that Bev suddenly becomes acutely aware of her own baggy-kneed tracksuit bottoms, her bobbly cardigan.

'Yes?' she says, tucking her hair behind her ears.

Bev thinks she must be a detective, this woman. But she's already spoken to the police, and they seemed satisfied enough with everything she told them. Yes, she used to work with JP Sharpe. Yes, she lost her job at Mermaid's Rest. No, she didn't bear any ill will. And what was she doing at the time of the murder? Asleep in her bed. No, she didn't have anyone who could confirm that, as her husband was working late. Unless you counted a mop-headed Cody slipping into her bed gone midnight because he had a nasty dream.

'I'm Cheryl Close, from the *Echo*. And I'd love it if you could spare me a few minutes to talk about what's going on up at Mermaid's Rest.'

Bev blinks. 'I don't think so . . .'

'You'll be paid, of course. I know how busy you must be, and your time's valuable. Your perspective's valuable.'

Bev hesitates. She wants to ask *How much?* but instead she says, 'I can't. I don't know anything about it. And we're just heading out.'

Cody appears then, hefting his scooter over the threshold, helmet skew-whiff. Jonathan behind him. They hardly bat an eye at the stranger, and instead head towards the garden gate.

'Boys, wait!' she calls.

'We could walk and talk?' offers Cheryl.

'But I've nothing to tell you. Not that's worth paying for anyway.'

'I doubt that,' says Cheryl. 'Here's the thing, Bev. Mermaid's Rest was in ruins long before that blaze took hold or JP Sharpe was murdered, that's what I'm hearing. Management at each other from day one. Bad attitudes and toxic culture. Staff in and out all the time. I mean you know, don't you? First-hand.'

'I don't have a score to settle, if that's what you're thinking.'

'Oh, it's not that sort of a piece,' says Cheryl, with a high laugh. 'Far from it. What I'm writing, Bev, is a portrait of the place, more than anything. A peep behind the curtain. Behind the cute name, the olde worlde charm, the fine-dining pretensions – what kind of a place is it really? It's captured people's imaginations, what with the murder and then the fire. That has to be more to it, doesn't there? I just want to tell that story.'

Bev pulls her eyes from Cheryl, and sees the boys practically ripping the gate off its hinges in their desperation to be off. They're good boys, waiting for her; others would have been halfway to the end of the road by now. She thinks of the letters to Santa. The shopping days still left. Their faces on Christmas morning. *You don't have to get us any extra presents, Mum*, Cody said the other day, his face pink with emotion. *We can just have what Santa brings us. If we've been good. And I'm pretty sure we've been good. Well, okay, anyway. Haven't we?*

Cheryl leans towards her conspiratorially and, as if she's been reading her mind, says, 'It's a pricey time of year, isn't it? And if I know kids, I'll bet those two are on at you for the latest this, or the newest that. Expecting you to magic up a mountain of gifts just like that.'

'They're not like that . . .' she starts to say.

'We pay well, Bev.' Then she gestures to the path ahead. 'Give me five minutes. Ten at the most. I just want you to say it as you see it. You could have Christmas sorted, just like that. Make it one to remember.'

Walking to the park, the boys careen ahead, coats flapping like capes. Anything that's not nailed down is ripe for the wind's taking; electric cables jump overhead, hedges tilt, they step round bins scattered like dominoes on the pavement. Beyond the wall the sea is as grey as a gun and just as angry.

As Bev takes a seat on a bench beside the journalist, she buries her chin in her coat. Her cheeks ache with the cold. Cheryl nudges close to her, nodding like her head is on a string, eyes lit up.

'I just got fed up one day,' Bev says, her hands kneading one another. 'Fed up of JP Sharpe treating us all like something he'd trodden in. I'd been seething with it my whole shift, then right at the end I was taking some plates out and I didn't realise how long they'd been sitting there, under the heat. I went to take one and it was red hot. I sort of flapped, dropped it instantly – it was that hot, you can still see the burn,' she says, holding up her fingers, 'but it skidded off and smashed on the floor. JP stormed over straight away. Started calling me every name under the sun. Said it'd be coming out my wages too – the cost of the ingredients as well as the plate. I was already tired. Dog-tired. And the burn was killing me. And then the way he showed me up like that. I was either going to start crying or just scream right back at him. So that's what I did. I snapped. Swear words I've never even used before came out. It was the stress of it all, you know? And that's what Phil heard, when he came in. Which probably meant half the dining room heard it too, because he just stood there in the entrance to the kitchen with his jaw to the floor. But when I said what'd happened – that I was only giving as good as I'd got – JP straight up denied it, and no one, not one person in that kitchen, backed me up.'

'Why? Because Sharpe ruled the roost? No one dared argue?'

Bev thinks of Dominic, JP's yes man: she'd never have expected anything from him. But Zolt the porter or the quietly straightforward Luke? She'd hoped for more. That's the trouble with Bev: she's always hoping.

'Phil's supposed to be the manager,' she says. 'He should have read the situation. He knew how JP could be, and he knew me too. A good worker. Keep my head down. Toe the line. But none of that mattered.'

'So, you don't just blame JP Sharpe for the fact you lost your job, but Phil Butt too?'

Bev hesitates; chews the inside of her mouth. She's been lying all this time, so to tell the truth, or part of it anyway, would be a relief. 'This is all just for background? Not to be printed?'

Cheryl nods.

'I blame myself,' she says. 'That's who. I shouldn't have let it get to me.'

'But you were pushed. Time and time again you were pushed. It's that kind of place, isn't it?'

Bev's eyes go to her boys. They're side by side on the swings, the wind's coming at them sideways, sending their trajectories haywire. She watches Cody's little legs, his red wellingtons, sticking up towards the sky then swooshing back down. Jonathan leaning so far back that his long hair skims the concrete.

'Careful!' she calls out. Their laughter sounds like church bells and her eyes fill at the sound. 'I say to those two all the time, turn the other cheek,' she says. 'Sticks and stones. I've got all the lines, as a mum. But when push came to shove, I did the opposite. And I could die of shame for that.'

Cheryl stares at her. She's obviously disappointed and who can blame her? How much is an answer like that worth? Not much probably. What's Bev even doing here, talking to this person? The fact is, she doesn't have anything to tell her. She's never been one for gossip – nor for sticking her head above the parapet. Earlier she described Phil to Cheryl as *weak-willed*, and she's already regretting putting her name to that. And JP Sharpe might be arrogant and even a little sadistic – yes, she used those words too – but she's not about to speculate on how he got himself killed.

Bev can feel her phone trilling in her bag, and she reaches for it. She sees Neil's name and feels a wash of guilt. She's pretty sure he wouldn't give a journalist the time of day, even one wielding a chequebook.

'My husband,' she says. 'Alright if I take it quickly?'

Cheryl gives a flick of her fingers, which Bev takes as acknowledgement.

'Hey, love,' she says.

'Now, I don't want you to worry,' he begins. 'But I'm headed down the police station.'

31

Saffron's crossing the square, and she's drawn towards The Wreckers Arms like it's a beacon. There are fairy lights in the tree outside, and as the branches shake it looks like a sky full of shooting stars. The glittering lengths of tinsel wound around the doorway have come loose and are waving madly in the wind. These weather-battered attempts at festivity strike Saffron as brave, and kind of heartbreaking.

She stands across the way, her chin tucked into the collar of her coat, watching. Through the brightly lit window Saffron can see the old familiars propping up the bar. It's late afternoon, speeding towards early evening; people having a pint of Cornish Cream or Doom Bar on their way home, or stopping in for an early tea with their kids. Though there's less of that in the winter, without the holiday crowds – in summer the beer garden is like a play park, children swinging and sliding, necking fizzy drinks and tossing chips to gangs of gulls.

Saffron can remember having tea in the pub as a girl, and it always felt like a treat. Tucked in a corner table, her mum going for a chilli jacket potato, or chicken pie, and Saffron always picking cheesy chips: come hell or high water, it was cheesy chips.

Ah, the Weeks girls! Paddy, who owned the place back then, would sing out as they walked in. The Weeks girls. As if they were sisters.

Saffron closes her eyes. She can see it like it was yesterday: the blue stripe on the plates; the red plastic straw sticking out of her bottle of fizzy apple. Her mum sitting beside her, the gentle nudge of their elbows as they ate, and the way she'd flop into her mum's side when she was done, feel the curl of her arm around her. Then, walking home together up the hill, heads dipping from the clifftop gusts; lights twinkling far across the bay. And it all feeling so ordinary but also totally magic.

Saffron knows her childhood was blessed, that she never had cause to doubt her mum's love or the safety of the home she gave her. She meant it when she said to Ally and Jayden that her mum was enough for her; that she never felt like there was a hole to be filled with a name or a photo – and certainly not an actual person.

But the sudden fact of JP Sharpe in her life – and that letter – has changed everything.

Even for just a short while, the absent figure of a dad was given a shape; a face. Even if it turned out to be the wrong one.

'If you'd received that letter by post, instead of in the way you did, would you still have wanted to know more?' Ally had asked.

And Saffron had to stop and think about that. In the end, she replied, 'I don't think I would. I mean, I know I can't call it, not really, I only know how I feel now. But honestly? I think I'd have thought, *No thanks. I'm good.*'

'So, what, you think it's partly the shock?' Jayden had said. 'Because of the way the news came to you?'

'Yeah, maybe. Like fight or flight. And . . . I guess I choose fight.'

But it was also Saffron thinking that her dad was suddenly dead. Somehow, that felt different to him never having existed at all.

Saffron had such conviction when she spoken to Ally and Jayden earlier. The one thing she didn't voice was the nagging worry that she's now betraying her mum. But it's okay for people to change their minds, isn't it? To feel completely different on one day, compared to, say, three years, two months and three weeks ago, sitting in a hospital room, looking her mum in the eye and saying, *It's okay, I don't want to know.*

The pub door swings open and the wreath dances, bells jangling.

It's Mullins. Mullins in a t-shirt, rubbing his hands together and bouncing on his toes.

Saffron thinks of shrinking back into the shadows, avoiding the chat, but no, it's Mullins – and he was kind to her last night.

'Where's your coat, mate?' she calls out.

'Left it in the car, didn't I?'

He comes towards her, a slightly nervous look on his face.

'Drinking on duty? Glad to see you're keeping up the old standards,' she says.

'It was Fanta. Anyway, I'm off. Did the night shift.' He looks sideways at her. 'You did hear, didn't you, Saff? What went on up at the Mermaid?'

She nods. 'Only what the news said. Insider info?'

'That bloke Phil Butt, the manager up there, was lucky to get out alive.'

'He started it, didn't he?'

'Yeah, the twonk,' says Mullins. 'Easily done, though. Fire spreads like . . .'

'Wildfire?'

Mullins gives it the big ho-ho. 'You should have seen it though. Flames all the way up to the sky. Like, massive. Took two showers to get the stench of smoke off me.'

'I really don't want to think about you showering, Mullins.'

'Yeah, yeah, okay.' He squints at her. 'You're different. Better. Feels good not to be Saffron Sharpe, is that it?'

She recoils. 'God, Mullins, just when I think you're turning over a new leaf.'

'Well, it's good news, isn't it?'

She hesitates. Ally and Jayden told her not to let on to Mullins that she's getting them involved.

'Not really. There's still a man dead.'

'And someone who thinks they're your dad got him confused with a letterbox.'

She shakes her head. *Seriously, Mullins?* But he's glancing at her awkwardly, and she can read him well enough these days: he's trying to find his way to saying something.

'What are you thinking, there, Saff? Are you still, you know, figuring you might want to—'

His phone goes then, and he plucks it from his pocket, with what looks like relief crossing his face. 'Work,' he says to her. 'Sorry.' Then, 'PC Mullins?'

He listens for a minute, head nodding in exaggerated fashion, elbow cocked wide.

A man on an important phone call: that's what his stance says. She gives him a little wave, making to go. She should be at home now, in that freezing house of hers. Ally and Jayden have given her a job: going through the last, the most precious, of her mum's things. Just in case there's something in there that might send them in the right direction. Something that she missed because, before, she simply wasn't looking.

'Saff, wait!' he calls.

She spins on her heel. 'Yeah?'

'We've taken someone in for Sharpe's murder. He's being questioned now.'

32

Inside The Shell House the fire is hypnotic, logs glowing bright white. The wind has temporarily dropped, and the waves push back in; to Jayden they sound like the thud of bass from a passing car.

He stifles a yawn. He's tired to his bones, but he needs to be fresh for this case. Doing right by Saffron is a pressure that he and Ally have to channel into their best work.

When he and Cat moved down here, there were a bunch of factors, but the one that his wife made a lot of was that her mum and dad would be able to help with Jasmine. But if Cat imagined on-tap babysitting then it hasn't exactly worked out like that. *I thought they'd offer more*, she often grumbles. *I shouldn't have to always ask.* And it's up to Jayden to talk her down, then; he doesn't want to take advantage of his in-laws. For all Cat's socially conscious talk, when it comes to her mum and dad, she can act a little entitled. So how does it work? He picks up all the slack that Sue and Cliff might have stepped in with. He says, *You take the day and go see your mates* or *I'll do the nights this week, you catch up on some sleep.* Jayden doesn't mind; it feels like his duty as the dad. After all, when it comes to balancing the scales, Cat has pregnancy, childbirth and breastfeeding on her side. When Kieran died, Cat carried Jayden, no doubt – and now he figures it's his turn to step up. It's going to be his turn for a long time, the way he sees it. And the truth is, the second he's with Jazzy he's all-in; the rest of the world can wait. A whole planet falling into line, just so he can lull her back to sleep or warm her a bottle or mush a carrot. So it goes.

But okay, he still feels the pull to other things, sometimes. Like Mousehole the night of the murder. Like being here now, trying to figure it all out for Saffron. Holding two completely contradictory feelings at the same time – is that parenthood?

Maybe Saffron is, deep down, feeling that contradiction too. Desperately wanting to know, but also afraid of what the truth might bring. Even if she hasn't admitted it.

'Okay,' he says to Ally, 'I said I'd be back at the farm by seven, so . . . I better make tracks soon. Shall we divide it up?'

Ally runs her finger down the list in her notebook. Adjusts her reading glasses.

'Well, Wenna has a soft spot for you. So I suggest you be the one to speak to her.'

When they asked Saffron if there was anyone in Porthpella who her mum was close to back in the day, she thought about it then said, *Well, I guess maybe Wenna?* And it's true, Wenna does know pretty much everything about what goes on round here. White Wave Stores is the epicentre of Porthpella, even more than The Wreckers Arms.

'All this time,' says Jayden, 'and what if Wenna knows exactly who Saffron's dad is? Easy as that?'

'It's possible,' says Ally. 'But I understand why Saffron doesn't want to ask for herself, when it felt so strange getting in touch with her mum's friends to ask the same thing.'

Jayden tosses another log into the wood burner and settles back as the flames jet. Maybe those tracks he's got to make can wait a minute or two. He stretches his legs out. *Man, it's cosy here.* Ally has some kind of a soup simmering away in the kitchen, the smell winding its way to his nostrils: something a bit sweet, a bit spicy. He thinks of his mum's corn soup. Happiness in a bowl. The same

168

recipe passed on from her mum, and her mum before that, split peas and corn, sweet potato and coconut milk. *Tastes like home*, his grandmother used to say, no doubt thinking of white sand and swaying palms and flame-red hibiscus. And it tastes like home to Jayden too: the tall red-brick house on the edge of the park; the banister where he once mistimed a slide and chipped his tooth; the back garden with the towering apple tree and the stone wall he used to fire his football at, staccato bursts of ball on foot on wall on head.

He can't wait to take Jazzy back to Leeds for New Year. They've got a full social schedule, including seeing Kieran's wife and daughters. Jayden's sister and all her lot. Old school mates. They're going to need sustenance to keep up the pace. Maybe he should message his mum and get the corn soup order in now.

'Carrot and coriander,' says Ally, reading his mind. 'Bill's recipe. If you can't stay, you could take some with you?'

'Al, you're a dream.'

As Ally gets up, Jayden says, 'I'm not dodging it, but I feel like Wenna might find you easier to talk to. If she knows anything, it might be . . . intimate.'

Ally hesitates; then nods agreement.

He's noticed, in their time working together, that Ally's more at ease with total strangers than with people she's known for forty years. They talked about it once and she said, *Oh dear, is it that obvious?* But the way she explained it made sense to Jayden: that people round here know her as Bill's wife, the one who keeps herself to herself; head down, walking the shore, doing her art, living that little bit away from everyone and everything. As far as Porthpella is concerned, she's nicely in her pigeonhole – and it's not easy to break out of that. Sometimes it sounds like she isn't even sure she wants to.

'Al, if we draw a blank with Wenna, then I reckon our best bet is whatever Saffron can find at home. If this was a movie there'd be a diary, right? Her mum laying it all out, just cryptic enough to keep us guessing, but enough to send us on the right path.' He shakes his head. 'But you know what, if there's nothing on record – and we already know the birth certificate doesn't list the father – then . . . all we have is what people say.'

'That's all we ever have, isn't it? We can't stop believing in that.'

'And I guess a DNA test. If it comes to it.'

Ally walks back through from the kitchen, a giant orange thermos in her hands. She hands it to him, and he hugs it to his chest like a hot-water bottle. Smiles his thanks.

'You know what, he might come to us,' says Jayden. 'Not literally to us, but to Saffron. I mean, he wrote the letter, didn't he? He wanted to make contact. He could follow it up, right?'

'Perhaps he doesn't know that it never got to her.'

'Yeah, true. The police haven't mentioned it in their press briefings, and they wouldn't, that kind of detail. Could be crucial.'

And they both know exactly what that means – if the police think the letter is key.

'So,' says Jayden, carefully, 'either he doesn't know that the letter didn't get to her, in which case he might be sitting there thinking that she doesn't want to know. Or . . . he does know. And for whatever reason, he's changed his mind about reaching out to her. And, Al, I still think there's something in the point that the letter wasn't signed or sealed. Why not?'

Ally pushes her fingers to her temples. 'I don't like this, Jayden. It's just a feeling I have. I want us to help Saffron, but the fact of the murder . . .'

'I know. But . . . she wants this. It's her choice, right?' Jayden starts to pull his coat on.

If he's really honest, he doesn't like it any more than Ally. But Saffron didn't come to them looking for good news, she came to them for the truth: that's what she said. It isn't up to them to tell her how to feel.

Outside, the wind is hurling itself around the headland. As Jayden moves to the window he squints out into the darkness. Nights like this, he can't believe that Ally's happy out here on her own. But he should know her well enough by now; there's nowhere she'd rather be.

He says it anyway: 'You okay, Al? This weather's wild.'

'I don't mind this weather. So long as everyone's safe. Drive carefully, Jayden.'

'You got it,' he says. 'Look, Saffron's at home going through her mum's things. You're going to talk to Wenna in the morning. So I'm going to keep looking at JP Sharpe. Because there *has* to be a connection, doesn't there? How else did he have the letter in his pocket? All those people up at Mermaid's Rest, it could be any one of them, couldn't it? The kitchen porter or some other chef, saying "Here mate, can you post this for me?" Someone there will know something, surely. Her dad could be one of the staff.'

Ally's face lights up.

'The manager, Phil Butt. I can't get his behaviour out of my head. That phone call. The trouble is, it's all but burnt down, Jayden. The staff will be scattered to the wind.'

'Then I'll find them.'

'When I told the police about Bev Potter, they said they'd already spoken to her. She's not a person of interest apparently, despite her obviously having an issue with the murder victim.'

'I definitely want to talk to this Phil. How old is he, Al? Is he a contender?'

'You mean is he old enough to be Saffron's father? I'd say late forties. You know, he didn't want me meeting the other chef either. Dominic, his name was. As far as Phil was concerned, I was just an enthusiastic customer, so why be so reluctant? He was younger, by the way, Dominic. Thirties, I'd say.'

'I'm on it, Al. Soon as you've spoken to Wenna, let's compare notes.'

He goes for a knuckle-bump. Ally obliges, with a laugh.

As she opens the door for him, the wind powers in. Jayden steps out on to the veranda. Black clouds swirl above the dunes. There are no stars about on a night like this.

'The police won't like it, you know, Jayden. You going round asking questions.'

He pops on his toes, the wind pushing at his back.

'I'll tread carefully,' he says. 'Float like a butterfly sting like a bee, right?'

33

The kettle at the station takes forever to boil. Mullins stands there with his mug, shifting from foot to foot, as it slowly reaches its whining peak. He's got a KitKat in his pocket too, and he's not afraid to use it. He feels his jaw click as another massive yawn takes over.

Mullins is knackered after the fire, but what's the point in just lying about at home when there's a murder suspect down the station? Plus, he owes it to Saffron to be here. Not that there's much to see. He's not getting a look-in.

'Ah, timing!'

DS Skinner comes striding into the kitchen. He snatches up a mug and helps himself to the just-boiled kettle. He sloshes water in, and only then casts around for the coffee. *Instant* coffee. It's down to Hippy-Dippy that he thinks of it like that now; before it was all just coffee. Mullins watches the sergeant as he lobs the grains in, and they swim on the surface like something nasty left in a toilet bowl.

As Mullins fills his own mug, the water only goes halfway and he growls internally. But he holds his tongue and says, 'So we've got a bloke in for the Sharpe murder, have we, sir?'

Skinner takes a slurp of his drink. 'You're not even on shift yet, Mullins. What are you doing here?'

'All hands to the pump, isn't it? Who is he? And is he talking?'

He feels his sergeant study him, and he shrinks back. Sometimes Mullins feels like he's two people. The one that other people see: sound, solid – okay, could stand to lose a pound or two – but a proper bloke and no doubt about it. Then someone else: flimsy as a net curtain. It's getting to him, that's the trouble: Saffron, fathers, Christmas in Mousehole. The way Skinner's looking at him, can he see it too?

'You did well up at the fire last night, that's what I'm hearing.'

'There wasn't much to do.'

'Secured the scene, spoke to witnesses, all with it raging in the background. You had your rest? Not exactly a normal night for us.'

Mullins doesn't even care about the half mug of coffee anymore. He's drinking in everything Skinner's saying; can feel it warming his insides.

'Yeah, it was nothing,' he says. 'Phil Butt was all over the place though. Drunk as a skunk.'

'And playing with fire. I've seen his statement, and it matches the investigator's report. Started from a candle up in the apartment. Synthetic furnishings, old building, once it got a hold, that was it. Well, he's shot himself in the foot there. Mermaid's Rest won't be reopening anytime soon.'

'Run of bad luck for that place, eh? You think that's all it is though?'

Skinner lowers himself into a chair. For once he seems willing to chat.

'Well, I wouldn't say there's no connection. Everything's connected. That's what DS Chang was going on about earlier. Phil Butt drinking too much after losing his head chef, that's a knock-on. Being clumsy with a candle and being too out of it to notice, well, that's a knock-on too. Connections. Nothing that'll help us with the murder though, far as I can see.'

Mullins eyes the other chair. It'd be too much to drop himself into it, wouldn't it? And he wants Skinner to keep talking.

'So, the suspect . . . do you think he's the one?' Mullins tries to sound airy, casual. 'Who is it, anyway?'

'Neil Potter. His wife left the Mermaid a couple of weeks ago, after a falling-out with Sharpe over an order. Definitely got an axe to grind. Whether that axe is our murder weapon though . . . that's another matter.'

'I thought it was a blunt object.'

'Very droll,' says Skinner.

'Is there any evidence on Neil Potter?'

'Not nearly enough. Yet. But he hasn't got an alibi for the time of the murder. And we've a witness – Dominic Brook – who said Potter got into a scrap with Sharpe over how his wife was treated. Still got the bruise here,' says Skinner, pointing to his cheek. 'But according to Potter, that never happened. Potter claims it was a chance encounter with a paint can.'

'Brook was the one who came up to the fire last night. He was mates with Sharpe. One of the few. Brook says he saw it, did he – the fight with Potter?'

'Not with his own eyes. But Sharpe talked about it the next day. I don't think Brook's lying about it. No, I think Neil Potter's lying. But I don't know why.'

'Er, because he killed JP Sharpe?'

'Well, that would be motivation to tell a porky, wouldn't it now? But if he was really clever, he'd be better off coming clean about the fight, but maintaining his innocence about the murder. But he's probably not that strategic.'

'Or maybe he's telling the truth?'

'You're very interested in all this, I must say. Don't tell me you're getting ideas about detective exams.'

Mullins can feel the tips of his ears go pink. He doesn't say anything.

'The cherry on the cake, of course, is that Potter has a record,' says Skinner. 'Two counts of ABH. A decade ago, but even so.'

'So, you're saying he had means, motive and opportunity?'

Skinner gets up, leaving his chair askew and his mug on the table. 'We'll make a detective out of you yet, Mullins,' he says, heading for the door. 'Just find me some evidence on Neil Potter and I reckon we've got our man.'

And Mullins can't tell if he's messing with him or not. He calls out, 'What about the letter, the one to Saffron Weeks? Did Potter write it? Were his prints on it?'

But Skinner's already gone.

34

Phil hates everything about the start of this Thursday morning. He hates the room that management hired, in somebody else's pub in Penzance, with its limp strings of tinsel and piped festive favourites. He hates the urn of hot water and cheap teabags and the hopeless plate of biscuits, still in their plastic packets, duos of shortbread that taste of nothing except the crushing blow of losing your job – or as good as, because no one here is fooled – right before Christmas.

Phil also hates that, apparently, it's becoming a habit. Only two days ago they gathered for him to deliver the news about JP. But somehow that felt different. It was on home turf, for one. And he didn't feel even the tiniest shred of guilt. Not like now.

'So, look,' he says, in wrap-up mode, desperate to get to the end of it, 'there'll be some form of compensation for wages. We have insurance for a reason. As soon as management confirm it then you'll know. Um, you'll know when I know.'

His eyes nervously skim the room. Quite why there isn't a representative from said management here today he'll never know; too busy sitting pretty in their offices upcountry. They probably scheduled the meeting deliberately early, to rule out anyone from head office attending. Plus, he's read between the lines: *This is your shit, Butt, so you face the associated storm.*

He sounded so pathetic when he used that word – *accident* – to his bosses. Like a whining child, dodging blame for breaking a vase, crayoning a wall, sending the whole kit and caboodle up in flames. But it was, wasn't it? An accident.

After JP, it was also very bad press. So that's another thing they'll be chewing over in their boardroom, no doubt, as well as Phil's suitability as restaurant manager at any venue, let alone the smoking pile of rubble that's Mermaid's Rest.

It's all a disaster. *He* is a disaster.

'They're not going to keep on paying us for ever, though, are they? Not without a place to work in,' says Cath, one of the waitresses. She's dressed in her uniform – black skirt and white blouse – and it might have broken his heart, if any part of that heart was still intact.

Phil's already regretting his own outfit; namely, his tie. He wanted to put a brave face on it, project a positive image – ha-ha-ha, his inner saboteur is rolling in the aisles at that one – but this shimmering purple and orange number, a long-ago gift from Melissa, is making him feel like he's turned up to a funeral in a tutu.

Misjudging things. Again.

Phil tugs at his collar and loosens the offending article. The radiators are up high, and the heat is suffocating. He can feel sweat pooling at his armpits, and he clamps his arms closer to his sides. He used to be a master fibber as a boy. *Course I've done my home-work, Dad.* Why is he finding it so hard to spin the truth now?

'We're looking at a few options,' he says. 'Exploring possibilities.'

'What possibilities?' says Zolt, the kitchen porter. 'What options?'

'Options,' says Phil. *I don't bloody know!* he screams inside. And for a moment he entertains the fantasy of doing just that: screaming the place down. Then collapsing in a heap on the floor. Because that's just the kind of behaviour that will bring Melissa running back to him, isn't it? Instead he says, 'Depending on the extent of damage to the building, we may reopen in the existing premises or . . .'

He catches Dominic's eye – his ally, thanks to him turning up last night. It'll probably come back to bite him, just like everything seems to these days. But Dominic was solid in the moment, and Phil appreciates that. Just like he's being solid now, relaxing back in his chair, like it isn't all bad news; like he wasn't up half the night too.

'How's that goin' to happen?' pipes Luke, one of the line cooks. A quiet, older guy, who should have risen through the ranks if he was actually any good. Another of JP's nonsensical hires. Sometimes Phil reckoned JP picked his kitchen staff based on who'd put up with his attitude. Just like Phil himself always did, he miserably concludes. A doormat. Melissa levelled that one at him once – not just with a wipe of her feet but with a grinding of her stilettoes.

God, he wants her back. Without her, he's nothing at all.

Phil tries to focus on Luke, who's still talking: 'I went past it on the way here, took a look for myself. Man alive, there's nothing left.'

'Alternatively, a new site might be sought,' says Phil. 'Take the essence of Mermaid's Rest and reopen elsewhere, in a new home—'

At the word *home*, his voice breaks.

Luke laughs, and the noise is a slap.

'Sorry, Phil, but I reckon maybe the head honchos are leading you up the garden path too.'

'So, anyway,' he says – attempting, once again, to draw things to a close. If he's lucky he'll make it back to his hotel to catch the last of the breakfast sitting. He hasn't eaten a thing all morning and he's queasy; running on empty. 'You'll be kept in the loop. You'll be paid for the foreseeable, certainly. And, um, as soon as management—'

'JP wouldn't have stood for this,' says Zolt. 'Well, he wouldn't, would he?'

'Yeah, what's happening there?' says Luke. 'Police need to pull their fingers out, don't they? He was murdered on the seventeenth; it's the twenty-first and there's nothing doing. How's that right?'

'I don't have any updates on the case,' says Phil, stiffly. He can't make this meeting about murder too – isn't fire enough? His anxieties move like clouds; when a new one blows in it blots out the others. Phil reaches for his collar again and tries to undo the top button. *God, it's hot in here.* He's actually at the point of wondering where his next breath is coming from. 'It's a traumatic time,' he says. 'A time of . . . uncertainty. What happened to JP was a shock to us all. Now this. Our leadership team are—'

'I tell you, JP wouldn't have stood for what's happening now,' says Zolt again. 'This so-called compensation but without the facts.'

'There's not a lot of choice, dude,' says Dominic, in a voice that's pure ice. And they are, Phil thinks, his first words of the whole meeting.

Phil nods in Dominic's direction, as if he's made an excellent point.

'That's it,' Phil says. 'There's not. We're all in the same boat here, by the way. Me included.'

A loud cough comes from the back, with two words smothered beneath it. Phil can feel colour shoot into his cheeks. *Ignore.* But a small wave of laughter, uncomfortable, bitter laughter, lifts and breaks.

Encouraged, someone pipes up again: 'I said *insurance job.*'

Phil can't even see who said it. But his money would be on bloody Luke; he seems to like the sound of his own voice this morning.

'Insurance job?' Phil repeats, blinking.

And it's as if the smoke is curling into the back of his throat, choking him all over again. He can feel the heat of the flames, see the wall of them, looking like special effects, not actual fire in the actual flat. He can still hear the scream that came from his lips, and the briny taste of whatever the hell he'd been drinking rising up with it, stinging his tongue. He remembers dropping to his knees outside, coughs coming like freight trains; he looked at the place engulfed by fire and thought of dragging himself right back in.

If he'd snuffed it, if Melissa had been called to identify his corpse, would she even have shed a tear? She was rattled about JP's death, that much was obvious. And whatever she claimed, it had something to do with her walking out on Phil two days later. But considering she and Sharpe had been intimate – *alright, meaningless sex, whatever, whatever, hands over his ears, la la la* – Melissa wasn't exactly in pieces. At the time, Phil took it as a good sign for their marriage: fool that he is.

'It wasn't a damn insurance job,' says Dominic, spinning in his chair. 'Phil could have died, yeah?'

And, for a second, he sounds like JP – but a reasonable version, and on Phil's side – with an inarguable authority among the troops.

Phil feels weak with gratitude. 'Now, any other questions,' he musters, 'address them to HR. Meeting terminated.'

'Still feels like funny business to me,' says Zolt, without blinking an eye. 'What with JP.'

'What really happened?' asks Cath in a quiet voice from the front row, apparently not understanding the meaning of the word *terminated* either. 'To start the fire, I mean, Phil.'

Phil finds himself looking to Dominic again – who nods. What does he mean by it, that nod? Permission to tell the truth? Not even Dominic knows what that is.

'I had a candle burning,' he says, 'and it got knocked over.'

'That was all?' she says, her mouth a small 'o'. 'Lucky Melissa wasn't there too.'

And it's just the kind of thing that people say, isn't it? A platitude, something well meaning, because the truth is, his wife isn't

181

popular with the staff; it didn't take them long to sniff out the fact that she didn't want to be there, stuck above a restaurant in the middle of, as she put it, *bloody nowhere.*

Or is there something more in it? Does everybody know about the affair after all? Phil can't stand the thought of that; how weak and pathetic it makes him look.

The gut-churning shame.

He sees that card of Melissa's, curling and blackening in his fingertips; the words disappearing before his eyes. *It's not about him.* Like hell.

'Okay, let's leave it there,' says Dominic, getting to his feet. 'Phil's had enough of a grilling.' He realises what he's said then and puts his hand to his head. 'Duh. Sorry.' The room breaks into laughter – but it's lighter, better, and Phil wonders about joining in. Should he join in? Would that look right? But he's too late. The moment has come and gone. And no one is actually happy, are they? Not one person in this room is happy right now.

As they're all filing out, Phil smooths his stupid tie with one hand and holds on tight to the back of a chair with the other. His throat's burning with kept-in tears. He reckons he can hold it together for about as long as it takes the last of them to leave.

Because what Melissa has never realised, what he probably never told her when they were together, is that Phil needs her. And he'll do anything for her. Anything at all. If he thought it'd bring her back, he'd set fire to Mermaid's Rest all over again.

35

'Now there's a question,' says Wenna, with a long sigh.

The shopkeeper regards Ally steadily through her glasses. Then she turns to the jars of sweets behind her: rhubarb and custard, sugar-dusted toffees, liquorice swirls. Wenna unscrews a lid, pops a foam shrimp into her mouth. When she tilts the jar in Ally's direction, she declines with a smile.

'You're talking a long way back, love. Stephanie was a private sort of person. Deep down, anyway, about certain things.' Wenna chews steadily, a look of consideration on her face. 'And our Saffron wants this, does she?'

Ally nods. 'She does.'

'Saffron's never once asked me about him, you know. After the funeral, I remember she said to me, "I'm all on my own now, Wen," and I said, "No, you're not, my love," and I gave her this whopping big hug. She was skinny as an imp then. Well, she still is, isn't she? But it was the worry, seeing her lovely mum so sick.' Wenna shakes her head. 'But I meant that I'd be there for her, that's all. But, you know, I suppose I was thinking something else too. I suppose I was thinking about her dad being out there somewhere.'

She knows, thinks Ally. *Wenna knows*. And she realises she's not surprised at all. Stephanie and Wenna were close, Saffron said.

Wenna goes to the door and flips the sign from *Open* to *Closed*. She smiles. 'That'll put a cat amongst the pigeons, closed on a Thursday morning.'

Ally reaches into her bag and draws out her notebook.

'Oh, you won't need that, my love. I haven't got a name for you or anything like that.'

'So you don't know who he is?'

'Steph wouldn't tell a soul. Said it was better that way.'

Of course. It would have been much too easy, the quickest investigation yet.

'But,' says Wenna, 'I remember when it happened. Steph was a young thing, just newly qualified in her nursing. Beautiful as sunrise, too – inside and out. Could have had anyone in the world, could Steph.'

As she speaks, Wenna's hand goes to the sweetie jar again. Another foam shrimp goes in. She chews slowly, looking into the distance, like a sheep at pasture.

'Oh, she said he was handsome as you like. Trap as old as time though, that.'

'Where did they meet?'

'Well, that would be telling. And Steph never did, not exactly, anyway. I got the impression it was down Penzance or Newlyn way. One of the rowdy pubs down there. He was a wild child, by all accounts.'

'A local man?'

'Oh, I should say so.' She smiles. 'Nothing to base that on, mind, but Steph was Kernow through and through.'

'Were they together for long, Wenna?' asks Ally.

'Together? Oh no, they weren't ever together. Not boyfriend and girlfriend like. A one-night stand, was what it was. And Steph falling pregnant, the bad luck of it! Though you can't say that when you consider Saffron. Nothing but good luck there.'

'Do you know if he was aware that he was going to be a father?'

Wenna pauses in her chewing; tips her head to one side. 'She didn't want to hear this herself? Saffron, I mean? She wants it to go through you?'

Ally nods.

'Well, I can understand that. Less emotional. Though it's always felt a bit odd, me knowing more than Saffron does herself. Steph's business though, that's how I saw it. And now Saffron wants to make it hers – and yours – well, that's her right, isn't it? You didn't want to send that lovely Jayden to see me then?'

'He's busy elsewhere, I'm afraid.'

'Pity. Ever such a nice smile. Now, where were we?'

'Did he know about Steph's pregnancy?'

'Oh yes. He knew alright. She told him straight. I remember it. I saw her the day after. She was on her way home from the surgery, exhausted as you like. Sick with it too, poor little love, as some of them are.'

Wenna takes off her glasses and wipes the lenses on her cardigan. It strikes Ally as a contemplative gesture, as if she's trying to see the past more clearly. She's always thought of Wenna as a bit of a busybody – good-hearted, but not necessarily someone you'd trust with the details of your life – but there's a gentleness to her now that Ally finds moving.

'Steph said that she was going it alone. That's how she put it. "I'm going it alone, Wen." After all, she hardly knew him, did she? She did say to him – this is what she told me after – she said, "Forget about me, you've got no obligation there, but do you want to be involved in this child's life?" And he went and said no. Just like that. He said being any kind of a dad wasn't for him. Fool.'

Wenna sets her glasses back on her nose. Blinks fast.

'Do you know if they stayed in touch after that?' asks Ally.

'No, no. Not a bit of it. That was the deal. As I remember it, that was what Steph agreed with him. I can just hear her doing it, because she was a forthright little thing when she wanted to be. She'd have said something like, "Now you listen here. You're either in or you're out. I don't want you messing with this child's head – or mine for that matter. And if you're out, you're staying out. And that'll be the end of it." Hah!' Wenna gives a sharp laugh. 'I can just hear her! Mind you, Ally, don't quote me on that. But that was the gist of it, I know that much. "In or out, mate, and that'll be the end of it." And he chose out, didn't he? He chose out.'

'And you've really no idea who he is?'

Wenna shakes her head. 'I don't poke my nose in other people's business.' She looks up sharply, lip twitching. 'Alright, alright, I know I like a chit-chat, don't get me wrong, I do like a chit-chat. But I don't go prying. Not where it matters, I don't.'

'Of course not,' says Ally tactfully.

'Besides,' says Wenna, 'she wouldn't give him up for nothing. The way Steph saw it, it wasn't fair on Saffron if anyone else knew and her own daughter didn't. She had a proper sense of what was right, did Steph.'

There's a knock at the door, and a face peers in. White Wave Stores is never shut on a Thursday. Wenna's on her way over, opens it so it's just ajar.

'Two minutes, love, just give me two minutes while I sort a delivery,' she says.

And Ally notes it: the ease of the white lie. Not that she thinks Wenna isn't telling the truth – but still.

'You must have wondered though,' says Ally, in a gentle nudge.

'Well, of course I did. I'm only human.'

'You never had any theories?'

186

'Only that he was a right plonker to have opted out of that child's life. That's who he is, if you want to know my opinion: a prime plum. And what, you're saying he wants in now, does he, after all this time? Sending her letters?'

'Just one letter.'

'But not man enough to sign his own name, hmm? Well, that's about right.'

Ally doesn't offer the suggestion that he might have left the letter unfinished. It only complicates things.

'Well, someone needs to tell him again what Steph said: you're either in or you're out, mate. Because neither halfway there is just what she was afraid of. God rest her soul.'

Ally's glad, too, that she left out the detail of how the letter came to Saffron. The existence of the letter on JP's body was being closely guarded by the police. They must think it important. Which worries her, and she knows it worries Jayden too.

'You've been very helpful, Wenna,' she says, 'thank you. And I've taken up too much of your time. You've customers waiting.'

'Oh, I know that one, she only comes in for the paper. Won't even buy a packet of biscuits from me.'

'You can't think of anyone else, can you, who might have known? Who Steph might have confided in?'

Wenna shakes her head. 'I think she only told me as much as she did because I happened to see her when it was all happening. We were good pals, me and Steph, but, like I say, she was private.'

Ally's hand is on the door handle when she says, 'Wenna, have you heard of a man called John Paul Sharpe?'

'What, the bloke who got himself killed over in Mousehole? Terrible business, that.'

And it's clear the name means no more to her than that. Ally touches the sign on the door, her mind already turning to how Jayden is getting on. 'Shall I flip this over?'

'Please. Let the stampede commence. Here, Ally, they haven't got you and Jayden working on that murder case too, have they?'

'Oh no,' says Ally. 'Not at all.'

'Good thing too. You stick to helping our Saffron. Though, if you want my opinion, I'm not sure he's worth the looking. You shouldn't have to smoke a dad out, should you?'

36

Jayden stands outside the hotel, planning his move. It's an ordinary-looking chain, not the kind of place he can saunter into, pretending to be swinging by for a coffee or brunch. Mullins tipped him off that since the fire Phil Butt's been staying here in Penzance. It isn't classified information, but nevertheless, Butt probably won't welcome the intrusion. Jayden reckons his best bet is to plant himself in a spot where he can watch the door and catch him in passing; make it look as casual as possible.

If Phil's passing, that is. He might just be holed up in his room, the outside world no kind of a temptation. First a murder then a fire: not good times for Phil Butt.

Jayden scans the street, the wind slicing his cheeks. There's no car parking round here, and it's way too chilly for just sitting on a bench. He decides to try his luck inside.

Ducking through the sliding doors he sees a tourist ahead of him at the desk, a man dressed in long khaki shorts and flip-flops, despite the weather. He's going deep with questions on St Michael's Mount and tide times, so Jayden takes a few steps on and looks through to the dining room. It's right at the tail end of the breakfast sitting, and just a few tables are still occupied. A little three-person family sit eating a yoghurt apiece, spoons moving in perfect time. A game-looking elderly couple are dressed up in hiking gear, maps spread out across the table. And there, in the far corner, on his own, is a man who looks like he doesn't want to be here at all. Jayden recognises him from his photo, the same one that has popped up in various news articles ever since the fire.

Phil Butt. A lucky break, but he'll take it.

'Can I help?' the girl on reception is calling out to him in a tone that's polite but questioning. She wears a shiny white blouse and a badge says her name is Anya.

'Morning,' says Jayden. 'I'm meeting a friend here.' He points to the breakfast room. 'Am I okay to just go on through?'

'Are you a guest?'

'No, but my friend is,' he says with a grin.

'Sure.' She smiles back. 'But you'll have to pay. £8.99 for Continental, £11.99 Full English. It's a buffet. And we're about to stop serving.'

'What about just a coffee?'

'That's included in the Continental.'

Her smile has a note of triumph in it, now. Well, fair enough. Jayden reaches for his wallet. It is, he thinks, a small price to pay for direct access to a lead.

'Alright, I'll go for the Continental,' he says, handing over a tenner. '*Bon appétit*, right?'

Phil is hunched over the last of his plate, shovelling egg into his mouth with no apparent enthusiasm. He's got his phone beside him on the table and his eyes are fixed on it, as if he's expecting a call at any second. There's a wet stain on the tablecloth, where it looks like he spilt his coffee.

'Phil?' says Jayden.

'What is it?' His head snaps up. His eyes are full of irritation or trepidation or both.

'Could we have a quick chat? I'm—'

'I've already given my statement. Twice,' Phil cuts in.

'I'm not with the police.'

'Yeah, well, I'm not talking to journalists.'

'I'm not a journalist either. Can I join you?'

Without waiting for an answer, Jayden pulls out a chair. It's kind of an intrusive move, but he has a feeling that if he doesn't take his chance, Phil will be out of here in a flash.

'I wanted to get a bit of info on JP Sharpe. It's in possible connection with a paternity case I'm working on. Well, not exactly a paternity case, that's the wrong lingo, but we're trying to trace a client's father.'

The relief on Phil's face is instant. Then he appears to sag, as if the last bit of adrenalin has left his body. 'Sharpe's dead.'

Jayden nods. 'Which makes it a lot more difficult.'

'What are you, a lawyer?'

'Private detective.'

Phil sets down his fork, adjusts it neatly with the knife; back and forth, as if he can't quite get it right. 'I can't help,' he says.

'You don't know what I'm asking yet,' says Jayden with an easy smile. 'Look, I really am sorry to be bothering you. I've seen the news. You've had a nightmare up there at Mermaid's Rest.'

Phil glances up at him, his hand still toying with the cutlery. And Jayden thinks that there's nothing past tense about the nightmare for Phil Butt.

'I guess what I want to know is whether JP might have helped someone out.'

Phil gives a humourless laugh.

'That a no?' says Jayden.

'Go on. This'll be good,' says Phil.

'Well, was he doing a favour for a mate, say? Delivering a letter?'

191

Jayden's clutching at straws big time – and doesn't he know it. He's still getting used to being without the uniform; trying to get people to talk because they want to, not because they have to. Ally reckons he's got the knack, but knack or not, you're still depending on a combination of people's goodwill, curiosity and sense of duty. Fear, too, sometimes. And for all his sudden bluster, there's something fearful about Phil Butt.

'Sharpe playing Postman Pat? Yeah, I don't think so.'

'Did anyone up at Mermaid's Rest ever talk about someone being an estranged father? Suddenly decide they wanted to trace their kid?'

Phil runs his hands through his hair. 'That girl came up yesterday,' he says. 'Was it yesterday? It's all a blur. No, the day before. Said JP might be her dad. Pink-haired girl. That who you're working for?'

'He's not her dad. But someone is, and we think they're connected to JP. We're trying to trace them.'

As he says it, Jayden feels uneasy. He doesn't like bringing Saffron into it. And he doesn't like the way Phil dubbed her the *pink-haired girl*. Labels, any labels, always get his back up.

'Can't help you,' says Phil.

'So, JP didn't mention any—'

'Strictly professional,' says Phil, his lip curling. 'There wasn't any *chat*.'

'You two didn't get on?'

Phil gives him a sharp look, then ignores the question. So, Jayden carries on. 'But he did have some friends up at the Mermaid? Work mates he'd share a beer with?'

Phil sighs, and it sounds like the last of the air slipping from a balloon.

'Dominic Brook. Sous-chef. He might know something.'

Jayden makes a note of Dominic's address.

'Bev Potter,' he says, thinking of Ally suddenly. 'Were Bev and JP friends?'

'You're joking, right?'

'What, more like enemies?'

'What's Bev Potter got to do with somebody's father? Thought that was all you were interested in?'

'You never know how things are connected.'

'Well, unless that husband of hers did the dirty on her twenty years ago, I think you're barking up the wrong tree there,' says Phil. 'Now excuse me but . . .' He gestures to his near-empty plate. 'I'd like to finish my breakfast in peace.'

As Jayden thanks Phil, he takes a look at him again, trying to figure him out. He's wearing a shirt and tie – an egg-stained tie, but a tie nevertheless – even though his place of work has burnt down. He's also wearing a heavy sense of dejection – or worse. Jayden knows how it feels to be brought down, to feel out of step with everyone and everything. Over at the police station, Phil Butt's face will be pinned to a board; even if he has an alibi, he'll be on the list. But Jayden's going to call it now: Phil doesn't seem capable of murder to him.

'Have you got someone to talk to?' he asks gently.

'I've talked to the police. Journalists can do one though.'

'I mean a friend down here. Or family. Someone to *talk to* talk to. Seems like you've got a lot on your plate.'

'My wife,' says Phil. 'I've got my wife.' He looks straight at Jayden for the first time, his bloodshot eyes burning with defiance. 'Now please leave me be.'

Outside, it's high tide and the sea's booming. Jayden can hear the rattle and clank of shifting boats at the marina, see the swirl of grey water. He shivers and pulls his parka closer around him. Really, he'd like to get in the car and boot straight to the address that Phil gave him and talk to this Dominic. But it's just a few days from Christmas and he still hasn't got Cat anything. He might as well make use of being in Penzance, and he can spare half an hour before going to see Dominic. He's already ahead of the schedule he sketched for himself: Phil appearing in the breakfast room was a stroke of luck. Though *luck* doesn't feel like the right word exactly. The residue of their exchange is still with Jayden. He's seen people at low points often enough, but Phil looked like a man who might just bend and snap.

As Jayden heads towards Chapel Street, he taps out a message to Ally. He describes Phil's dejection, and the chat with Dominic to come.

How did it go with Wenna? he adds.

Ally phones back straight away and gives him the lowdown on her White Wave Stores visit.

'Wenna thought perhaps they might have met in Penzance or Newlyn. In "one of the rowdy pubs", that's how Wenna put it.'

'That's pretty good intel.'

'She knew a fair bit about the circumstances, but precious little of the detail. Still, it's something to go on, isn't it?'

'Sure. Rowdy pubs in Penzance and Newlyn. I'll sort us a bar crawl.'

'Twenty-four years ago, mind. It's changed a lot in certain parts.'

'And it's subjective. Wenna's idea of rowdy might be someone else's quiet night down the local, right?'

'We could ask Saffron for a photograph of her mum and try to find out if she was a regular anywhere? Though I think Wenna would have said. I got the impression she enjoyed being given the chance to talk about it after all these years.'

'I'll bet she bit your arm off.' Jayden grins.

'I think she was rather disappointed I wasn't you though.'

'Hah.'

Jayden's now on the very un-rowdy Chapel Street. Cat's favourite spot. He eyes a window display of bright neon candles, then another with art prints of wild swimmers and leather bags in cool colours. He's pretty sure that Cat would like any of this stuff but his head's full of the case, and he feels indecisive.

'So, you're saying Wenna had a hunch that he was a local man, but doesn't know it for sure?' he says.

'That's right. I don't know why, but I'm inclined to trust her hunches . . .'

Jayden's walking on, thinking he'll just go to the end and back, when he spots the bright blue buggy. *That's the same one as ours*, he thinks. Then he sees Cat's green jacket and flyaway blond hair. Cat didn't say she was going to Penzance, but then nor did he.

'Now, tell me more about Phil Butt,' Ally's saying. 'You think he's hiding something don't you . . .'

'Hang on, Al, I've just seen Cat . . .'

He's about to call out to his wife when he hears her laugh, and a tall man in a leather jacket steps into view beside her. Jayden watches as this guy sets his hand on Cat's shoulder.

'Jayden? Are you still there?'

On the other end of the phone, Ally's voice feels a long way away. Jayden watches as they walk on side by side, Cat pushing the buggy. And she's looking at the guy, not down at Jasmine. They go around the corner – and then they're gone. Jayden's left frozen to the spot.

'Still here, Al,' he says with uncertainty.

37

Trip answers the door warily. That's how he is now: a bag of nerves. His nails are bitten to the quick.

'Hello, my love,' says Dawn, thrusting a box towards him, 'this is for you.'

It's spilling over with all sorts of things: a six-pack of beers, chocolate biscuits, a pineapple, some pricey-looking crisps in a pink bag that are, apparently, lobster flavour.

'Silly stuff,' she says. 'Things you wouldn't buy yourself. Well, the beers might be an exception. But the rest.'

'I can't take this, Dawn.'

'Stop that. Rough weather like this, you're not out earning. And when you're not earning, you don't say no to help.'

He holds up a tin of mint toffees. 'Just the essentials, eh?'

'Don't tell Wilson, he'll think I'm daft as a brush. But Christmas should be about the little treats, shouldn't it? Having nice things in the cupboard. I'm just sorry it's not a paycheque.'

Trip shakes his head. She's too sweet, Dawn.

'I'll be eating like a king. Thank you.'

'And you're coming to us like always?'

She means for Christmas Day. And of course he is; for all the uncertainty, Christmas is Christmas. Before he can answer she says, 'I don't mind saying, I'm dying for a cuppa, Trippy.'

'I'll get the kettle on. Come in.'

As he gets busy with the tea, Trip's phone beeps and he reaches for it. He stares blankly at the message from Leo: *I've asked about a bit. Nothing on JP Sharpe. Apart from a little recreational usage* – winking face emoji inserted here – *his nose was clean, mate.*

So, the elaborate story Trip's been telling himself – JP falling foul of dealers – looks less and less likely. He glances back through at Dawn, watching her settle on the sofa. And he feels uneasy; he can't help it. She's always been easy to read has Dawn, not one to hide her emotions. And right now, she looks all good. Doesn't she? And that has to be a sign, doesn't it? But still, he can't help scratching the itch.

As he brings the two steaming mugs through, he says, 'Sorry your dinner out got ruined, Dawn.'

'What's that?'

'Your sister. And her son-in-law. Wilson said there was trouble.'

'Oh, there was. And then my dear old sister getting in a flap about it. I should know by now she's over the top, but it's the angina, see. When she gets stressed, she thinks she's about to pop off and then I get the fear big time. So, we abandoned ship, rushed over. And course then it'd passed. Storm in a teacup. Dear me, I'm grateful for Wilson though. Solid as a rock, he is, and that's why I married him – I told him so last night as well. Drama everywhere but not under our roof. No thank you.'

Dawn takes a sip of tea. She hardly flinches at the heat of it and goes in for another.

Trip's about to say something when Dawn carries on: 'Course, there was a cloud over the meal before we got the call. These fancy places think they know best, but I can tell when pork's not done right, and I tell you, you don't mess about with pork. That chef, the one who went and got himself killed, well, I don't mind saying, he was a high-handed sort of bloke. Didn't like being told he'd got something wrong. Tried to tell me it was the best way to have it.

Pink pork! That cooking it through was old news. Or like food poisoning is a good look.' She chuckles. 'Bit of a ding-dong, if I'm honest. Mind you, terrible to think he went and died that same night. Awful, that.'

Trip sets down his mug with a clunk. 'You went to Mermaid's Rest?'

Dawn claps her hand to her lips. 'Oh, me and my stupid big mouth. Wilson didn't want you knowing. Not at any cost. He knew what you'd think about it.'

On account of the fish contract. That's what she means, isn't it?

'And you talked to JP Sharpe that night?' he says.

Unease is swashing in like tidal waters, Trip's heart sinking fast.

'Well, when I got a word in I did. I told the waitress, "Sorry, love, I can't eat this, it's all pink in the middle, just look at it." She was nice as pie and took it back to the kitchen. A minute later he's storming out. Straight through the dining room, loud voice, like he wanted to embarrass me. Said there was nothing wrong with it at all. And Wilson just sits there through it, looking about a hundred miles away, and did he say anything? Did he heck. I said to him afterwards, "Where was my backup then, husband?" But then it didn't matter, because our Sally went and called and all hell broke loose.'

'And you went straight over to theirs?'

'Dashed out. Well, you would, wouldn't you, when she's panting down the phone? The restaurant lot probably thought our noses were out of joint. We were that flustered we nearly left without paying. Wilson was halfway out the door when he remembered. I said don't you go leaving a tip though.' She shakes her head. 'All in all, a night to remember. Or best forget.'

And then JP Sharpe was murdered.

'Poor Wilson, he felt bad, I think. Bad that he hadn't stood up for me. I did get on at him on the drive to Sally's. It was the stress of it all, I didn't mean it. And it was supposed to be a nice treat and all that, the meal. A special night for us two old love birds. That's why I had to tell him how grateful I was for him. He's my safe harbour, always has been, and I told him so as well. I thought he was going to cry at that, though keep that bit under your hat for goodness' sake.'

As Dawn chatters on, all Trip can think is, *Why didn't Wilson mention any of this?* His boss always plays his cards close to his chest – it's Dawn who's the talker – but not saying anything about what happened at the Mermaid? Trip's heart is racing, and sweat's pricking at his brow. *Just ask her*, he thinks. *Just ask her where Wilson was later that night.* She'll say they were tucked up in bed together, and then his brain can take a hold of that and level things out a bit inside his head. Because a man can't be in two places at once, can he? And Dawn's right: Wilson is a safe harbour.

'Must have been a relief to get on home after a night like that, Dawn,' he says.

She nods. Swirls the last of the tea in her cup.

'I should think it was. I stopped over at Sally's, felt I should, after the fuss of it all. But I said to Wilson, "You go, love. It doesn't need both of us here. You go on home to your bed."'

Trip stares at her.

'Well, what? Don't look at me like that, love. It's not so much of a shock that I can be a little bit thoughtful, is it? We all know Wilson's not one for the drama, and my family is drama with a capital D. Tucked up in his own bed, dreaming of that steak dinner he half finished, was the best place for him. Well, wasn't it?'

38

Bev sits at the table with the boys. She tries to focus on what's right there in front of her and think of nothing else: felt-tip pens, A4 paper; comics for Daddy.

'You need to actually say what the fish are,' says Cody, and there's a whining insistence to his voice that is, Bev thinks, about more than his brother's drawing. A sensitive little lad, she's pretty sure he's picking up on whatever's hanging in the air, as if worry, and guilt, and stress are lurking in every room in the house; as if innocent children could walk right into their spores. 'You need to write them in, Jonathan.'

'I don't need to write them in. Everybody knows.'

'No, they don't. Not if you don't live in Cornwall you don't. What if you live in, in . . . London? Or America. Or Plymouth. You don't know what the fish are then.'

'Are they all the places you can think of? The exotic land of Plymouth?'

'Jonathan, be nice to your brother.'

'He's never nice,' mumbles Cody. Which isn't true, but Bev can't put it into context, not today. It was stupid of her to expect harmony of any kind.

The memory of last night surges back. It was already bad enough that Neil was called down to the police station – *But what were you talking about for five hours? I don't understand why they wanted to speak to you, Neil* – but then what happened afterwards, in the small hours, that time when the mind goes to all the worst places, was even worse. They were in bed together. Not wrapped round each other like they often were, but both on the far edges of the mattress. Neil shifted in his sleep; groaning, twisting the bed sheets off them both. And it woke her instantly.

'Gerwhasscomintuhyou.'

She held her breath. His voice was slurred, but there was nothing sleepy about it.

'Gedditgonnageddit.'

His leg kicked out and caught her ankle.

Then, clear as day, he yelled out, 'Sharpe!'

Neil sat up in bed, bolt upright; panting. Was he awake? Still asleep? She'll never know. Because her response was to close her eyes tight shut; drop her breathing low and steady. The coward's choice.

Bev's tried telling herself it was a natural reaction to Neil being questioned about the murder: just his mind trying to process events. We can't be held to ransom by our dreams, can we? Or we'd all be in trouble.

They must have been looking at his record, the police. They must have seen that ancient history and thought it meant something.

They were going around in circles, love, chasing their tails. I could have walked out any time I liked but I half felt sorry for them.

But the fact is, Neil doesn't have an alibi. And if they called him in – called him in, when they didn't call her in – they must think they're on to something.

Bev thinks of Cheryl Close and her article; all the things she might be writing. Bev hasn't heard a peep from her since their chat in the park and she's had an uneasy feeling about the whole thing ever since. But, to be fair, it's joining a whole club of uneasy feelings.

She can feel her breathing ratcheting up, so she tries again to focus. But the boys keep leaving the lids off the felt-tips, and now another one's rolling off the table on to the floor with a clunk, and Bev can feel the stress pulsing at her temples. She wants, so badly, to disappear into the moment. For it to be like when they were newborns, and she'd press her face to their warm heads and just breathe them in; how it'd centre her, like nothing else, the weight and scent of her darling boys, reminding her of what really mattered.

'And Cody, will you pick up that pen? And *please* will you put the lids back on.'

She can't help herself. What does it matter? But her anxiety is like an octopus, every tentacle of her life vibrating. Even with these sweet boys and their Tom Bawcock's Eve comic books.

Cody ignores her and Jonathan gives a howl of laughter. 'That is the worst, literally the worst, Stargazy Pie I have ever seen! Who would eat that fish head? It looks like a poo! A poo with eyes!'

Bev wraps an arm around her little son, expecting him to lunge out at his brother. He's her tiny spitfire with a temper he can't always keep a lid on – and who does he get that from, eh? But, instead, Cody dissolves into tears.

'Cody, baby, it's okay, he didn't mean it. He didn't mean it at all.'

And suddenly she wants to cry too. Great, heaving sobs, if she's honest.

'I was only joking,' says Jonathan. 'It's not actually like a poo. Maybe not a fish, but not a poo. *What*, Mum? It's not.'

Cody lifts his hot little face, his cheeks burnt up like two round oranges.

'Why did the police take Daddy?'

Bev feels a stab to her chest. Right in the centre, sharp as a knife.

'Oh baby, I already told you, they didn't. They didn't take him. He was just helping them. He was helping them with a case. That's all. It's done with now.'

Cody slides his way on to her lap and she slowly exhales. The weight of him; this is what matters. She reaches for Jonathan's hand and holds it tight.

'You know that too, don't you, Johnny?'

'Course I know it. And don't call me Johnny.' But there's a wobble at his lip.

'Listen, you two,' she says, 'let's keep on with these comics. Brave Tom Bawcock, fearless Tom Bawcock who saved the village. Then we can show them to Daddy when he's home later.'

'But what if he's in jail? Can we take them to him if he's in jail?'

'Cody, shut *up*!'

'He's not in jail, you sillies,' says Bev. 'He's back working up at the Pollock house.'

'But we didn't see him when he came home last night and he was gone again this morning,' wails Cody. 'How do you know he's not in jail?'

'Cody, you are such an idiot . . .' says Jonathan, his voice revving up again like an engine.

Bev closes her eyes as the two boys start shouting at one another. She tries to picture something calm – and, for the life of her, she can't. Because in his sleep last night her husband was fighting with a murder victim, and what would the police have to say about that?

'It's just like I said already,' she says, resetting herself. 'The police had some questions, and Daddy told them the answers. And now he's at work. But later he's going to come home and have his tea and read these amazing comics with us,' she says. 'That's what's going to happen.'

'He didn't tell them everything, did he?' says Cody, a new shadow of worry falling across his face.

'Of course he did,' says Bev. 'That's what good people do.'

Why does she even say that? What seed of bitterness, or fear, sprouted that pointless statement?

'But Daddy's got a secret that he promised not to tell,' Cody says. His voice falls to a fierce whisper. 'I only know it because I saw something I shouldn't. That's why I had to be quiet.'

'Shut up, Cody, that's not even true. Daddy doesn't tell you secrets,' snaps Jonathan.

'He does actually. He said if anyone found out, it would all be ruined.'

Bev looks from one son to the other. She realises she needs to breathe. So, she makes herself. In then out; in then out.

'Cody, what would be ruined?' she says, as calmly as she can.

39

Dominic's legs are burning by the time he hits the coast road. Two more bends, a hellish bit of hill, and then the drab little house he's been renting since late summer will come into view. It's been ages since he took his bike out, but he needed to clear his head. The staff meeting brought it all home: they're anchorless, now. No JP, no Mermaid's Rest. The latter feels like an act of God, a reaction to the first. But no, it was just stupid Phil playing with candles. And meanwhile Neil Potter, Bev's husband, is apparently in for questioning over JP.

JP's *murder*.

He can't quite bring himself to say the word.

Just three days ago Dominic told Lena that he'd give up the job at Mermaid's Rest in an instant if she wanted to keep living in the city – though it was a nice place to bring a kiddie up, down here, wasn't it? Rock pools and all that. Sandcastles. But little did he know as he said it that the decision would be taken out of his hands so easily. Tragically easily. The truth is, there's nothing left in Cornwall for Dominic now.

JP has been a presence in his life – no, more than that, a force – for so long, he can't believe he's really gone. He hasn't cried yet. Should he have cried? He's never been a crier, not even as a kid. But Dominic feels an ache in his chest as he mounts the hill, and it's more to do with his thoughts than the physical exertion; though he's breathing way too heavily, so maybe it is a bit of both. That's another thing he'll have to sort for Lena. You've got to keep up with a child; no good being the out-of-shape dad, puffing around the playpark.

It's been hard, not contacting her these last few days, but Dominic's decided he has to be selfless about it. First, he promised to give her space. Second, she really doesn't need the stress – and it would be stressful, no matter how gently he told her about JP – and it's Dominic's job to look after her and the baby now. He's so sure of this, that it's making everything else a little easier to cope with. It's given him perspective.

You've got to deal with what's in front of you, JP always said. He was talking about flapping junior chefs, losing their minds under the heat of service, orders building up, just a few seconds making the difference between perfection and disaster. But it works for actual life-and-death situations too: you have to deal with what's in front of you.

It isn't like Dominic's always wanted to be a dad or anything. He can't claim that. Even when he and Lena were at their happiest, he wasn't picturing a buggy, a playmat, a yowling creature in the mix. But he does have this one distinct memory from childhood: the school nativity play. Seven-year-old Dominic on all fours, sweating under a sheep's costume, his skin flaring and itching from the scraggy wool – and feeling such a sharp desire to be Joseph instead. Joseph who got to sit beside Mary. It was always the prettiest girl in the class who got to be Mary. And it was always the alpha male – even at primary school the social strata were forming – who got to be Joseph. He can remember the pair of them cradling the grubby plastic baby doll, with the too-big head and creepy eyes that rolled and clunked when it was tipped upside down. But still, to seven-year-old Dominic it was an idyllic picture and he wanted to be in it, not scrabbling around on all fours, baa-ing without conviction.

So maybe, deep down, he did always want to be a dad? He laughs at the thought as he cycles this last stretch. A nice distraction, as the wind blasts in off the water and the lactic acid balloons in his calves.

He wonders if, when he checks his phone, there'll be a message from Lena. There's every chance that she's seen the news by now anyway. It's gone national, hit all the headlines, because murder in a pretty place always makes a good story. As much as Dominic wants to protect her from the stress, the baby too, the thought of sharing his emotions with Lena is actually a welcome one. Extreme circumstances always draw people closer, reminding them what's important. He wouldn't be surprised if she got the next train back down to him. They didn't talk about where she was spending Christmas this year. Maybe, just maybe, she'll make it in time for the big day. And maybe that's when his tears will finally come.

Dominic's legs are starting to cramp now. He takes the last bend and there's the house, built hard to the road, windows greasy with fumes and sea salt. Well, it's only a rental. Handy for work – as was. Maybe because he's fatigued, but Dominic feels loss, then, like a sudden punch. That's how the thought of JP keeps striking him: sharp blows out of nowhere, and just when he thinks he's righted himself, or successfully distracted, another comes along.

Bam.

It's in these moments that Dominic thinks of the future with Lena – and it immediately resets him. Then he finds himself mulling over Phil. Funny how thoughts shunt up like that. Phil, who's trying to pretend that his wife is on a shopping trip to Bath instead of having walked out on him. Or at least that's what Dominic reckons has happened. Dominic's never had a whole lot of sympathy for Phil, not day-to-day. But to be shamed in that way? Yeah, Dominic can feel sorry for Phil for that one.

No matter how much reason he has to hate JP, Phil is too pathetic to be capable of murder. Dominic knows that, but maybe the police are thinking differently. And there's a whole lot of other people to look at too. Most of the Mermaid's Rest staff aren't even pretending to be sad about JP. Shocked, sure, but that's different.

Dominic's just pulling up to his front door, that last thought still in his head, when a man steps out. His wheel skids and somehow he tumbles forward, smacking his chest on the handlebars. He swears noisily, instantly blaming this lurking person.

'Hey, sorry. I didn't mean to make you jump. Are you alright?'

Dominic grunts, one hand rubbing at his chest.

'Are you Dominic?'

Dominic narrows his eyes. His ribs are sore from where they hit the handlebars but, below them, there's now a thrum of unease too. After Phil's sad little staff meeting, Luke and Zolt were whipping up the waitresses: *All we're saying is that trouble comes in threes.* But Dominic's hardly going to lose sleep thinking someone might come knocking at his door, is he? That's no way to go through life.

Now though, here's a stranger.

'Who's asking?' he says.

He hasn't seen him before. He's smiling, but what does that mean? Anyone can smile. And it feels like there's something combative in it. If it comes to a fight, Dominic's not sure he'll come off well.

'Jayden,' the guy says, 'Jayden Weston. I'm a private detective.'

'Forget it. I've told the police what I know.'

'It's not about the murder or the fire. We're trying to trace a father.'

Dominic feels a stabbing pain in his chest again. His hand goes to it, and he rubs back and forth. 'What?'

'We're trying to trace a father and we think JP Sharpe might be the connection.'

Dominic stares at him, this man who was lying in wait. He's panting slightly, and he can feel a trickle of sweat at his temple.

'Can't you see I'm knackered? I've ridden a shedload of miles. I can't talk to you now, about some dad or other.'

'But I haven't asked you anything yet,' says Jayden. He smiles again; maddeningly calm. 'Our client is trying to trace her father, and we're following up a lead that he might be connected to JP Sharpe.'

And it falls into place now. Dominic remembers the girl who came to the Mermaid, the same one who was full of the news of JP. That's what this is.

'I'm sorry for your loss,' says Jayden, 'that's how I should have started. I'm told that you and JP were good friends, as well as co-workers. I know this isn't a good time, but my client—'

'It's alright,' says Dominic, leaning his bike against the wall. 'Your client came to the restaurant, when there still was a restaurant. She wanted to ask about JP. Said she thought he was her dad. But I wasn't exactly in the mood for making chit-chat, you know? Not that morning. That's how I was told he was dead. By her.'

'JP Sharpe isn't her father. But we do think there's a connection. That maybe JP knew who her dad is.'

'Well, I wouldn't know anything about that.'

'It's a long shot, I know, but did JP meet anyone in the days leading up to his death? He might have casually mentioned it, or . . .'

Dominic unclips his helmet. Despite the cold day, his hair beneath the helmet is sodden with sweat. He runs his fingers through it. 'When JP was working, he didn't do small talk. He was focused. Like . . . a conductor in an orchestra.'

'What about away from work though?'

'You do know what time of year it is, right? Working in a kitchen, coming up on Christmas, there is no *away from work*.'

'So, you can't think of anything out of the ordinary in his behaviour?'

A camper with a cargo of surfboards on its roof blasts past then, the wing mirror narrowly missing Jayden's shoulder. But the guy is so focused on Dominic's response, he hardly notices.

'Look, the police asked all this same stuff,' says Dominic, moving towards his door. 'And now they've got a bloke in for questioning. Thanks to what I told them, as it happens. Neil Potter.'

He sees this is news to Jayden and feels a shot of satisfaction. He sticks his key in the lock, kicks the door open with his foot.

'Husband of a waitress that got the sack. Pretty much thanks to JP not liking her, though she did mouth off at him one night in front of everyone, which probably helped. Looks cut-and-dried to me, but hey, I'm not the police.'

'How old is Neil Potter?' asks Jayden suddenly.

'I don't know. Forties? What, you think he could be the dad? Anything's possible, mate.'

Dominic picks up his bike and lumps it over the threshold. He wants to be under a hot shower now. Then what? Job listings, probably: South-East region. He isn't going to sit around while Phil and the management lot twiddle their thumbs. He slips his phone from his pocket. Nothing from Lena. As he's staring at it, he sees a text message buzz in from Phil. He clicks on it.

'You don't seem all that invested,' says Jayden, looming in the doorway, 'in whether Neil Potter is guilty or not.'

'Invested?'

'Don't you want to know who's responsible for your friend's death?'

Dominic stuffs the phone back in his pocket and lets the bike drop against the wall. He turns to face Jayden. And suddenly he feels taller, does Dominic. Suddenly he feels like he can look this guy right in the eye.

'You don't know anything about me or how I'm feeling.'

Jayden holds up his hands. He looks like he's about to apologise, but Dominic's on a roll now. Anger surges in him.

'I'm not going to get all excited or emotional because the police are talking to someone who's fallen out with JP. You want to know the truth? There are plenty more where Neil Potter came from. JP wound people up, that's what he did. On any given night of service, there'd be noses out of joint. And that was just what I saw.'

'Yeah, okay, but to murder—'

'I knew how he ticked, okay? It didn't bother me. But people working with him for the first time, or oversensitive people . . . they didn't. Suppliers? Yeah, he knew how to upset them too. Boy, did he. And customers complaining about the food? Some tiny thing not being right? He'd eat them for breakfast. You talk to Phil Butt, he knows.'

'I've talked to Phil.'

'Well, maybe talk some more. Or maybe don't, and let the police do their job. Because who cares about some random girl's father, when there's a murderer on the loose? Huh?'

For a horrible second, Dominic thinks he might actually cry – that this will be the moment when it happens. But instead of tears, a thought comes to him, and he eyes this guy Jayden differently, wondering if this has been his play all along.

If he is, in fact, working with the police.

'Unless they're the same person. That's it, isn't it?' He almost laughs. 'You're not just looking for someone's dad, you're looking for the murderer. And when you find one, you reckon you'll have found them both.'

And Dominic can tell from the look on Jayden's face that he's hit the nail on the head.

40

Saffron's phone rings just as she's pulling on her coat to head for The Shell House. She immediately thinks of Ally, or Jayden; or even him – whoever he may be – having somehow got her number. Because it's possible, isn't it? But it's Broady.

Broady in Ahangama. With the perfect peelers, the pelicans and puff-headed palms. And Dee. Living the life, the lot of them. A life that is so purely in the moment – the next wave, the next cocktail – no weight of family pressing down.

Another world altogether.

Saffron wants to speak to Broady more than anyone, but she still doesn't know what words to use.

'Hey,' she says. 'Hey, how are you?'

Broady's face fills the screen. It's night-time over there, and the light in the room is low. She recognises the slatted blind behind him, and the wooden headboard. It's the bed they shared. With the tie-dye cover and creaking springs.

Another world.

'Babe,' he says. 'Where have you been?'

So, she leans against the wall, and there in the hall, with the heaped trainers and her quiver of skateboards, she tells him. The murder. The letter. The hiring of Ally and Jayden. She can't read his expression as he listens; she half wonders if it's even sinking in, or if it all sounds like too crazy a story.

'So . . . I've been kind of busy since I got back,' she wraps up, throwing him a grin. And she expects one back, because that's what she and Broady trade in: good times, good vibes. Right?

'That's . . . wild.'

'Tell me about it.'

He runs his hand through his long, sun-bleached hair. 'But, babe, you've been home for three days. How come you haven't told me?'

There's a deep groove in his brow, and Saffron feels an urge to press her thumb against it; to smooth it. She can't remember having seen it before.

'I guess I wanted to figure things out. Figure out how I feel.'

There's a beat of quiet, then another, and she thinks the screen is frozen. But then she can hear someone calling out to him in the background, and he turns his head. He says something she can't catch.

'Look,' she says, 'the connection's bad, maybe let's—'

'I didn't know it was a big thing for you. Your dad.'

'It wasn't. Not at all.' And the words come out all wrong; hard stones in her mouth.

'Saffron,' he says, 'are . . . you okay? Are the girls there with you?'

'Everyone's here,' she says. And she knows how it sounds – *except for you* – and instantly kicks herself. 'I'm all good.'

'How was your mum's birthday?'

A day that feels so far away now. Waking up that morning, feeling like the worst that she had in store was a walk to the churchyard in ice-bright sunshine.

'The sun shone,' she says, simply.

And, again, it's like he's frozen.

'Look,' she starts to say, but then he interjects.

213

'And are you doing your Tom Bawcock thing? Or is that off the cards, with . . .'

Saffron had forgotten she told him about that, her and her mum and the stargazing fish. The pre-Christmas celebration that she loved almost more than Christmas itself; their beach walk, no matter the weather, then home for pie. How for the last three years she's made the pie for Jodie and Kelly, even though they'd gag at the sight of the fish heads and hardly touch their plates. But then they'd all dance and drink beer and even though it was so different from with Mum, it was okay, it was fun, it was their Tom Bawcock's Eve.

'Oh no, it's still on,' she says. 'Course it's on.'

They pretty much wrap up the call after that. Saffron wants to be the girl who asks about his day, the surf, but she can't quite stretch to it. She knows he must be uncomfortable, too, with all this heavy stuff. That's not Broady. He must want to get off the call as much as she does.

'Saffron,' he says, 'do you want me to—'

'All I want,' she says, gusting energy into her voice, 'is for you to have enough fun for both of us.'

Saffron rides hard and fast to the beach, the wind whipping tears from her eyes. Darkness is falling as she gets to The Shell House and its warmly lit windows beckon her in. She takes a minute, drying off her face and catching her breath. The marram grass rustles all around her, and sand sifts over her shoes. It's wild out here, but she feels at home, just like she knows Ally does.

She heads up the path, her feet making the wooden steps creak. From inside she can hear Fox's bark start up before she even knocks.

Saffron knows Ally will think she's here about the case, and when she hands over the postcard, Ally's sure to think it's a clue. So Saffron hopes it won't come as a disappointment. Because the truth is, her search through her mum's things, or what she's kept of them anyway – the cedar-wood engraved box of childhood drawings; her cowrie-studded jewellery tin with the trails of love-beads; even the pockets of her long green woollen coat – didn't show her anything that Saffron could connect with a man in her mum's life. Not even close.

But she did find Bill Bright.

The card had been ripped at some point and a piece of yellowing Sellotape holds it together, but Saffron recognised the art style immediately, from posters and biscuit boxes and even the little tins of Cornish sardines that you see in delis. The back of the postcard says *Stanhope Forbes (1857–1947), The Lighthouse*. A picture of two men in a wooden dingy, the younger of them sculling towards the harbour, the older one sitting in the bow with a fishing line running through his fingers. The older man is sandy-haired and bearded, with a thick knitted jumper. And he's the spitting image of Ally's husband.

'Saffron, hello, my dear. Come in.'

'I can't stop,' she says. Though as she peers in, her heart is pulled. She sees shadows flitting on the white wooden walls. The popping colour of Ally's collages. The fire will be going too. Wine on the table. Ally's quiet, easy company; that warm smile of hers – when it comes – is always so inviting. Ally is someone who's lived through loss, is living through it still, but seems to treat every day as if it were a gift. As if she's figured out just what life is all about.

How could Saffron ever leave, if she went in now?

Besides, she knows Ally values her privacy. Until Jayden came along, Saffron can hardly ever remember seeing her out and about, except as a distant figure along the shore.

'I found something, that's why I'm here. In Mum's stuff.' She sees the look on Ally's face and quickly adds, 'It won't help the case, but . . . I wanted you to have it.'

Ally takes the postcard and gives a small smile of recognition.

'Bill,' she says quietly. 'Isn't it?'

'You've seen it before?'

'I have. We even tried to see the original over at the Penlee Gallery.' Ally looks up, her eyes shining. 'It really does look like him. Not so much the features, but . . . the build. The posture. Even he admitted it.'

'And the beard.'

'And the beard. Saffron, thank you. You're very thoughtful.'

'It's kind of tatty. Don't keep it if you don't want to. You can just chuck it. But I thought . . .'

'I wouldn't dream of chucking it.' Then, 'Are you sure you won't come in? I don't have anything much to update you on, but . . . you'd be very welcome.'

'It's okay,' says Saffron, bending down to pet Fox. 'I've got to jet. I'll wait until you have something. If you have something.' She turns to go then stops. She wants to say what's been bothering her ever since she sat on the floor in her mum's old room, surrounded by her things, desperately looking for something that might tell a story. 'Is this all mad, Ally?'

'Mad?'

'There was nothing in Mum's stuff. I knew there wouldn't be. And I expect you've spoken to Wenna, because she's the only person round here who'd know anything and . . . she doesn't. I'm sure of it. So . . . what else is there? I feel like I've been stupid expecting you and Jayden to . . . I don't know . . .'

216

She loses her drift.

'There's the JP Sharpe connection, Saffron. That's our best lead.'

'Yeah, I know it is.' And she feels a shiver run through her.

'We can stop, you know. We can stop any time.'

'No. I want to know.' Saffron finds a grin. 'Hey, Ally, are you doing anything on the twenty-third? Tom Bawcock's Eve?'

'I don't think so.'

She's said it now; she has to follow through. 'Mum always went big on Tom Bawcock's. I'm making the Stargazy Pie. You're invited.'

Ally hesitates. Her face is all kindness, and Saffron's glad of the twilight as she feels her eyes prick. 'Are you sure you're up to it?'

'It's a good distraction. And it's tradition. Y'know.'

Saffron shifts on her feet; sniffs. That's the point of tradition, isn't it? You can rely on it. When everything else is uncertain, ritual keeps you steady. It says, *Okay, wild things happen, but we'll keep showing up anyway; keep laying places at the table, keep lighting the lights.*

'Do you know, I don't think I've eaten Stargazy Pie for twenty years. The last time was with Evie, when she was home from university. I remember it. We all went over to The Ship.'

'I'm going to ask Gus. And Jayden and Cat too, of course.'

'Gus was thinking of going to Mousehole to see what it was all about,' says Ally. She stops. 'Not that you . . .'

'I'll tempt him with my boutique version. Mum always preferred it that way, anyway. Cosy.'

'Well, I'd love to,' says Ally.

Saffron pops a thumbs up, then turns and walks quickly down the path. She can still feel the glow of The Shell House at her back and Fox gives a small whine as she swings the gate shut. As she jumps on her bike, Saffron glances back. Ally's framed in the doorway, holding the postcard close to her chest. At least something good has come of her search.

It's really something, a love like Ally and Bill's.

That's what Saffron holds on to as she puts her head down and pedals off. Trying not to think of Broady, five thousand miles away by the beach in Sri Lanka.

41

As Mullins reaches the harbour, a gust of wind fills his coat, blowing him up like a Michelin man. He sets his hands on the railing and watches as the tide surges in. The three ships – the centrepiece of the light display – are rocking and rolling on their moorings, while above his head, the strings of lanterns dance chaotically. What a night. He watches a family of four cramming together for a photo; sees a couple with a buggy, the plastic covering all but taking off, and the baby inside crying like a lost thing. There aren't the same flocks of tourists as you'd get with the calm, but there's no rain – apart from the odd half-hearted splatter – and that's got to be a win.

It's been three nights since the body was discovered, and there's an energy about the station; everyone wants the case solved by Christmas. Including Mullins. It's already 21 December and you can't have a platter of sausage rolls in the middle of an unsolved murder, can you? No blinkin' chocolate logs either. And the top brass always bought in the chocolate logs. So even though it's Mullins's night off he's spending it here, walking the streets, just like the Major Crimes lot did: treading JP Sharpe's path.

It was slamming with rain in Mousehole on the night of the murder. No one was out who didn't need to be out. You wouldn't have had anyone hanging around by the harbour wall, getting soaked with sea spray on top of the downpour. The Christmas lights were all switched off, and the pub would have been shut up too, the last few drinkers hurried home to their beds. JP would have parked on the wet dark cobbles of the harbour car park, then worked his way through the boats, packed in stern to stern. Then . . . whammo.

Mullins plods his way towards the other side of the harbour. Passing the pub, he hovers a moment – with its misted windows and twinkling lights it calls to him, he can practically smell the beer and feel the warmth – but then he shoulders on by, head down. He wants to take a good look at the boat. The blue tape is gone now, all evidence gathered – which is, by the way, diddly-squat: no prints, no DNA, no murder weapon. But he still wants to see it with his own eyes.

On TV shows, cops always have breakthroughs at sudden moments. They do that staring-into-the-middle-distance thing, then *I've got it!* And that's why Mullins is here. It's not Skinner he's trying to impress, and it's not the Newquay lot either. But he'd really, really like to be able to tell Saffron that they've figured it all out. Because she's in the middle of this, and that isn't right. Saffron is sunshine. Hippy-dippy daisy chains. Spoky-dokies on her flip-ping bike. How can this trouble have landed at her door? Even if Sharpe isn't her dad, it's still Saffron's name in a dead man's pocket. So, he's returned to the scene of the crime, a move straight out of the dumb criminal's playbook – except he, Mullins, is here for the vibes. Or that's what Hippy-Dippy would say, anyway.

When he gets to the gently sloping car park Mullins weaves between the boats and vehicles. He's near to the harbour wall here, and he can feel a light splatter of spray on his cheeks as further along, the waves hurl themselves against it. He's never liked being close to the water at night; not that he'd admit it, but it gives him the willies, big time. Those sucking waves, all that endless darkness: no, thanks. His eyes flick back to the lit-up pub again, and he imagines dumping his rear end on a stool, tucking into a pint and clearing out a bag of roast beef crisps; the sea shut out beyond the windows, just as it should be.

But on he goes.

Sea Pup has her blue tarp pulled back over her, and two faded pink buoys hang from her side. Mullins shines his torch over her, from bow to stern and back again.

'You know who did it, don't you, old girl?' he says, patting the edge of the boat. 'If only you could talk.'

'Oi, what are you doing?'

Mullins jumps. The shout comes out of nowhere and is followed by quick footsteps. He spins round, flashing his torch into the face of a fast-approaching man.

It's the fisherman, Trip Stephens. Mullins saw him wide-eyed, all innocent, saying, *What? A body?* the night that Sharpe was found in his boat. Now Trip's fists are clenched at his sides and he's got a look on his face that immediately makes Mullins think of the board back in the incident room with the pecking order of suspects. Well, it might need a little adjustment now.

'I said, what are you doing sniffing round my boat?'

Mullins is about to reach for his badge, when he stops. *He doesn't recognise me.* Because Mullins is in his green anorak and jeans. Decent pair of trainers, too. The word *undercover* flashes into his mind.

'Sorry, mate,' he says now, all easy-breezy. 'Didn't know it was yours.'

'What are you doing then?'

'Just looking. I saw it in the paper. That murder.' Mullins tweaks his hood as he says it. Bloke to bloke, this could work. He could get some vital information.

'Yeah, well, there's been enough trouble. I don't need rubber-neckers on top.'

'Bet they've been knocking on your door, haven't they? The police? As the owner.'

Too much. But Mullins thought the detectives were a little too quick to agree that, yes, you'd have to be really stupid to hide a body in your own boat.

Because maybe Trip Stephens *is* stupid.

Trip is squinting at him as he rubs his hand across his face. He looks as jumpy as a frog.

'I'd take it pretty personally, if someone dumped a body in my boat,' says Mullins. 'I'd want to know who's setting me up like that.'

'You can stop talking now,' growls Trip, stepping closer, 'and you can get out of here. Before I make you, alright?'

He's wearing those clumpy boots that all the guys down the harbour wear, and his toe scuffs the edge of Mullins's foot.

'Before you *make me*?'

A little flame jumps inside of Mullins. Once upon a time he didn't mind a bit of fighting talk. Only playground stuff, really. As soon as he left college and went for the police, he needed his knuckles clean. Trip's about his age, could have been the same year group, different schools though, if he was a Mousehole boy. He looks as skinny as a rope and about as strong as one too. You don't want to fight a fisherman, don't want them sinking their hooks in, hauling on your bones.

But Trip's pushing up close to him, so close that Mullins can feel the heat of his breath. Cigarettes and alcohol, like Trip charged out of the pub without even grabbing his coat first. Mullins is almost willing the guy to throw a punch. He sticks his chin out; locks his jaw. Assaulting a police officer. That's a hefty charge, isn't it? Or does it not count, if the police officer is in a wet anorak and trainers and didn't flash their badge? Either way, it's a reaction. And that's what Skinner and the Newquay lot said they were looking for: reaction.

'Or do you want me to call the police?' says Trip, his voice level again. 'See what they have to say about someone suspicious lurking round?'

'Or how about I beat you to it,' says Mullins. And he's reaching for his badge then.

Trip stares at him, then the badge, then back to him. Swears.

'So,' says Mullins, shaking out his shoulders, making himself bigger. 'How about you tell me why you're getting so wound up?'

Trip pulls at the zip of his hoodie, tracks it to the top. 'I thought you got what you needed from the scene,' he says. 'They said I could carry on as normal.'

'True. But there's still a killer on the loose. And we're not going to stop until he's caught.'

Trip steps back, folds his arms tightly across his chest. 'Well, good. Nothing more I can say.'

'When you saw me down here, did you think I was connected?' asks Mullins. 'Is that why you came down? You were in the pub, weren't you? Night off from fishing? But you put down your pint and came down here fast as a race car.'

Trip's brow is bunched and grooved as Mullins speaks. And for a second Mullins feels like he's putting it together here, telling a story. And he likes how it feels.

'No one likes anyone sniffing round their boat. And they're all frickin' nights off right now.'

'What do you mean?' asks Mullins.

Trip gives him a look like he's stupid. 'Haven't you seen it? Too rough to fish.'

'So, you're not earning?'

'Not a penny, mate.'

Mullins rubs his chin. 'It's a run of bad luck, isn't it? A body in your boat, and being stuck on land?'

Mullins hasn't exactly mastered his interview technique, and the questions land somewhere between taunting and fake-matey. Neither of which seems to go over well with Trip Stephens. His face is as stony as the harbour wall.

'No comment,' he says, eventually.

A massive wave slams at said wall then, and sends spray splattering across their shoulders, raining down on the tarp of *Sea Pup*. Mullins doesn't flinch. Instead he watches Trip carefully. *No comment?*

'What aren't you telling us?' he says.

'Nothing. No comment.'

'You can't keep saying "no comment",' says Mullins, not even sure if this is true.

But this time Trip says nothing at all, and instead stalks off into the darkness, boots scuffing over the cobbles. Back to the pub, back to his pint, back to tell his mates at the bar that there's a plod sniffing round the harbour and he's getting nowhere fast.

Mullins drums his fingers on the wet tarp. But he did get somewhere, didn't he?

He got his reaction and then some.

'See,' he says, a grin spreading across his damp face as he taps the boat, 'you did tell me something, old girl. Your captain let the cat right out of the bag.'

Because Mullins is pretty sure that if he got out a textbook and looked in the index under *Man who has something to hide*, he'd see a picture of Trip Stephens staring right back at him.

42

On Friday morning, the day before Tom Bawcock's Eve, Ally lights a candle and sits with her coffee. Dawn light is a fair way off so instead the glow comes from her little Christmas tree in its red pot. Fox is in his basket beside it, nose tucked into his paws. Her dog sleeps soundly despite the rain drumming on the roof, despite the wind – the wind that seems like it'll never stop blowing – swirling across the dunes, rattling the edges of The Shell House.

Ally studies Saffron's postcard. She holds it close to the candle, the flickering light showing her Bill's likeness. She looks at the concentration on his face as he holds the line; the confidence of his pose, showing he's done this a thousand times before. The silvery catch in a basket at his feet. The light on the water is beautiful; glossy, inky blues. The lantern in the lighthouse burns brightly. Is it dusk? It looks like dusk. The young man sculling them back to the safety of the harbour before the night comes down.

Ally and Bill once went to Penlee Gallery to see the original painting, but it turned out it was held in Manchester, not Penzance. They bought a replica postcard just like this one, though goodness knows where it is now. And that's the important point, isn't it? Ally didn't press the card between the pages of a book or prop it on a shelf. It was lovely, but not precious; not back then. Now though, she runs her fingers over the picture. The kindness of Saffron, to think of her, of Bill, in her own hour of need: that's what Ally was focused on last night. She didn't realise what she was given. What she's *perhaps* been given. A clue. A clue that is, at least, worth discussing with Jayden. Though he did end their phone call rather abruptly yesterday, and the message he sent after his meeting with Dominic was brief. She hopes he's not feeling gloomy about the case because losing heart isn't Jayden's style.

Ally decides to call Wenna too, as soon as light fills the sky and the ringing of a telephone isn't going to come across as an alarming thing.

She fingers the edges of the Sellotape. Was Stephanie the one to tear the card in two? Because it's a definite tear, not just a folded corner or a frayed edge. Someone ripped it up, then stuck it back together again. And it was stowed away amongst Stephanie's most cherished things.

Now Ally looks not at the man like Bill, but the other one. The handsome young man in a peaked cap. And the rip that cuts him clean in two.

Just as pink light is swilling into the sky, Ally picks up the phone to call Wenna.

'Could he,' she asks, 'have been a fisherman perhaps?'

Ally can practically hear Wenna thinking on the other end of the line. 'Well,' she says eventually, 'I suppose he could have been. What makes you ask that?'

'Just an idea,' says Ally.

She picks up her magnifying glass again, holds it over the young man's face. His dark hair, low brow, strong chin. Handsome, by anybody's reckoning.

'You said you thought they might have met in Newlyn or Penzance. Was Steph ever friends with any fishermen?'

'Not especially, not as far as I know.' Wenna gives a low laugh. 'The only fisherman that I could swear was in Steph's life was dear old Tom Bawcock. She never missed marking the day. I hear Saffron's got something planned for tomorrow night too, the sweet

226

thing. She invited me but I already promised myself to Beryl down in Mousehole; we'll be at The Ship like always. And I expect she'll have her young friends with her, will Saffron. She won't want—'

'Did Steph ever go to Mousehole for the celebrations?' Ally cuts in.

Ally can hear a faint chomping at the other end of the line. What morsel could have found its way to Wenna's mouth this time? She waits, biting down a smile.

'Do you know what, I don't think she ever did.'

'Saffron said she preferred it cosy.'

'Oh, and it's the best kind of hullabaloo down Mousehole. Lantern parades and harbour games and beer flying around like nobody's business. And the pies of course. Tray after tray of them. I wouldn't miss it. It's a fine thing, to stand at that harbour's edge, and think of old Tom making his way home with his monster catch.' Her voice creaks. 'A fine thing, Ally. The whole village out, and plenty more besides. A special place and no mistake.'

'Isn't it a little strange then,' begins Ally, 'that Steph—'

'Well, now you say it, it is strange she never went. And a bunch of us came down from Porthpella, every year. Piled in together, we did. But never Steph. But then she did always do things her way. But now you mention it, to honour Tom Bawcock, to make the pie, and never once go to the heartland, as it were . . .'

'Perhaps she didn't like crowds,' says Ally.

'Oh no, Steph wasn't funny like that. She loved a crowd. Moth to a flame, in that way. No, no, it wouldn't be that.' Wenna swallows. 'Oh, hold on now, I see what you're saying. You're thinking he might have been a Mousehole man, aren't you?'

'Perhaps.'

A Mousehole man and a fisherman. Who, once upon a time, looked just like the young man bringing the boat home in *The Lighthouse*. Well, it's a place to start, isn't it?

Ally thanks Wenna. Then she photographs the postcard and messages it straight to Jayden.

~

Jayden gets to The Shell House just as the frying bacon is sending its magical wafts into the ether. Just as the coffee pot is a beat from whistling.

'Good timing,' says Ally, as he shakes the rain from his coat at the door.

'It's my thing,' he says, but not quite with his usual energy. The smile he gives her feels a little forced. *Another long night with the baby*, Ally thinks. Bacon and coffee will set him right. And maybe this new clue – if you can call it that – will too.

Soon they're sitting at the table, across from one another. Doorstop sandwiches and steaming mugs. Ally's itching to get on to the postcard, but first she asks him again about Phil and Dominic.

'Yeah, they were both off. Neither of them wanted to speak to me.'

'Did they think you were the police?'

'No, I made that clear. It was when I said we were trying to connect JP to someone's father. Dominic, especially, looked shocked at that. But, I don't know, maybe it was just a general kind of shock. Dominic's the closest JP had to a friend down here.'

Jayden picks up his coffee; blows on it then takes a sip. Normally he'd say *Good coffee, Al*, or *That's the stuff.* But he just sets the mug down with a clonk and stares off into the middle distance.

'I don't know,' he says again. 'And Phil just seemed . . . desolate. I felt bad after.'

'Do you think either of them knows more than they're saying?'

Jayden lifts up his sandwich and puts it down again without taking a bite. 'Dominic got excited when he thought that whoever killed JP might also be the dad we're looking for. Bad taste, if you ask me, seeing as he's actually met Saffron. Though maybe he just didn't love a random stranger turning up on his doorstep asking questions.'

Ally frowns. 'How did you get to that point in the conversation?'

'Him putting two and two together and making five.' Jayden shrugs. 'Or four. In which case the police will do our job for us, won't they?'

'Jayden,' says Ally. 'You don't mean that.'

He shakes his head. 'No. Sorry. Of course I don't.'

Ally watches him. He almost looks as if he's about to cry. She rests her hand lightly on his arm.

'We'll get there. Maybe it'll take a while, but we will. And we'll do right by Saffron.'

'I know,' he says, looking up, fixing her with his dark eyes that are full of something Ally hasn't seen before. 'It's not that.'

43

Jayden didn't mean to say anything to Ally. He meant to talk to his wife, like a normal human being, say, *Hey, I saw you in Penzance, who were you with?* But when he got back to the farm after seeing Dominic, Cat was buzzing happily around the house, Jasmine high on her hip, and it was like someone had opened a window, fresh air breezing in. Jayden was hit by such a sinking feeling that instead he tiptoed round it and asked her how her morning was. *Jazzy might have got her daddy something secret so no more questions please, Jay.* Said with a smile, and an accompanying bubble of laughter from his daughter.

Later, Cat asked him if he was alright, a hand dusting his shoulder, and Jayden said he was caught up in the case, that was all. Worried about Saffron – and it was true, even though he felt bad using her in this half-lie. Why didn't he just say he'd seen them in Penzance? Afraid of the answer? Some detective he was. He didn't even follow the pair of them on the street; he'd been rooted to the spot, unable to move.

'Things have been tough, I guess,' he says to Ally, after explaining everything. 'And I know we've both been so focused on Jasmine, that maybe we've forgotten about us. Couple stuff, you know. But I thought that was just a phase. Something we were in together. And both okay with.'

It feels like the pair of them are heads down in a storm, pushing on together, side by side, focusing on the next step and the next, knowing that one day soon they'll be in the clear. But maybe new parenthood is like that for everyone.

'Talk to her, Jayden. You may have misunderstood it.'

'I know what I saw. It just . . . had a vibe about it.'

'Didn't Cat go to school in Penzance? They could be old friends who just bumped into each other.'

'But then why didn't she mention it?' He groans and picks up his coffee cup. 'I will talk to her. Course I will. I'd have just preferred it if . . . she'd said it first, you know what I mean?' He glances across to Ally. 'And it will be nothing. Like you say, a chance meeting. Old mate.'

'Exactly.' Ally gets up. Laying a hand on his shoulder, she says, 'More coffee?'

'More coffee. More coffee would be great.'

As Ally moves to the kitchen, Jayden sinks back in his chair. His eyes go to the picture above the fireplace, the smiling Bill. His striped barbeque apron and the creases round his eyes. And Jayden thinks, not for the first time, that he wishes he'd known him. Maybe he'd even have wanted to join the force down here, if a boss like Bill Bright had been on the scene. Or maybe not.

'You and Bill,' he says. 'Did you have your moments? When Evie was a baby, I mean. In the tough bit.'

Ally doesn't answer straight away and he wonders if he's crossed some line he shouldn't have. But right from the start, he and Ally got into the heavy stuff. Life and death. It's part of what brought them together.

'I struggled after Evie was born. Baby blues they called it then. I suspect it would be called depression today. Bill was . . . well, Bill was everything. He looked after the pair of us.' She sets the coffee pot on the stove. Flicks on the gas. 'It was part of why we moved down here. We were stuck in a tiny flat in Falmouth. Bill thought the space, all of this' – she gestures to the window, the dunes, the water, the sky – 'would be a lift. And it was. I spent so much time out of doors. On even the blowiest days I'd bundle up Evie and out we'd go. Lay our tracks on the sand and see what we could find.'

'I don't think Cat's depressed,' he says. 'But I think, sometimes, she wants her old life back. I think she misses freedom.'

'Do you feel that way too?'

Jayden rubs his face with both hands. 'No. Not really. I like . . . having a job to do. Jasmine's my job. And she's the best job in the world. Being her dad . . .' He stops, feeling his voice break. 'But it's been hard work. We're both knackered. She's never slept well but it's been crazy lately. But you know that, I'm always going on about that. It's boring.'

'It's not boring. It matters. Jayden, listen. When you asked if Bill and I had our moments, of course we did. Every couple does. It's the ebb and the flow. And you'll find your way through them. But you've got to talk. I haven't always been good at talking, I don't have two words to rub together a lot of the time, but I was lucky because Bill was very good at it. You need one of you to be like that. I always bottled things up, but Bill . . .' She gives a low laugh, passes Jayden his coffee. 'He always let it all out. Like it was easy.'

Jayden takes the mug from her and inhales its scent. 'Perfect, Al, thanks. And consider me briefed. I'll talk to Cat later.'

'You don't want to go home now?'

'I want to work on the case now. Let's talk about that postcard. I've taken a good look at the pic you sent. What are you thinking?'

She hands it to him. And he puts down the coffee and holds it in both hands; peers close. He runs his finger over the Sellotape. Then he looks towards the photograph hanging above the fireplace. Bearded Bill, smiling down.

'No, the younger one,' says Ally, 'the man ripped in two.'

232

And she explains her thinking. 'It's not much,' she says, 'but it could be something.'

'And it didn't occur to Saffron?'

Ally shakes her head. 'She said she wanted me to have it because of the Bill likeness.'

A thought flashes into Jayden's head then. It's crazy, but nevertheless, in the beginning it's about not ruling anything out. Bill was in his sixties when he died, which means he'd have been in his forties when Saffron was born. Jayden glances at Ally: has she gone down this route too? Because if they're going to consider the card as a possible lead, then they should be looking at both men. The rip isn't necessarily accurate.

'I know it's a long shot,' says Ally.

'Stephanie might have kept this card for any number of reasons. And yeah, okay, it is a leap to think it's connected to Saffron's dad, but, if we are looking at it in that light, then . . .'

'It's the Sellotape,' says Ally. 'That's what does it.'

'I hear you.'

Jayden turns the card over, and there's no date on it. No suggestion of when it was bought.

'Did Stephanie and Bill know each other?' he says carefully.

'Only in the way that Bill knew everyone round here. He went to her funeral.'

Jayden holds Ally's eye. *She's still not getting what I'm saying.* Ally the bottler. Didn't she just say that you need at least one person to lay it out?

Plus, it's his job: detectives have to ask the difficult questions.

'What I mean is,' says Jayden, 'if we're thinking this card means something, then shouldn't we look at both men equally?'

'But one's the spitting image of Bill. And he's old, even here. The beard.'

'Yeah, but we don't know when Saffron's mum bought this card, do we? It could have been just five years ago. Ten years. The older man in the picture might be the one who meant something to her.' Jayden sees the look on Ally's face and starts to backtrack. 'But it could also be totally irrelevant. Just a nice bit of art.'

Ally doesn't say anything for a moment. Then she looks up, slowly takes off her reading glasses.

'I take your point,' she says. 'The thought didn't even occur to me. Not for a moment.'

The thought didn't occur to me that Cat would be meeting a man in Penzance. But it's a whole other thing, a whole other scale, and he knows that. He's had a rubbish twenty-four hours, and maybe his faith has been a little shaken. He's hardly naive. You don't get to be at the frontline of city policing and be naive. He's been called to enough situations, seen enough people's fury and hurt and sorrow, to know how complicated it is to be human. But Jayden also knows it's possible to live alongside someone – to think you know what's going on in their head and in their heart – and really, have not the slightest clue.

So, he chews the end of his thumb and says, 'Well, if the card is a clue, Al – and it is a big if – then isn't Bill as possible as anyone else?'

44

'Look at it,' says Phil. 'It's a living nightmare. A dead nightmare.'

He watches Dominic stuff his hands deep in his pockets and stare up at the burnt-out carcass of Mermaid's Rest. Metal fences surround it, with 'Keep Out' notices hanging at intervals. Phil swears he can still smell smoke and he coughs awkwardly; scuffs his feet in the gravel. He's so knackered he could drop. To say he didn't sleep well last night is the understatement of the year.

'Tell me again why you wanted to meet here,' Dominic says. 'I can think of more salubrious spots.'

It was Dominic's suggestion to meet this morning. After Phil tried calling him yesterday to say he might get a visit from a private detective, Dominic phoned back to say, *Yeah, thanks for the heads-up, shame I didn't actually get it in time.*

So much for gratitude.

And yet there still is gratitude, on Phil's side, anyway. But it's not quite pure; it's cut with suspicion. To be honest, it doesn't quite make sense.

'Because it's the one place we won't get earwiggers,' Phil says. 'Or rubberneckers. Or press.'

'Schoolboy error, isn't it? Returning to the scene of the crime.' Dominic rolls his eyes when Phil fails to laugh. 'Joking, obviously, mate.'

Phil decides to be honest – partially. 'Yeah, okay. Maybe I need to stare what I've done in the face.'

'So, the fire was deliberate?'

'No, it wasn't bloody deliberate.'

Phil plants his rear on the edge of his car bonnet; folds his arms. If he closes his eyes, he can see it all just as it was. The gabled windows. The slate roof. From their bedroom they could see nothing but fields and sea. When they first arrived, he thought Melissa would love it here. He glances sideways at Dominic. An unexpected ally, but beggars can't be choosers.

'I looked that private detective up, you know,' says Phil. 'Jayden Weston.'

'Yeah, I looked him up too. Him and someone called Ally Bright.'

'They've made a bit of a name for themselves over in Porthpella.'

'Household names. In their own households.'

'The local press loves them. Calls them the Shell House Detectives.'

'Local press loves everything, place like this. Bake sales. Pony clubs. Kittens stuck up trees.'

'The bloke was in the police before. Up north somewhere. And the woman . . .'

'Was married to the local plod. Which is obviously a universally recognised qualification. Phil, what's up? Why are we really here?'

Phil pinches the bridge of his nose. His eyes are watering, and he can feel his chest constrict; it must be the memory of the smoke. There was so much smoke.

'This guy Jayden,' he says, 'he told me that he was looking into something that's nothing to do with JP's death. Is that what he said to you too?'

Dominic smiles to himself. And it's a strange sort of smile; Phil can't decipher it.

'I wouldn't say that. Maybe that's how they justify it, making out like they're staying out of the police's way or something, but . . . I got the impression that whoever's the father of that pink-haired girl who came up here – and it's not JP, apparently – he's chief suspect.' Dominic turns his eyes on Phil. 'I don't care who cracks it, but someone needs to. Sometimes I feel like I'm the only person who cares if someone's actually held to account for JP's murder.'

'That's not true,' Phil murmurs. 'But . . .' He chews on his nails and thinks about how to say it, and then, again – for about the fiftieth time – whether to even say it at all.

'I do know, by the way,' says Dominic. 'In case that's what you're wondering.'

Phil snaps to attention. He spits a shard of nail from his lips.

'Know what?'

'Melissa. And JP.'

Phil feels an odd rush of relief. Then he gives a small nod. 'She's gone.'

'Not shopping in Bath, then? Figured as much.'

'Said she's staying with a friend. That she needs space.'

And Phil winces at the memory. As he held the card to the candle and watched it catch, he saw his wife's words flare blue then yellow, then gone. So much destruction.

'It was over between them,' says Phil. 'It had been for months.'

'Sure,' says Dominic.

'You don't believe it?'

'Does it matter?'

'It was over,' Phil says again, his voice raised. 'She didn't even like him as a person.'

It wasn't about JP, Melissa told Phil, which makes it worse, in a way. It could have been anyone – so long as it wasn't Phil.

He wipes his nose with the back of his hand. 'She wasn't even that sad when she heard the news of his death, you know.' Phil sees the look on Dominic's face. Says, 'Sorry. I didn't mean it like that. I just . . .'

Just what? Want to persuade someone that my wife never really felt anything for JP Sharpe?

'Did he tell you, then?' says Phil. 'Did he gloat?'

Dominic nods. 'He told me.'

'I always thought that was part of it. That he wanted to get one up on me. Lord it about the place. I pretended not to know it was happening.' The shame burns in his throat like indigestion. 'I didn't want to give him the satisfaction.'

'How could you carry on working side by side?' says Dominic. 'That's what I don't get.'

'Because I'm a coward,' says Phil in a voice that's as pathetic as a wrinkled balloon. 'Isn't it obvious?'

He waits for Dominic to protest. Brothers in arms and all that.

'I couldn't have just carried on like that,' says Dominic, with feeling. 'If I found out another bloke had been messing with my wife, I couldn't just stand by. No man could.'

And Dominic is right, of course he is. But so much for allies.

'You heard anything from her since she left?' says Dominic.

'Not a peep. But she will call. She wouldn't just . . . disappear on me. She . . .'

Dominic's looking at him sideways. 'Phil, you don't think she . . .'

'She what?' says Phil.

'Crime of passion,' says Dominic, scratching his head. 'I don't know. Have the police even spoken to her?'

They stare at one another.

'That's a really stupid thing to say,' says Phil in the end. He heaves a breath. 'What I don't understand, is why didn't you tell the police what you knew. You told them about Bev Potter. Why not me?'

'And I told them about Bev's husband, Neil. Up here, throwing his weight around. You know he's in for questioning.'

'When was he up here?' Phil shakes himself. What does it matter about Neil bloody Potter? 'So why didn't you tell them that JP had an affair with my wife? Because that's just the kind of thing they love, the police. I'd have gone straight to the top of their list, wouldn't I?'

Dominic looks at him – almost with pity. Phil grits his teeth hard; feels a pulsing at his jaw. He hates pity. It's the last thing he wants. And the thing is, he already knows the answer to his question. Because Dominic doesn't think he'd ever have it in him; a coward like Phil Butt wouldn't exactly go and kill a man for sleeping with his wife.

Not in a million years.

'It'd been over for ages, hadn't it?' Dominic shrugs. 'Listen, they're going to find who did this to JP, with or without the Shell House lot. And it won't matter then, will it, if he slept with your wife or not.'

Phil blinks. Dominic's words about it not mattering are caught like a string of meat in his teeth; he needs something sharp to get them out. Before he can answer, Dominic gives him a quick tap on the shoulder.

'I am sorry though, mate. Alright? It's rough.'

'But JP always did what he wanted. That's what you're going to say.' *And maybe he finally paid for it*, thinks Phil.

'I was actually going to say that it's not over until it's over. With Melissa. Maybe she'll come back, realise she's made a big mistake.'

'You think?'

Dominic shrugs. 'When I moved down here, I'd just broken up with a girl. I was properly in love with her too. But the whole

239

long-distance thing, you know? It looked like it wasn't going to work. But we're getting back together, because we both want it. Well, there is a bit more to it than that, actually. She's pregnant. She held off telling me, wanted to get to twelve weeks and all that, but then she jumped on the first train down here to break the news.' He stops, grins. 'Here's where I pause for you to congratulate me.'

Phil shakes his head. He isn't exactly interested in other people's good tidings right now. 'Congrats,' he says. 'Cracking news.'

'How does that saying go? Where there's love there's hope. Or where there's life there's hope? Well, both work, don't they? And where there's new life, there's definitely hope.'

Phil looks at Dominic. He feels entirely empty. 'Where there's life there's hope,' he repeats.

'But you've got to fight for it, Phil. You can't just give up and roll over. What you need is a grand gesture. Actions speak louder than words.'

'Does setting fire to a pub count?' Then, 'Joke.'

Just then Phil's phone rings in his pocket, and he makes a grab for it. But it's a number he doesn't recognise. Still, it could be management with a new plan. It could be a job opportunity. Neither of those things fills him with hope, let alone love. Not when all he wants is Melissa.

'Phil Butt,' he says, abruptly.

'Phil, it's DS Skinner. We wanted to have another chat with you.'

Phil darts an anxious look at Dominic. Mouths, *Police.*

'We'll come and pick you up, save you the trip,' says Skinner, his voice all friendly, but there's something in it that Phil doesn't trust.

'What, a chat at the police station?' says Phil.

'That's right.'

And for a moment he doesn't feel like Phil Butt – dead pub, failing marriage – at all. He feels like someone completely different, like a character in a film or TV show. Only no one's given him his lines, and he's not sure what to say next.

'Um, okay?' he says.

45

Ally stands with Jayden outside Penlee House, the wind tearing through the tattered palms in the garden. It was full summer when she last came here with Bill, years ago now. They had an ice cream apiece, just like a couple of holidaymakers, and walked along the promenade afterwards. It didn't matter when the curator explained that Stanhope Forbes's *The Lighthouse* was on display in Manchester, not in Penzance, at all – the whole outing was just a bit of fun. Not like today. As flimsy as the postcard feels, it's their only lead.

Ally tightens her scarf around her neck as another gust shakes the palms.

'Well, she was helpful,' Jayden says, with an attempt at brightness. 'It was worth coming. Wasn't it?'

They talked to one of the gallery attendants, who gave them a potted history of the Newlyn School artists. All things Ally's heard before, but Jayden listened intently, almost demonstrably so. He'd been quiet on the drive over and kept glancing at Ally from beneath his lashes, like a little boy who thought he'd done something wrong – when it wasn't like that at all. Jayden was just doing his job. Asking the right questions. But the thought of Bill fathering another child is ludicrous.

'A lot of folk see people they recognise in the works,' the gallerist said. 'Forbes, like many of the Newlyn School, painted from real life, using local people, not models. And, of course, there's a naturalness about it – not just the faces, but the postures, the clothes, the circumstances of the entire image – that invites relatability. In the fisher community there will be genuine connections too, recognisable ancestors, as used by Forbes and the others. It's a wonderful documentation of social history.'

The gallerist looked at the torn postcard, and when Jayden asked if the young man standing in the boat had drawn any particular attention or enquiries over the years, she simply shook her head.

'What about him?' Ally said, pointing to the bearded man. To Bill.

'Like I said, the works have always invited connection and identification. It's their particular power. Ordinary people doing ordinary things.'

And that was pretty much that. Ally proffered thanks and gently steered them away.

'So, what now?' says Jayden. 'To the harbour?'

Ally's eyes travel over the gardens and out towards the sea. It's the day before Tom Bawcock's Eve and they're looking for a fisherman. 'To the harbour,' she agrees. 'Newlyn first, then Mousehole.'

'All the boats are out of the water at Mousehole. Old Fran said pretty much no one's working it these days. Not commercially, anyway.'

'It's still worth showing the card around, isn't it?'

Jayden rocks on his heels. His chin is dipped into his jacket. 'Yeah, it is. If we're on the right lines with the fisherman thing, and it sounds like Wenna thinks we could be, then . . .'

'Well, she didn't exactly say that. It all comes back to the postcard. And Tom Bawcock's Eve. Take away those two things and he could be an estate agent. Or a teacher. Or—'

'Al, let's keep our focus and head to the harbour. If it turns up nothing, then . . . we'll regroup.'

Unless the police turn something up first. He doesn't need to say it – they both know.

* * *

In people terms, it's eerily quiet down on the docks, but the place is full of the sound of the sea. The water in the harbour sloshes at the quayside, while beyond the walls, the open ocean lifts and churns. It's always a spectacle, an angry sea, *but not if you have to go to work on it*, thinks Ally; *not if your fates are bound up in it.*

One of the harbour staff, Terry, gives them their bearings. There are trawlers the size of cruise ships, with intimidating-looking machinery; jaunty smaller craft, in bright colours, their moorings rattling like a tireless percussion section. Along the quays, rainbow-coloured plastic crates are stacked high, curls of net and, everywhere, slews of clued-in gulls, no doubt disappointed by recent pickings. But with the weather so rough, there's precious little coming and going. And precious little was traded at the morning market, apparently. The derricks – huge, iron structures – stand silent and still. The few men that are around – suited up in oilskins and heavy boots – are busy with maintenance.

'People just want to get back out there now,' Terry says. 'There's not a lot of chat going on.'

When they explain their purpose, it's clear Terry thinks it's all a bit pie in the sky.

'Can't say I've heard any of the blokes talking about a lost daughter.'

'And the name Saffron Weeks doesn't mean anything to you?'

He shakes his head.

'What about this picture? Do either of the men resemble any-one you know – past or present?'

He takes a good look. 'That Forbes bloke, isn't it? His pictures are on our pilchards. Good on him, that's what I say. Whatever sells.'

'But the men in the picture,' Jayden says, 'do they look like anyone down here?'

'Nah, could be anyone. Look, I've got to get on. You're alright taking a look around, just watch out. There's not a lot of movement going on, but be careful just the same. Give me a knock on the way out.'

And then they're on their own.

'Okay,' says Jayden. 'Let's go door to door. Boat to boat. See who's in. Split up or stay together?'

'Stay together,' says Ally.

'Okay, let's do this.'

Half an hour later, and they're cold to the bone – with nothing they can use. People are busy, hard-working, and it all sounds so whimsical, this mission they're on. Only when they've mentioned JP Sharpe has interest been piqued.

He hasn't got a good reputation round here.

Jumped-up little chef from the Mermaid? Doesn't appreciate what's on his doorstep.

'Pillock,' says one man. Despite the wind chill he's in a t-shirt, a faded Miami Dolphins cap on back to front. His cigarette bobs up and down in the corner of his mouth as he talks. 'And that's a polite word.'

'And there's no one down here who was particularly close to Sharpe, who might have told him about trying to connect with their daughter?' says Ally.

The man pulls on his cigarette. Shakes his head. 'What's all this got to do with the police investigation?'

'It hasn't,' says Jayden. 'Not necessarily, anyway.'

245

Ally's taking out the postcard when she feels a light tug on her arm. She turns to see Jayden staring at the next boat along.

'What is it?'

'See what I see?' he says, quietly.

Ally looks. It's a thirty-foot boat, maybe. Painted bright red, with yellow trim, and the name *Night Dancer* written on the bow. It looks, to Ally, not a lot different to any of the other boats on the quay here today. Better-kept than some, maybe, and the name has a romance about it, but that's hardly enough to catch Jayden's eye.

She steps a little closer. She looks up at the wheelhouse, with its slew of papers and coffee cups.

'Whose boat is that?' she hears Jayden say.

'That? That's Wilson's. Wilson Rowe. But he's done his leg in. Trip's been skippering since.'

'Trip Stephens?' says Ally, turning quickly, and when the man nods, she and Jayden swap looks.

JP's body was found in Trip Stephens's boat.

'See it now?' calls Jayden to Ally, a note of undisguised triumph in his voice.

She looks again.

Up there in the wheelhouse, leaning against the glass, there's a turquoise coffee cup. It's the smart recycled kind that people use for takeaway. And it has the Hang Ten logo on it.

46

Bev's reading the email from Cheryl Close. Her hand is pressed to her forehead, stress lashing through her.

> *Piece in today's paper, up online later. Editor loves it.*
> *Budget slashed but we'll honour the fee. Send your invoice*
> *for £30, usual terms, payment in 30 days. Regards, C.*

Thirty quid. She's not going to say no, but so much for paying for Christmas. And shouldn't Bev see what Cheryl's written, before it goes to print? She's cycling back through all the things she said, trying to think if there was anything that could bite her – or anyone else for that matter. And what if the piece mentions Neil? What if this Cheryl somehow found out that he's been into the police station? And that he has a record? That maybe there's another angle to this whole article, with Bev and Neil at the centre of it? Maybe Cheryl Close and her newspaper don't care about the truth. Whatever the hell that is.

Just when Bev thought her worry quota was all filled up, now this.

Her finger hovers over the Reply button, wondering what on earth to say. Then she hears the front door.

'Neil?' she calls out.

She hears the clunk of his boots hitting the mat; the pad of his socks down the hall. She drops her phone, as if she's been caught doing something she shouldn't.

'Forgot my sarnies,' he says, as he comes into the kitchen.

She passes them to him, a neat foil-wrapped package. Not that they're worth having, heavy on the margarine, cheese sliced so thin you can see through it.

She knows she has to talk to him now. She has to drop some of what she's carrying – the old stuff, the new stuff, the really scary stuff – knowing it could make for an even worse mess than the one that's already in her mind.

'Thanks, love,' he says, already turning for the door. 'Head like a sieve.' Then he stops. 'It's a bit quiet, isn't it? Where are the boys?'

'Playdate,' she says. 'Round at Tommy's.'

'Enjoy the peace, hey?'

In the stillness of the house, she studies his face. He's tanned even in winter. Paint flecks in his greying hair. The bruise on his cheek is so faint now you could miss it.

Bev leans against the worktop, feels the reassuring press of it against her back. Beneath her cardigan, her heart goes like a drum.

'What have you told Cody?' she says.

'What's that?'

He stands in the doorway, sandwiches clasped in his hand. Is it her imagination or can she see the paper wrinkling as he holds them tighter?

'Cody,' she says. 'What secret have you told him?'

The boys were so excited to see their dad last night, and the Tom Bawcock comic books went down a treat. Neil pored over the pictures with them, asking all the right questions, saying all the right things. And Bev stood by, watching, waiting; knowing that she had to face this ugly, unwanted moment at some point.

'Bev, you've hardly asked me what went on at the cop shop the other day. They had me in for five bloody hours. And instead you're going on about Cody.'

'I was counting every single one of those hours. And I did ask you, Neil. But you did your usual "everything's cool, babe."'

'Because everything is cool.'

'Oh, it is, is it?' Her voice is shrill, and she hates the sound of it.

They stare at each other. How many secrets can they count between them? Each one a malignant cell. Multiplying. Taking over.

'So, why are you talking about Cody again?' Neil says finally.

'Because you told him something, a secret, that you said would ruin everything if it got out.'

Neil shakes his head. *He looks tired,* she thinks. He leans against the door and crosses his ankles, and it's his fuzzy, knitted socks that make her want to cry. He always takes his work boots off so carefully at the door. He's her Neil. Isn't he?

'You're as bad as the boys. You shouldn't go prying round Christmas time.'

'It's not about bloody Christmas, Neil!'

And she can taste the tears burning the back of her throat.

Neil draws a breath, and she watches his chest swell with it. He's got his old fisherman's jumper on too, the lumpy blue knitted one. She thought he was one, when they first met down in Penzance, and he said, *Used to be, used to be, but I started getting sick. What kind of fisherman can't stand to be at sea?*

'So, tell me what it's about,' he says.

'It's about how you got this,' she says, pointing to his cheek. 'And what happened afterwards.'

'Paint can.' Then he starts unwrapping his sandwiches; takes a hefty bite from one of them.

'Paint can?'

He nods, his mouth full.

And then she's uncoiling, springing across the room, grabbing the sandwiches from his hand and hurling them at the wall. They come apart in mid-air: a streak of margarine coats the cupboard; cheddar slides beneath the washing machine.

Is this how it feels, she thinks, *to really lose control?* Because if it is, she needs more than this. More than a bloody cheese sandwich to take it out on.

'Neil, I need you to stop lying to me. It might work with the police, but not with me.'

And the irony isn't lost on her, but this is different; this is a whole other league to the lie she told.

He looks as startled as if she'd slapped him. 'Jesus, Bev. What are you talking about, lying to the police? This isn't—'

'I think you got into a fight with JP Sharpe last week. I think it was Sharpe who gave you that bruise.'

And in all their nine years together, she's never looked at him like this: with blatant accusation. And he's never looked back at her like he's a man made of paper, who'd crumple and tear at the slightest touch.

He buries his face in his hands, and when he looks back up his eyes are red with tears.

Bev's hand goes to her mouth; she can hardly breathe.

'Okay,' he says. 'I lost it with Sharpe. Last week. Because the way he got you sacked, it wasn't right. I couldn't stand by and let that happen, could I? What kind of a man . . .'

And guilt fires through her like a jet engine. But still she thinks, *A sensible man, that's who. A smart man.* And despite everything, she hates herself for it.

'So, you went after him?'

'He started it,' says Neil, petulant as a child.

'Oh, come on!'

'He threw the first punch. And the last punch, because they were one and the same. World's shortest fight, it was. I walked away.'

'You walked away?'

'I'm not saying it was easy, but I did.'

'Where was this?'

'Outside Mermaid's Rest. Late afternoon. I knew it'd be quiet. I wasn't going to make a scene. I went around to the back, to the kitchen. There was no one else around. I had a go at him, told him what kind of a bloke I thought he was. He came out swinging.'

'Just like that?'

'Just like that.' Then, 'Some men are like that, aren't they? Talk with their fists.'

'I hate men like that.'

'I know you do.'

Their galley kitchen suddenly feels like the smallest room in the world. She holds a hand to her forehead, feels herself burning up.

'So why hide it?' she says. 'If you were so squeaky clean, why hide it?'

'I didn't think you'd appreciate me fighting your battles.'

'Not like that I wouldn't.'

'I told you, I didn't—'

'I know.' Bev swallows. 'But you have, haven't you? Before us. Before the boys.'

Her voice is so small it's barely there.

Neil's red eyes spill now; she watches a tear track its way over his stubbled cheek. He brushes it away with his sleeve, but another follows it.

It was her friend Sara who told her. They'd just started dating, her and Neil, and she was full of him: his looks, his charm, the sound of his laugh. *I heard he likes a rumble*, was how Sara put it. And then she told Bev the stories she'd heard. That once Neil spent a night in jail, because of his fists. All dressed up in a suit and tie, standing on the steps of the courthouse too. *Drunken stuff*, Sara said, *back in the day. Angry young man stuff. And only ever blokes.* And Bev meant to ask him, to say that violence – no matter what kind – wasn't acceptable. But the moment passed somehow. She was too busy falling for him, she supposed. And then she fell pregnant too. And the way he reacted, the out-and-out joy that beamed from him, and he proposed to her just like that, as she stood there with the test in one hand, that blue line, and his lips pressed to her other hand: *Marry me, Bev.* And he never once gave her reason to doubt him. His patience with the boys. His gentleness with her. She's never doubted him.

So why now?

'ABH,' he says. 'Two counts. That's why the police got me in. They had my record. But it was old, old stuff. Some idiot in Plymouth who thought it was okay to hassle women, and he didn't like it when I told him that it wasn't. Then a stag-night thing, years ago. Group of blokes set on us, no reason. Smashed my mate Tammo into a window. I had some drinks in me, and I fought back. Didn't know my own strength. Ancient history, Bev. I put it far behind me.'

'Always someone else starting it, hey?'

'It was.'

Bev heaves in a breath. 'The night JP was killed. You weren't at home.'

'No. I was working. You know I was.'

'Because you were behind on the Pollock job. You were working until gone midnight.'

'I was.'

'You've been behind on jobs before. You've never worked until midnight.'

'They want to be in for New Year.'

252

'And then suddenly you're ahead. Coming home early the other day.'

'Wait, you knew about the ABH charges? All this time, you knew I had a record. But you married me anyway.'

'There was Jonathan.'

'Don't say that.'

She bites her lip.

'All these years,' he says, 'all these years I've sweated it. Hating that I was hiding it from you. But not knowing how to say it. In case . . . you thought twice about me.'

'But here we are,' says Bev.

Neil drops his head. There's no fight in him, not now. He looks like a much older man than his forty-six years.

'You can't seriously think I killed someone?' he says.

She hesitates. Fatally. And Neil sees it. Then he's making for the door.

'By the way, I know you weren't sacked, Bev,' he says, spinning on his heel. 'You walked out. There's not much in it as far as I'm concerned. They're arseholes up there at the Mermaid, I don't blame you one bit. But if you want to talk about lying, I'd look a little closer to home.'

And he's out of the door before she can stop him; the slam carrying like a clap of thunder.

47

As Jayden and Ally approach Bay View, a neat-looking bungalow perched on the outskirts of Mousehole, Ally stops. She suddenly looks hesitant.

Momentum has carried them here. After Jayden spotted the coffee cup, they went back to the harbour office where Terry called over an old-timer, Neville. Neville peered close and said, *You know who that's the spit of, that's Wilson back in the day.* The same Wilson who owns *Night Dancer*. And Jayden and Ally looked at one another, both feeling *this is it.* Because the coffee cup alone wasn't much more than a nothing, but the cup put together with the card – well, that's something.

And, added to it all, the fact that Wilson Rowe is directly connected to Trip Stephens, whose boat the body was actually found in.

That is more than something.

'It has to be this guy Wilson,' says Jayden now. 'It's too much of a coincidence otherwise.'

'It's definitely worth the conversation,' says Ally. 'I'm just not sure we should rush into it.'

And Jayden wants her to drop her guard, because they've cracked it, surely. Wilson Rowe has to be Saffron's father. He's in his early sixties now, which would put him in his late thirties or early forties at the time Saffron was born. Bit of a wild child in the old days, with looks, charm, and the kind of temperament that only settled at sea – that's what the old guy Neville said. And why else would he have a Hang Ten coffee cup in his boat? Porthpella is out of the way if you're living in Mousehole.

On the short drive from Newlyn to Mousehole, Jayden scanned Google for Wilson Rowe, but little could be found except for a couple of mentions of him being part of an alliance of Cornish sardine fishermen. Then he messaged Saffron, saying: *We might have something. Do you want details now, or when we're sure?* Her reply was instant: *Only when you're sure.*

'Let's talk to him, Al. Then we can be *certain* certain. Saffron doesn't want speculation, she wants facts.'

'Just . . . he wrote the letter but never sent it. He never even signed it. And why did JP Sharpe have it? It feels . . . odd. Doesn't it?'

Jayden feels a flicker of frustration. 'And these are the questions that Wilson is going to answer,' he says, gesturing at the house.

There's a smart little car parked in the driveway, a collection of gnomes fishing by the pond. He notices a movement at one of the windows. A flick of a curtain? They do look kind of suspicious, loitering by the gate.

'Wouldn't it have been sensible to have told the police first?' she says.

'The coffee cup and card are good for us, but it's not exactly proper evidence, is it? And there's zero to say that Wilson Rowe has anything to do with the murder.'

'Except that there's a definite connection between him and the boat where the body was found.'

'Trip Stephens's boat. Not Wilson's. And the police will be looking into him, and everyone connected to him, as first priority. Look, we've made it here. This is good detective work, Al. We've actually found him.'

And while Jayden knows he's hurrying a little, it feels so good to achieve what, at certain points, felt impossible.

'Okay,' says Ally. 'You're right.'

And with that, they walk up to the front door.

Wilson Rowe's eyes are fixed on the horizon. It's a killer view from the bungalow's conservatory. Jayden notes the binoculars on the side table. The well-worn armchair. He imagines the fisherman spends a lot of time here, when he's off the water. The guys at the harbour said Wilson is in his early sixties but to Jayden he looks older than that. He's in faded jeans and a loose jumper, strong in the shoulders but with a slight paunch. His face is well-worn and sun-creased; shaggy grey hair and stubbled cheeks.

His eyes, though. Wide and sea-green, with an arched brow. They're Saffron's. Surely Ally has clocked the resemblance too? Jayden feels a swell of emotion. They've done it. They've found him.

After they explain who they are and why they're here, Jayden asks the question outright. After a long beat of quiet, Wilson answers it.

'Yes, then. It was me who wrote the letter.'

Jayden looks at Ally and Ally looks at Jayden.

Job done.

'But,' Wilson scratches his head, in cartoon style, 'how the hell did anyone find out about it?'

After they explain that too, Wilson gapes. 'It was *what?*'

They sit, letting it settle. Wilson draws back in his chair, his hand rubbing his stubbled chin. His letter in a murder victim's pocket.

'Can you think of any reason for that?' asks Jayden, carefully.

'It doesn't make any sense,' says Wilson. 'Unless . . .' He shakes his head, his bewilderment genuine. 'Unless he had my coat on? Though why he'd have my coat on, I don't know. But that must be it. Nothing else it could be.'

'Why would JP Sharpe have your coat on?' says Ally, her voice heavy with doubt.

'Because I left it behind there, didn't I? We were eating up at Mermaid's Rest. We had to leave in a hurry, Dawn had a drama with her sister. It was on the back of my chair and in the mess of it all I clean forgot. I was going to call back up there to get it, but then there was the fire. I figured it'd be gone. Gone, and the letter with it.'

Jayden pictures it. It feels a stretch, for JP to put on someone else's coat, but he must have had a reason for it. Maybe it was a damn nice coat, and he liked the look of it? Though Wilson doesn't exactly look like a style leader.

'That must be it,' says Wilson.

Ally gives a brief tilt of her head. Jayden can't tell if she believes the man or not.

'You'll need to tell the police,' he says. 'Identify the coat.'

'Not sure I want it back,' he says, gruffly. 'Bless my soul, it's a strange one. Murdered in my coat? With the letter . . .'

'Why didn't you sign the letter?' asks Ally. 'You sound very sure of the fact you're her father in the letter, but then you don't sign your name.'

'I hadn't got around to finishing it. I got interrupted.'

'Interrupted by who?' says Jayden.

'My wife. Dawn came in just as I was getting to the end and . . . I stuffed it in the envelope. I was going to tell her before I did anything with it, but it had to be the right moment. Good job I didn't sign it, seeing as it wasn't ready to be sent. You're telling me Saffron doesn't know it's me?'

'She doesn't know,' says Ally.

He looks away from them, back out to the sea. It looks calm enough from here, a slab of granite-grey; tough and unyielding. Wilson takes a long breath.

'That's a sign that it's for the best, then. I'll get in touch with the police if that's what you want. Tell them about my coat, clear that one up.' He shakes his head. 'What are the chances . . .'

'And what about Saffron?' says Jayden.

'Dawn . . . I can't.' Wilson blinks. 'I had it planned. She wanted a fancy dinner up at Mermaid's Rest and I couldn't refuse her. Not that I'd be seen dead in there, normally. But we went, and . . . well, I was going to tell her then. Explain about it. Nice bit of steak, wine, I thought that'd be a good time. And then, when I had her blessing – I suppose that's what I wanted, her blessing – I was going to finish off the letter and stick it in a postbox.'

Wilson picks up an empty coffee cup and stares at it blankly. Sets it down again.

'It was all years before I met Dawn. But still, I always knew I had a daughter, and I never told her that. I made my choice years ago, and once I did, I had to stick by it, because that's the way Saffron's mum wanted it. I was in no position to be anyone's dad. It just wasn't for me.' He pulls at his beard, eyes down. 'I was gearing up to tell Dawn the other night, but we had a bit of fuss with her pork. It wasn't cooked right, and she was upset about it, the way that chef, Sharpe, came barrelling out the kitchen to put her in her place. I couldn't do it straight after that, could I? Then her sister Sally phoned. Having a panic attack. Nothing but stress, that family of hers, time and time again. And we were out of there and rushing over to Sally's – that's when I left my coat. Her no-good nephew causing trouble again with his sleeping around. Dawn said to me in the car, "What I love about you, Wilson, is that you're solid. No drama. From the minute I met you you've been my safe harbour."'

Wilson taps his fingers on the arm of the chair. There's an obstinate set to his jaw that wasn't there before.

'You think I was going to chuck a grenade at her, after she said that to me? Tell her that all these years I knew I had a daughter living just over in Porthpella? I couldn't do it.'

Suddenly Wilson looks as immovable as a harbour wall.

'But you do still want to contact Saffron, right?' says Jayden.

48

Saffron stands at the top of their garden mini ramp. She loves this spot. They built it two summers ago, clubbing together for materials, a carpenter friend of Kelly's doing them a favour. On a blue-sky day, with the palm tree overhead, you can imagine you're in Southern California. But, really, why fantasise when you're right here in Porthpella: Kernowfornia, baby. On pink-light nights, Saffron's mates gather, ice-buckets and beers, fairy lights twining the garden, the clatter of skate wheels and hollers of *yew!*, trippy beats drifting, just low enough to keep her neighbours happy – though it probably helps that old Mrs Marcus on one side is hard of hearing.

Skating and surfing are always fun, but in the months of her mum's illness, they gave Saffron something essential: a place where she could go and temporarily – astonishingly – forget. Out there on a wave, or bending gravity on her skateboard, there's nothing but the moment; and the moment is so simple. It made her braver and tougher and happier. Even though she felt guilty sometimes as she returned to reality, wringing the salt water from her hair or hurrying back from the park. And after her mum was gone? Well, let's just say she skated the hell out of this ramp. The rhythmic turns, the total immersion in a mindless – and totally mindful – activity; plus the occasional full body slam to keep it real.

Right now, Saffron positions her board for the drop-in. She glances at the sky; the wind has softened, and the dark clouds have yet to spill their load. Back in the day she spent hours practising this move, and she can still remember the terror of the first time. It was like she was trying to walk on water. These days it's pretty much effortless, but the combination of board and ramp is a fair-minded one: it doesn't care who you are, or how much time you've spent here, it'll treat you just the same. Get it right, you'll fly, but get it wrong, and you're going down.

And her head's not in it, not today.

Because it's Tom Bawcock's Eve tomorrow and she's promised people a party. Because somewhere she's got a dad who wants to find her, and she's asked Jayden and Ally to get there first. Because of Broady, and all the things she wanted to say to him on the phone yesterday, but she didn't because . . . Good Vibes Only. Because the murder, the *murder*, and her name in JP Sharpe's pocket. And because her mum really should be here for all of this.

Saffron drops in, the clunk of her landing carrying across the gardens. Her weight isn't ideal, but she holds it, and sucks her legs up as she goes up the other side. She performs a neat little backside kickturn, then she's into the rock to fakie. She's hitting her groove now, the dance of it, legs, shoulders, all in harmony. Into a quick slash grind, her wheels clipping the coping at the top of the ramp, then her favourite, the fakie tail stall, when time seems suspended. She's holding this little lip trick, and coming out of it fast, then something happens – she doesn't even know what, but the board is gone from under her, like the magic swipe of a tablecloth, and she lands hard. No time to catch the fall and turn it into a roll; no time to suck up the impact. Just a hard, clean slam that takes the wind from her.

She lies at the bottom of the ramp, looking up at the darkening sky.

And it comes to her with total clarity then: whoever wrote those words – *Could you give me half a chance?* – she knows that her answer is already yes. Whatever this dad of hers has done, or not done. And it's scary, that thought, because she knows she's throwing herself wide open.

As Saffron slowly brings herself to her feet, tiny stars flit in and out at the edge of her vision. She casts round for her board and sees it lying on its side on the grass. She walks gingerly over to get it, testing every part of herself as she goes.

'I think I got away with that,' she says out loud.

But she knows that's the session ended. Because she's spooked now; the fragility that was already in her head is in her body now too.

She can feel a tear running down her cheek, and for a minute she feels like a child in the playground who's taken a tumble and wants their mum.

She really, really wants her mum.

She lets the tears roll, because who cares, there's no one here to see. She picks up her board and hugs it to her. Hugs it harder than anyone should hug anything that's not going to hug back. Then she trudges back up to the house.

She's just inside, leaning carefully on the door frame, easing off her Vans, when she hears the doorbell.

She goes to answer it, one hand whisking away the tears. Then she takes a breath – one that's gusted away, the second she pulls back the door and sees who's standing on her step.

'I couldn't tell if you wanted me to come or not,' says Broady. 'So, if you want space, I'll give you space. But if . . .'

And as he opens his arms, Saffron steps straight into them.

49

Wilson stands out on the patio, hauling air into his lungs. He's bundled up in his coat – not the donkey jacket that wound up as a shroud for JP Sharpe, terrible thought that, but his seafaring coat. The one he wears on the coldest nights, bent in the wheelhouse studying constellations on the sonar, the boat tipping and dropping, caught between the black depths of the sea and the sky.

Wilson knows where he is in this coat.

Except he doesn't. He's trapped on land, and land problems are swashing over his boots, rising to his middle. He hasn't got the legs for land; he never has.

The detective pair have just left. And what could they say, in the end? It isn't up to them. The ways their faces looked as they left. Maybe they're only getting paid if they land the big fish, find the father and serve him up on ice.

He has to admit they're canny though, tracking him down.

Against the odds, Wilson found himself wanting to explain things. The young bloke had kind eyes, and one way or another the older lady made you want to split yourself wide and start talking.

He told them how it used to be, back in the day, when Newlyn wasn't what it is now. He was working for one of the big trawlers then, away days at a time: tiny bunk, same blokes, the infinite mirror of the ocean. It did something to a man, all that. By God, he loved it. Life lived at full speed. Steaming back into the harbour, seeing the tops of the houses, the lighthouse, cars – cars! All normal land things, and none of them for him. Feeling so out of whack being back, swilling about onshore, money in his pocket, blood rising. Distractions were always easy to come by; the pubs were full of fighters in those days. Money on the bar and pushing and shoving, then outright war now and again. The white-hot pain of a punch landing square – sometimes Wilson took it just to feel it. It made him feel alive. Because at times back then, without the water beneath the hull, he didn't feel very alive at all.

And women. They were a distraction too.

He didn't have time for a lot of them, figured all they wanted was to get their hooks in and keep you there, living that boring life made of tea at the table and carrier bags stuffed with shopping and sex now and then if you were lucky. But Wilson was always honest, at least. He never let anyone believe that he wanted more.

And then came Stephanie Weeks.

She was unremarkable, at first. She could have been more or less anyone. What can he remember of her? Strawberry-blond hair and a face of freckles. A good smile. There was laughter, he can remember that. The way she stood out though, was how she acted afterwards. When she knew she was expecting a baby. Man, she was as cool as a cucumber. Said, *In or out, Wilson Rowe. Because I don't want half measures for this child.* She knew what they were to one another, you see. A man and a woman who had bumped into each other one night and ended up with more than they bargained for.

But she wanted to keep the child, he could see that. There was love in her eyes already, and when she spoke to him it was with one hand on her belly.

In or out. So, he chose out.

And he's hardly thought about her since. Off and on, here and there, but mostly with a feeling of having been let off the hook. And the child? Yeah, sometimes. Like when the boat was puttering back in with a belly full of pilchards, the rosy light of dawn, and he thought how it might be to climb the stairs and drop a kiss on a still-sleeping little one, and say, *I'm home.* But it was silly story-book stuff, because that wasn't who he was, and nor was it what he wanted. Ninety-five, ninety-six per cent of the time it wasn't.

He got his own boat, *Night Dancer*, twelve years ago, and that's when he and Dawn got serious. She was already past the fifty marker and had been married before. She had a whole life of her own on the land and was happy living it. Dawn didn't mind the hours he kept, or how he came and went, or how his heart belonged most of all to the sea. It was too late for children of course, and that was fine by Wilson.

Ninety-five, ninety-six per cent fine.

Then he heard about Stephanie passing. With her living up there in Porthpella, and him so often at sea, it was possible for the two of them to have been as separate as planets. He hadn't seen her once since the day it was decided, *Okay, out then.* There was a note in the paper – *Survived by her daughter, Saffron* – and he tried out the name then. Said it aloud over the turning of the engine and the churning of the waves and as packs of gulls swooped in on the nets. *Saffron.* He half thought of getting in touch, offering his condolences, but he didn't want to give the girl something else to deal with when she already had enough on her plate.

That was what he told himself, anyway.

Then he saw her for himself last summer. She was in the paper again but for a good reason this time: a splashy piece about the cook-outs on the sand and her café in Porthpella, and the surfing sessions for people going through a bad patch. *The sea helps*, she was quoted as saying, and Wilson looked at the picture of her – with her pink hair and skinny shoulders and green cat's eyes that were straight off his own mum – and thought, *Dear God, that's my girl, that is.* So, he went to her café, just as the season was finishing up.

No intention of saying anything, just wanted to see her for himself. No harm in that was there? He felt as out of place as anything stepping into that trendy little café, but the smile she gave him as he walked in near enough made his heart stop.

Does she know?

But she didn't know. That was just her way, he realised. A great big smile.

He bought one of those coffee cups, not because he was sentimental – okay, a little bit because he was sentimental, call it old age – but he couldn't stay in there, he couldn't be that close to her, she was burning so bright he was afraid he'd go up in smoke, so he said *Takeaway*, and she offered it to him – a nifty blue cup with a rubber lid – and he'd said, *Go on then.* Then he got out of there, a brownie in a brown paper bag and a hot coffee in his hand.

Outside, he leant against the railing and doubled over like his heart was giving up.

And maybe that would have been it. Maybe he'd have left it there. One look was enough, then on with his life. Because he had made his choice twenty-four years ago and Wilson was a man of his word – a sturdy man, when it came down to it. Especially when Stephanie wasn't around to okay it. But then came his accident on the boat. The week in hospital. The handing-over of his skipper's hat to young Trip. The slow healing of old bones and yanked ligaments. Sunk in the chair in the conservatory, binoculars pressed to his sockets, seeing all the boats heading out of Newlyn without him. Dawn hoovering up around his feet and those damn dogs yapping. Being stuck on land, his head turned to land things. And it was her. Always her.

So, one day, he wrote.

But he never finished it, did he? Ten seconds more, and he would have.

Well, that was a damn sign, just like he said to the detectives. Dawn came flying in just as he was about to sign off and he gathered it up and stuffed it in the envelope. Because he wasn't quite ready to tell his dear wife. Not yet. But he would.

Then came the phone call at the dinner, at that place they should never have gone to. All hell breaking loose with her family, and whatever he had to say not getting a look-in.

Well, that was a sign too.

Those words of Dawn's. *You've always been my safe harbour.* And, *You never bring the drama, Wilson.* Another sign. Never mind her sister's angina, Dawn was no spring chicken herself. And it wasn't just about delivering a piece of news that might stress her, it was about Wilson becoming – in that second of him telling her about Saffron – a different person to the one she loved. Nothing like the spilling of a secret to shoot a hole in the hull of a marriage. He was a fool to have ever thought to tell Dawn. To have imagined for a second that she'd be okay with it.

And if he wanted more signs? Well, what about leaving the coat up at the Mermaid with its precious cargo in its pocket? Then the whole place going up in flames?

And instead of that letter being turned to ash, it turning up on the body of a dead man?

Well, if all of that didn't constitute a bloody sign then he doesn't know what does.

Now, Wilson turns from the cold garden and makes to go back inside. He's had his minutes to himself, and he's ordered the bits that were flying round his head. He can carry back on now. It doesn't matter that Saffron's gone looking for him – and hired those two detectives too, for goodness' sake, what is this, California? It doesn't make a difference to anything. He's changed his mind and that's up to him. Because he wants to keep life easy for the woman he loves, and that has to be the right thing. In fact, he's surer now than he was this morning, or yesterday. Because Saffron clearly wants something from him. And whatever it is, he's pretty certain he can't give it.

Doesn't have it.

It's not fair on Dawn.

No, the only thing that Wilson will be doing now is going to the police and clearing things up about his coat. What a business.

He's just about to pull off his boots when the doorbell goes, so he makes to get it, treading garden prints through the house and across Dawn's floor.

'Trip.'

He's standing there looking like a lost boy, and Wilson's getting this flashback to a decade ago when that was just what Trip Stephens was. *How about you come out on the boat with me, get you fishing?* The guys down on the quay gave him this look like he was coming over all fatherly. But not him. He just needed another pair of hands and there the boy was – willing, cheap, Wilson could build him up in his own way.

But Wilson hasn't got the space in him to ask *What's up?* right now. It'll be the weather, the not fishing, the lack of money in his pocket. Trip's got a right to be pissed off at that.

'I'm just heading out,' he says, more gruffly than he means. 'Got to go and see the police. Don't ask.'

But Trip yanks his hands out of his coat pockets and pushes them against Wilson's chest. They're as hot as a couple of irons, and Wilson's mouth twists in surprise.

'No, I'm going to ask,' says Trip. 'I have to.' Then, with a tear in his voice, 'You didn't do it, did you?'

50

The silence in the car needs breaking, but neither Ally nor Jayden seems to want to do it.

They're in the steep lanes headed back towards Porthpella, scraggy winter hedgerows scratching the metalwork. As Jayden drives, Ally keeps her eyes on a bird of prey lifting on the wind. It flies alongside them then suddenly drops like a bomber and Ally imagines a helpless creature snatched in its talons. In Fox's younger days, he once brought a baby rabbit back to The Shell House and laid its soft body on the rattan mat like an offering. Bill had words, in that soft-strong way of his, and it didn't happen again. That's how Ally remembers it, anyway: a story of Bill's persuasive powers and Fox's biddable nature. She doesn't know why she thinks of this now, but she does.

'We need to tell her,' says Jayden, eventually.

'We can't.'

'We can't not,' he says. 'We found him, Al. We know who he is.'

Ally shakes her head. 'It would hurt her. It would hurt her so much. Besides, Wilson's changed his mind.'

He was immovable in the end, fixed as rock. Ally had to suppress the urge to tell him all about Saffron; say that if Wilson only knew her, he'd realise what a mistake he was making. She knew it wasn't her place. *It's my loss*, Wilson said, as if reading her mind. *And my choice to make.*

And this was the worst of it: Ally liked Wilson. When he talked about the sea, what it meant to fish, he had music in him. Same when he spoke about his wife, who he didn't want to hurt. But when he talked of being a father, Wilson was as tight as a clam. Ally could see it was no good. Just like she could see that Jayden, sitting there beside her, was quietly furious with him.

She glances at Jayden now, sees his hands tight on the wheel; the flicker at his jaw. It isn't often that they disagree.

'The chance of it though, don't you think?' she says, trying to meet him on shared ground. 'A lost coat. What an extraordinary way for the truth to come to light.'

'And it's wrong to keep Saffron in the dark.'

'But Jayden, what good would it do to tell her? To say, *We know who your father is, he lives just down the coast, he's been there all this time, but he's changed his mind about wanting to know you.* Have you any idea how much that would hurt, to hear a thing like that? Isn't it better to say that we tried but failed? That there simply wasn't enough to go on. Saffron will understand that. Whereas . . . I don't think she'd understand the other.'

'But it's a lie.'

'A white lie.'

'Oh, and white lies are okay? White lies are all good? Yeah, course they are. Come on, Al. That's not us. Saffron came to us because she wants the truth.'

'We gave Wilson our word.'

'No, *you* did. You gave Wilson your word. I didn't.'

'*Jayden.*'

Wilson was showing them out when the man said, almost as an afterthought, 'Everything considered, that letter wasn't destined to be read. And I'd appreciate it if you honoured that.'

Jayden was already out of the door, the disappointment and frustration coming off him like steam. Ally hesitated.

'What I mean is,' Wilson went on, 'I want my privacy respected. My identity . . . protected.'

'There's really no one else who knows you have a daughter, Wilson?' Ally said.

'No one. And it's what Stephanie wanted too, isn't it? For her own reasons.'

And how did Ally answer? She honestly can't remember. But they shook hands on parting. Which Wilson probably took as tacit agreement.

This is where Ally would have given anything to turn things over with Bill. Where did the lines of confidentiality lie? A doctor took an oath to do no harm – well what about detectives like them? As far as Ally can see, telling Saffron about Wilson Rowe would only lead to harm – for both of them.

'Saffron hired us,' says Jayden, slamming on the brakes as a pheasant darts across their path. 'She put her faith in us. We can't let her down now.'

'I don't think she thought it through.'

'That's pretty patronising, Al.'

'I don't mean it to be. But telling her about Wilson will only do more harm than good. He doesn't want to know her, and he made that clear. Don't you think it's kinder just . . . to let it go?'

Jayden shakes his head. 'I don't agree.'

'I think we need to agree. We need to decide this together.'

'What if we can't?'

'Then . . . Then we've a problem.'

The trilling of Jayden's phone fills the car. Ally glances down at the screen.

'It's Cat. Do you want me to answer it for you?'

'No, thanks,' he says stiffly. 'I'll talk to her later.'

'*Talk to her* talk to her?'

'Oh, so suddenly you're about the honesty?' And Jayden sounds nothing like himself as he says it. Instantly, he corrects himself. 'Sorry. I'm sorry. Just . . .'

'I know. Jayden, I don't think there's any malice in Wilson's change of heart, he just wants to protect his marriage. He loves his wife and he doesn't want to upset her . . .'

'What, by keeping a secret that he's got a daughter living down the road? Yeah, that's really loving that is.'

'It's not up to us to judge.'

'But it is up to us to tell Saffron. Because that's why she hired us.'

The grey rooftops of Porthpella are just coming into view, and Jayden slows for the turning out to the dunes.

'I can walk from here,' says Ally.

Jayden shoots her a look. 'Al, I'll drop you at home. It's no trouble.'

'No, really, I'd like to. I want to stretch my legs. Clear my head.' Then, 'Shall we talk more later?'

'We can't know more about Saffron's life than she does. I'm not okay with that.'

Ally has her hand on the car door. She hesitates. 'Let's sleep on it,' she says.

'But tomorrow's Tom Bawcock's Eve. It's a big deal for her. We can't tell her then.'

'There's no rush to tell her anything at all.'

'Then it's Christmas Eve. Christmas Day. Boxing Day. New Year. There are no good times, only less bad times. And I think today is the last of the less bad times. Now or never. And it can't be never.'

Ally sighs. 'I just don't . . . I can't agree.'

'So, I'll be the one to do it. Then you haven't broken your word. Anyway, what do you think Saffron's going to do? She's not going to go knocking at Wilson's door on Christmas Day. She's not going to broadcast the fact that there's this fisherman who—'

'Jayden, we can't possibly know what she's going to do.'

He drops his head on the steering wheel for a moment. When he lifts it again, he looks quietly devastated.

'We didn't think this through,' he says. 'When we took this job, I mean. We didn't think of all the ways it could go.'

'I know. And there was me afraid that we'd uncover a murderer.'

'Exactly. Al, if we don't tell Saffron about Wilson, and the police never catch this killer, then she's going to go the rest of her life wondering if her dad was involved, isn't she? We can't let that happen.'

'The police will surely have a breakthrough soon.'

'Yeah, and what if they don't?'

'So, offer to help,' says Ally, 'talk to Skinner. See if he can use an extra pair of hands.'

Jayden almost gives a shout of laughter. 'It doesn't work like that. What happened with Lewis in the spring was different. We knew more than they did that time. With JP Sharpe, we don't know anything. Except that the letter to Saffron has got absolutely nothing to do with any murder.'

'So, let's change that,' says Ally. 'Let's find something.'

'You want us to solve a murder, so we don't have to tell Saffron that her dad doesn't want to know her? That's the dumbest idea I've heard . . .'

And it is a foolish idea, but what else is there? They're between a rock and a hard place. Is it their naivety that's brought them here? Or perhaps it was always going to be difficult, because Saffron is their friend. They can't possibly be objective, neither one of them.

Ally climbs out of the car. She stands with the door open, peering back in.

'I don't know what more to say,' she says.

'Look, being a detective is all about having the difficult conversations, Al. It's part of it. It's not just looking at old postcards and running around art galleries . . . you've got to face the hard stuff head on, and if you don't want to do that . . .'

Then perhaps you're not cut out for it. Those are the words that Ally fills in.

This unspoken thought hangs in the air between them. She looks down at her boots.

'It's part of it,' he says again. 'That's why—'

There's a sudden gust of wind then and it whips the car door from Ally's fingers and slams it shut. It's as if she's hung up the telephone or walked out of the room mid-conversation. And Jayden must have thought the same, because, before she can say it was the wind that did it, he's already driving away.

51

This is not Phil's first time in a police station. They were in London once, on a weekend break, and Melissa had her handbag stolen. One minute they were enjoying an afternoon drink in an over-priced pub and the next his wife was casting round for her bag.

There one minute, gone the next. *Never nice for anyone*, he thinks bitterly.

They reported it at the nearest police station, which happened to be on Savile Row. Phil felt a little bit grand as he walked Melissa in there – *We'd like to report a crime!* – not exactly expecting red carpet treatment but at least the acknowledgement that this was at best inconvenient, and at worst distressing (even though she'd stopped her cards, Melissa loved that handbag, and the eight hundred odds and ends it apparently contained). But they were met with long faces and even longer forms. And now here he is – seven, eight years later? – at a two-horse outfit in a nowhere town, sitting on a split plastic chair, chewing at his thumbnail, still waiting to be seen by whoever called him in in the first place.

Don't they know he has places to be, people to see?

Who's he kidding?

Phil takes his phone from his pocket and looks at it again. Nothing. Every single one of his messages has gone unanswered. It's like screaming into the void. And it's enough to drive a person mad. Phil wishes that he was worried something had happened to her, because somehow that would be better than knowing what the silence really means. Which is total indifference.

Dominic's 'where there's love there's hope' line is all very well, but it doesn't matter how much one person loves, does it, or how much they hope, if it's met with nothing in return. That particular bumper sticker is clearly only sported by people who've got what they want. The rose-tinted, 'I'm alright Jack' brigade.

A wash of woozy exhaustion comes over Phil. He hardly slept last night. He looks to the bloke sitting behind his desk.

'Excuse me, can you tell me what the delay is please?'

But the officer's eyes are on his computer screen, and they only flick to Phil when they're good and ready, and even then, it's as if it's by accident. As if they're roaming the room and they happen to land on him.

'Did you hear?' says Phil.

And the man looks like he might just do him the courtesy of a reply, or at least is thinking about the possibility of it, when the phone rings and he answers that instead.

Phil gnaws at the inside of his mouth, a habit since boyhood. His nails are already bitten to nothing. Maybe all these little tics are just to prove to himself that he does, indeed, exist. There were days, plenty of days – even before everything with Melissa – when JP Sharpe made Phil feel invisible. Yet he was the manager. In charge! But it wasn't just JP, was it? It's always been near enough everyone, forever. Phil is just one of those people that don't matter. It doesn't make a difference that he has a job title, a decent car, a good few suits in his wardrobe – not Savile Row, their visit there was brief and unfruitful, but suits none the less. And a wife, a wife, a wife.

None of it's ever been enough though.

He stares at his phone. Giving in to another body-wracking yawn, Phil scrolls back through all the messages that Melissa has ignored. It's too painful, this. Really, he should delete the lot. But the last time he tried to erase the existence of a thing – that damn card – the whole pub went up. What would happen this time?

Dominic was right, wasn't he, that only a coward would put up with working alongside JP after what he'd done.

What if Melissa thinks the exact same thing? What if all these weeks she's been waiting for Phil to do something – to prove that he actually cares about their marriage, and won't stand for anyone messing with it? He thought he was being the bigger man – well, alright, the less confrontational man – but what if Melissa was desperate for him to stand up to JP? What if she's now thinking, *My pathetic husband never even showed me how much our marriage means, and now JP's dead anyway?*

God. That's it, isn't it?

Perhaps he does have one more text message in him after all.

I'm with the police, he taps out. *You're my one phone call, Mel.*

Then Phil fixes his sights on the officer on reception again. He watches him hang up the phone and go back to his computer as if Phil isn't there at all.

'I was brought here,' he says, standing up, 'I don't see why you'd bother getting me to—'

'Ah, there you are,' says Detective Sergeant Skinner. 'Thanks for your patience, Phil. Come on through.'

And the way he says it is man-to-man. Companionable. Respectful. Phil nods, then follows the detective's broad back. As Phil walks, he can hear the soles of his shoes squeaking on the linoleum, as if announcing his arrival, after all. He shoots the man on reception a look as he passes; a look that says, *See, I'm pretty important round here.*

Then, over the sound of his shoes, he hears his phone buzz in his pocket.

'Phones off please,' says Skinner, over his shoulder. 'House rules. Thanks.'

Phil pulls it out. And it's her. It's bloody her.

For the first time since this whole thing, Phil feels a jolt of power; it fizzes through his fingertips like electric charge.

He was right. All Melissa was waiting for was for him to do something.

52

Saffron and Broady are crossing the wind-whipped square together. His arm is around her shoulders and she's leaning into him, their footsteps in perfect synch. The Christmas tree outside The Wreckers is twinkling its welcome, and for the first time since Saffron's been back in Porthpella she feels a glow of true festivity.

When Broady turned up earlier, he was pretty much the last person Saffron had expected to see. But there he was, so solid, sun-streaked hair touching his shoulders, a tanned face full of laughter lines; surfboard under his arm, rucksack on his back, both of which he'd dropped right there on the doorstep as he folded her into a hug that smelt of salt water and sun cream and him, just him. Saffron stayed in that hug for about as long as it was possible to without needing to take out planning permission.

'But what about the rest of the trip?' she said into his t-shirt.

'There's no way I was going to stay there. Not with you here, not with all this going on.' Then, 'But I couldn't tell if you wanted me or not. It was a punt.'

They're about to duck inside the pub when she recognises Jayden's car parked outside White Wave Stores. Then he's walking out, arms full of groceries, loading a monster bag of nappies into the boot.

'Hey, Jayden!' she calls out.

Jayden's face, as he looks up, is all weirdness. He's never looked like he isn't happy to see her before. Then it's as if he quickly adjusts; finds a grin.

'Saffron, hey. And Broady, how's it going, man?'

'I'm glad to be back home with this girl, that's for sure.'

Saffron smiles, but her cheeks feel cold and tight. Jayden's dodging eye contact; he never dodges eye contact.

'Emergency call from Cat,' says Jayden, snapping the boot shut and going around to the driver's door. 'We're all out of nappies. I'd get my blues and twos going if I had any.'

As Jayden says it, he shoots Saffron a look. If he didn't, if he'd just bundled into the car with a quick wave, then she'd have left it. She'd have carried on with Broady into The Wreckers and tucked in for fireside pints and cheesy tunes on the jukebox. But for a split second, Jayden's eyes hold hers.

And she knows.

'You've got something to tell me, haven't you?'

He shakes his head. 'Erm . . . we need more time to figure—'

'You said you had a lead about a man in Mousehole,' she cuts in. 'What did you find out?'

Jayden hesitates, then closes the car door. He comes around to her side. At the look on his face, unease shivers through her. Because she recognises this look. She saw it from people when her mum fell ill. It was a careful look, an assessing look. It says, *Is Saffron going to be able to handle this?*

She thinks of JP Sharpe. The unsolved murder. And her stomach drops.

'I mean,' she begins, 'I don't want to make you late or anything. If Jazz needs her nappies . . .' Then she draws in a breath, tells herself that this is her doing, that she wants it. Whatever it turns out to be. 'I'd just really like to know.'

'Saffron . . .' he begins; his voice is all kindness, but that con-
flicted look is still there. 'I think it's probably best if Ally and I—'

'What?' she says, her eyes filling. 'Jayden, please tell me. I need
to know.'

She sees Jayden glance at Broady, and it gets under her skin.
She feels, suddenly, *managed*.

'Jayden, listen,' she says. 'Asking you and Ally to look for my
dad, I know what a long shot that is. You've had nothing to go on.
No records, no DNA, no secret letters from my mum. What does
that even leave?'

It leaves the murder investigation. She rubs her hands on her
jeans, her palms pricking with sweat. Broady's arm tightens around
her shoulders, while inside her chest her heart goes like a drum.

'Yeah, what does it leave?' says Broady. 'He could be anywhere
in the world. He could be on a yacht in Thailand. He could be . . .'

Jayden's dark eyes glitter with sadness. 'Saffron, we found him,'
he says.

Saffron watches Jayden drive away. She holds up her hand, because
she knows he'll be looking back in his mirrors. Her tears are suspended like a wave about to break; she can't hold them any longer.

He was in Mousehole this whole time.

He's changed his mind about knowing her.

He was in Mousehole this whole time.

He's changed his mind about knowing her.

He saw her in Hang Ten, drank her coffee, wrote her that letter,
but now, given the chance to think better of it, he's done just that:
thought better. Wilson Rowe – he even has a name – has cashed in
his cooling-off period.

'Saff, baby?'

She doesn't turn to face Broady. She feels, weirdly, like she can't move at all. The wind sweeps across the square, stinging her wet cheeks.

'Mum never wanted me to . . .' she begins to say, 'but I . . .'

And that's all she's got. Because this is it, she gets it now, the feeling that her mum tried to protect her from. It's rejection – and it's hit her like a truck.

53

Jayden parks in the farmyard. The lights are on in the main house, and he knows at this time of day his in-laws will be sitting down to a pot of tea, probably a mince pie. He kind of hopes Cat and Jazzy are with them, though their cottage is lit up too.

He hesitates, just sitting at the wheel. If he goes in, Cat will ask him about his day, and he'll have to tell her that it's been rubbish. Will he take that moment to ask her about Penzance? Really pile it on himself? No, he'll wait until their daughter's in bed to go anywhere near that. But, nevertheless, the topic will hum about the room like a mosquito; one that only he can hear.

Ally was right. Maybe. Possibly. Was there such a thing as 'right' here anyway? Ally definitely thought she was, the way she slammed the car door on him like that. That wasn't Ally's usual style at all.

The fact is, when Broady said that Saffron's dad could be in Thailand – or anywhere the world over – Jayden could have taken that and run with it; batted away the notion of the Mousehole man altogether. And Saffron would have been okay, because with Broady just now she was looking happy – for the first time since she got back.

But, instead, Jayden told her the truth: Wilson Rowe doesn't want to know.

He groans, knowing he'll have to tell Ally. She isn't an 'I told you so' kind of person, but he can't help feeling he's let her down. They're supposed to be partners, which means deciding things together. But he wants her to understand that being a pair also means that only one of them has to handle the difficult conversations, or, even better, that they can handle them together. That's what Jayden wanted to say to Ally before she slammed the car door. *That's why there's two of us.*

His phone rings just as he's reluctantly gathering himself to get out of the car.

'Saffron, hey,' he says, closing his eyes.

'I'm sorry I didn't take it well,' she says.

'You did,' he says. 'You took it about as well as anyone could. I'm just really sorry.'

Stoical, that's the word that comes to mind. And that was the worst of it: Saffron's quiet sorrow. She went completely pale earlier, and very quiet. *Okay*, she said, a tremor in her voice. *Thanks for telling me.* But the look that Broady sent him – Mr Chill, the easy-breezy surf guy – said it all. *Mate, seriously?*

'Jayden, I know it wouldn't have been easy telling me that. But I'm glad you did.'

He feels very close to crying. This is just like Saffron, to set herself aside and make other people feel better. He wants to tell her to forget about him, but he doesn't have the voice for it.

'You know,' she says, 'with JP Sharpe, and the DNA result, there was this weird moment when I got it and it turned out that it wasn't him. I felt . . . disappointed. I know, I know, it's not that I wanted it to be him. I mean, apart from anything else he was . . . dead. But . . . I'd been thinking about him, reading about him, talking about him. He'd become real to me. A real person. Not just a newspaper headline.'

'I know.'

'More real, in some ways, than . . . this Wilson. Wilson Rowe.'

And Jayden hates that she can barely say the name. That she will be carrying it with her now – a trigger-point, a weight, complicating everything.

'They still haven't caught anyone, have they, the police? I checked in with Mullins this morning.'

'I don't think so,' he says. 'They had a guy in for questioning, but he's been released without charge.'

'They need to find who did it.'

'They will, Saffron.'

'Help them, Jayden. Can't you? I know I've asked for so much already, and you've *done* so much, you and Ally. But look, you found this . . . Wilson, Wilson Rowe . . . out of nowhere. Surely you can find who killed JP Sharpe?'

'I don't think we can. There's no way in for us. We know there's no connection between JP and the letter now.'

Jayden knows part of this is Saffron swinging to something else, trying to *do* something when, really, there's nothing to be done. But he means it. If there were a way in, Jayden would take it like a shot. And he knows Ally would too.

No matter how JP Sharpe ended up wearing Wilson Rowe's coat that night, it has nothing to do with the case. The guy accidentally left it on his chair. It was a cold, wet night, the seventeenth, maybe JP saw it as he was leaving and thought it looked warmer than his own, so he took it. Whatever happened, the police would have that info now – or soon enough.

'JP Sharpe hasn't got any family,' Saffron says, 'or none that care. Mullins said there's a cousin somewhere, but they fell out years ago. Maybe there's a reason, maybe he's a nightmare . . . but there's no one pushing for justice. There's no one down here, not resting till someone's caught.'

'The police will do the best they can with what they've got,' says Jayden. 'It doesn't matter how much the family is, or isn't, pushing.'

But Jayden knows that isn't always true. Media pressure, certain families, it all plays into it. Just like in so many parts of society, some people are better served than others. JP Sharpe is hardly underprivileged, but Jayden gets Saffron's point about family.

'It's just . . . he was someone's baby once,' she says. 'That's what I keep thinking about. A little boy who just wanted to be safe and loved, just like everyone wants. And then he grew up into a man who was murdered and, well, no one really seems to care. Apart from the people who are paid to care.'

'I think Dominic Brook cares. And I think—'

'Jayden, if you and Ally found Wilson bloody Rowe, then you can find who did this too. I know you can.'

And then she rings off.

Jayden looks to the cottage again, sees the silhouette of his wife moving past the window. He can't remember any other time when he hasn't wanted to walk through his own front doorway. He sits holding his phone in his hand – a small beam of light – as outside the dusk starts to gather.

He types in *John Paul Sharpe*.

Then he scrolls through the hits, clicking on images, thumbing down through them too. He brings up the portrait shot from the Mermaid's Rest website: chef's whites, folded arms, the determined set to Sharpe's mouth and the challenge in his eyes. Jayden tries to imagine how Saffron felt as she looked at him, thinking . . . *could he be?*

Jayden goes back to the main search page. He taps on the team shot from a London restaurant called The Peppercorn, the one with Dominic Brook in it too. He focuses in on JP again here. It's a far-fetched thought, but did JP have a different set to his face, before he moved to Cornwall? Was his attitude, the one that's so obvious in

286

the Mermaid's Rest picture, with him during his London cheffing days too? JP's close-up face fills the screen, and yep: same guy, same vibe. It wasn't Cornwall that changed him.

Jayden clicks his tongue, never feeling more like an amateur. Here he is, speculating over photographs, looking for clues in two-dimensional faces. The fact is, even though he spoke to Phil Butt and Dominic Brook, the two people who were closest to JP down here, Jayden doesn't feel like he knows JP Sharpe at all. Could he go back to them and try again? Not without getting in the way of Skinner and co., that's for sure.

As much as he sees where Saffron is coming from, there's no way in.

Jayden zooms back out again, his heart rock-heavy in his chest. He's just about to click away from the page when something – or, specifically, someone – at the edge of the picture catches his eye. A different face this time. He enlarges it. Gives a small gasp.

'You,' he says, with absolute conviction. 'I've seen you before.'

54

Ally has all but missed the sunset. It wasn't a showstopper, there was too much heavy cloud around, but it's a ritual of hers to get out in it anyway. Especially since Bill died, marking each day with the movement of the sun. Their beach at low tide is like a giant mirror, and as she stands out on those sandflats, the roar of the surf in her ears, an implausible spectrum of colours streaking the sky, it feels as if the distance between this world and the next isn't so much after all.

The next. She doesn't even know what she means by that. And that's okay.

There's a lot we don't know, Al. That was one of the things Bill used to say. And he used it for matters both practical and spiritual: he was never someone who had a problem acknowledging the limits of his knowledge.

Nor is Jayden. And she knows that the ways in which Jayden is like Bill, as well as all the ways in which he's different, are part of what first drew her to him. Ally never thought that at the age of sixty-four, her best friend – could she call him that? Though she wouldn't expect it to work the other way – would be a man who is only just thirty. Jayden brings so much energy with him: the way he pounds up the steps to The Shell House, throwing open the door, *Hey Al!* Sunshine coming off him in waves.

And now they're at loggerheads. They've never been here before.

As Ally thinks about Jayden, she feels in her pocket for her phone and realises she's left it in the house. And it's actually quite a nice thought, to be untethered. This situation they're in, it's so emotionally complex, how would anyone know the right thing to do?

She thinks, now, she should have trusted Jayden. He's much closer to Saffron in age. Perhaps it's a generational thing, the inclination to process difficult truths. Or just a question of character? Ally feels suddenly old, and tired, and out of step.

Jayden's probably right, too, to doubt her ability as a detective. She already told him she has a tendency to avoid difficult conversations. She knows this about herself. My God, the way she panicked, when she sensed Gus wanted to say something important to her the other night.

Fox has broken from her and she's on her own as she pushes through the marram grass to reach the beach. Her feet slip in the soft ledge of sand. Winter storms have hurled the place about – hunks of driftwood, white as bones in this half-light, are strewn all over. This is the best time for wrecking. It would be nice to turn something up that might give her a sign. To reassure her of the right thing to do. *And now I sound like Wilson Rowe.*

She and Jayden must be united; that's the most important thing.

As Ally walks towards the water, she feels gusts swirl around her, and she leans into them. She imagines a leaf floating on currents of air. Her knitted hat is pulled down well over her ears, and even so, she can feel the cold pricking her temples. It's dusky, dim, and somewhere there's the early moon doing its best to break through.

When Ally sees the dim figure of an approaching man, she knows exactly who it is. She thinks about turning back, then stops herself. She walks towards him instead, her feet heavy in the wet sand.

'You're late today,' Gus says with a smile. 'The sun wouldn't wait. Rude of it, I thought.'

She gives a low laugh. Says, 'It's the case.'

'I know. I saw Broady in the village just now.'

'Broady's back? Oh that is good.'

'You did a great job, you know,' he says. 'Even so.'

'What do you mean?'

'Finding Saffron's father. That's some decent detective work.'

Ally looks at him sharply.

'Don't feel dreadful about it. I knew you would, the minute Broady said it, and I wanted to come and see you to say . . . don't. You couldn't have known how the man would react.'

Ally feels, suddenly, as if the tide has a hold of her, is pulling her out.

'Ally, look. It was always a risk. He's a complete stranger. No one knew anything about him. You can't hold yourself responsible for how he—'

'Is this where you say I told you so?' she says, her words more clipped than she means. She sees the surprise in Gus's face.

'It's where I say that I've been here. Not exactly here. But . . .' He steals a glance at her, then passes his hand across his mouth. 'It was why I wanted to talk to Saffron. When I was around her age, I got in touch with my dad, even though my mum told me not to. And, Ally, I've regretted it just about every day since. I think it's possible to know too much, sometimes. Maybe it's old-fashioned, that whole blissful ignorance thing, but . . .'

Gus looks down at the sand.

And Ally has so many questions, but she can't make space for this now – Gus, and his dad, all that regret? She knows the right thing to do is to ask him more, but she can't. Not when her head is full of Jayden telling Saffron.

'Have you talked to her?' Gus asks. 'Saffron, I mean. Broady said she's pretty cut up.'

'It was Jayden who talked to her.'

Gus raises an eyebrow, hearing the discernible spike in her voice. 'You mean you haven't yourself yet?'

Ally looks past him towards the water. A new set's rolling in and it's huge. Furious. The sound of it booms in her ears. She feels a rush of unease and calls out for Fox. And when he doesn't appear, the call becomes a shout. She feels Gus's hand on her shoulder.

'Ally?' The gentle enquiry.

Suddenly Fox is there, hurling himself against her legs. Ally reaches down to him.

She needs to call Wilson Rowe and tell him that Saffron knows after all, because the man deserves that much. But she doesn't explain this to Gus. Because she's cross with Jayden. And, inexplicably, she's cross with Gus too.

So, she just says, 'Fox and I need to get back.'

As she walks away, the hurt she sees in Gus's face – passing like a shadow – makes everything worse.

55

Mullins wanders down the corridor, his mug of soup clasped in his mitt. It's scalding hot from the microwave and he blows on it, his stomach rumbling impatiently. He's outside one of the interview rooms, and he's not eavesdropping; no, not him. Mullins just happens to be standing in this prime spot, blowing on his soup.

Things have got a little bit exciting round here, you see. And, finally, he's back in it.

One of the Newquay lot had a breakthrough with the phone records earlier. Someone thought to go back just a little bit further than the last three months – and, sure enough, there it was: a message from Melissa Butt to JP Sharpe. And another. And another.

'The end of the affair!' Skinner declared in a show-off voice, and DS Chang winked at Mullins, saying, 'It's a novel, Tim, and don't worry, I haven't read it either.'

What followed was a brief conversation where Skinner said that, no, it was a film not a book, until DCI Robinson brought things back to what really mattered: JP Sharpe had had an affair with Phil Butt's wife. This was big. Did Phil know? And wasn't it a little bit strange, that Melissa had left town not long after Sharpe turned up dead? Yeah, this was very big.

'He did it, didn't he?' Mullins said. 'Jealous husband. He must have.'

'Or spurned lover,' Chang said. 'We can't rule out Melissa.'

'First things first, let's get Butt in,' Skinner said. 'And then talk to his wife. She was his alibi too, wasn't she? That needs checking again. On both sides.'

And just like that, there was a buzz about the place. Mullins was going back through his report from the night of the fire – what exactly had Butt said? – when suddenly he was called out to a farm on the moor. A stolen quad bike. He reluctantly took the patrol car, but all the way up there – the vehicle rocking on its chassis as gusts whipped down off the moorland – he thought about Phil. How upset the man had been the night of the fire. How it was Dominic Brook that Phil had called, not his wife.

Mullins is pretty sure that Phil Butt knows about the affair and is hiding it from them. And that's based on not much more than a bloke's intuition for when one of your own has been sucker-punched.

When Phil Butt stood outside the burning pub, a blanket over his shoulders, he looked like someone who'd lost the thing he loved most. At the time, Mullins thought it was pride in his job, or something like that – and a bit of feeling stupid too, because the plonker burnt the place down by knocking over a candle. But Mullins can see it clearly now – Butt lost his wife to JP Sharpe. Maybe after Sharpe's death, Melissa saw no point in sticking around. Maybe she isn't out of town for a couple of days, as Phil said in his statement; maybe she's *gone* gone. Was the fire deliberate, then? Was he raging mad, and flames were the only way he could let it all out? Mullins talked to a teenage arsonist once, and the boy's words stuck in his head: *I just wanted to burn something.*

Mullins takes a cautious sip of his pea soup. It's still on the hot side. He shifts a little closer to the door, but he can't hear a thing.

The thing is – as Mullins was thinking on that long moorland drive earlier, through mist as thick as porridge – Phil Butt doesn't really seem the murdering type. Neil Potter, with his ABH and his

293

obvious grudge, is more likely. But what does Mullins know? That's why he isn't going to be looking into those detective exams any time soon – or ever. Maybe DS Chang is right, and the mysterious Melissa bludgeoned Sharpe, no one so much as glancing in her direction as she swanned off out of town, while her sad husband stood around in the ashes.

Mullins takes another sip of soup. It's just making up stories really, isn't it – detective work? Making up stories, then going after the facts to drop in afterwards. Funny old business, really.

He presses his ear closer to the door just as someone on the other side throws it open.

Mullins jumps back, splattering his murky green soup all over his shoes, the wall, just about everywhere.

'Mullins? What the hell,' spits Skinner.

Mullins licks a blob from his wrist and waits for the tirade. But instead Skinner claps him on the shoulder and shows all of his teeth in a creepy kind of grin.

'We've only gone and got our man.'

'What – Butt?' says Mullins, soup still slopping in his cup.

56

Jayden's driving. Driving and thinking. He wants to go to The Shell House, but he can't, not yet. He doesn't want Ally to know that he's told Saffron about Wilson Rowe until he's got something positive to balance that out with.

And he's close. It's at the tips of his fingers; he just can't grasp it.

The woman from the photograph: Jayden knows he's seen her before. And even if he's got just a tiny scrap to go on, he'll take it.

As the lane splits, he hesitates. Does he turn right to head out to the dunes, or keep on going to Porthpella? Jayden chooses the road to the dunes, knowing there's a pull-in coming up any second with an immense view of the bay. He swings into it, making a wide turn in the parking area, then stops the car. Dusk is coming on fast, the electric sky darkening by the second. As Jayden climbs out, the wind buffets him.

Ally always says that when you don't know what to do, look out to sea and the answer will come.

Think, Jayden. Think.

He loves the drama of this spot. Locals call it The Drop, and there's always a bit of awe, and fear, in the way they say its name. When Jazzy was tiny, Jayden used to take her out driving just to get her off to sleep, and he often wound up here, easing his car up to the barrier, sinking back in his seat and watching the view as behind him his daughter slept, all cosy in her car seat. He's come to know pretty much every inch of rock and crag.

As the light fades, the waves are losing definition. Far below, out of sight, water crashes hard against the cliff; he can hear the fizz and boom. He shivers, pulling his coat closer around him.

The woman in the picture has to be significant, because Jayden knows he's seen her somewhere around here – and recently too. It's too much of a coincidence that someone who once worked with JP in London was in Cornwall the same week that Sharpe was murdered. Was she already on the police radar? Maybe he could tap up Mullins to find out. Phil Butt mentioned Dominic, but he didn't say that anyone else down here had a connection to Sharpe. And nor did Dominic.

Jayden realises, then, that Dominic is exactly the person to call and ask.

He slips his phone from his pocket. Before Dominic though, it has to be Ally. The phone signal's dodgy up here but he knows a spot where it works. He strides to the barrier at the cliff's edge. Two bars: score. But when he calls Ally it rings and rings, then goes to voicemail.

'Al, it's me. I need to talk to you. I don't know but think I might have something. Something that connects someone else down here to JP. Call me back and I'll explain.' Jayden hesitates, then says, 'And I've got to tell you, Al: I saw Saffron. I ran into her and Broady. By total chance. She asked me if we had anything to tell her and I couldn't lie. And, yeah, it went about as well as you said it would. I thought it was the right thing to do, but I still don't know if it was or wasn't. I feel rubbish about it. We should have agreed a way forward together, and I shouldn't have driven off when you slammed the door. I'm sorry. So, yeah, I guess that's it. I hope we're good, Al.' He's just about to ring off when he adds, 'Sorry if this message is super noisy by the way, I'm at The Drop. It's windy

296

as hell out here. But it's a good thinking place, you know? Anyway. Talk soon, okay?'

Jayden ends the message. Then, with a breath, he finds Dominic's number and hits Call. The chef answers straight away.

'Dominic? Hi, it's Jayden. We spoke yesterday about JP.'

'Sure, how can I help?'

Jayden turns his back to the wind.

'If I send you a link to a picture, could you tell me the name of the woman on the right-hand side? The one with the long blond hair? You and JP worked with her back in London, at The Peppercorn. JP's namechecked in the text beneath the picture, but no one else is. It just says *JP Sharpe and team.*'

The wind gusts then, and he loses what Dominic says.

'Say that again?' he says, cupping his hand to the receiver. 'Sorry, it's wild out here, but there's no reception back at the car . . .'

'I said sure, no problem. Go ahead and send it. What's it about?'

'I don't know yet,' says Jayden – and it's kind of the truth. 'Thanks, Dominic. Appreciate it.'

He hangs up and sends through the message. He can see that it's delivered, then waits a minute or two for Dominic to open the picture. As the three dots show, meaning Dominic's typing a reply, Jayden feels a thrum of anticipation. The message pings in.

She's called Anna Collins. She was with us for a few months as a waitress.

Jayden starts to tap out a response, asking if Dominic knows if Anna has been in Cornwall lately. But something stops him. Instead he writes: *Cheers. That's helpful. Does she still work at The Peppercorn?*

297

No idea. We didn't stay in touch.

Did JP and Anna stay in touch?

I doubt it.

Then Dominic again: *You know if the police are any closer?*

Saffron was wrong; Dominic cares. Maybe Anna Collins cares too. Maybe Anna Collins cares a little too much. No, Jayden's getting ahead of himself. But the excitement of feeling that he's on to something is building. His thumb hovers, thinking about his reply. He sees Dominic start to type something more, then stop again.

I've no idea, types Jayden. Then adds, *But I hope so.*

Makes me feel better if Shell House Detectives are on it. I heard you guys are good.

Jayden can't resist a grin. He sends a thumbs up emoji, then pockets his phone. He ponders his next move.

He thinks of Anna Collins again, and where he could have seen her. He tries to bring her into focus but it's like she's a figure on a distant stage, the scenery behind her indistinct. It wasn't Porthpella, he's pretty sure of that. It was somewhere out of the ordinary, where he doesn't normally go. But where would that be? Penzance yesterday? No, it was further back than that. But not a lot further back. Where else has he even been? Only to Mousehole.

Mousehole.

Mousehole to see Old Fran. Not the other day but before, with Cat and Jazzy.

He saw Anna Collins in Mousehole.

A mental picture comes into focus, and he lets out a whoop.

She was leaning on the railing overlooking the harbour. She noticed him and Jazzy, and she struck up a conversation with Jayden about him being a hands-on dad. That was her, he's sure of it. The angular features, the dead-straight hair. She wasn't flashing a smile like the one in the picture, but it was the same woman.

He's certain. Like, ninety per cent certain. Ninety per cent certain that he talked to Anna Collins in Mousehole, and then, just two days later, JP Sharpe was found dead in the same village. Just a few steps away from where they were standing when they talked. If the police aren't speaking to her already, then they really need to be. The only thing Jayden has to decide now is whether to call the station or try Ally again first.

Jayden's just about to head back to the car when his phone rings. He's hoping for Ally but it's Dominic.

'Jayden, I've been thinking about it. About Anna. I need to tell you something about her.'

'Okay.'

'Have you talked to the police yet?'

'Not yet.'

'Good. It's just . . .' He hesitates on the other end of the line. 'It's sensitive. You'll want to hear this before they do, I think.'

Then Jayden just comes out with it. 'Dominic, is there any way Anna could have been in Cornwall when JP was killed?' He doesn't answer, so Jayden adds, 'I'm pretty sure I saw her in Mousehole. Randomly.'

'Okay,' says Dominic. 'I definitely need to speak to you. Face-to-face. Where are you?'

'Over in Porthpella. Well, just outside. You know The Drop? But I'll come to you.'

'No, I'm not far from there. I'll meet you. In fact,' his voice, suddenly, has a note of urgency, 'the lookout point above the village? I know it. Perfect. I'll meet you there in fifteen minutes.'

And Dominic hangs up before Jayden can suggest a more convivial spot.

He rubs his hands together; pops up on his toes. *Something sensitive about Anna Collins.* This is going to be worth hearing. Jayden isn't going to wait for Dominic before he calls the station though. The police can get started on checking her out, and he can always feed in any new information later.

He starts dialling, excitement climbing in his chest.

57

Phil sits in his cell with his head in his hands. What can he do now except wait?

I did it. It was me.

He said those words to DS Skinner and the other bloke, DCI Robinson, without even knowing that they were going to come out. And maybe that was how these interviewers got you: they talked and talked and, in the end, just to make it stop, you said what they wanted to hear. Maybe that was how it went for some people.

But not for Phil.

He knew exactly what he was doing – and he'd never been more in control. It felt so good: that cut-diamond power.

It was partly the way they talked about him, the version of Phil Butt that they saw. And there was something about hearing it laid out for him like that. He said, *Yes, that's how it was.*

It was almost as though he'd stepped outside of himself – and it felt so good to speak up. To finally have the guts to admit the anger and the passion.

You don't mess with Phil Butt.

So, yeah, he told them that he couldn't stand the thought of JP Sharpe with his wife. Professionally, Sharpe was rude, abrasive, didn't respect Phil's authority. He upset the staff and even, at times, the customers. But when Sharpe crossed that personal line, when he started seeing Melissa, well, Phil had snapped, hadn't he? He wasn't going to take that.

'What man would, officers?'

Phil had known that talking to Sharpe wouldn't work. In the short time they'd worked together he'd learnt that appealing to JP's better nature, expecting him to see things from anyone else's perspective, was pointless.

As Phil said all this, Skinner and Robinson nodding along, he almost felt like the three of them could have been down the pub, sharing a couple of pints. They got it. They understood.

'You'd had enough, hadn't you, Phil? Fed up of being treated as if you didn't matter.'

'Yes,' he said, 'that's exactly it. I'd had enough.'

So, Phil told them how he'd planned it meticulously. He said how he'd followed Sharpe home that night, and when Sharpe had parked, he'd parked. How Phil was behind JP as he crossed the harbour car park, and it was easy, so easy, because the rain was slamming down and the wind was howling and no one in their right mind would be out in that, would they?

'Did he turn to face you, Phil? Did you tell him just what you thought of him?'

Phil sucked in his breath at that.

He wanted to say yes. Because Phil really wished he'd told JP what he thought of him. But what difference would it have made? So, he told Skinner the truth.

'I didn't have the words. I was too angry.'

He'd hated JP Sharpe. The man had belittled him in every possible way. People shouldn't be able to get away with that, should they? They should be held to account.

'So, you killed him?' Skinner said.

And, at those words, Phil felt a surge in his chest, like fire – but the good kind, not the terrifying, shameful kind that had taken hold at the Mermaid. He imagined Melissa watching a replay of this interview, her hand held to her mouth. Would something like fire be climbing in her chest too, as she realised what he'd done? The lengths he was capable of going to.

'Yes,' he said. 'I did.'

'What I want to know,' the other officer, Robinson, said, 'is why now? According to their messages, Melissa and JP stopped seeing each other two months ago. Why the wait?'

And Phil didn't answer that one. He wasn't going to hand them everything on a plate, was he? So, he clamped his lips together and said the thing they said in all the films: 'No comment.'

Now, in his cell, Phil pushes his nails into the palm of his hand. He pushes them until he sees the string of white crescents and feels the sharp and piercing pain. The adrenalin is ebbing away. He drags in a breath, but his body doesn't seem to want it; he judders like a car with a busted engine.

Will there be other questions? Well, he'll *no comment* his way through them as well. And surely there won't be too many. If the police have someone sitting there saying he did it, they'll take the win all day long.

A cry for help. Funny how that phrase rolls into his mind at this moment. Long ago a teacher levelled that one at Phil, when he was in trouble for putting a cricket ball through the headmaster's window. At this thought, his eyes start burning, and it's like he can smell the smoke of the fire again; see those words of Melissa's catching light – and then the whole damn place behind it. The fire was no cry for help, but even if it was, help didn't come. Melissa didn't even bother checking in to make sure he was okay.

This though? This is different.

They'll have told her by now: *We've arrested your husband for the murder of John Paul Sharpe.* Wherever Melissa is, she'll be taking her car keys, and getting on the A30. She'll be coming here, knowing what passion he's capable of, knowing that you don't mess with Phil Butt, knowing that he must really, really love her, to do a thing like that.

And it's that thought, that single thought, that has Phil lifting his head up out of his hands and looking at the four walls of the cell and thinking, *Yes, I did the right thing.*

But he feels a flicker of uncertainty, like a whiff of gas. You could either ignore it, or you could try and catch its scent again – convince yourself it's there and it's a problem.

Did I do the right thing?

He rubs his nose with the back of his hand. What will Melissa say when she finds out? And what will happen then? Nausea swirls in his stomach. A dim memory of that cricket ball comes back to him, the perfect arc of the other boy's throw; how Phil's hands were stuffed deep in his pockets as the glass shattered.

He stands up, gulping in air. Then he makes his way to the cell door. He slams his palms against the metal – and he starts to pound.

58

Bev is standing outside the Pollock house. Neil's been working on it for months, but she hasn't seen it properly before. It gleams and glitters, from the first brick to the last. She wonders if it feels strange for her husband to spend his days labouring at a vast house like this – all light and magic – then coming home to their two-up two-down, with its smells of washing powder and oven chips and shoes littering the hallway. Though perhaps it's no stranger, to be fair, than when she was up at the Mermaid, setting down immaculate plates, pouring wines she could never in a lifetime afford to drink. That's just how it is.

Bev isn't one for envy, but standing outside the Pollock house – with its soaring roof and wide windows – she feels something a little bit close to it. What would their lives be like, spread out inside a place such as this? With all that light pouring in perhaps everything would feel brighter. Maybe she'd stand a little taller – a sunflower, catching the best of everything – and be able to say the hard things as well as the easy things.

Like, *You can't just charge out, Neil Potter. Not when you're a father. A husband. No matter how much you're hurting or raging. You just can't do it.*

And then, *I'm so sorry for what I said. And, also, what I didn't say.*

Bev needs to tell him both of these things, with equal importance. And she knows she's passing the buck if she thinks living somewhere like the Pollock house would make it any easier.

Earlier, Neil convinced her that he wasn't lying. Maybe he had form for untruths – he'd kept the convictions in his past hidden, after all – but Bev had made her peace about it without the two of them ever having the grown-up conversation, so maybe that wasn't ideal either. It takes two to tango.

As to her own lie. Well, she's got only herself to blame for that one.

The fact is, Bev was too ashamed to tell Neil that she wasn't sacked; that, despite knowing how much they needed the money, she left her job of her own accord. She should have put her family first and sucked up everything else: the humiliation of what happened in the kitchen, the dressing-down from Phil afterwards. But she didn't. She quit. Afterwards, it was easy to say she was sacked. And spineless Phil seemed happy to tell that story too, because it made him look tougher than he was, probably. *She had to go* was what he told the other staff, apparently. And that was true, at least: she *did* have to go.

But she should have had the guts to tell Neil. Because, deep down, she knows he would have supported her. And maybe then he'd never have gone after JP Sharpe and got himself that bruise, that stupid scrap that got him hauled into the police station, opening up all those other cans of worms.

Or maybe he would have, anyway. And it all would have unfolded just the same.

Bev walks up to the wide wooden door. She knocks and waits.

She's about to knock again when she hears a hammering noise from somewhere behind the house, beyond his van. She moves towards it, her feet crunching on the gravel. The sound is coming from a sizable outhouse, with pure white walls and a grey slate roof. As she passes Neil's battered old Transit, something on the dashboard catches her eye.

The *Echo*.

Yanking open the door, she grabs the newspaper. She flicks it open, and the headline shouts at her with all its might.

INN CRISIS: COASTAL WATERING HOLE HAS TROUBLE ON THE MENU.

After the terrible argument with Neil, the stupid article dropped from her mind. She scans it, looking for her name. That's all she cares about at this exact second: what they've said she said.

Two days after the murder of its head chef, Mermaid's Rest goes up in flames. While reports suggest the blaze started accidentally, the proximity of these two tragic events has shone a light on this upmarket watering hole. We ask, where did it all go wrong for Mermaid's Rest?

Bev reads on. Then she sees this:

Bethany* (*name changed for anonymity) was recently fired from her waitressing role after running into the sharp end of the head chef's infamous temper. 'I blame myself,' says Bethany, showing the extent of the working culture's toxicity.

Bev scans down the article, but there's no more mention of this browbeaten Bethany. Instead it talks about faceless management companies, disconnection from community, and ends on a sensational – and Bev thinks pretty tasteless – question: *Will trouble come in three courses for Mermaid's Rest?*

No wonder they slashed the budget. Were they even worth £30, those words of hers?

But, somehow, it feels costly. A piece of her own life – and so far from the full story.

'Bev.'

She jumps.

'Or Bethany, is it?' says Neil.

'Don't.'

He gives her a deep look, and she feels her eyes fill again.

'You don't mean it, do you?' he says, gently. 'What you said in the rag. That you blame yourself?'

'Not like that. Not like they wrote it.'

He looks down at his paint-splattered boots, and when he looks back up his eyes are as red as her own.

'Bev, I'm glad you walked out. I'm proud of you for doing that. I wish you'd told me yourself – I'd have preferred not to have heard it from that weasel Sharpe – but hey. It's nothing. Nothing to what I kept from you.'

She exhales; feels her breath leave her in one heavy wave of relief.

'Can we walk a little way?' she says.

Neil nods, and together they wind their way down the drive. Neil's hand is warm in hers.

'I was afraid the journalist would have found out that the police called you in,' she says, pausing at the gateway. 'Named you as a suspect or something. Tried to take what I said and . . . and twist it, turn it into something else. I'd never have talked to them if I thought for a second that . . .'

'That I was involved?'

'I didn't really think you were. Of course I didn't. It was just with everything . . . I mean, all those late nights, were you really always here?'

He nods. 'I was here. You can trust me on that.'

'You haven't worked so late like this on other jobs,' she can't help saying, as they head into the lane.

'No,' he says, carefully. 'But this one's . . . different. There's been a lot to do. It's important to get it right.'

She can feel her face screwing up into a frown because even after everything they've been through it still feels like Neil's hiding something from her. Something that he seems to think, by the twinkle in his eye, is almost funny.

No. More. Secrets.

'Neil . . .' she begins, stepping back from him into the lane. 'You can't just—'

The next thing she knows there's the roar of an engine right on top of them. Neil grabs Bev, pulling her towards him so that the two of them stagger backwards. She clings to him as the car blasts on up the hill. In its wake the hedgerow trembles and the stench of exhaust fills the lane.

'Idiot!' he yells.

And by the tremor in his voice Bev knows just how close a call it was.

'I didn't hear it, I didn't see it,' she says, shaking. 'Neil, I . . .'

She buries her face in his jumper. One step more, and she'd have been hit – and this certain knowledge makes her cold to the bone. She feels Neil's arms wrap around her as safety returns.

'I saw it, alright,' he says. 'It was that other chef's car. You know, Sharpe's number two.'

Bev lifts her face up. 'You mean Dominic? Did it have stupid go-faster stripes all over it?'

'Yeah. And someone needs to take them off him before he gets himself killed, or . . .'

'. . . before he kills someone,' Bev finishes.

59

Mullins is on the phone to Anna Collins and he doesn't want to say *what did I tell you?* to Jayden, but also, he really does.

He was so excitable, Jayden, when he called in with this 'potentially vital information', as he put it. And yeah, okay, Mullins had to agree it was a little unusual that someone who knew JP Sharpe happened to be in Mousehole at the time of the murder but didn't come forward. But the case would be closed any minute now: they had their man. Of course, Mullins couldn't tell Jayden that, though he did feel the name pushing dangerously close to his lips: *Phil Butt!* Not until a press conference was happening anyway, and they were getting on to that now, the brass. So instead, he did his duty and promised to take Jayden's info to Skinner.

The gist of the conversation that then followed with his boss was: *Fill your boots.* Skinner said that if Mullins wanted, he could follow up with Anna Collins himself. He was in 'we cracked it' mode – chest out, triumphant – all because Phil Butt had buckled under his questioning.

So here Mullins is, filling his boots. He's also eying the end of his shift, and the time always goes more quickly if he's busy doing something.

Besides, he knows that with Jayden it won't be enough to tell him that Skinner ruled it out. He'd expect Mullins to take it into his own hands: follow his nose. Or whatever other *sleuthy* speak him and Ally use when they have their heads together.

And so Mullins has tracked her down. Anna Collins, living in Walthamstow, twenty-nine years of age. She remembers her days working at The Peppercorn less than fondly – *I was glad to get out of the place* – and yeah, she read about the death of JP Sharpe in the press.

'You don't seem very sad to hear he's dead,' says Mullins, kicked back in his chair, ankles crossed. Then he adjusts himself; he doesn't need the whole office seeing his snowman socks.

'Honestly?' says Anna, 'I'm not even that surprised. I know that's, like, a really bad thing to say but . . . he pushed people. That was his thing.'

Mullins asks her if she has an alibi for the time of the murder and Anna says she was at work and didn't finish her shift until 1 a.m. In Covent Garden.

'People that can back that up?' Mullins trips off, thinking that there's no way this woman was in Mousehole. Jayden obviously eyed up some other blond-haired beauty. Not that he'd admit it.

'Erm, yeah. My workmates. Look, where's this coming from?'

He notes down Anna's place of work, though doubts he'll bother following it up. Jayden's barking up the wrong tree with this one; in fact he isn't even in the right forest.

'So, you weren't in Mousehole on either the sixteenth or the seventeenth of December then?' he says, just for fun really.

'Mowzel? What kind of a name is that? No. No, I wasn't.' Then, 'Why would you even think I was?'

'You were in a Peppercorn team photograph with JP Sharpe. Someone recognised you. Thought they'd seen you in Mousehole.'

'What photo?'

311

Mullins brings it up on his screen. 'It was part of an article about the new ownership. In a magazine called *Dine*. From two years ago.'

'But I wasn't in that picture. I was off sick.'

'You are, I'm looking at you now.' Then, hurriedly, because that sounds creepy, 'I've got it up on screen.'

'*Dine* magazine? I wasn't. And I was gutted about it. It was JP, Dom, Lennie, Ricky and Shiv. Not me.'

Mullins shakes his head. First Jayden's seeing things, and then she's not even in the picture in the first place. The Shell House Detectives need to check their sources. Typical bloody amateurs.

There's a brief outbreak of noise at the other end of the office, and Mullins looks up. DS Skinner is charging in, his face thunderous.

'And now he's gone and changed his mind,' Skinner announces.

'Who, boss?' asks Mullins, because this looks like trouble and Anna Collins – this person of no interest whatsoever – can wait a minute.

'Phil Butt. Phil Butt who didn't, apparently, murder JP Sharpe after all.' Skinner groans, loud as a tractor engine. 'Silly beggar, wasting police time. So, listen up, people, it seems we no longer have our man.'

And on the word *man*, Skinner slams his hand against the wall.

Mullins's eyes widen. On the other end of the line, Anna's saying, 'Are we done?'

Are they done? He thought they were. But now he's not so sure. Not Phil Butt, after all?

I saw her, Jayden said. *She was right here in Mousehole.*

'Anna,' he says, thinking on his feet, 'if I quickly send you this photograph, can you tell me who the woman with the blond hair is on the right-hand side?'

'I can tell you without seeing it,' she says. 'I told you, I was annoyed not to be in it. And Lennie and Shiv kept going on about it. It's Lennie. Lena. Lena Prior.'

Mullins writes the name down, then underlines it three times.

Lena. He wonders, is that a name that means anything to anyone?

60

Back inside his car, Jayden looks at his watch. It's been twenty minutes since Dominic called. *Something weird about Anna Collins. It's sensitive.* He has a feeling – deep in his gut – that this conversation is going to count.

Since he and Dominic spoke, Jayden's been trying to remember if Anna said anything else when he saw her in Mousehole. *Not often you see a hands-on Dad.* With that slightly strained look in her eyes.

Mullins sounded like he was going through the motions when he said he'd take the info to Skinner. It felt like there was something more that he wasn't saying, too. Maybe the enquiry's moved in a different direction. Or maybe they already know all about her: Anna Collins is old news.

Jayden thinks about trying Ally again, but instead he taps out a quick message to Cat. She'll be wondering where he is. He's avoided thinking about the conversation they still need to have, but he knows he'll have to face it soon enough.

Impatient, he climbs out of the car and looks down the hill towards Porthpella, watching for headlights. If Dominic is driving from Mousehole, that's the direction he'll be coming from. Despite the knock-out view from The Drop it's a quiet road, especially at this time of year. Jayden's still getting used to the way that parts of Cornwall fill, then empty. The fact that people use it for their own ends – pleasure, sure, but also investment – means others don't get a look-in. All those second homes with lights off through the winter: ghost-town vibes, some places. He knows how lucky he and Cat are to have the cottage on the farm. Even if he doesn't particularly want to think about Cat and the cottage on the farm right now.

He walks up and down, flapping his arms to keep warm. The wind's whipping up and over the headland. Jayden kind of likes it, this assault from the elements: it fits his mood. The truth is, he needs this to be a lead, he needs Anna Collins to matter. Because then, at least, he can tell Saffron, and Ally, and it'll mean some actual good has come of them being involved in the case.

Jayden walks to the edge, side-stepping gorse. There's a run of dark grass, a flimsy sort of barrier, then a sheer drop, interrupted only by a ledge of rock about three metres down. He can hear the water swirling far below in the darkness and it makes his stomach lurch. Jayden plants his hand on the railing and feels the damp, soft wood give slightly under the pressure. Country people think cities are dangerous, but right here, you could die a hundred ways without even trying. A slip on the cliff path, a rip current, and no one would even hear you scream.

He feels, then, a pang for Leeds. He thinks of his mum and dad prepping for Christmas, counting down the days until he and Cat and Jazzy visit for New Year. The tree will be in, and because his mum always goes for the underdog it'll be a lanky one, or super stumpy; she'll have felt sorry for it and taken it home to give it its moment to shine.

His phone rings.

'Ally.'

'Jayden. Are you alright?'

He goes to lean against the barrier then changes his mind.

'I'm alright. Can you hear me okay up here?'

'Just.' There's a hesitation. 'I got your voicemail. It was an impossible situation. You only did what you thought was right.'

315

'You're not mad?'

'I'm not mad. Not now. I do wish that we'd talked, or that you'd called me the moment you left Saffron.'

'I know. This only works if we're a partnership.'

He sees headlights then, flashing up the hill, and feels a flare of anticipation. It has to be Dominic.

'Al, the other part of my message, being on to something. I really think I am. I'm about to meet someone . . .'

'You're not still at The Drop are you?'

'Yeah, and I'm going to have to go in a sec, but let me just tell you quickly . . .'

As the car's headlights bounce off the hedgerows and beam into the clearing, Jayden steps out and waves. But the vehicle's coming on too fast and he drops his arms. *It's not Dominic*, he thinks, *it's some lunatic trying to turn around.* He steps back, wary suddenly. He's a lone figure in a remote spot at nightfall; if the car's swinging in to make the turn then the last thing they'll be expecting is someone standing in their way.

'Jayden?' Ally's voice sounds very small and far away.

'Hold on, there's something . . . Jeez!'

The car hasn't seen him. It is, in fact, driving directly towards him. Jayden's dazzled by the headlights as they swoop over him.

'Hey, watch it!' he shouts, stepping quickly to the side. His foot skids on the wet grass. Surely the driver's seen him now? He waits for the door to open, expecting a flood of apologies. But nothing. He hears Ally's distant voice and presses the phone back to his ear.

'Jayden? What's going on?'

'Sorry, Al, I've got to go. Some nutter's trying to run me over.' He laughs. 'Look, I'll fill you in later, I—'

The car has stopped in front of him, its engine ticking over. All of a sudden, unease thrums in Jayden's chest. He has the impression of a cat about to pounce. The headlights dip, and for a split second

Jayden plainly sees the figure behind the wheel. He gives a shout of surprise.

But then the lights lift again, and he's blinded by their glare.

'Al, wait, don't go!' he gasps. 'It's Domin—'

The engine guns and his words are lost.

Jayden takes a step back but behind him is nothing but the edge of the cliff. That sheer drop. Fear rushes in hard as the madness of the situation hits him. This driver wants to hurt him. No, wants him dead.

'Al, it's Dominic!' he yells.

On the other end of the phone, a million miles away, Ally cries out Jayden's name.

Suddenly the car's surging forward and, as it does, time slows. He feels the heat of the engine and the dazzling burn of the headlamps. He's a mouse caught in a cat's paws, a cat's jaws. No way out.

Unless.

Jayden spins his head, orientating himself. The barrier. The Drop. He makes a lightning-fast calculation and, just as the car is inches from him, he flings himself sideways. It's a desperate act, but he's always been quick-footed – on the football pitch, on the dance floor – and even thinking these things, in this moment, is that his life flashing before his eyes?

He's airborne. Dropping fast, into nothing.

And, just like that, the car – that violent hunk of metal and its murderous driver – feels, by far, the lesser of two evils.

61

Trip is on the dark road up to Porthpella. He came here a few years ago, to meet an old school mate at The Wreckers Arms, but not since. And never on this kind of business. In fact, he hasn't been anywhere on this kind of business before.

Trip's truck wheezes as it struggles on the hill, headlights bouncing off the drizzle that's being blown horizontal. This weather really needs to do one. And, if the forecasts are to be believed, it's finally on its way out. Perfectly timed, too: tomorrow, Tom Bawcock's Eve should be fine and clear. Still a decent wind, but nothing like this, and nothing that'll stop him getting back on the boat and netting a decent catch. Knowing this, Trip feels lighter than he has in days. But perhaps that's more to do with Wilson than the weather.

He idles at a crossroads, sees the sign for Porthpella, then dips into a lane so narrow that it feels like an unlit tunnel. In his mind, Trip runs over everything that happened with Wilson earlier.

It was a lot.

The way Wilson said the word *police*, and the look on his face as it left his mouth – like he was carrying the weight of the world – opened the floodgates for Trip. Standing there on Wilson's doorstep, he let rip at him. Told Wilson that he knew he was keeping stuff from him – and he was afraid, so afraid, that he'd killed JP Sharpe. Wilson looked genuinely baffled.

Son, why on earth would you think a thing like that?

Trip told him everything then. Sharpe's drugs talk back in the summer, letting him on the boat, the smashing of the little black cat.

My little black cat?

The bad luck that followed: the dismal run of catches, the boat needing that new engine, Wilson's accident, this weather.

And you think all that was enough for me to kill the bloke that broke my little black cat?

Wilson was caught between laughter and out-and-out disbelief.

Alright, I'm superstitious. But not murderous. And I didn't even know about Sinbad.

Sinbad was the little black cat.

Now, Trip hits the brakes as something darts across the path in front of him. A rabbit? He changes gear as the hill climbs. The lights are on full beam but his head's still back in Mousehole. Because what Wilson told him has blown his mind.

He said he had a daughter, just about the same age as Trip. But that being a dad – any kind of dad, no matter how remote – wasn't for him. Just as Wilson was explaining all this to Trip, his phone rang and it was Ally Bright, one of the Shell House Detectives. She told him that the cat was out of the bag: Saffron Weeks now knew who Wilson Rowe was. Wilson hung up, blinking.

What would a superstitious man make of timing like that?

'What now?' Trip asked, watching him carefully. This man who never let anyone know how he was feeling; who'd slipped and gone down that night on the deck, and then said, *I might need a hand up*, even though the agony must have been a knockout, and he fainted soon after.

'She knows,' Wilson said again. And there was a light in his eyes that Trip hadn't seen before. Wilson Rowe was shining like a lighthouse.

'But Dawn. I don't want to hurt her. Dawn counts on me.'

'And I reckon you can count on her. She's made of stern stuff, your Dawn. Plus, anyway . . .'

'Plus, anyway what?'

'Dawn loves you, doesn't she.'

That's why Trip's here, on this mission. Driving out to Porthpella to knock on Saffron's door before it gets much past six o'clock.

It was his idea to do it.

'And say what to the girl exactly?' Wilson said in response.

Trip rubbed his hands together; knitted his thoughts. He's never been all that with words.

'I'll say to her . . . that he's a good man, this Wilson Rowe. And that it's not like him, to switch in the wind and go changing his mind. That Wilson means it when he says it this time: if you want to know him, Saffron, then he wants to know you.'

Wilson looked at him long and hard. Then said, 'That sounds alright, that does. Wouldn't it be better coming from those detectives though? I don't want it to be too much, you turning up at her door.'

'They wouldn't say it like I'd say it. They don't know you.'

And that was enough.

As Trip was heading out the door Wilson caught his sleeve. He gave him a half-hug, a sort of knocking of chests.

'Good lad.' Then, with an uneasy smile, 'I'll tackle it with Dawn when you're back. I'm thinking . . . can you add that it would be an honour? The honour of my life. If she wants to know me. Something like that.'

Now, Trip thinks back on this moment. He won't be saying it to Saffron, it wouldn't be right, but the truth is Wilson has been as good as a dad to him. As good as a dad – and a good dad at that. Trip puts his foot down for the hill, a satisfied smile spreading across his face. He has no doubt that Wilson will be the same kind of good for this girl Saffron too. Better, even, because he'll be making up for lost time.

Deep in this reverie, the other vehicle comes out of nowhere.

It's on top of Trip before he can do anything about it. Blinding headlights, smashing metal. Then silence.

62

Jayden closes his eyes then opens them again; he doesn't know which is worse. Pressing his back hard against the cliff, he curls his fingers around tufts of vegetation. Far below him the sea roars and lunges. Spray explodes over the rocks, a twilight firework display that at a distance he'd admire but here it punches the air from him, making fear lodge in its place. The wind wants a piece of him too, clawing at his coat.

He struggles to get his breath.

Part of Jayden is full of relief. This was, after all, the plan. If you could call it that, anyway. A plan made in the white-hot fear of a moment – the image of a ledge, a swift gauge of where it was positioned, then a leap of faith.

And he's nailed it.

He's not smashed on the rocks below or dragged by the waves to certain death. He's safe. Ish. Jayden feels his face splitting into a grin, but then he shudders with a sob that he didn't even know he was holding on to. Because what wasn't part of the plan was his phone slipping from his fingers as he fell.

His only way of getting help is gone.

Jayden wipes his face with his hand and tastes salt: the wind's hurling in straight off the sea. The rain is half sea water. He wracks his brain: did he tell Ally he was at The Drop? Their phone call is scrambled in his mind. His brain's crowded with sounds and pictures: headlights rearing up at him, the roar of an engine filling his ears. The one thing he does know is that he yelled the name *Dominic*. He hurled it, a desperate throw from the outfield, and he knows Ally will have caught it.

Because they're partners.

This thought is like an energy shot. He carefully twists, trying to work out how high he has to climb. If his body – sore from the fall – is even capable of it. From the clifftop the ledge looked close enough; he'd seen it enough times in daylight and wouldn't have attempted the jump otherwise. Though, to be fair, what other choice was there? But now that he's on the ledge, it's a different thing. His hand runs over the cliffside, and there's nothing to get hold of. His fingers fasten on a stone, but it comes away in his hand and soil rains down into his face. He clamps his eyes shut. For a moment the ground beneath his feet appears to tilt. He sinks to his knees, scrabbling for anything solid. When he eventually steadies his breathing, he realises nothing has slipped. The ledge is still the ledge.

He's safe.

But he's screwed.

He can't risk trying to climb up. His only option is to last out the night and by daylight reassess the situation; see if he can see anything close to a handhold or foothold, or even try to edge sideways and down. But for now, the smart play is to stay put, his back pressed against the cliff. And try not to panic. The silver lining is that there's all the time in the world to think about why Dominic Brook wanted to kill him, right? And what it has to do with Anna Collins and JP Sharpe. *Keep busy.* Meanwhile, Jayden just has to hope the weather gets no worse. He'll tough out anything, but if the wind gets up or the rain pools on the ledge and destabilises it, he's done for.

But it won't come to that.

Why won't it though? snaps the voice in his head. Because bad things happen to good people every split second of every day. Why should he be any kind of an exception?

But the one thing Jayden does know for sure is that if it comes to it, he'll fight. He'll fight all the way down. And with that thought he lets out a roar of such defiance that for a second even the wind seems to drop back. So, he yells again. And again.

63

Ally slams the door of The Shell House and runs down the steps, Fox at her heels. He thinks it's a game and twists between her legs yapping. She stumbles, and snaps at him.

Ally never snaps at Fox.

Once inside her car she guns the engine and blasts down the track, headlights bouncing over the dunes. With one hand on the wheel she tries calling Jayden again, but it just rings and rings. Meanwhile her mind fills in possibilities.

As soon as she lost contact with Jayden, she called 999.

'I think my friend might be in danger,' she said, her voice uneven. 'He was waiting to meet Dominic Brook, the sous-chef at Mermaid's Rest. We were on the phone and Jayden said there was a lunatic in a car. I think he said it was Dominic. I heard the engine, then I heard Jayden scream, then nothing. And now he's not picking up.'

She gave the location and then she hung up. What was she supposed to do next?

Grab her keys and run to the car, that's what. Because they were partners. And if anything had happened at The Drop, she could get there quicker than the police.

Ally passes the dark hulk of the empty Sea Dream and then Gus's house, where the windows glimmer with light. She briefly considers asking him to come too, but she can't waste a moment.

Ally knows just what an excellent officer Jayden must have been back in Leeds too. He has the physical ability, as well as the mental; in the spring, Jayden not only prevented another murder and apprehended the killer, he put the whole case together too. But she worries sometimes, that he forgets he's not part of something bigger: that his automatic backup isn't a fleet of panda cars and trained officers but a pensioner in a dune house. Not that Ally thinks of herself like that, but it's only natural that he must from time to time.

As her phone starts ringing her heart leaps, but then it drops again as she sees it's Skinner.

'What's this about you and Jayden getting mixed up in the Sharpe case?' His voice is all anger. She can hear fast footsteps in the background, the slamming of a car door.

'Please tell me someone's on their way to The Drop,' she says, ignoring his question.

'We've had a confession,' he says, ignoring her right back. 'So Dominic Brook being any kind of a suspect is tommyrot.'

'A confession? From who?' But then Ally refocuses. If Skinner had heard the way Jayden yelled Dominic's name down the phone, he wouldn't be taking it so lightly. 'Jayden thinks he's got something—'

'Meanwhile someone's called in an accident on the road down to Porthpella,' cuts in Skinner. 'It's blocked the lane. Mullins is on the way there now. Which means I'm going the long way round.'

And she's already thinking, *What if it's Jayden?* Instead she says, 'You're on your way to The Drop?'

Skinner grunts. But a detective who's just closed a murder case doesn't return a 999. He must think there's something in it.

'I'll get there first,' she says.

'You stay away, Ally. I mean it.'

She stops talking and concentrates hard as she swings into the tiny lane, one that climbs and climbs, vegetation scraping the sides of the car. *Please can I not meet anything coming in the other direction.*

She thinks of how Evie broke her arm when she was ten, and as they drove her to the hospital Bill had to reverse five times back down the lane, all the while Evie whimpering in the back. *Where are the blues and twos when you need them, eh?* Bill laughed then. And, miraculously, Evie laughed too. Ally just folded her arm around her little girl, anxiety climbing in her chest.

She feels it again now. That crackle of worry.

She knows something's happened. Jayden wouldn't scream like that otherwise. And he wouldn't not answer his phone.

Skinner's ended the call. Well, what more was there to say? She puts her foot down. As the car spins to the junction and joins the slightly wider road, her lights dance over the space up ahead: The Drop. Beyond, the lane ahead carries on, eventually winding back down to Porthpella.

Is this the site of the traffic accident that Mullins is on his way to? In this wild, remote corner of the world, could there be two incidents, one on top of the other? Or is it one and the same, and Jayden is in the crash?

Ally pulls in – and straight away sees Jayden's parked car. Is that a good sign or a bad sign? She climbs out, Fox protesting it.

'It's okay,' she says, over his whine. 'I'll be back.'

Outside she staggers, throwing out her arms for balance. The wind is tearing up and over the cliff, and it catches her, pushing her forward. She plants her feet heavily, takes a few paces, shining her torch over the empty car. When she tries the door, it's unlocked.

Ally walks on further and, bending closer, sees distinct tyre marks.

Then she casts her torch beam in the other direction and kneels down. She sees footprints; scuffed stones.

'Jayden!' she shouts.

But the gusting wind takes her voice and rips it to pieces. She yells again. Then, with her hand cocked to her ear, she hears something.

Not the sea booming against the cliff. Not the whistle of the wind. Something else.

Adrenalin rockets through her.

Ally moves to the cliff edge, as near as she dares. The grass is wet and slippery, and she lowers herself to her knees with care. Wind catches her hood and yanks it halfway across her face, and the temporary disorientation sends fear blasting in.

'Jayden!' she yells again. 'Jayden!'

'Al!'

Tears jump to her eyes. 'Jayden!'

She leans closer to the edge. Her torchlight picks out rock, clumped grasses.

'Where are you?' she cries. And it feels like they're hurtling through space, and she's yelling into the abyss. What reply can she expect out of nothingness?

But it comes. A hoarse sound – something like a cry too, or a laugh, or both.

Her heart is hammering so fast now, her breath so uneven, that she thinks of Bill. How can she not? She always will. But this moment isn't death. This is life. This is Jayden.

'I'm here!'

Her cheeks are wet with tears as she crawls along the cliff edge, her hands steadying her way, her torch gripped between finger and thumb.

'I'm coming,' she says. 'I don't know where you are, but I'm coming.'

And then she sees him. Ten, twelve feet down. Her torch picks out first the green of his parka, the blue of his jeans. Then his upturned face. His unlikely smile.

Ally thinks she's never been so happy to see anyone.

But his perilous position quells her joy. He's on a jutting section of cliff, a natural platform that's probably as wide and long as The Shell House veranda but, with the drop on three sides, appears to Ally to be as thin as a pencil.

'I did try climbing up,' says Jayden, 'but it's hella slippery. Thought I'd best stay put.'

She sees him exhale then and press his hand to his chest. Her torchlight picks out his wet cheeks. He's sitting with his back against the cliff, his hands holding on to rocks on either side. If he extended his legs out, his feet would be over the edge.

Ally stretches out her hand to him. She knows she can't reach him, but she wants him to know that she's there.

'I'll call the coastguard,' she says. 'They'll bring you up. Jayden, you're safe. Just don't move. Don't move a muscle.'

'I'm going nowhere, Al.'

He wipes his face on the sleeve of his coat, and then he tells Ally what happened. That, faced with no choice, he made a calculation in the heat of the moment: one that was no less accurate for being panicked.

'I've seen it before. This ledge. I've parked up here loads with Jazzy as she's napping – time to kill, you know? I noticed it.'

He says he knew that if he went over the edge at this exact point, if he didn't leap too far back – or catch an unlucky gust – he'd land on it. *The ledge of dreams.* And that Dominic would presume he'd fallen.

And that's exactly what happened.

Ally doesn't realise she's been holding her breath. 'But, Jayden, a step or two in either direction . . . Or if you'd landed and then rolled . . .'

She can't even finish the sentence.

'I know. Fortune favours the . . . desperate. This time, anyway.'

They hold each other's eye, and it's as if there's a length of rope stretched between them, each of them hanging on tight.

'Get your phone out, Al. But, before you call the coastguard, call the police. Dominic Brook tried to kill me. And I think it's because I made the Anna Collins connection. She used to work with Dominic and JP Sharpe back in London, and I saw her in Mousehole the day before Sharpe was killed.'

'Skinner's already on his way. He says someone's confessed to Sharpe's murder.'

'Someone's confessed? Who? It's not Anna Collins, is it?'

'I don't know. Skinner didn't sound all that jubilant about it.'

'So, why's he on his way then? He could have sent anyone.'

'There's been a crash on the road from here to Porthpella, and Mullins is at the scene. You don't think it could be . . . ?'

'Brook. Could be. He left me for dead, and the way he roared away . . .'

Ally sees Jayden shiver and wrap his arms around his knees. She knows that once the adrenalin fades, he'll realise the immensity of what has happened. They both will.

'Jayden, I've a blanket in the car, let me throw it down to you.'

'Please call Mullins, Al. Call him direct. Ask if it's Dominic Brook in the crash.' Jayden's voice is steel. 'And if it is, make sure he cuffs Brook. No matter what state he's in.'

64

When Dominic first opens his eyes, he doesn't know where he is. The pain in his head is both dull and searing, a thump and a knife stroke, and it runs down his neck and shoulders, and doesn't stop there. He hears a bovine-like moan, then realises it's coming from his own mouth.

He lifts his head, blinking into the dark. It takes several beats for him to compute that the thing he's slumped into is an airbag. He's in a car. A crashed car.

How am I in a crashed car?

A seed of panic sprouts inside him. Somewhere, Dominic can hear a voice. It sounds very far away. Surely it's not him again, crying out? When he closes his eyes, he sees shifting constellations but it's like a bad trip, because of the pain – there's so much pain – so he tries to keep them open. His vision tips and blurs.

'Hell's coming.'

And that low moan of his becomes a shout. *Hell's coming?* No. He doesn't want to die. Dominic starts to struggle, realising he's pinned, that something's trapping him in place. The door is open beside him, and the cold air that rolls in makes him shudder.

The voice comes again and this time he hears it differently.

'Help's coming.'

Help. He starts to try and move, to fight past the airbag, shift his legs. If he can only get out of this car then he has the idea that he will be free.

He unclicks the seat belt with a cry of triumph.

To be free feels very important. Like, the most important thing. Not just away from this cramped, dark, pained space, but *away* away. Dominic doesn't know why it matters so much – there's something right at the back of his head, a thought, and he can't quite reach it. But he does know he's got to go.

He sees JP's face then, looming up in front of him, but he trusts himself enough to know it's his mind playing tricks. Because JP went down so easily that night by the harbour. One hard strike was all it took. The others were just because once he'd started, it was hard to stop. JP went down so easily that Dominic didn't even have a chance to say his piece. And he did have a piece – a very important one – even if, now, he can't catch hold of it. It was about love and betrayal and JP taking something that was Dominic's. That's what it was.

There are blue lights filling the car now, other vehicles pushing closer.

'Help's here,' he hears.

But it's not. He knows that. Even through the fog of pain he knows that help is not here. In fact, it's the opposite of that.

But how can anyone know? That Shell House guy is dead. Run off the cliff, smashed on the rocks or taken by the tide. Whichever, Dominic doesn't care; he knew too much.

Dominic hauls himself up out of the car and this other man puts out a hand to stop him, so he tries to bat it away. He takes two steps and staggers. The man's there again, trying to catch him, and so Dominic swings at him, his loosely balled fist scuffing his shoulder. The move sends Dominic off balance and he has to fight to stay up.

'Easy there,' the man's saying. 'You take it easy, okay?'

Dominic bares his teeth, stamps through the pain and hurls himself at this man, this wall, this *thing* that's in his way.

'Oh no you don't,' the man says, his body hardly shifting. 'You're not going anywhere.'

And Dominic feels a strong grip on his wrists, so he hisses, like an alley cat, kicks out. 'Get off me.'

'You're injured. You need to wait here, mate. Get it together, okay?'

'I said get your hands off me or I'll . . .'

What? What will Dominic do? Nothing he hasn't done before. Twice now. And it's all for Lena. He feels a surge of energy: a murderous charge. He burns with it. But the man only holds him tighter.

'I said you're going nowhere, mate. You were driving like a madman. As good as totalled my truck – could have killed me, or yourself, or both. Call it a citizen's arrest, alright? Plus, you need to be seen by someone. You're concussed, you are.'

Then there's a noise in the lane, louder than the roaring in Dominic's ears, and suddenly blue lights are dancing all over them. As Dominic struggles in this man's hands – his stupidly strong hands – he can see a police officer coming towards him. He can see the hi-vis coat, the stripes, the weird light cast in front of him. Dominic feels a rush of nausea.

He has to get away.

The officer's torch beam catches Dominic full in the face. He can feel his knees buckle. The only reason he doesn't fall smack down on the hard road is because he's still being held upright. His fight ebbs.

'Dominic Brook,' the officer says. 'We've been looking for you.'

65

Mullins sits in the back of the ambulance as it swings down and round the lanes. He is aware that this is a Big Deal. He's belted in, but ready to spring into action if he's needed. When Skinner didn't pick up his phone, Mullins left word with one of the Newquay lot back at the station, but right now, it's still just him. Mullins. Handling this one all by himself.

Well, alright, with a little bit of help from the fisherman Trip Stephens. *Citizen's arrest* he called it, as Mullins got on the scene. But Mullins was the one to turn it into an actual arrest. No doubt about that.

Dominic Brook grunts and groans.

'You alright there?' Mullins asks.

But Dominic just shakes his head and closes his eyes again.

Mullins keeps watching him, feeling glad of the proximity of the paramedics. Brook looks green about the gills, and he's tilting and leaning with every movement of the vehicle. Right now, Dominic looks more pathetic than dangerous.

Mullins checks his phone again. Skinner's going to have questions for him. In fact, there are a hell of a lot of questions swirling around in the air, full stop. And very few answers being netted.

One question is why did Dominic look at that team photograph and lie, saying that the long-haired blond girl was called Anna Collins instead of Lena Prior? Ally said they reckon it was deliberate, to throw everyone off the scent, because Jayden told Dominic he'd seen the woman in Mousehole.

Anna Collins obviously wasn't on their list of suspects. But more to the point, nor was Lena Prior. Lena Prior wasn't even on their radar. But she flipping would be now. Because as soon as the report of the traffic incident came in and Mullins was despatched – shrugging on his coat, chucking back the last of his coffee – he gave Skinner the name as he passed his desk.

What do I want with a Lena Prior? his boss scoffed, still annoyed about Phil Butt's false confession. But Skinner wrote it down anyway. Probably because DS Chang was watching. Maybe they've even followed up on her by now.

Mullins checks his phone again. Has he ever before, in his whole life, wanted Skinner to call him? Not likely.

Even Jayden didn't know about Anna actually being Lena, until Mullins told Ally on the phone.

'Arrest him,' Ally said.

'For dangerous driving?' he asked.

To which she replied, 'For attempted murder.'

At that point Jayden was still clinging to the cliff-face, the prat. Lucky prat, at that. Coastguard wouldn't hang around in getting him to safety. And it was proof in itself, wasn't it? If Dominic was prepared to kill Jayden for asking about a girl in a photograph, then he must be hiding something pretty big. Or the two of them together were: Bonnie and Clyde. Dominic and Anna. *Lena.* Dominic and Lena.

For a moment Mullins imagines that the back of the ambulance is an interview room. Tape recorder running. Shiny-suited solicitor. *Officer present, PC Tim Mullins.* What if he cracked the case before they even made it to the hospital?

Tell me about Lena Prior.

That's how he'd start things. In that fake-casual way that detectives have.

Or, *Why did you bloody try to run my mate Jayden off a cliff?*

And it's as if Dominic is reading his thoughts, because he suddenly looks up, and stares straight at Mullins with a pretty murderous expression on his face. Or maybe just an angry sort of look. A *loaded* look, anyway.

'She wanted to get back with me.'

'Who?' says Mullins.

'Course she did. Otherwise why would she have come?'

Mullins nods as if in agreement. He's not really sure what the right move is here. Suspects aren't supposed to just start talking at you, are they?

'I said I'd be all the dad that kid of hers needed. I'd do that for her, despite everything. But she was scared he was going to want to be involved. And there was no way she wanted that.'

Mullins can feel his brow knotting. With Dominic talking about being a dad he can't stop thinking of Saffron, but that can't be right, can it? This guy is way too young to be Saffron's dad. Mullins scratches the back of his head, figures the guy's age and does the count. Brook would have been a teenager. Well, it did happen. Not that Mullins was getting a sniff of anything back when he was in his school uniform. The situation hasn't massively improved in this uniform either, to be honest.

He focuses back in on Dominic.

'Who are you talking about?' he says.

'JP betrayed me. He knew Lena was mine.' And he sends Mullins a look of appeal: man to man – or something.

Mullins nods as if he knows exactly what he's talking about.

'He had to pay for that. And I had to get him out of Lena and the baby's lives too.'

Oh my God, thinks Mullins, with an internal squeak, *has he literally just confessed to murder? And I've got nothing to show for it.* Actually, he can't swear that the squeak wasn't audible.

'Two birds, one stone,' says Brook.

Was that one stone then lobbed over the harbour wall, washed clean, shunted up on to the beach with all the rest? A murder weapon hiding in plain sight.

Dominic's head drops. 'I'm saying nothing else.'

Mullins's phone bleats in his pocket then and, with some difficulty, he yanks it out. It's Skinner.

'Sarge?' he says. And he's full of relief. Sort of. He still thinks he might get in trouble for all this. But he's been following procedure, hasn't he? It isn't his fault that the suspect started talking all on his own. Stones and birds and such.

'What's this I hear about you arresting Dominic Brook?'

It's a bad line, and it's difficult to hear Skinner. He sounds like he's standing out on a clifftop, not tucked up in the station with a cup of tea and a scowl for company.

'I'm in the ambulance with him,' says Mullins. 'He's concussed, rambling on a bit. What happened was—'

'And I'm with the Shell House Detectives, as they like to call themselves. One of them nearly got himself killed tonight. Says it was Dominic Brook.'

'That's right,' says Mullins. 'Mrs Bright called me just as I was getting to the crash site.'

And Mullins feels on safe ground here. Skinner makes some sort of noise, but it's lost in the wind.

'That name you gave me as you were headed out the door. Lena Prior, was it?'

Mullins stiffens. Heat floods his cheeks as he realises what he's done. He told Ally about what happened when he traced Anna Collins and this Anna confirmed the real identity of the woman in the photograph. He should never have passed this detail of the case on to members of the public – even if it was Ally. And now she's comparing notes with Skinner. Mullins winces, waiting for the reprimand.

'How's your poker face, PC Mullins? You'd best slap it on now. Because apparently someone called Lena Prior just called in, in a bit of a lather, saying she's got a pretty good idea of who killed JP Sharpe. And it just happens to be the bloke you've currently got in handcuffs.'

Mullins's mouth drops. *Easy as that!* So much for his poker face. His eyes go to Dominic. Dominic, who still has his head sunk in his hands, luckily.

'You check you put those cuffs on nice and tight,' says Skinner. 'And meanwhile I'm sending backup to meet you at the hospital. Don't say anything to him.'

'No sir.'

But what if he's already started talking to me?

Then Mullins twigs. When he arrested Dominic, the guy was still reeling from the crash. Maybe he didn't hear the caution properly. Maybe he heard *attempted murder* as *murder*. Maybe Dominic thought they already knew whatever there was to know about JP Sharpe, and Lena, and whoever the hell else was involved in this case.

Skinner says something that he doesn't quite catch. The wind again.

'What's that?'

'I said good job, son.'

Then his boss delivers a set of barking instructions – back to business as usual – and rings off.

Good job, son, though.

For just a second, Mullins is all lit up like a Christmas tree.

66

Lena is curled on the sofa, her hands resting on the small dome of her stomach. Her mobile – the one she called the police on – lies face down on the carpet. Beyond her window the lights of South London shimmer through the rain.

'I've done the right thing, haven't I?' she says. But the baby's too small to kick yet, so she gets no sign in reply.

A tear rolls down her cheek. Just one. And who is it for, exactly? It could be for any one of them in this sorry story.

It could be for her baby, who will grow up with either a terrible truth – that their father was murdered – or a well-meaning lie; a piece of their history missing altogether. A less tragic truth is that that same father was also capable of being an utter arsehole and Lena should never have slept with him in the first place, but everyone makes mistakes, don't they?

Did Dominic Brook make a mistake? You could never call it that. Because if it was true, if Dominic did kill JP – and who else would have, all the way out west in a tiny little village called Mousehole? – there would have been nothing mistaken, nothing accidental, about it. Lena saw it in his eyes when she told Dominic about the one-night stand: pure intent. She just didn't know what it meant at the time.

It was a late summer's night when she and JP had ended up in bed. Lena and Dominic were already broken up and he was in

Cornwall, but JP was back in town for a couple of nights and the cocktails were slipping down easily. One thing led to another. Of course, she didn't go into all of that with Dominic, but she had to remember it for herself, to track it back. She hadn't even fancied JP. But she'd liked the feeling of how much he wanted her. That night, it was that simple.

'Whether you're a boy or a girl,' she says now, her hand on her bump, 'be better than your mum. Always think about the consequences.'

Consequences. But how could she have imagined this? Talking to a detective in a Cornish town, telling him that her ex-boyfriend killed her one-time lover – and that he almost certainly did it for her. Lena made a point of saying to Dominic that she didn't want JP having any claim on her or the child – mostly because she thought it made the whole thing more palatable for Dominic. She knew it was a fine line; yes, they'd been broken up, but only just. And Dominic liked it, she could tell, this talk of hers: *I don't want him in this baby's life.* And the stupidest thing of all? It probably wasn't even true. She wouldn't have kept JP Sharpe from his child, not if he wanted to be involved. So maybe that one tear of hers is for JP. Not only because he's dead, but because he never knew he had a child coming into the world. He never had the chance to show the kind of man he could, perhaps, be.

Consequences. One night that meant nothing at all has led to a tiny person growing inside Lena – a person who already means everything.

Maybe the tear is for Dominic. Her stupid – but not evil? Surely not evil – ex-boyfriend. The same man who took her for a walk on the South Bank on their first date and bought her a bag of churros and chocolate sauce. Who had a mum he didn't speak to, a long-dead dad, and said that of all the things about cheffing it was making soup that he liked best. She thought that cute once:

her soup-making boyfriend. Despite the way she's thinking about him now – the sick feeling that keeps rising in her stomach – she knows that for the five or six months that they dated, things were okay. Never good enough to make her think they'd go the distance though, no matter what Dominic thought. The truth is, Dominic was possessive, all green-eyed and hackles rising when other men paid her attention. He'd try to come off all macho but then around JP he was like a whipped dog. He'd always idolised JP, a bromance that anyone could see was one-sided. Lena explained these things away to start with: so Dominic was a little insecure? Well, who wasn't? But over time she found herself losing her patience with it. And when Dominic got the job with JP down in Cornwall, it was a good time to cut and run. But even as she was breaking up with him, she wasn't sure it was properly sinking in. Because that was another thing about Dominic. She doesn't want to use the word *deluded* – not in, like, a clinical sense – but he sees the world through his own blinkered eyes, that's for sure.

Why did you choose to tell Dominic about the baby? That was one of the questions the officer asked on the phone.

And it felt like salt in the wound, because it would have been so much easier to stay quiet. The truth is, she was trying to do the right thing: because of the months they'd had together, and Dominic being basically an okay guy. But what a stupid thought that is now. And, selfishly, she fancied a dose of sea air. People said it cleared the head and focused the mind. She'd never been to Cornwall before, and Lena can safely say she won't be going back now. Apart from a court appearance, maybe. She doesn't know how these things work.

She closes her eyes. Does she have any doubt that he did it? While she has no evidence, with Dominic she's given the police a motive that they didn't know existed. And deep down, she knows.

Regret pulses like a headache. She should have kept her baby a secret: the truth of the pregnancy hers and hers alone. That single tear is joined by another, and another.

Why didn't you come forward sooner? the police asked. So, she told them.

Once Dominic had absorbed her news, he went very quiet and stayed that way. Lena left early and he insisted on seeing her to the station, giving her this suffocating hug. He said he knew she had a lot of thinking to do and he'd give her the space to do it. She thought it was weird at the time, like he was reading something different into the situation. Dominic surely didn't think she wanted to get back with him? On the train home, she turned off her phone. She didn't want to deal with a string of messages. But soon enough she had a whole other worry filling her mind, as when she went to the toilet on the train, she looked down and saw blood in her pants.

Fear gripped her all the way back to Paddington. She couldn't lose it. Because that's the one thing Lena's known all along: she wants this baby.

She went in for a scan as soon as she could. A darkened room, cold gel streaking her stomach. The kindness of the nurse – *don't worry, sweetheart, relax*. And how it seemed like forever before the nurse spoke again, Lena filling that space with alternating thoughts: *it's OK, it's not OK, it's OK, it's not OK.* She held her breath. Closed her eyes.

'It's OK. Look, there's your baby.'

And her tears flowed then; big drenching sobs.

The scan at fifteen weeks showed just the same as it had at twelve: a blurry miracle with a domed head, a prominent foot and a beating heart.

Walking back out of the hospital, her coat buttoned tight against her stomach, Lena felt like she'd been given a second chance. She vowed that from here on in, she'd do nothing but the best by her baby.

So maybe these tears are for herself. Because for that short-lived moment, Lena was stupid enough to be happy. Relieved, too, that the only message from Dominic since her visit was a heart-filled emoji one: emojis were easier to ignore than actual words. But then she saw the news on the television, and the shock of it was a sucker-punch. She doubled over, her hands going to her stomach.

JP was dead.

She could literally feel the stress vibrating through her body. She was scared, so scared, for her baby. Surely Dominic wasn't capable of murder? Sharpe's little shadow, an okay-enough boyfriend for a bit but, really, a killer? She tried to push it from her mind, to think instead of her breathing, playing music to this hardly-there bump, eating all the vegetables, even the ones she didn't like. But after waking again in the middle of the night, barely able to catch her breath, Lena knew she had to do the right thing. To face her fear and call the police.

Lena wipes her sleeve across her eyes. Then she tugs her blanket closer and starts to softly sing a lullaby for her baby. She sings it again. And again. She'll go out and get a Christmas tree tomorrow. Just a small one, but a real one, her first ever. She'll string it with lights and put a star on top; cross her fingers. Lena will think good thoughts, despite all the reasons not to. And she'll try to forget about Cornwall.

67

Phil stands outside the police station, zipping his coat all the way to his chin. He'd take it up over his head if he could. It's bitter out, *and it's just as bitter inside as well*, he thinks.

Because, what now?

His phone call with Melissa did not go well. Numerous variations on *You did what, Phil?* Some part of him still wonders how she would have reacted if he really had killed JP Sharpe. How could saying you'd done something be considered worse than actually having done it?

As Phil filled out yet another round of forms – turns out false confessions were quite admin-heavy – there was a bit of excitement in the background. Someone else was charged with JP's murder. Phil wonders dimly who and why, but in truth, he doesn't have enough left in him to care.

Now, he hears the door go behind him and out steps DS Skinner, a cigarette between his lips.

'You're still here?' Skinner says. 'You should have been gone hours ago.'

Phil doesn't need another verbal kicking, that's for sure. *I should do you for timewasting. Serious charge, that. If you're so desperate to get yourself a record.* And that look of disdain; like Phil was something Skinner was trying to wipe off the bottom of his shoe.

'I'm going,' he says.

But where? Where exactly is he going? Back to the hotel, to sit in that tatty, beige room to wait to hear what management have in store for him – if they've anything at all.

He flicks a look at the detective sergeant, with his big shoulders and square jaw and the kind of hair that people call salt and pepper, never just grey. His natural air of authority. It felt so good, temporarily getting this man's attention, his approving nod as Phil started to talk. The fact is, some people just take up more space than others; some people deserve more space. Just like some people are destined to be happy, and others are not. Phil sees the glint of a wedding band as Skinner sparks up. *Of course.*

Phil shivers, feeling cold to the bone. 'I'm going,' he says again.

Skinner's looking at him carefully. 'Don't go doing anything stupid. Anything *more* stupid, I should say.'

Phil shifts from foot to foot. Was this cop a mind reader? It isn't like Phil is thinking of pills, or belt straps, or all that black sea. He wouldn't go that far. But, if he's honest, he doesn't feel a lot like living right now. It's all a bit bloody bleak, isn't it? And there are other ways to shut it all out. A bottle of cheap whisky would be a start. Not gin, mind. Never again gin.

'We got our man, by the way,' says Skinner. 'Dominic Brook, if you're interested.'

Phil just nods dimly. Drops his head. So much for Dominic and JP being mates. You couldn't trust anyone, could you?

Skinner blows out smoke. 'Look, do you want to talk to someone? I've got a card somewhere. I can make a call.'

'Talk?'

He's done enough talking, hasn't he? Far too much. *Stupid, stupid Phil.*

'Get yourself some support. It's not easy sometimes,' says Skinner. 'Not easy a lot of the time, for a lot of people. And this time of year, too . . .'

There's no sign of Christmas from where they're standing. But go around the corner, Phil knows he'll be met with the full blaze of it: shiny lights a-go-go. All that brightness. If you're not feeling it, it only makes the dark darker.

Phil thinks again of that little room that's waiting for him, with the sticky TV remote and the curling lino on the bathroom floor. And he wonders what the hell he's going to do.

Melissa is never coming back – he knows this now. And his eyes prick with the hurt of it.

'My wife left a year ago,' says Skinner. 'It's no picnic, having the rug pulled from under you like that.'

Phil blinks. He glances again at Skinner's wedding band.

'You find your way back though,' the sergeant goes on. 'In the end. Maybe you even change things up a little. It's yoga for me now.'

'Yoga?'

'For pity's sake don't tell anyone round here. Look, I'll get that number. Don't go anywhere.'

He squints at Phil then, and it's in quite a kindly way, all things considered. Phil's throat burns; his eyes ache with not crying.

'In fact,' says Skinner, 'do you want to come back in. Wait inside?'

So, Phil goes back inside the police station. Skinner's hand on his back briefly guides him. A bit like you might guide a small child, or a very old and helpless man.

'Wait,' Phil says, 'it's not a yoga number, is it? Because that's not . . .'

He didn't mean it as a joke but Skinner laughs, a proper booming wash of good humour. And Phil can't help joining in. Just a little bit. But even that much surprises him.

68

Jazzy is asleep in bed. For once, she's gone off easy, and Cat was full of this win when Jayden got home. When he came into the sitting room, with his scraped cheek and wet clothes, she didn't look shocked exactly, she just did a double take and said, *You okay, Jay?* So, he told her the full story, which added up to yes, he was okay now. Although it turns out Cat has kind of a different definition of the word.

Leap of faith, he said with a grin.

But then he started crying, and as they held each other, it all came rushing back to him. The Drop. The ledge. How it went one way, but it could have gone another. How Dominic had left him for dead. But then Ally came. What if he hadn't left her that voicemail? What if, when she phoned back, they'd carried on their argument on the phone? Or what if she'd been so fed up with Jayden for telling Saffron that she hadn't called him back at all?

But Jayden did phone her. And she had phoned him back. And they had both said they were sorry, both of them reaching out in the dark. And even though he can't remember saying it, he told her that he was at The Drop. So, it wasn't the coastguard that saved his life, hauling him back to safe ground. It wasn't even the ledge that caught and held him. It was telling Ally where he was – and all that that meant.

Cat squeezes his hand. They're lying on the sofa now, side by side, feet twined. It's way past their bedtime. Cat brushes the pad of her thumb against his palm. She's doing her 'angry but loving' face. It's one that he thinks might be unique to her – or, more accurately, unique to him and her.

'You and Ally,' she says, 'you get yourselves into things. Way over your heads. Ally should—'

'You know it wasn't like that.'

'I know.' Cat breathes deeply. 'But still.'

'Yeah,' says Jayden, with a grin, 'good idea, let's just be still.'

And he closes his eyes. As tiredness washes over him, the facts flow in.

Dominic Brook will be charged with attempted murder, as well as the murder of JP Sharpe. Because the woman Jayden saw in Mousehole – whose actual name is Lena Prior – phoned in of her own accord. *Finally got around to it,* Skinner said. And the story she told made Brook look like a shoo-in in the guilty stakes. Plus, according to Mullins, Dominic as good as confessed it in the ambulance.

If Jayden had suspected Dominic for a second, he never would have agreed to meet him on his own, in that lonely spot. He said this to Ally, and to Cat too. Was it a hundred per cent the truth, though? Because he also knows that he really, really wanted to help solve this case. Sometimes you have to calculate the risk and take it anyway.

Earlier he messaged Saffron to tell her that the arrest had been made, but of course she already knew. Mullins beat them to it. Well, fair enough, he was the one to catch Brook. With a bit of help from Trip Stephens – which had a kind of poetic justice to it. Saffron said she'd sleep easy now – and that she really was okay about the 'dad thing'. Jayden doesn't know how true that is, but he can hope.

'Hey, I spoke to Old Fran today,' says Cat. 'She said they're going to Bernard's sister in Brittany in a few weeks, and did we want to house-sit? Well, parrot-sit, I guess. But it'd be fun to be in Mousehole, wouldn't it? Jazz would love it.'

'Jazz would love it,' he agreed. 'And maybe it'd be good for us, to have a change of scene.'

Cat snorted. 'Yeah, because it'd be such a change of scene. Maybe we should gatecrash their Brittany trip. Leave Jazz to stay in Cornwall and look after the pet.'

He laughs. Then, without even thinking, he's saying it – and trying to sound all even and fine. 'Hey, I meant to mention, I saw you in Penzance the other day.'

Cat wrinkles her nose. 'Did you?'

'You, Jazzy, and some guy. On Chapel Street.'

She gives him a look. 'Jay, what is this, a surveillance operation?'

'I thought it was weird, that's all. That you didn't say.'

Cat lets go of his hand. She pulls her hair out of its band and reties it.

'Cat?'

'That was Matt.'

'And who's Matt?'

Jayden's trying very hard to keep his voice cool, casual. *Perspective! You fell off a cliff tonight, right?*

'We went to school together. Years ago. I mean, obviously it was years ago. It was school.' She gives a little self-conscious laugh. 'We ran into each other and thought we'd grab a coffee.' Then, 'He's a nice guy. A personal trainer now.'

'A personal trainer?'

'Jay, don't look like that. I've actually been thinking I want to do something since Jazzy, do something for me. A personal trainer could be just what I need.'

'You're in great shape.'

'Yeah?' She shakes her head. 'Look, it's not even about that. It's how I feel. So, we swapped numbers. I'm going to book a session with him in the new year.'

'Cool.'

'Cool.'

So why doesn't it feel even slightly cool?

'I just wish you'd told me. You looked pretty matey. That's all.'

'Because he's my mate. Or was. Will be again, I hope. Oh Jay, come on, don't look like that.'

Jayden chews his lip.

'I'll get him over here, okay? We can have some drinks. Well, probably not drinks, he's very . . . well, it's probably all smoothies and vitamin shakes. You'll like him though, I promise.'

Jayden nods. He tries not to make it sound mechanical when he says, 'If you do, I'm sure I will. And I think it's a great idea, doing something for you.' Because he does mean it. Definitely. He just wishes that Cat had been the first to mention Matt the Personal Trainer. Or, better still, that there wasn't a Matt the Personal Trainer at all. That would probably be ideal.

He shifts himself off the sofa.

'Where are you going?'

'Checking in on our little girl.'

She pats the sofa. 'I'll keep your space.'

'You better,' he says. He leans down and kisses her on the cheek.

'Er, lips please, Weston.'

One kiss with his wife later – a longer kiss than they've had in ages – and Jayden's upstairs by Jazzy's cot. She's got a night light shaped like a seashell that Ally gave her, and it sends out a delicate golden glow. Beneath it, his baby daughter seems to shimmer. Who's he kidding? She always shimmers.

He knows that Cat will kill him if he wakes her up, but tonight he's willing to chance it; another calculated risk. If he could climb inside and lie down right beside her, he would, but instead he makes do with pressing a kiss to his fingertips, then reaching through the bars and delicately touching her forehead.

Jayden feels love – such deep love – humming through his body, and he's felt it every single day since his daughter came into the world. Did people tell him that, before he became a dad? Maybe they did and he just didn't believe it; couldn't imagine how it would actually feel.

JP Sharpe never knew that there was a baby on the way. And Wilson missed all this with Saffron; Wilson is missing everything still. But Jayden is here. He's here with bells on. His wife is downstairs. He's kissing his daughter goodnight. All good.

He lifts a lock of her hair and Jazzy pouts. Those rosebud lips; he almost laughs at how perfect she is. Will he always look at her with this adoration, even when she's slamming doors and staying out late and arguing the toss?

He has a funny feeling that he will.

69

Outside The Shell House the winds have dropped and the quiet is almost eerie. Thank goodness for the sound of the sea. Ally closes her eyes and hears the push and pull, the push and pull.

Against all odds, Jayden is safe. Dominic Brook is caught. And in a few months' time, JP Sharpe's child will be coming into the world, perhaps never knowing the complex circumstances around her journey towards life. How much Lena Prior will one day tell the child, and how much the child might one day ask, will be up to them.

Wilson was gracious when Ally called to tell him that Saffron knew who he was. He didn't say a lot, but he didn't rail either. Ally knew better than to try and persuade him to rethink anything. But afterwards, a feeling of guilt lingered; guilt that she hadn't made the attempt. And a continuing uncertainty about whether she and Jayden should ever have got involved in the first place.

Sometimes the demands of their detective work shock her still. To be so enmeshed in another person's business is as exhausting as it is exhilarating. Her life has been so quiet, for so long. It was always Bill out there, exploring the frontiers of human existence, flying the flag for the community. Meanwhile, The Shell House was, literally, Ally's shell, and one she often retreated into, as hidden as a mollusc. All this – the complexity of Saffron and Wilson's situation, Jayden's instincts butting against her own, even picking Wenna's brains and walking around Newlyn harbour commandeering strangers who might be Saffron's father – has left her scattered.

She can't even think about what happened at The Drop. Calling Jayden's name into the howling darkness. Fear burning inside her, from the tips of her fingers to the ends of her toes, as she crawled along the clifftop. And then the moment when they found one another. *Relief* isn't the word. Maybe *miracle* is.

A Christmas miracle.

The adrenalin has long since ebbed, and in its place, she can feel the old urge returning, to slip away to a quiet place. To resume that old childhood nickname: Ally All Alone. She reaches down and her hand finds Fox. She runs his ears through her fingers and feels the raspy lick of his tongue. Her little rock.

Ally still has the postcard of the Stanhope Forbes lighthouse painting and she picks it up now. *Bill.* Looking just as he did before he died: solid, bearded, her best friend and only love. And, sitting in the front of the boat with a paddle in his hand, the man that looked like a young Wilson Rowe. Whatever Saffron's mother had felt about Wilson, when she came across a picture that resembled him, she'd kept it. Ripped it – whether accidentally or intentionally – then taped it back together; like the Japanese art of Kintsugi perhaps, where pottery is mended to show the breaks. Embracing, not hiding, the flaws.

Ally picks up her phone and turns it in her hand. Then she taps out a message.

> *Hello Gus. I'm sorry I was grumpy before. It'd been a long day. But you deserved better. A x*

He's a bit of a night owl, Gus. He'll be wide awake now in his little house along the dunes. Maybe working on his novel, his reading glasses sliding down his nose; or perhaps sunk in the armchair by the fire, a paperback in his hands, a glass of something cold beside him – or maybe warming, on a night like this.

Her phone buzzes straight back.

Not a bit of it. I'm looking forward to my first Tom Bawcock's. Don't worry, I won't bring any mince pies. Gx

She completely forgot about tomorrow and Saffron's party plans. Surely they wouldn't still be on, with everything that's happened? If Saffron doesn't feel like celebrating then perhaps Gus can go to Mousehole after all. He'll be keen to see how the village marks it. Ally pictures Gus as he was just a few nights ago, when they were there together, before the body was found in the boat. His cup of mulled wine and sparkling eyes. The words he started to say.

But Ally loves Bill. She will always love Bill. Letting go of him, even just a little bit – enough to let someone else in – doesn't feel like something she can ever do.

Her phone beeps again, and she thinks it's Gus with a follow-up message, but no: it's Saffron.

Ally, hey, I know it's late, but can I ask a favour?

Ally already knows that whatever it is, she'll say yes.

70

Tom Bawcock's Eve dawns merry and bright in Mousehole. The sun sends its rays over the harbour wall, lighting up the faces of the cottages that ring the quay. The sky and the sea shimmer in shades of pink and gold as gulls spin and dance through the pyrotechnics. The harbour lights – the Stargazy, the three ships, the strings of lanterns – are naturally illuminated, a sunrise show for anyone who's lucky enough to catch it.

And it's Bev and the boys; her three boys.

They're waiting for the café to open, for a breakfast of hot chocolates and marshmallows and buttery croissants. Auntie Deb's treat, she insisted, pressing a crisp £20 into Bev's hand. And it was Bev's idea to get to Mousehole early – shrugging the boys out of their pyjamas, hustling Neil along in the bathroom – to see the sun come up.

'Seeing the sunrise is one of the gifts of being alive,' Bev said, as Cody ran his remote-control car over her feet and Jonathan turned on the telly and Neil flushed the toilet. 'Come on, slow coaches. Or we'll miss it.'

She doesn't know why, but it feels important to see it today. A new day dawning.

Bev breathes it in, as if she can take all this colour, all this light, and hold it inside of her, carrying it always. When she glances at her littlest, Cody, he's doing just the same. Meanwhile Jonathan's assembling a stack of pebbles, one on top of the other.

'And we'll be back again later,' she says, nudging him. 'To see the *other* lights.'

'And have some pie,' says Neil. 'A ruddy great wedge of pie.'

'Do I have to eat the fish head?' says Jonathan.

'You are the fish head,' says Cody, and both boys collapse into giggles.

Neil reaches for Bev's hand and holds it tight.

The boys will be waking up to Lego on Christmas morning, thanks to Bev spotting a Gumtree ad – *original boxes; as good as new!* – and Neil jumping on it with lightning speed. Their wishes answered, but especially Bev's: Santa will be bringing his magic.

'You've got the best surprise coming,' says Cody, whispering his hot little breath in her ear. 'On Christmas Day, Mummy.'

And she smiles and hugs him to her.

It won't be a surprise, but that doesn't matter. Yesterday, after the shock of nearly being hit in the lane – by the murderer, no less; no wonder Dominic Brook was driving like a bat out of hell – Neil said she needed a pick-me-up. So he gave up his big surprise, his top Christmas secret. *Okay, the game's up. Bev, I love you. And this is for you.* In the middle of the Pollock house garage – with its poured concrete floor and flawless walls, soon to be filled with stupid great Range Rovers and BMWs and the like – there was a sculpture of a seahorse. The wood was dark gold; the colour of sand after rain. Bev ran her hand over the ridged back, the long nose, the flicked tail. Shavings were scattered at the base, and she could see that it wasn't quite finished on one side. But, to her, it was already perfect.

Her hand went to her mouth.

'I know I shouldn't have been working on it here, but no one else was using it, were they? They're not in until New Year. I've been doing a little bit here, a little bit there. After hours, mostly.'

So many things fell into place, then. Bev was a fool for ever suspecting him, but she'd had her reasons, and her reasons had made sense. She knows that and Neil knows that.

'Bev, I should have told you I'd gone after JP Sharpe after you got the sack,' he said. 'My pride got in the way.'

'And the rest,' she said.

'And the rest.'

She turned back to the seahorse and felt tears pricking, a swelling in her chest. It was the most beautiful thing she'd ever seen. It should be in a gallery, with a price tag of thousands of pounds. Neil was a proper craftsman, though he'd never call himself an artist. They'd make a space for it in their living room; she knew just where to put it, where the light streamed in.

'I think the sun's up in the sky now,' says Jonathan. 'Can we please go and have our posh hot chocolates.'

'And our posh marshmallows,' says Cody.

'And our posh croissants,' says Neil.

They scramble back over the rocks and head up to the café, the boys racing ahead. They push open the door, the jangling bell announcing them. Their shyness pulls them up short as soon as they're inside. Neil plants a hand on each of their shoulders, steers them to the counter. The Potter family are the first customers of the day.

'Morning,' he says to the woman at the till. 'We're on a hot-chocolate mission.'

Bev stops in the doorway, a notice in the window catching her eye.

Waitress needed ASAP! Enquire within.

She feels herself breaking out in a smile. She's got one of her feelings again – but this time it's a good one.

71

It's a fine evening. There's a whisper of wind, nothing like what's been blowing lately. And it's clear too, the skies above studded with stars. Trip thinks of it as neck-crick night, when if you're standing idle, you'll only be looking upwards; drunk on starlight. But he's far from idle tonight, and about as sober as a man can be. It's on. On, after being off for so long. And he can feel it, it's going to be a good one. Whatever they net, it's going to be a good one. Because they're fishing.

The throb of the engine is sweet music, and the lifting of the boat as it cuts through the water feels like a dance. His crew, Wilson's crew, is beside him, and they're itching to get going as much as Trip. They grin and nod at each other.

If Wilson were here, he'd send a look in that little black cat's direction, if it was still in one piece: just for luck. Wilson and his superstitions. Sometimes those beliefs of his give him what he needs and sometimes they keep him prisoner. Wilson has taken the crash as yet another sign. A bit of balance being restored: it wasn't just any bloke hurtling head-on into Trip, but Dominic Brook, the idiot who'd decided Trip's boat was the one to dump the body in once he was done killing. When Trip held on tight to him in the lane, not letting him go, not letting him get away with it, he had no idea who the man was; no idea he'd netted himself a whopping great shark. It was soon clear when the police turned up though. Talk about coming face-to-face with consequences.

But the sign that Wilson is making such a big deal of is that, according to him, the universe really didn't want Trip making it over to Porthpella. So, the visit to Saffron is now, according to Wilson, on ice. Meanwhile, Dawn is still none the wiser – which the silly old bloke thinks is some kind of a good thing.

Wilson and Trip exchanged views on it, before Trip left for Newlyn earlier. Not an argument, exactly, but Trip said this: *I think you're looking for a way out.* Then he added, before Wilson could say anything: *Not because you don't care. But because you do.*

Wilson made a noise in response that Trip couldn't quite decipher.

You're not doing Dawn any favours either. Give her some credit and fess up.

And then it was time to leave, so, he clapped his friend, his boss, on the back and headed off down the harbour. He was a stubborn bloke, Wilson. But hey, never say never, and soon it'd be a whole new year. And Trip knows one thing: he's not going to let Wilson forget it.

Trip glances down at the sonar and holds his course. The colours on the screen shift and move and he feels it pulsing through him; it's like the trails that unicorns leave. He knows just where to find the shoals tonight, and they're coming for them. They'll spin vast rings around them, throwing down their nets, hauling sacks of glistening catch, *one more time around, lads!* And the gulls will rush in, screeching and flapping and following them all the way home. It's hunting, it's courting, it's everything, isn't it?

The land, and all its complications, is at Trip's back, those last twinkling lights growing smaller and smaller until they're all but gone. And he feels a lightening of the spirit. How can he describe it? He probably can't. Just that, out on the water he feels right. Wilson felt like that once, but Trip isn't sure that he does anymore, not in the same way – but maybe that's good for the people around him. For Dawn. And maybe for this daughter of his, if Wilson can ever find the heart and bones to face her.

One thing's for sure: Trip can't go on about bad luck anymore. The crash in the lane left him with hardly a scratch. Instead of crumpling at the wheel he climbed out of his pickup, rolling his shoulders, thinking, *There's no way that lunatic driver's getting away*. As far as the police are concerned, Trip's an unintentional hero. Well, he'll take that. Now here he is, less than twenty-four hours later: hitting open water on Tom Bawcock's Eve.

He starts to hum 'I Saw Three Ships', and before long he's broken into full song.

72

Saffron crouches by the oven, watching the pie crust turning to gold. She stands up, wipes her hands on her denim apron. It looks perfect.

Her mum had her own recipe, and Saffron has followed it faithfully. Okay, almost faithfully. She added leeks, because she likes the softness they bring, and the way the pale green ribbons remind her of strands of seaweed. And she went a little heavier on the parsley too.

It felt weird at first, making Stargazy somewhere other than their kitchen. But this morning Daz declared the Sun Street boiler as dead as disco, and Saffron can't exactly welcome her guests to a freezing house – no matter how much rum she plies them with. So here she is at The Shell House, in Ally's kitchen.

'That smells divine,' says Ally, standing in the doorway. 'In fact, it hasn't smelt this delicious in here for . . . a long time. It was Bill who really loved to cook.'

Saffron puts her arm around her. There are people missing tonight, and nothing can make up for that. But Christmas is about being grateful for what you do have; counting every blessing and holding them close.

Ally squeezes her right back. 'What is this?' she says, tipping her head, pointing to the air, as if the musical notes are flying by. 'I like it.'

'Mum's favourite,' says Saffron. 'And mine.'

Jayden appears then. 'What's this? *What's this?!* Come on now, Al . . .'

He takes Ally's hand, whirling her into a few quick steps. Ally goes with it, Saffron laughing in delight as she watches the two of them spin their way across the kitchen floor. She turns up the music. Her mum loved Sister Nancy. Jodie and Kelly and Saffron love Sister Nancy. And they always play Sister Nancy on Tom Bawcock's. It's their thing.

'Party in the kitchen?' says Broady from the doorway.

'Better believe it,' says Saffron, grabbing his hands, pulling him close. 'Actually no, the pie, the pie, it's just cresting.' She peels away, back to the oven. Broady keeps throwing his moves. He is, she thinks, glancing back, an extraordinarily good-looking man.

If she's thinking of silver linings, everything that's happened in the last few days has brought her and Broady closer together. It's made her realise that he's not only there for the sunshine. And that she'd been doing him – and herself – a disservice to imagine that he was.

It's not about dodging the hard stuff, she said to him last night, *because that's coming for all of us, sooner or later. That's life. It's how we show up for it, right?*

And Saffron has decided to show up for it with a dinner for her friends. A pie full of stargazing pilchards. And toasting a brave fisherman who was there for the people around him when they needed him most. She will do this last with no trace of bitterness, because she's spent twenty-four years figuring out that she doesn't need a father. Her mum was right all along.

Ally and Jayden made the fisherman connection, and that was what led them to the letter writer. All these years, and Saffron never suspected that Tom Bawcock's Eve meant anything more to her mum than the same thing it means to a lot of people in their little corner of the world: a chance to get together and celebrate courage and kindness, generosity and connection. Maybe there was something about the occasion that both drew and repelled her mum: she'd always wanted to mark it – only not in Mousehole.

Because, apparently, Wilson Rowe lives in Mousehole.

Saffron deliberately hasn't asked Ally or Jayden any questions. Except one, earlier this evening. *Did you like him?* she asked. And their faces were equally matched in hesitation. *It's okay*, she said, *be honest. Guys, I can take it. I'm just curious. And it's the only question I'm ever going to ask.* And then, without even looking at one another, they nodded.

They liked him.

'There's people need topping up,' announces Mullins at the top of his voice, steaming towards her with a tray of cups. He's wearing a Rudolph Christmas jumper, the fluffy red nose smack in the middle of his belly. 'That cider of mine is going down a treat, Saff.'

Saffron sees Mullins shoot a sideways look at the still-dancing Broady. Mullins is the type of bloke who is suspicious of good looks in other men. And rippling biceps. And general coolness. *Dear old Mullins*, she thinks fondly, actually meaning it. In the other room, Cat, Jodie and Gus have been tucking into his offering by the fire: hot mulled cider. Well, actually, Mullins just brought a big bottle of cider, and one sip made Saffron's eyes water: smooth it was not, with an aftertaste that was more dung heap than apple orchard. So, she added lashings of apple juice, brown sugar, cinnamon and cloves, set it gently warming on the stove, and now – apparently – it's a hit.

'Hey, this is ready,' says Saffron, drawing the pie from the oven. 'Everybody to the table!'

Ally's made the dining room look beautiful. Thick church candles throw shadows. There are scatterings of seashells, their ridges picked out with a lick of gold paint, and sprigs of holly in enamel cups. Wenna is in Mousehole tonight but she sent a giant jar of sweets, and there are tall glasses filled with pink foam shrimps set at either end of the table. And now, in the middle, a huge and golden Stargazy Pie, the heads of ten glistening pilchards peeking out.

'Do you want to listen to something more festive?' Saffron says, just as they're taking their seats, reggae still drifting from the kitchen. She saw Ally's Mousehole Male Voice Choir record on the side.

'No, this is perfect,' says Ally.

'*Yes*, Al,' says Jayden. 'Now you're talking.'

So, they stick with it, and they tuck in, and some people are squeamish about the fish heads, but hey, that's how it always goes.

Saffron looks around the table. She feels tears welling, but they're the good kind. Broady squeezes her knee and mouths *I love you*. The three little words they said to one another for the first time last night. She doesn't think she'll ever get tired of hearing them from him. Or saying them back.

'May I?' says Gus, glancing at Ally, raising his glass. 'To Saffron, with thanks for the feast. And to Ally, for opening her home to us all.' He smiles in that kind of shy and Gus-ish way. 'And to all you very good friends indeed.'

An hour later, the candles are burnt low, and the plates cleared. Cat and Ally are yawning. It's not quite half past nine.

'So hey,' Broady says, 'Paulo's down in Mousehole. He says it's going off. Do you want to head over?'

Saffron stops and thinks about it, and then she says yes. Because wouldn't it be nice to be there for actual Tom Bawcock's, for once? To see the harbour lights, so close to Christmas. To do things a little bit differently, and for that to be okay.

'I'm in,' shouts Mullins.

'Anyone else?' says Broady. 'I'm good to drive.'

'How about you guys?' asks Saffron, looking to Jayden and Cat. Jayden hesitates, and Cat tells him to go if he wants to, but personally she's dead on her feet. Jayden scoops her up in his arms and says, 'Home then, m'lady.'

'Ally? Gus?'

But Ally's tired. And Gus, who doesn't look tired at all, says, 'Next time.'

Jodie's off meeting her boyfriend, so it's the three of them who drive to Mousehole in the dark, Mullins leaning forward from the back seat like a busy child. They're soon parking on the outskirts of the village, walking towards the shimmering lights. The lantern parade is long finished, but the harbour is still thronged with people. Music and laughter and wafts of woodsmoke fill the air. The windows of the pub are all steamed up, and when the door swings open, a wall of bodies fills the space inside.

Mullins surges through, the crowd opening for him then closing again. Broady mimes taking a breath and pinching his nose, as if he's a kid ducking under the waves. He holds out his hand for hers.

'You know what,' she says, 'I'll see you in there.'

'Are you okay?'

'I just want to take a minute. Get me a drink, I'll be right behind you.'

Then it's just Saffron.

She turns and weaves through the crowd outside. The air is biting-cold, and she pulls her beanie down. When she looks up, the sky is loaded with stars, giving the harbour lights a run for their money. She whispers something, to way up there, and it makes her feel sturdier somehow. It's low tide and the sand down on the harbour beach glimmers with reflected lights. She wants, suddenly, to get a lucky shell; to slip it in her pocket and remember this night.

As she makes for the beach, she passes a sweet little family huddled together with cones of chips – the kind of family that makes her think not of the past, but of a possible future – and she smiles at them.

'Cody, look, I'm putting five in at once,' she hears the older boy say, his mouth full of chips.

She weaves through the cluster of people by the railing. At the top of the steps there's a bearded man with a pint in his hand, and he moves to one side as she says, 'Excuse me.'

'Sorry there, love.'

She thanks him and, as she passes, Saffron hears his sharp intake of breath. She glances back, her look questioning. And the expression on his face – like none she has ever seen before – is all the answer she needs.

In that moment the whole of Mousehole – the lights, the music, the people – fades into the background, as they look each other in the eye.

'Hi,' she says. Then, carefully, deliberately, 'We don't know each other, or . . . do we?'

73

'Al, Cat and I are going to hit the road.'

Jayden's found Ally in the kitchen, where she's tidying up a few things. But, really, there's nothing to be done here; Saffron, the consummate professional, has wiped all the surfaces and set the dishwasher, leaving it immaculate.

Ally can't help thinking how much Bill would have loved a night like this. And, also, how surprised he'd be to discover that it's happened without him. The Shell House hopping with people, reggae music drifting over the dunes, laughter and stories and Ally at the centre of it. But here is the thing: if Bill were alive, there wouldn't have been this night – not like this, anyway. Just like if Saffron's mum were still here, she and Saffron would have been up at Sun Street together, not down in the dunes. In fact, would Ally and Saffron have ever come to know one another? Saffron set up her café with the money her mum left her, and a promise to do, above all, what made her happy.

And Jayden, this friend of Ally's beside her now. If Bill were still here, maybe her path might have crossed with Jayden's in a faint sort of way. Perhaps Bill would have said, *I've heard there's a former constable just moved here. I'm going to see if I can talk him into joining us down the station.* Because Bill recognised good people when he saw them. Maybe Ally would have glimpsed Jayden from afar with his baby daughter, or trying to catch a wave in the warmer-water months, and exchanged a pleasantry in passing.

Now Jayden leans in and kisses Ally on the cheek, then follows it with a bear hug.

'Mullins says your statement, even without Lena coming forward on JP Sharpe, would have been enough to convict Brook for attempted murder,' she says.

'Yeah, it was all part of my plan. Honeytrap kinda thing. Lure Brook to a remote spot then outstep his moving vehicle. That was totally, a hundred per cent, my intention. The cliff bit was just so he'd give up the chase.'

'Of course it was,' she says. Then she grips his arm. Holds on to him, as if she never wants to let him go. She sees Jayden's eyes fill.

'No one would have predicted that Brook would do a thing like that,' she says.

'Yeah, I know. But, from now on, we do things together.'

'Yes. Even when we disagree, we're still there, side by side.'

'Holmes and Watson.'

'Cagney and Lacey.' She's still holding on to him. 'I'm serious. I'm only sixty-four. I can do the action bits too.'

'So you think there's going to be more action for us? Not just puzzles to be solved? What, stake-outs, high-speed pursuits . . .'

'I think,' she says, 'that I'm learning to expect the unexpected. Now, you take that family of yours home.'

'See you Christmas Day?'

She still hasn't fully decided. But then she hears herself saying, loud and clear, 'Yes. See you for Christmas Day.'

Gus is the last to leave. Ally says goodnight to him on the veranda and they linger for a moment. The tide is all the way out and, after the tumult of the last few days, the sea feels gentle, the waves shushing on to the sand. The marram grass stirs and whispers.

'Oh, look up,' breathes Ally. 'That sky.'

Constellations glimmer and glint. The North Star winks like it knows every secret. It has, she thinks, never looked more beautiful.

'I am looking up,' says Gus, stepping back towards the doorway. 'Did you hang that there, Ally Bright?'

She sees the sprig of mistletoe; the red ribbon.

'No, I did not.' Then, 'Did you?'

'Me? No. But . . .' Gus shifts on his feet, smiles. 'Seeing as it's there . . . it's probably bad luck to eschew tradition and—'

Before he can finish, Ally steps forward. She lays one hand lightly on his shoulder and lays one kiss lightly on his cheek. Then, somehow, they're holding hands. She feels the warmth flow between them.

'Thank you for your friendship this year, Gus,' she says. 'I've come to treasure it.'

He smiles. 'As have I, Ally. A great deal.'

For a moment, he looks like he might be about to say something more. Instead, he dips his head, squeezes her hand. Then they part.

Ally watches as Gus slowly pads down the steps. With a wave of his hand, he's up and over the dunes, silver moonlight marking his path.

She feels Fox nudge her legs, and looks down at him.

'Oh, what?' she says. And Ally swears he gives her a knowing look in reply. 'It's well past our bedtime, boy. Say goodnight to the sea now.'

Her dog tips his nose, and Ally does the same: breathes it all in. Tomorrow, Christmas Eve, will be a day of stillness. She'll walk the shore, work on her pictures, and phone Evie to reassure her that she is going to be fine, absolutely fine, this Christmas.

Ally gives the night sky one last glance – that so-bright star, shining for anyone who needs to see it – then she goes back inside The Shell House.

Acknowledgements

It's been a total joy writing this second book in the Shell House series. The characters feel like old friends, and inhabiting the world of Porthpella is pure wish fulfilment. However, a number of real people and real places have also helped make my writing process a happy one and proved immeasurably important to this novel.

First, thanks to my brilliant agent, Rowan Lawton at The Soho Agency, I'm so appreciative of your continuing support and enthusiasm. At Thomas & Mercer, I'm indebted to the editorial dream team of Victoria Haslam and Laura Gerrard: it's such a pleasure and a privilege working with you both. Vic, I thank my lucky stars for the day that you fell in love with Ally, Jayden and the Porthpella gang. Thank you, too, to the wider team at Thomas & Mercer, including Sadie Mayne, Gemma Wain, Silvia Crompton, Rebecca Hills, and the fabulous Sophie Goodfellow at FMcM. I'm grateful to Deborah Balogun for the very much-valued cultural read, and also to Marianna Tomaselli for the stunning cover illustration.

Thank you to my husband Robin Etherington and friend Lucy Clarke for reading my first draft and giving such energetic and thoughtful feedback. It means the world. Big thanks, too, to Emma Stonex for reading a later draft: your shining enthusiasm was just the boost I needed when I was deep in edits.

Thank you to Peter Taylor, chairman of the Mousehole Harbour Lights committee, for sharing your experience of what is such a special annual event. Thanks, also, to Rob McBurnie at Padstow Harbour Office, for chatting to me about the fishing life, one blustery March day by the quayside. Any inaccuracies – on both of these fronts – are mine alone.

While I wrote most of *The Harbour Lights Mystery* at home in Bristol, I was lucky enough to go to Cornwall for several writing retreats during the drafting process. These trips to Mousehole, Padstow, Gwithian and St Ives filled my soul (not to mention the pages of this book). Thank you to Megan Wilkinson-Tough and Lucy Clarke for your stellar company. In Mousehole I hunkered down on my own. I ate chocolate for breakfast, and saw in every sunrise and sunset down by the water. It was November, so I was too early for the Christmas lights, but the village is always luminous to me.

Writing in a new genre, and launching a series, is a nerve-wracking thing, and undoubtedly the early response to *The Shell House Detectives* has made such a difference to how I felt writing this follow-up. A number of generous authors gave their time to read advance copies of the first book and offer endorsements, and for that I'm incredibly grateful. So (at the time of writing) thank you to Amanda Reynolds, Claire Douglas, Elly Griffiths, Emily Koch, Emma Stonex, Ginny Bell, Hannah Richell, Jill Mansell, Kate Riordan, Lucy Clarke, Lucy Diamond, Rosanna Ley, Rosie Walsh, Sarah Pearse, Sarah Winman, Susan Fletcher and Veronica Henry. Your words mean more than you can know.

Lastly, I owe many thanks to my family – the Halls, the Green-Halls, and the Etheringtons – and to my husband Robin and my son Calvin. I'm very, very lucky to have you.

About the Author

Photo © 2022 Victoria Walker

Emylia Hall lives with her husband and son in Bristol, where she writes from a hut in the garden and dreams of the sea. Her debut crime novel, *The Shell House Detectives*, was published in summer 2023 and is the first of The Shell House Detectives Mysteries, a series inspired by her love of Cornwall's wild landscape. Emylia has published four previous novels, including Richard and Judy Book Club pick *The Book of Summers* and *The Thousand Lights Hotel*. Her work has been translated into ten languages and broadcast on BBC Radio 6 Music. She is the founder of Mothership Writers and is a writing coach at The Novelry.

You can follow Emylia on Instagram at @emyliahall_author and on Twitter at @emyliahall.

Follow the Author on Amazon

If you enjoyed this book, follow Emylia Hall on Amazon to be notified when the author releases a new book!
To do this, please follow these instructions:

Desktop:

1) Search for the author's name on Amazon or in the Amazon App.
2) Click on the author's name to arrive on their Amazon page.
3) Click the 'Follow' button.

Mobile and Tablet:

1) Search for the author's name on Amazon or in the Amazon App.
2) Click on one of the author's books.
3) Click on the author's name to arrive on their Amazon page.
4) Click the 'Follow' button.

Kindle eReader and Kindle App:

If you enjoyed this book on a Kindle eReader or in the Kindle App, you will find the author 'Follow' button after the last page.